# EXACTING ESSENCE

## SHROUD
### IMMORTAL NIGHTMARE CYCLE
#### BOOK ONE

### JAMES WYMORE

*SLCC '14*
*James Wymore*

A Division of **Whampa, LLC**
P.O. Box 2160
Reston, VA 20195
Tel/Fax: 800-998-2509
http://curiosityquills.com

© 2014 **James Wymore**
http://jameswymore.wordpress.com

All rights reserved, including the right to reproduce this book or portions thereof in any form whatsoever. For information about Subsidiary Rights, Bulk Purchases, Live Events, or any other questions - please contact Curiosity Quills Press at info@curiosityquills.com, or visit http://curiosityquills.com

ISBN 978-1-62007-554-8 (ebook)
ISBN 978-1-62007-555-5 (paperback)
ISBN 978-1-62007-556-2 (hardcover)

*For my daughter*

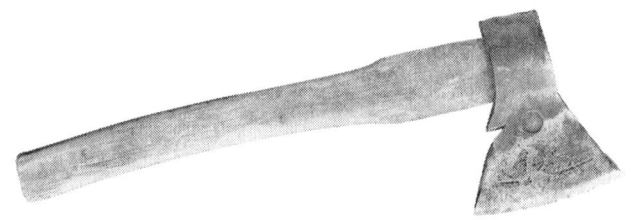

# TABLE OF CONTENTS

Chapter One ........................................................................................... 6
Chapter Two .......................................................................................... 11
Chapter Three ....................................................................................... 17
Chapter Four ......................................................................................... 21
Chapter Five .......................................................................................... 24
Chapter Six ............................................................................................ 27
Chapter Seven ....................................................................................... 31
Chapter Eight ........................................................................................ 35
Chapter Nine ......................................................................................... 38
Chapter Ten .......................................................................................... 45
Chapter Eleven ...................................................................................... 52
Chapter Twelve ..................................................................................... 58
Chapter Thirteen ................................................................................... 65
Chapter Fourteen .................................................................................. 71
Chapter Fifteen ..................................................................................... 75
Chapter Sixteen ..................................................................................... 79
Chapter Seventeen ................................................................................ 83
Chapter Eighteen .................................................................................. 89
Chapter Nineteen .................................................................................. 94
Chapter Twenty .................................................................................... 98
Chapter Twenty-One ............................................................................ 103
Chapter Twenty-Two ............................................................................ 110
Chapter Twenty-Three .......................................................................... 114
Chapter Twenty-Four ............................................................................ 119

Chapter Twenty-Five ............................................................................. 123
Chapter Twenty-Six................................................................................ 129
Chapter Twenty-Seven .......................................................................... 133
Chapter Twenty-Eight............................................................................ 140
Chapter Twenty-Nine ............................................................................. 144
Chapter Thirty......................................................................................... 152
Chapter Thirty-One................................................................................ 156
Chapter Thirty-Two ............................................................................... 161
Chapter Thirty-Three............................................................................. 165
Chapter Thirty-Four............................................................................... 170
Chapter Thirty-Five................................................................................ 173
Chapter Thirty-Six.................................................................................. 176
Chapter Thirty-Seven............................................................................. 182
Chapter Thirty-Eight.............................................................................. 188
Chapter Thirty-Nine............................................................................... 190
Chapter Forty.......................................................................................... 195
Chapter Forty-One................................................................................. 201
Chapter Forty-Two ................................................................................ 206
Chapter Forty-Three.............................................................................. 211
Chapter Forty-Four................................................................................ 215
Chapter Forty-Five................................................................................. 220
Acknowledgements ................................................................................ 223
Glossary.................................................................................................... 224
About the Author................................................................................... 227
A Taste Of *Salvation*, by **James Wymore**........................................... 228
More from Curiosity Quills Press ........................................................ 249

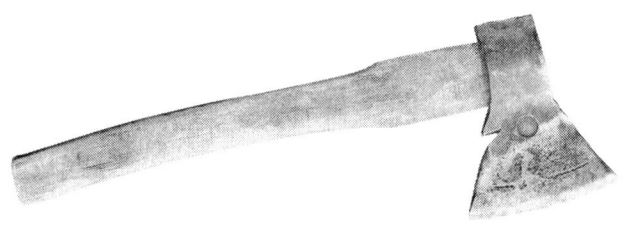

# CHAPTER ONE

Late in the night, Megan Howell sat in her bed, looking at the flowing patterns of light on her wall. A steady patter of rain coated the window behind her with a thin sheet of water. Cut by sharp shadow lines from Levelor blinds, the light from the streetlamp outside warped through the water into dancing yellow moiré patterns on the wall. Occasional bolts of lightning disrupted the flowing design with shocks of blue.

When nearby thunder made her jump, she turned to the window and saw a ghost staring back at her. She held her breath until she realized the misty image was just the warped reflection of her tired face and mottled hair in the window. The dark, sunken eyes were her own.

She willed herself back into the rhythmic window display, fighting to keep the fading trance. As the shimmering lights waned, a deep exhaustion filled the space. Without consent, her body had eroded into so much rubble on the bed. Her eyelids stayed closed for a full second after she blinked.

She couldn't surrender. She had to stay awake. She forced her thoughts to be abrupt and powerful.

"Don't think about it." She spoke aloud to the rain, which had been dominating the conversation so far. For so long now, terrors had riddled her nights. Despite repeating the doctor's advice, she couldn't force the horrible images from her mind.

"Stop!" she said, muscling her eyes open. She couldn't fight it forever. Hope ebbed. "The doctor said not to think about it." He was the only one she had ever told about the circus nightmares. She only told him because he promised never to tell her mother.

Shock registered in the psychologist's voice. "You see these monsters every night?"

It amused Megan to get a reaction from the middle-aged man who was usually so calm and clinical.

"Every night, all night," she said.

"Is that why you started cutting yourself?" He lifted his glasses to get a better look at her arms and indicate the scratches had not escaped his attention.

"I didn't do that," she said. "They did it."

"Megan"—his voice became flat and clinical as he sat back in his desk chair and cleaned his glasses on the sleeve of his plaid, button-up shirt—"you know nothing from your dreams can hurt you in real life. Those had to come from you."

She nodded and looked down, folding her arms to hide the thin, red lines crossing the inside of her forearms.

"I don't think you are doing it on purpose. Maybe you're scratching yourself while you sleep."

"Not on purpose," she said.

"These things are all in your mind. You are in control of your mind. Accept the message your mind is trying to tell you and then move on."

"What if I can't stop them?" she asked.

"We have some new medications we can try. They're stronger, and they'll keep you asleep, unlike the last one. And if you're scratching yourself while you sleep, maybe you should wear gloves to bed."

That had been a week ago. She had another appointment with him tomorrow. If she couldn't make this work tonight, she'd ask for the medication. She pulled on the long gloves intended to protect her from scratching herself. Megan imagined her mother hugging her with a big smile and the doctor shaking her hand. She wanted to show them she could beat these imaginary monsters. Seventeen was too old for bad dreams.

Letting herself relax, she thought of happier times. She remembered coming out early on a dark Christmas morning and the excitement at seeing all the presents beneath the unlit tree. She thought of the trip with her mother to the beach last summer with the serenity of rhythmic waves and the warm sun. She relived her friend's birthday party where a boy had kissed her during a game and sent shivers up her spine, starting a month-long crush. The happy memories filled her, and she let them carry her into a cradle of sleep, which she needed more than an addict after a drug-free week.

*At first, the color gray dominated her mind. Then, details slowly filled in around her, and Megan found herself at school. Only a few of her friends came to*

class today. They were all wearing matching uniforms with white blouses and black skirts. Since her school didn't have uniforms, this worried Megan. She started brushing chalk dust off the skirt and checking to see if the others thought it was strange. The desks littered the room chaotically in defiance of the usual order at school, so she had to push a few out of the way to join her friends. Only dim sunlight from one small window lit the room. Jessica gazed out longingly.

"What's going on?" Megan asked. "Where's everybody else?"

"They're all outside," Jessica said.

"Why?" Meg continued. "What are they doing? Aren't they worried they'll be late for class?"

"No," said Erin, the dark-haired girl beside her. "The teacher's out there, too. They all are."

"Let's go outside," said Jessica, gazing intently out the tinted glass. "It looks fun."

"Can I see?" Megan asked.

Erin crowded in, blocking the view. "Wow! It's a whole carnival." She turned from the window and walked toward the door. "I wish I had more money."

"Where are you going?" Megan asked. She didn't want to go to the carnival. Something told her to stay away. Her hands began to shake a little.

"To have fun with the others," the three girls said in unison.

"Let's stay in here," Megan suggested, her voice faltering.

They slowed their pace only a moment at the door. Jenny, the shortest, said, "And miss all the fun? No way. I love carnivals."

"Please stay with me," Megan begged.

"Forget it," said Erin as they disappeared. She called down the hall, "If you're going to stay, you're going to do it by yourself."

Emptiness surrounded her. The fear of being alone in the dark propelled her out into the hall. She jogged to catch up. They were far ahead. She couldn't lose her friends. She could feel the fear rising inside her as she edged closer to the door. Light was pouring in, the light at the end of a dark tunnel. She couldn't make out any details until she reached the doorframe. She paused again, clinging desperately to it, hoping there was another choice—anything.

When her eyes adjusted, she saw a cotton candy stand, a small roller coaster, a fishing game, a dunking machine, and other attractions all in red and orange booths. There were people all around, but she couldn't see her friends anywhere. With her arms folded for comfort, she meandered through the swarm. People bumped into her as if they couldn't see her. Several times she found herself fenced in by groups in line or having conversations over top of her. The harder she pushed to break free, the more they backed into her and shifted to block her.

Suddenly, she stopped. She covered her mouth to catch a small gasp before it escaped. Before her was a huge carousel, taller even than the school. Dark paint covered the animals, which raced around in circles while sporting horrible sneers and eerie grimaces. Macabre fascination kept her from running in fear, just like the moment before jerking her fingers away from a hot stove.

One moment was all it took. Before she could bolt, she saw them. Erin rode on a black grizzly bear with huge claws. Behind her, a pine-green snake was bobbing up and down, carrying Jessica, who grinned widely. They waved when they noticed her. The metal and boards creaked and popped as if the whole contraption was moments from implosion. Jenny motioned for her to come up.

Megan couldn't step on the rotating platform. Nothing in the world would ever make her get on the merry-go-round, even if it meant losing her friends. Fear dragged her away. She turned to run, but instead jumped back with a short scream. A short, fat clown blocked her retreat. He dressed in a puffy red suit with yellow dots, covered in dirt and oil. His horrifying face featured a large, red mouth painted into a sneer. She couldn't look away from his two side-tufts of green hair.

She wanted to dart but found herself paralyzed like a statue. She couldn't even breathe. The clown reached up and touched her cheek. His sweaty finger left a line of white, greasy makeup, which itched. There were tears on her face, but she refused to scream. Some unvoiced wisdom told her it would make him even happier if she did.

The clown pulled out a floppy balloon. Sputtering globs of spit from the sides of his mouth, he blew air and rigidity into the rubbery blue line until it expanded into a long curve. Meg tried to look away as he began twisting it with a grating sound. She wanted to see or hear anything else, but the balloon drew her attention in a new way. It had shimmering patterns of yellow light. It seemed to be flickering in a familiar moiré pattern between parallel shadow lines. It was hypnotic. As he tied the balloon, his hands left smeared fingerprints of the same greasy makeup all over it. Only when the clown was done could she look away from the lights to see what he had made. It was the shape of a knife.

Instantly, her hand shot up to hold back a scream. She turned on her heels and sprinted, running off the pavement with her hand still clenching her mouth. Hurtling over the rocks lining the perimeter of the parking lot, she was determined to escape. As she rushed away, she entered longer grass before passing bushes and trees.

She stopped as soon as she realized she had sprinted into a dead forest. Dried sagebrush punctuated the black shadows of gnarled, dead trees. Only a few dead leaves clung to the twisted branches. She stopped once the balding clown was out of sight. She tried to retrace her steps, only to discover she was lost. The lines on her cheeks from dried tears parted around the greasy paint on her cheek. Now those lines filled again with new tears.

The sun abandoned her, and the wind began to whistle through the thin branches. Some small rustling sound drove her into a panic again. She chose a direction and ran blindly. It was hopeless, she knew. The ending was inevitable. She didn't run to escape now; she ran because if she stood still, she would go crazy. Soon the trees thinned and opened around a large tent with huge red-and-white stripes running up it to a single sharp point.

The circus. Out of the frying pan, into the fire. She remembered how this tent used to make her so happy. It hadn't for a long time. She knew there was no escape. She let the numbness of shock wash over her. It was too late to resist now. It had happened so many times. She didn't fight it anymore. Next time, she could try again to escape.

She stumbled slowly through the dirty front flaps of the tent door, dreading what waited for her.

# Chapter Two

Megan stopped the scream before it could get out—slapping one hand over her mouth the instant she woke. Even so, a soft whine escaped her lips. Her eyes wide, she looked at the wall to see the rain had stopped now. She never let herself scream anymore. It just woke her mother and sisters up, and she didn't want to talk to her mother. There was no reason for both of them to lose sleep. Megan wasn't a child anymore, and her mother's touch and soft words wouldn't help. Besides, she didn't want to add any more sorrow to her mom's already great burden. Megan wanted desperately to be free of this horror. She wanted her mother to be free of the constant worry, too.

An ache set in behind her eyes. It always happened if she didn't get enough sleep. It wouldn't keep her awake now, but it would make school hard tomorrow.

She rolled over so her face wasn't touching the part of her pillow still wet from crying. The other side crackled with last night's dried tears. She made herself comfortable and began thinking. I have to beat this. I have to get past it. She started again, remembering nice things and good memories, with little hope. She'd been having these nightmares since before most of those memories even happened.

After a long night of horrors, Megan was incoherent when someone began shaking her gently. She knew sleep deprivation was a kind of torture and whoever was waking her up was the person responsible. When she finally surrendered and allowed images to bombard her brain, she saw the harbinger of doom—her mother announcing it was time for school.

"Come on, honey. I've already gotten a letter from the school once. You just can't be late anymore."

"I'm sick," Megan said flatly. It was true. Her stomach always felt twisted and sour after a hard night.

"Megan Howell, you are not sick. Did you have bad dreams again?"

Megan hoped it would help her case enough to gain a few precious moments of sleep. "Yes," she admitted. Her voice had quivered. She wanted to sound like she didn't care except for the need to sleep. Yet she found it impossible to sound tough when she was exhausted.

"Well, you have another appointment with Dr. Gund today. Hopefully, he can help."

"He wants me to take new sleeping pills," Megan said.

"Maybe you should try them," her mother said sympathetically. "Maybe they'll do the trick."

"I tried other ones before." Megan looked to the side. "The pills keep me asleep, but then I can't wake up to escape the… nightmares." It had been the worst night of her life. She remembered the two-week prescription of lorazepam. After one night, she refused to touch them again.

"Maybe this time will be better. Maybe they're better pills. You just have to get more sleep," her mother said. "I know the pills aren't great. But your teachers say you sometimes nod off in the middle of class. Your grades are getting worse all the time."

It was an exaggeration. Her grades couldn't get any worse.

Megan opened her eyes bitterly, breaking the salt crusts trying to cement them shut. She wanted to lash out her mother for failing to protect her.

She rolled out of bed and dressed, shambling like a zombie. She wondered if death might not be a solution. If nothing else, she would finally get to rest. She had been working up the courage to try it until they read Hamlet in school. Once she heard the whole, "To sleep, perchance to dream," thing, she decided to wait. The thought of dreams she could never wake from scared her more.

Later, she asked a minister, in confidence, what happened to people who killed themselves. She hoped for a sweet oblivion. He told her in heaven there were no dreams. He told her you go to hell if you commit suicide. Then he said hell was worse than any nightmares and they never ended. You could never wake up from them. Just like the pills the doctor was going to give her today… never-ending dreams. Hell pills. So the minister had won the suicide debate.

As Megan went through her closet, she pushed aside a light blue shirt with Princess across the front in glitter letters. Her mother liked that shirt.

Megan didn't. She had a kind of tunnel vision, blurred at the edges. It made simple tasks like picking a shirt into a chore. She chose a gray, hooded sweatshirt because it looked warm like a blanket. Then she brushed her shoulder-length blonde hair until it was straight.

"How about a little makeup today?" her mother said from the hall. "Boys notice how cute you are when you wear makeup."

Megan rolled her eyes. Boys didn't seem to notice her—with or without makeup.

Nothing felt real. Megan was numb. School passed in a stupor of exhaustion. The events of the day flowed around her the same way the cars and buildings flowed around the minivan on the way to the psychiatrist now. She moved between them without making contact, like a ghost.

Soon she sat in a waiting room decorated with watercolor paintings of flowers. Then she sat alone with Dr. Gund in his office. Yellow walls surrounded her, and a solid wood bookshelf took up the space to the left. She settled onto the comfy leather couch, which was far too short to lie down on… although she would be willing to try if she thought he'd let her. A white noise machine in the wall made blowing sounds that seemed to drive any thoughts from her brain. He kept his small desk clear except for a pad of yellow paper he wrote on and a big, flat sandbox. There were wavy lines in the sand and a few rocks. He said it was some kind of meditation thing, but she didn't understand or care. She was in survival mode. Silly decorations pretending to be deep didn't impress her.

Dr. Gund was probably the same age as her mom, but he had more wrinkles and darker skin. He wore a brown suit jacket that matched his dark hair and bright brown eyes. He smiled to cover the sadness Megan could see in his face. She was one of his first patients, and she suspected with time he would become less emotionally involved in his clients' problems.

"Your mother said you had bad dreams again last night." His voice was polite, unassuming, and warm.

Megan almost scoffed as she realized he actually thought he could fix her.

"Yeah. Every night. I don't usually tell her." Megan looked at the floor, winding one of the ties from her hoodie around one finger. She didn't want him to feel bad for her. She wanted him to fix her or stop making her come to these silly sessions. She knew her mother couldn't afford to keep going on like this.

"So does that mean you're willing to try a new medication?"

"I don't want to. They just make the nightmares go on and on. I can't wake up from them if I take the pills." She was trying to sound brave, but the whininess of her own voice was annoying even to herself. "Don't you have pills that make it so I can't dream?"

He didn't answer her question. "Did you think of what these dreams could mean? Like we talked about last time?"

"Yes," Megan said. "I thought about them a lot. I don't know if they mean anything. I think they're like twisted memories. We've been through all this before. When my parents divorced, my mother said my father went off to join the circus. I took it too literally and started to dream about it."

"But that doesn't explain why you're hurting yourself," Dr. Gund said, nodding at her arms. Megan looked down at the pink scratches and brown scabs, which poked out beneath the sleeves of her hoodie at strange angles. Even though she insisted she never scratched herself, they looked like they came from fingernails. She nervously rubbed the soft fabric against the itchy wounds.

Megan crossed her arms. "I told you it isn't on purpose. It happens in my sleep. I dream the clowns are cutting me, and then when I wake up…" She rubbed her eyes, unwilling to start crying again.

"What concerns me is how it has changed lately," he said. "You were fine for years, and now the dreams have turned to nightmares and you're waking up with real wounds. It doesn't match the usual traumatic stress disorders or repressed memories. What we need to understand is what changed with you."

Megan thought about the differences. At first, there had been many clowns. Then there were just twenty or so. Now she only ever saw the same ones. There was a roller coaster, which always had broken rails. If she ever got on, she had to live through the terror of knowing she was probably going to die when the train hit the broken spot. She could never stop it.

She felt the lap bar closing down on her legs. It was rusty and cold with no padding. Her heart skipped a beat as she realized what was about to—

"Megan?" The doctor's voice roused her. "You seem to have dozed off there." He smiled. She was just glad she didn't have to see that horrible roller coaster ride through to the end. At the same time, the constant need for sleep nagged at her.

"So I'm nuts, right?" Megan probed. "Can't fix it, so I gotta take pills."

"You're not nuts," the doctor reassured her. "Sometimes our minds do things that we can't control. Nobody knows how different people would react to the same situations. You can't blame yourself for something biological that happens in your mind as a result of such strong outside forces."

"So I have to take sleeping pills and live through hell every night because of it?" She surprised herself when she said that. It was stronger language than she usually dared to use with adults. It felt good.

"No. But that's one option."

"There are other options?"

"Would you mind inviting your mother in?"

Meg opened the door and called out into the waiting room. The doctor had never done this before. She was curious and worried at the same time. Meg sat down, and her mother stood behind her after closing the door.

"I was hesitant to bring this up because I have some reservations about it. But in light of the fact that I have not been able to help you, maybe you would be better with another doctor."

"You're giving up on me?" Megan's voice broke. She closed her eyes while her heart raced.

"No, I'm not. But maybe there is somebody else that can help you more. I found someone that specializes in cases like yours. She's a new doctor. She responded immediately to my inquiry and wants to meet you as soon as possible."

"Is it expensive?" Her mother had never complained about the doctor bills, but Megan knew they didn't really have the money for this. They certainly couldn't afford anything extra.

"Surprisingly, it's not. She said she's working on a grant. She needs the research data, so you won't have to pay anything."

Megan's eyes opened a little wider. "Where is it?"

"Actually, she wants to come here. Apparently, it's a pretty huge grant. She wants to stay at your house." He tapped his pen loudly on his yellow paper. He wagged his head slightly as if he couldn't believe it himself.

"Our house?" Meg and her mother asked in unison.

"Yes. If you aren't comfortable with it, you shouldn't do it."

Was Dr. Gund jealous?

"I want to do it." Megan said it before she thought about it. It would be creepy having some stranger watch her all night as she faced her nightmares. However, at this point anything different was good.

Megan looked at her mother's brow, furrowed beneath her dark bangs. She knew her mother hated this idea, but nodded to support her daughter's reckless acceptance.

"Okay," he said after a pause. "She asked me to tell her about the nature of your dreams. I won't give out any information without your permission."

"That's fine. Tell her whatever she wants to know." Megan dreaded the thought of going through that story again with someone else. She scratched her arms absently, filled at once with hope and worry.

Dr. Gund seemed a little bit disappointed. "I don't want you to get any false hope, Megan. This is experimental treatment and often unsuccessful. When she's finished, you can start coming to me again."

"What if it works?" her mother asked.

"We'll decide that afterward. But again, I don't want you to expect a miracle."

"I understand," Megan said flatly. She had already decided to hope. What choice did she have? "How soon can she come?"

"I'll have my secretary fax a transcript of my notes from our sessions up to this point. Then your mother will have to schedule with her when she can come." Megan was quiet until he said, "You're brave, Megan. I hope this other doctor can help you. If you wouldn't mind waiting in the lobby while I talk to your mother…"

"Okay." Megan's heart raced. The clock ground to a stop as she waited. She had to believe in something. She had to hope that there was a way for the torture to end. She wanted to taste freedom again.

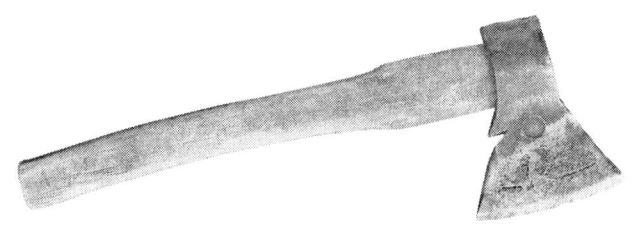

# CHAPTER THREE

As a child, when Carrie Gretsch thought about what she wanted to do with her life, she never imagined she would be in the business of dreams. That wasn't precisely accurate. When she began working for Intershroud, they told her it was the business of dreams. Instead, it turned out she spent all her time working on the ugly side of things—nightmares. She glanced suspiciously out the open door of her small office. Straightening her gray jacket and thin-rimmed glasses, she forced her eyes to scan the nearby cubicles while trying not to look suspicious. Her light hair slumped to one side. Her makeup was blotched in places. She closed the door with her nameplate on it, Ms. Carrie Gretsch, and then picked up the phone.

She pretended to dial but didn't bother pretending to talk. This cluttered closet of an office had only one small window in the door. She knew it was so they could watch her. Someone always did. So she couldn't just put her head down and rest. She at least had to make it look like she was working.

Carrie tried to sit up straight. The best she could manage was a sideways slouch that disarranged her jacket again. She hoped the caffeine would kick in soon, so she could get back to work. Until then, all she wanted was to curl up in a ball on the floor and cry herself to sleep. It wouldn't help. She knew what was waiting for her on the other side. She hadn't slept properly in days. She was so close to the end of this project. All she needed was one night of good sleep and she'd have him.

Todd Price. The elusive rogue that had so far evaded the vast reaches of this company would soon be in her grasp. He was one of the top ten most wanted enemies on Intershroud's list. The upper management considered him more than just a thorn in their side, but she thought of him as her golden ticket. When she caught him, she could get out of this cracker-box and into a proper office—one with windows to the outside world.

It was just one night's sleep away, but for the last few nights, she hadn't been able to sleep at all—a dark Nightmare kept waking her.

She had plenty of resources, of course. She could order a team to eradicate the Nightmare. However, she wanted to find whoever had sent it after her, which complicated things immensely. She didn't have the authority to reassign an agent. They were so rare that if she did get approval to use an agent, it might be weeks or months before the availability of a single night's use. If she destroyed the Nightmare, she would never know who sent it. Therefore, she was trying to figure it out on her own. She knew it had to be somebody nearby. Probably one of the people assigned to her team. It could be any of a dozen coworkers.

She had been manipulating the investigation expertly. None of the employees who worked for her knew everything. They knew the overall goal, of course. Each group only worked on bits and pieces, so that none of them had all of the information. She was reasonably sure none of them knew how close she was to the final prize, but one of them must have at least suspected. The timing of this Nightmare's arrival was more than coincidence.

In the business of dreams, a personally attuned monster amounted to nothing more than a sophomoric prank. They probably only expected it to work for one night, and then she would destroy it and move on. So what had they hoped to gain? Was it really just a distraction so they could hack her computer and try to turn Todd Price over to upper management in order to beat her to a promotion? If so, it had failed. Carrie was too smart for that. She never wrote the key pieces of information down anywhere. She had to make only one final contact.

Fidgeting in her chair with her head tipped back and the phone about five inches from her ear, she knew this had gone on too long.

After her promotion, her first assignment would be to recommend somebody on the team below her for this position. She didn't want to promote a dream saboteur who would try to supplant her again.

It wasn't working. The last couple of nights had been torture. Now she realized it was all becoming some kind of personal vendetta and she couldn't afford that. There were too many manipulative people in this office to take them all out. She would have to use their scheming against them if she wanted to succeed. She had ideas about who it was, of course. She suspected Brian, but it might also have been Tyler or Mary. Those two had been giving her a lot of trouble in meetings lately.

Sitting back up, hoping the small swell of energy was from the caffeine and not an overactive desire for revenge, she put the phone down. Yawning, she stretched and cracked her neck. She wasn't getting any younger. A couple more years and she wouldn't be able to rely on good looks to help her climb the corporate ladder. She wagged her head again. How had she become so deeply entrenched in this dream business? Intershroud. It had sounded so exotic and a little bit mystical when she first started. Since then, it really had been one long, hellish nightmare.

She picked the phone up for real this time and dialed.

Half a ring and then a perky female voice chimed, "IS information. How can I help you?"

Carrie wanted to scratch her eyes out just for being so peppy.

"Forward me to Dale Burns in Native Affairs." Native Affairs meant people who dealt with Nightmares.

"Right away." The perkiness dropped out of the young woman's voice. Despite being in the business of dreams, many employees still didn't like Nightmares.

"IS Native Affairs," said another female voice, lower and more careworn. The ever-changing phone tree of Intershroud was a life-form of its own. Too many offices were in a constant state of flux with people being promoted and transferred all over the place. There was a computer program used by the secretaries to track it all, but it was still more common to be transferred to another secretary than anywhere specific.

"Is Dale Burns in?" Carrie didn't know Dale Burns. She had looked his name up yesterday in preparation for this call.

"I'm sorry, Mr. Burns is in a meeting. Can I take a message?" Everybody was always in a meeting. If a call came for Carrie right now, the secretary would say the exact same thing.

"I have an urgent situation. Upper management asked me to have a Nightmare dissipated ASAP." It wasn't true, but if you wanted anything done, you had to put some weight behind it.

"Everything we do here is urgent, Ms., uh, Gretsch." The secretary was reading that off the computer's caller ID. "Do you want me to have Mr. Burns call you on your direct line or e-mail you?"

"Have him call me direct." Carrie didn't let the bureaucratic nonsense bother her anymore. Red tape was her bread and butter. "How long before you expect him to be out of his meeting?"

"Probably less than an hour."

"Okay, I'll be here. Thanks." Most people around the office didn't use niceties, but Carrie found them to be a convenient camouflage. Sometimes people actually did something you asked because of it. Gullible.

They both hung up.

How had she gotten involved in all of this? Dreams and Nightmares. It was crazy, right? It was too late to turn back now. She was crazy by association.

Carrie hung her head. She didn't have anything else to do until she got that call. If she could swing it, she'd try to order the Nightmare destroyed before noon, leave early, and go take a nap. Everything else was in place. If she had her wits, she would have called a few meetings to see if she could flush out her tormentor. She was too tired to pull off anything that subtle. She just needed to get some sleep so she could finish this project. Then, when the whole thing was over and she had her promotion, and her new office, she would conduct a proper witch hunt.

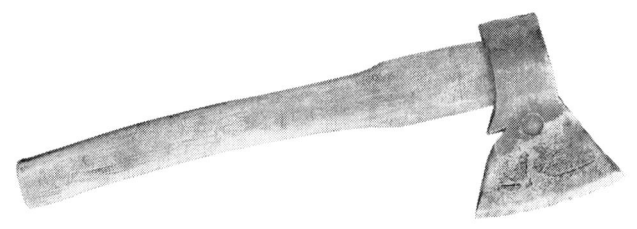

# Chapter Four

On the way home from the doctor's office, Megan couldn't stop smiling. The window was down, and cool air blasted her in the face. She had the radio on, playing obnoxious music as loud as her mother would let her. She felt good for the moment. She felt like there was a tiny glimmer of hope and it would carry her a little further through her gloomy life.

"You seem unexpectedly happy," her mother noted with a smile.

"Maybe," Megan said without much thought. "I just feel good."

"See, that's different."

"Thanks again for agreeing to have her come."

"What else could I say? But don't get your hopes up. If she's very busy, it may be weeks or months before she comes."

"Don't say that," Megan said, rolling up the window. "I can't make it that long."

"You've made it years," her mother said.

"It's getting worse," Megan confided. She turned the radio off. The silence added sorrowful emphasis to her words. "Promise you'll call as soon as we're home."

"I will," her mother said with an exasperated sigh.

When they pulled into the driveway, Megan jumped out of the van and ran for the door before her mother had completely stopped the car. She looked back to see her mother still in the minivan, holding the card Dr. Gund had given her in one hand and dialing with the other. While she watched, Megan saw her mother bite one of her nails. Megan grinned. Her mother's manicurist would flip when he saw that. Megan went inside, her emotions churning. This call made her so nervous she thought she might throw up.

Surrounded by carnival horrors, Megan was trying hard to control herself. The coal-black sky morphed with the silhouette of the leafless trees that surrounded Megan, trapping her with the clowns—there really was no place to run. The spinning carousel played some ghastly song. It was devoid of children, so the creatures bound to the spinning platform by metal spikes through their bodies took the opportunity to sneer and glare. The roller coaster, some lights burned out and some flickering, ran continuously without occupants. Clowns and game masters circled around her, poking at her with sharp fingers if they got close enough, as they taunted and laughed like she was the freak show and they were the audience. They corralled her to this place—the same place they always brought her. She held them off much longer this time with her running and hiding. The end was inevitable, but she fought with renewed vigor. Again, she stood outside the dirt-smeared tent. The large stripes rose to the high point in a nauseating pattern of grime and tattered edges. The front door flaps flipped open and closed in the wind that reeked of feces.

She had known these tormentors for so long. She even gave them names. She called the tallest Stilts. She hated Greasy, the short one with a round belly, more than the rest. Pie, Knife, Bearded Lady—she spent more time with these monsters than with her mother or anybody else. No matter what, the struggle always ended here at the big top tent.

She knew what awaited her inside; it hadn't changed in so long. She had dreamed this nightmare so many times that it was the most constant thing in her life. She had spent more time with it than she spent in school. The terror that built from the myriad of scenarios that all led her to this same place was more familiar than her own reflection. Fear was the filter that strained her every thought, awake or asleep.

She used to fight it. She used to struggle, hit, and bite. She used to scream for help. She used to beg for mercy. She'd tried every rational and irrational response she could imagine, but nothing had ever stopped this moment. She'd played different roles in the dream: soldier, rock star, orphan, martial arts expert. Once, she'd even been a clown, hoping to blend in. It never worked. Nothing would prevent it now, either.

"This is the last night," she said calmly to the contorted freaks around her.

"No, there is tomorrow night," Stilts said, cackling atop super-long legs. Meg had looked once; there were no stilts under those striped pants that went over ten feet up. He really had legs that long.

"This is the last night," Meg repeated. "After tonight, you won't be able to do this to me anymore."

"Why?" asked Bearded Lady with sweat rolling down over the greasy, white paint they all seemed to bathe in.

"Because I have a new doctor. She's going to fix everything."

"We have a doctor, too," said Greasy, the horrible, fat clown with green tufts of hair. He pointed to a tall, white-gowned monster with telescoping eyes and dentist-tool fingers.

The circus doctor said, "You had a doctor already. It made no difference."

"This one will," Megan replied. "So I hope you all had fun because this is the last time."

One of the little monsters started to look worried. She was a tightrope walker with a smile so stretched that it left wrinkles all over her face. Megan heard the lion tamer next to her saying, "It's not true. She always comes back."

"Not this time," she said. "Never again." Then she stepped into the doors of the tent, fully aware of what awaited her. She knew it would terrify her until she woke, but she didn't care. Despite the horrors, she finally felt there was a small beacon of hope in the future.

Inside the cavernous tent, six small fires cast garish shadows of the only occupant. There, in the middle, where he always waited for her, stood the Ringmaster. Dressed in midnight blue, deep maroon, green ochre, and other tones so dark he looked to be in a black suit until you got close, the Ringmaster was tall and broad. He carried a long stick. Though he had his back to her now, she knew what would happen when he turned around. She didn't dwell on it. She just waited, heart racing, until it was finally over.

# Chapter Five

The young widower stood alone, his hands deep in the pockets of a tan trench coat. Icy rain fell like tiny bullets from the dark sky. Bits of hail collected in the low parts of the cemetery grass and the unfilled vases of memorials. Gravestones radiated away from the party of mourners grouped around a wooden casket exposed to the elements. Most of the family and friends of the departed were on metal folding chairs under a canopy.

Over the rim of small, round glasses, tinted dark by the sun despite the stormy weather, he looked at the white flowers atop the gold-trimmed casket. Bitter lances from the sky pierced and tore the petals, just like his life. The cold air was still warmer than the young man's heart. He thought, *Elaine is in there*.

Somebody was talking to the gathered people. He didn't listen. They didn't know her. Nobody knew his wife as he did. For such a precious, short time, they had been happy. Words had killed her. So he refused to take any comfort from words. They were a weapon of war. They were a device of destruction. Words could never heal.

He knew that this was his fault. They had gotten to her because of him. All she had ever done was love him. There was no way he could ever prove it, but he knew they had done it. She was sick. She needed surgery. The hospital had made them sign bulletproof release waivers. What choice did he have? She shouldn't have died on that operating table. He could have prevented it.

The memory of his failure still burned hot despite the frosty weather. One day on the subway, a stranger had said quietly, "If you're not careful, people you know could get hurt." Then the large man pushed several people out of the way and quickly exited the train.

Listening to tiny snapping sounds as the balls of ice occasionally bounced off the stained wooden lid before him, he couldn't pretend he didn't know what the threat meant at the time. He just hadn't believed it. Everything had been so perfect. He was the hottest up-and-coming reporter in the city. He had the perfect scandal story. The paper was printing a daily spot that was creeping closer and closer to the front page. Bad people were afraid. The good guys were winning... until now.

Elaine had needed a simple operation, just an appendectomy. Most people didn't die from it, but there were always exceptions. He'd dropped a fortune on lawyers to find any loopholes in that waiver. He'd paid for an independent autopsy. He'd interviewed every doctor, nurse, janitor, and administrator at the hospital. Nobody would break. His evidence was no more substantial than fumes of exhaust. The ones who knew would never tell. This exception had torn his blissful life to shreds.

His hands, buried deep in his pockets, curled around the items he always kept there. His right hand held a pencil and his left a notebook. He used to keep a lighter and pack of cigarettes there, too. He wished they were still there. The sadness that was weighing on him made the cravings so much worse.

Elaine had made him quit. Now she was gone, and he knew the desire to smoke would never leave. It would remind him of her every day, but he would never smoke again. If he did, it would take away something good she had done in her short life.

A frozen raindrop managed to miss his glasses and hit his eye, breaking free the tear that had been hovering there, undetected. It rolled halfway down his cheek before stopping cold. He tipped his neck back so his short brown hair blew upward instead of flattening against his forehead. It didn't matter whose fault it was. None of that mattered now. He didn't want people to see him crying.

Behind the canopy of people, two new cars pulled up. Three large men in suits got out and made their way slowly toward the group. The ice in the young man's heart cracked. How could they come here? Could they not give him even a moment's peace to mourn? Their message was clear. If he didn't stop publishing the information he had, he would be next.

They didn't realize they had overplayed their hand. He didn't care what they did to him now. They had no more leverage. He would publish everything he had and bring them all down. There would be investigations, trials, and prison. Once that was in motion, he would publish his unproven suspicions as facts to smear their name and spread their infamy.

He blew one silent kiss toward the grave of his love. He buried his old life and name with her. He already had a false identity cultivated. Once his articles hit the papers, his real name would never be heard again. From now on, he would be Todd Price.

Then he turned and walked briskly away before the hired goons could close too much ground. The frozen grass crunched beneath his footsteps. He knew Elaine's family would think he was rude, but he didn't care. He would never see any of them again. The men following him tried to work their way around the canopy without being obvious. He didn't look back. The cemetery ended at a copse of trees and a brick wall that was the back of a strip mall.

Todd Price would become a ghost. They followed him into the trees, but they couldn't find him. All he lived for now was to haunt the ones who had killed his only true love.

Once Todd Price left the cemetery, the rain lightened. As he held on to the pencil and paper in his deep pockets, worry lines grew on his face. He'd started to show his age. He knew he was dreaming. He knew this funeral had happened long ago, but it came back to him in his sleep—bitter memories from his defining moment. Would he ever be free of it?

He had work to do tonight. There was no time to wallow. He turned the corner and disappeared.

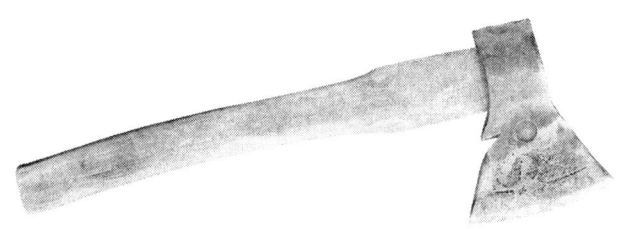

# CHAPTER SIX

"Wow," Megan said as she looked at the china with hand-painted lilies all set formally on the dark table. "It looks like Thanksgiving. Are we having turkey?"

"Very funny," her mother replied. "I just want to start things off right with our guest." She straightened the napkins beneath the silverware.

The doorbell rang, and they both jumped.

"I'll get the door," Megan said.

"Remember what I told you?"

"If anything weird happens, I scream," Megan repeated for the twentieth time. She brushed her hands down her skirt to straighten it and pulled the door open.

Before her stood a woman in her midtwenties who could have passed for a teen. She had black-rimmed glasses and shoulder-length hair with auburn streaks. She wore Levi's and a sage-green sweater. She was about the same height as Megan. She didn't wear any makeup except for a hint of lip gloss. Even though the woman was smiling, Megan felt those eyes boring into her soul. Despite everything seeming perfect for this first impression, Megan suddenly felt self-conscious when she realized this stranger knew all her darkest secrets.

"Hello. I'm Rose. Are you Megan Howell?"

"Yes. I'm pleased to meet you, Dr. Jayne." She reached out to shake hands.

"Please call me Rose."

Megan laughed nervously, trying to relieve some discomfort. She finally said, "Please come in," and moved out of the way.

As she stepped up, Rose scanned the house.

Megan looked down at her blouse and skirt. She suddenly felt a dire need to explain it wasn't her style. "My mom made me wear this." Then she felt stupid for having said anything.

"I understand," Rose replied softly. Then she turned and said more loudly, "This is a very nice house."

Megan's mother came in with a rigid smile.

"Thank you. And thank you again for coming, Doc... Rose."

"It smells delicious. Is it Italian?"

"Fettuccini Alfredo."

"One of my favorites."

"If you'll excuse me, I'll throw the garlic bread in and we'll be ready soon. Megan, take Rose's bag to the other bedroom and then get your sisters."

Megan took the one small bag and then called out, "Time for dinner!" She was back in seconds, leading two younger girls. They wore dressy clothes like Megan, a testament to her mother's determination to make a good impression.

Megan's mother brought hot pans in one at a time before she sat down. Rose followed Megan to the table. "Well, I can see a lot of psychological problems already," Rose said seriously.

Everybody gasped.

Then Rose smiled and laughed. "Just kidding! This is all very nice. Thank you for having me."

After dinner, they moved to the living room. Megan made sure to sit next to Rose on the couch. Megan's mother sat in the recliner across the room. She fidgeted nervously through the small talk.

Rose finally changed to a more formal discussion. "I should give you some credentials before we begin. I'm a psychologist. I have a doctorate, but I haven't gone to medical school like Dr. Gund, so I'm not a psychiatrist. My work is university research, not medical practice."

"So you aren't a real doctor?" Megan asked. She had a sinking feeling as if her hope were in vain. She noticed her mother biting a manicured nail.

"Amanda," Rose said, "you don't need to worry. I'm not here to judge you. None of this is your fault."

"What do you think is wrong, then?" Megan's mother asked. She lay back, no longer trying to keep a formal posture.

"Oh, it's too early to make assumptions. I'll have to do some observations before I know for sure."

"So it's not something you can fix tonight?" Megan thought of her vain oath to the clowns about not coming back and regretted it.

"Honey," Amanda said. "These things take time before…"

Rose made a quick wave to stop her.

"If it's that important to you," Rose cut in, "this is a good time to begin. I can't promise we will succeed in one night, but I can tell you that it all depends on you. The more open you are, the faster you accept that you are in control, the sooner you will have the power to conquer these nightmares."

Megan's mother made a knowing nod and excused herself.

Once they were alone, Rose concentrated on Megan's face. Megan looked down at her feet, trying to maintain composure. Her emotions were so high that she was just trying not to burst. Rose reached a hand out and put it on her shoulder, squeezing gently. Megan fanned the tears out of her eyes and gritted her teeth. She took two deep breaths and rubbed her forearms through the sleeves of the blouse.

"Take your time," Rose said. "You've been under enormous pressure. We don't have to do anything until you're ready."

"I'm ready," Megan said. She made eye contact and sat up straight. "I'll do anything to make this stop."

Rose nodded her approval and went on. "I've read what you told Dr. Gund. Is it true that you have the same nightmares every night? And you wake up with scratches on your arms?"

"Yes. At first, Dr. Gund said I had coulrophobia. But then later, he said my mind was trying to give me a message and once I understood it, they would go away."

"I don't think so," Rose said.

Megan looked up. "Really? Because that always sounded like bull… Uh, it sounded wrong to me."

"It's okay," Rose said. "Say what you feel. I'm not a teacher."

Megan nodded but didn't repeat herself.

So Rose continued, "This has been going on too long for a simple answer."

"You don't talk like him. You don't sound like a shrink." Her voice held admiration.

"I'm not. I'm a researcher. But I do know those words won't help people like you. They don't make the nightmares go away."

"What will?" Megan clenched her fists and knit her brow.

"I'm going to tell you something that's very hard to believe," Rose said. "I'm going to tell you something that Dr. Gund doesn't know. Your mother doesn't know it. Your friends don't know it, either. You probably won't want to believe me when I tell you. But as soon as you believe what I tell you, you can learn to make the nightmares stop."

"Anything," Megan said as her gaze darted to the side. "I'll believe anything."

She saw Rose nod. This doctor was too clever to be tricked by an enthusiastic lie. "It's not something I can tell you. It's something I have to show you."

# Chapter Seven

It was hazy outside the wood-paneled rambler where Carrie grew up. Everything looked gray and drab. There was a chilly wind, but Carrie didn't shiver. She breathed in deeply, trying to grab just a moment of peace. She wanted nothing more than to relax and wander about the garden, looking for ripe strawberries or tomatoes. If there weren't any, she could always pull a tender young carrot from the earth.

Her mother was inside knitting and chatting on the phone with a friend. Carrie felt guilty that she didn't visit more often, but today, she didn't have time. She had so much to do... Except now she couldn't remember what it all was.

Suddenly, as if on cue, a deep roar came from the garden. Carrie knew that roar. It featured in all her dreams lately. Low and predatory, the growl lingered. She began to feel the cold, and it made her gasp. She wanted to run, knew she should be running already, but she waited. Something big was going to happen.

A wave of shrapnel and a cracking explosion flew at her face and cut her skin. Fragments of the wooden fence blasted past her head on every side. Time seemed to slow as the dust clouds plumed. Ivy leaves and splintered boards were scattered everywhere. If she had been thinking straight, she would have been surprised that none of the boards hit her. Instead, the numbing shock held her transfixed while the breeze pulled the shroud of dust off the Nightmare.

The hulking shape of a large black gorilla came into focus like a ship through the fog. It was nine feet tall, and each of the gigantic fists it leaned on was as big as a chair. Its smooth skin was almost glossy in places, and the ripples of anatomically strange muscles—unlike any real primates—glistened in the dim light of an overcast sky.

Dread filled Carrie the moment recognition dawned. This thing had been hunting her for days. Why wouldn't it let her sleep? It raised both fists in the air and bellowed a cry so fierce Carrie felt her knees go weak. Her heart raced, and sweat stuck to her skin. She wanted to scream, she wanted to run, she wanted to curl up and cry. She knew nothing would save her.

Then the monster, grinding huge, square teeth like fingernails on a chalkboard, brought its fists down with titanic force. Carrie didn't even feel the impact on her body. She felt the ground shake beneath her feet. The monster's hands went straight through her and brought up chips of rock and dirt, renewing the cloud of dust. The last thing she saw was the satisfaction in the beast's huge eyes.

Carrie jerked awake. She caught herself before falling out of her office chair. She snapped to attention, attempting again to straighten her hair. When the moment had passed, she glanced around. The door remained closed, and she didn't detect anybody that might have noticed through the window.

While her heart slowed and she deliberately took deep breaths, she picked up a pen and began to write on a yellow sticky note. This had to end. She couldn't take any more of it. That was no simple Nightmare, and she was not a child. Somebody had spent a lot of time on that monster and geared it to her personally. Why? What had they hoped to gain? It didn't even keep her asleep and torture her as Nightmares usually did. It just woke her up, quickly and deliberately. There was no doubt. This was intentional.

Her anger welled into a vendetta. Her revenge would be harsh. Right now, though, she couldn't let it control her. She was too close to finishing this deal, too close to making all her dreams a reality. Revenge would have to wait.

This wasn't working. She couldn't let people at the office see her like this. It was too competitive around here to show weakness of any kind. She also feared the motive behind the Nightmare. If she stayed, she might be playing into their hands.

She picked up the phone and pushed the speed dial for her secretary again.

"Can I help you, Ms. Gretsch?"

"Yes. I've got a contact to meet soon. But I have a very important call that I don't want to miss. When Mr. Burns calls, please forward it straight to my mobile."

"Okay. No problem."

"This is the highest priority. Make sure whoever covers your lunch understands the importance if the call hasn't come before then."

"I will. Is there anything else?"

"No, that's all." Then Carrie had a new thought. "Wait. There is one more thing. Can you keep an eye on my office? I have some sensitive information out that I need to remain undisturbed."

"Do you want me to call up a guard to watch the door?"

"No, that would just draw attention. Just let me know if anybody is loitering by or goes into my office."

"Okay," she said, her voice marbled with bewilderment. "I can do that."

"Thanks." Another nicety. Even half-unconscious, Carrie could manage that much. She hung up. She scribbled fake information on the Post-it. It detailed a time and place, which anybody spying on her would assume was a meeting.

*Spaghetti Barn at Trolley Square*
*12:45*
*Bring Cash!!!*

She had played it a bit heavy-handed with the secretary. It didn't matter. Whether the secretary was or wasn't a confederate with her enemies was irrelevant at this point. It was probably Tyler and Mary together. She suspected they had been seeing each other outside of work. She would remember to verify that when things went back to normal.

If she had been fully on her game, she would have gone there herself to try to catch whoever was following her. In her present state, however, the best she could hope for was a diversion to keep them off the trail until she could get some sleep and finish this. Eyes on the prize.

She checked her makeup and patted her dirty blonde hair once more. It was past her shoulders but pulled back to keep out of the way. She yawned, using the stretching motion of her arms to slip on her coat, which sat over the back of her office chair. The warmth of it tempted her to try another nap. She ignored the impulse and walked casually, all the time looking forward to the blast of cold air outside that would help keep her sensible. She smiled to the unknown faces in the elevator, nodded to the doorman, and floated seamlessly through the rotating glass door.

The air was every bit as refreshing as she had hoped. Filling her lungs with bitter ice, it shocked her nicely awake. Despite wearing sensible shoes, she slipped twice as she approached the curb. The sleet lay on the frozen concrete like graphite ball bearings. A taxi idled nearby, but the light was off, indicating it was waiting for a fare. Carrie raised a bare hand to the biting sleet and leaned over to wave down a new one.

Almost instantly, a yellow car down the street slowed and moved toward her. Her cell phone rang. It was the call she had been waiting for. She retracted her hand quickly to the shelter of her pocket. In that moment, the tiniest bump from someone behind her... Suddenly, it felt like a dream as her feet slipped and she tipped slowly toward the road. Her shoes cut through inches of slush on the road before landing. Her body lurched as her feet slipped under her. The phone, still ringing, fell free when her hands instinctively reached forward to catch herself as she toppled. The cabbie stomped on the brakes, but the car didn't slow at all. It slid forward in eerie silence. Carrie couldn't get any traction with her feet. The moment turned into a thousand still photographs as the dirty bumper closed the frictionless space. At the last second, she closed her eyes. It sounded strangely like a mousetrap snapping shut. Finally, she embraced the complete relief of sleep.

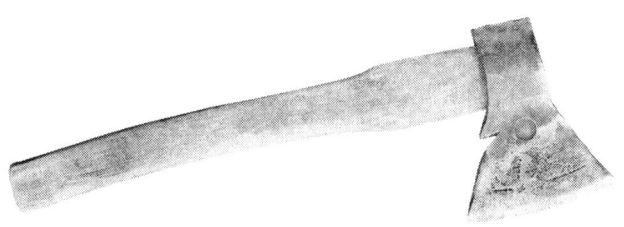

# CHAPTER EIGHT

Megan looked up with her head tipped to the side and asked, "What are you going to show me?"

"I'm going to show you that dreams are real."

"Of course they are. They wake me up every night."

"No. I mean, they are really happening. They aren't just pictures in your mind. When you sleep, you wake up in a different place. It's still your mind and your body, but you are in a real place. You can see other people there that are also dreaming."

Megan looked back down at her feet, feeling betrayed. Knowing the awful things happening in her dreams were not real kept her sane all these years. If they were real, it all became so much worse.

She rocked in place on the couch and held back tears. The horrible dreams felt real enough. She could believe in those feelings.

Eventually, she lifted her eyes and in a breathy voice said, "I can believe you."

Rose pursed her lips and said, "Good. Because tonight I'm going to meet you in your dream."

"What?" Megan asked. Her mind started tumbling as if somebody had pulled the carpet out from under her sanity and there was no ground beneath it to fall on. She looked at Rose again, certain this stranger's eyes would finally reveal insanity. Rose remained steady, looking back in a way Megan suddenly found creepy. She didn't want this weirdo knowing all her terrible secrets.

Rose continued, "I can help you, but I have to see what you're dreaming. If you can meet me in your dream, I can fix what is wrong. Do you believe me?"

Trying not to flinch and failing, Megan said, "Yes." What else could she say?

"Good," Rose said. "The next thing you need to know is that these nightmares you're having are real. They aren't figments of your imagination. They are real, living beings. They don't disappear when you wake up. They continue to live and breathe all the time. I won't know more until I see them."

"You don't want to see them. They're awful." Megan decided to play along. If this doctor wanted to be in Megan's world, she was more than welcome to have it all. "They suck the life out of you. Can't you just make them go away?"

"I'm afraid not. If you really have been seeing them over and over for years, they're probably very strong."

"They are strong. And mean. I told them last night that it was the last time. They laughed. But if I ever have to go through that again… I'd rather die." Her voice was quiet and dark.

"I can't promise that, Megan," Rose said. "We may have to try several things. You have to promise me you can live through it again. You can beat this. Don't throw away your life for a rash promise."

"Okay," Megan said, exasperated.

"Now we need a place to meet in your dream," Rose said.

"The school," Megan said. "No matter what I dream, I always end up at the school."

"I have to see this school, then. I have to see it now before we go to bed. Do you think your mother would drive us there?"

"Sure, it's not far." Megan jumped up and ran to her mother. "Mom, can you drive us over to the school?"

Amanda said quietly, "I'm not sure I want a stranger knowing where you go to school."

"I'm a senior, Mom. It's not like she's going to abduct me."

Megan's mother nodded. "I'll get the keys."

As Megan showed Rose around the empty parking lot, she noticed her mother frowning as she waited behind the wheel of the white minivan. Unlike her dreams, the parking lot didn't evoke any feelings. The moon and tall lamps cast a thin, but steady, light on the yellow lines above the asphalt. Megan realized she'd never been here at night when she was awake before. The real school didn't sit next to a forest, of course. Fences and suburban houses sat beyond the football field.

"So your dreams always start here?" Rose asked.

"Sometimes in the school, sometimes in the forest. All that," Megan said, as she pointed to the oblong track and baseball diamond, "is filled with dead trees. The circus rides and creeps all hide in there before they come up here. It sounds crazy to say it now."

"No. It's not crazy. I've seen much stranger."

"Like what?" Megan asked.

Rose stopped smiling. "Like caves that were actually giant mouths and a castle sitting right in the middle of a big city, but nobody even noticed it."

"Is that what normal dreams are like?" Megan asked.

"No, but we're not going for normal. We're going for exceptional."

Rose made sure her air mattress was ready in the living room. Then she went to talk to Megan. The bedroom remained dark except for the yellowish lines projected from the streetlight on the wall next to Megan's bed.

"Okay, this is the most important time, Megan. The only way I can share your dream is if you concentrate now. You have to concentrate so hard that it is hard to sleep. You cannot let your mind wander. You can't think about me or your nightmares. You have to think about the parking lot at the school and meeting me there."

"I will," Megan said. "Rose?" It was louder and more direct than her previous words.

"Yes?"

"If you wake up first, will you wake me up? That way they can't finish with me." The words had fallen to a whisper. Her voice trembled.

Rose was flooded with sympathy for this tortured soul. "I promise," she said softly.

"Thank you," Megan said. "Parking lot. Mom's picking me up from…" Megan's voice went quiet as she drifted off.

Satisfied, Rose left the door open and slipped down the hall.

# Chapter Nine

Carrie felt groggy. Her head felt stuffed with cotton and every movement of her body felt like she was swimming in grease. It was a dark day with tiny spots of snow threatening to break loose a quiet storm. The world seemed to be taking a long time to come into focus. Then slowly she noticed a nip of cold and the smell of dry leaves. Only then did she feel her feet were standing on uneven lines. It took a moment for her eyes to focus and for her to realize a fencing board lay under her heels.

Beyond the breached fence, some kind of animal was rooting around in the garden. Carrie didn't feel fear or curiosity. She felt like she had just broken a fever and by staying still, she hoped to heal more. It came much faster than she expected. Her strength returned, not just her own strength, a new, greater power. She knew she could climb Everest or wrestle alligators.

How it had happened so suddenly, she didn't know. She wasn't tired at all. In fact, she felt like running for the thrill of it. She knew she should visit her mother, but that could wait. She started a deep breath and then cut it short when she heard a low grunt.

The pointed and wrinkled head of a huge, black gorilla peeked around the side of the large gap in the fence. Fear brought back exhaustion. She suddenly remembered being in the road and now, an instant later, she was dreaming. This wasn't fair. It wasn't right. She was so close to finishing this deal. If not for this stupid ape, she would be done already.

The monster stepped out, revealing his massive shoulders and arms. Carrie closed her eyes. The moment of power was gone. She just waited for the Nightmare to wake her... as it always did.

The gargantuan roar made her shudder. Flecks of spittle hit her arms as the blast of air from its lungs rushed past her. The monster reared back and then brought down two fists to crush her. They pushed down on her shoulders, locking her knees and hips. The ground rumbled, but she didn't wake.

The monster let out a surprised whelp. Then it furrowed the lines of its face and began winding up for a powerful punch. This time Carrie looked. Each fist was almost the size of her torso. When one hit, she fell over. It hurt in a dull kind of way, but it didn't throw her twenty feet as she expected. It was as if the very fabric of space bent to protect her from the unimaginable force of this assault.

The enraged gorilla smashed again and again. It jumped up and down on her head with feet the size of skateboards. It picked up a board and swung it like a bat, all the while roaring. The pain throbbed. But it was like a sore thumb or a headache.

The fear began to leave her as Carrie became more curious about the situation. The monster flexed its muscles, pacing and howling. It leapt at her and pummeled her again. Now that she was lying down, it didn't really affect her. She felt the wind. Her feet tickled from the vibrations on the ground. The fence was torn to splinters and the garden smashed by the dark creature's ranting. It persisted for quite a while until the creature exhausted its fury.

Carrie could swear it shrugged as it turned its attention elsewhere and walked away on its knuckles, heading up the street. She sat up. What just happened?

She remembered slipping into the road. She remembered the taxi hitting her. Then she was here. Wait, was she dead? Was she a Ghost?

No. If she were a Ghost, the Nightmare monster would have killed her. Moreover, if she was merely asleep, it would have scared her awake. What was different now? Why couldn't the monster hurt her?

The truth of her strange circumstances settled slowly into her mind. She wasn't dead or sleeping. Her job training finally kicked in. She must be in a coma.

She wasn't an agent or even much of a Free Dreamer. She knew about dreams, but she had still kept the focus of her mind on material things. Now the sad truth began to dawn on her. She might not wake up for a long time. Sometimes coma victims never woke up. She thought back to what they taught her at Intershroud, trying to remember what this meant. Coma victims were like people who took sleeping pills. Nothing in their dreams could ever wake them. Their mind was completely in the dream as long as the hospital maintained their body. So, as long as she remained in a coma, she was nearly invincible.

A smile crossed her lips, but it rapidly turned down. She was powerless to do anything in Materia to protect her body. If somebody intended to kill her, it would be frightfully easy. She had no idea who had sent the Nightmare after her. She still didn't know what they ultimately wanted. What would happen if her body died while she was dreaming like this? Would she become a Ghost or just die? She knew those were the only two options.

She turned and ran after the shiny black gorilla that had been following her constantly for nights in a row. "Hey!" She didn't know what else to call it, so she yelled again, "Hey! Stop!"

The monster turned to look at her for a moment and then continued its slow trundle forward, looking for something interesting to do. Carrie didn't know how to interrogate a monster, but it was her only lead on who had sent it, so she had to figure it out fast.

"Wait!" When she finally caught up to it, the gorilla turned with an expression of annoyance that could easily become violent if she bothered it. "Who sent you after me?"

"I go where I want and do what I want," it said. It was still a low, gravelly voice despite its surprising eloquence.

"Okay, but who told you about me or set you on my trail?" She was trying to look authoritative, even though she was looking almost straight up at a creature with ten times her body mass.

"Yellow Hat."

"That's his name?"

"I don't know what a Vitae would call him." So it was a male? She didn't know what "Vitae" meant, but she wasn't sure how much time she had, so she persisted.

"Why did Yellow Hat send you after me?"

"Food. Why else? Vitae dream about food so much. Strange you don't understand it more." The massive gorilla looked to the left and right as if searching for food of its own. She knew Nightmares fed off human emotions. She had never tried rationalizing with a Nightmare before. In fact, she had never consciously talked to one like this.

"Food for you. But what was Yellow Hat's reason?"

The gorilla wound up a large fist and casually brought down another crushing blow from the sky. The asphalt fractured around her and sent up tiny curls of steam. Carrie remained unaffected. "You can't hurt me," she explained. "I'm not sleeping in the usual way."

"Obviously," he growled, turning to look at a small bird that had landed on one of the houses in her mother's neighborhood. Carrie grew up in this neighborhood. Her mother didn't live there anymore. In Materia, she lived in a nursing home.

"Did he say anything about why he wanted this to happen?"

"No." The monster grunted that and began moving forward again. "He just said it was a free lunch."

"That's all? He just showed up one day and told you how to find me?"

"No. He worked with me for a while. He gave me a lot of essence. He had other Vitae helping him—made me strong and big." Carrie's brow furrowed. That was definitely intentional. An Intershroud team had doctored this Nightmare and attuned it especially to her.

"How long did that take?"

"Many dream cycles."

"And all you had to do in return was keep waking me up?"

"That was the easy part."

"What's the hard part?" Carrie was beginning to think this conversation wasn't going anywhere.

"Now it will be hard to find food."

"Because I'm not scared anymore?"

"Yes." Of course. Nightmares literally fed off human emotions and thoughts. They had attuned him especially to her. Now that she was no longer available as a food source, he would have a hard time finding any kind of sustenance.

"Can't you just go scare somebody else?" She didn't care if the thing lived or died. In fact, she was glad it would have to suffer a long time for what it had done to her. Still she needed it to keep talking.

"Maybe." The gorilla found a twig on the side of the road and sat down with a thump. He began chewing on it. Small threads of white fog trailed out of his mouth and dribbled onto his shiny chest before disappearing.

"What's your name?" Carrie asked. She needed to get more information.

"Furious George."

Carrie half smiled, half grimaced. This thing had started out in children's dreams as a mischievous little monkey with no tail. It probably played with them at first. Then when their attention lagged, he scared them half to death.

"How big were you before Yellow Hat came?" Yellow Hat, whomever that was, was playing along with the monster's *raison d'etre*.

"Smaller than you." The huge primate bellowed with self-pity now. They had put a lot of essence into this Nightmare. It wasn't a small investment. Somebody in the company had misappropriated a lot of resources. That or it was somebody very high up. She couldn't accept that anybody above her would need to go to these extreme measures. They could just fire her. It had to be somebody under her with contacts from whom they could draw favors.

"Did he take you someplace when he gave you so much essence?"

"No. They came to me."

Carrie sat down next to the big monkey in the middle of the street and scratched her head. What were her options? She could contact an Intershroud office in Essentia. They should be able to help her, but if she didn't know the name of the person out to get her, it would only be a matter of time before he destroyed her body. She still suspected Brian, but she needed some kind of proof. Having the wrong person killed would probably mess up her promotion. Even though she had the power to do it, she'd never had anybody killed before. She wondered at her mind suddenly jumping to the option now. Should such a deplorable act upset her? Why wasn't it bothering her? Suddenly, she patted George on the back, which made him smile. "It's not wrong to kill in a dream," she said, matter-of-factly.

George grunted through a half smile. It was still weird to have such a primitive creature fully understand her. She didn't have any allies in the dream. She didn't even really know where an Intershroud office might be. She was a natural leader, so she knew how to collect the help she needed. Right now, this monster was the only resource she had.

She jumped up. "Come on, Furious." The huge head tipped to see what she was going on about. "Come and show me where Yellow Hat came to meet you." It was a long shot, but it was all she had.

"Why should I?" the monster moaned.

"Because I'm the only source of food you've got. You can't scare me awake. But you creep me out. It may not be a lot, but if you stick with me, you're bound to get a little something out of that."

"And what happens when you leave? Vitae always leave. Only Intenui stay here all the time." Despite the protest, Furious George rose up on his great knuckles.

"I'm not going to wake up," Carrie said. "I can't wake up."

"Why not?"

Carrie started walking. She wanted to pull on the monster to bring him along, but it was too big for a small gesture like that. "It's a long story. I'll tell you on the way. But first, I think you should start explaining all these funny words you use."

George took one step for every three of hers. He said, "You're right. You are repulsed by me. It's better than nothing."

Carrie tried to mask her revulsion. She was used to pretending she liked people. However, Nightmares fed on feelings. She couldn't hide that with nice words. It was primal—part of their nature. Fortunately, this one wanted her to be disgusted. So it was symbiotic. "What do Vitae and Intenui mean?"

George smacked his chest proudly and said, "Intenui." Then he pointed to Carrie with a huge finger. "Vitae." She sensed George liked how his voice unsettled her, so the Nightmare launched into a very long speech. "That's Godrathan talk. When I was new, I did pretty well for myself. But after a while, there was a lull in dreamers interested in my story. I was contacted by other Intenui and given the chance to join them. I am an Intenu."

Carrie looked around at the buildings near them. The last thing on earth she wanted was to listen to a big monkey telling his life's story. Despite her revulsion at every detail, she paid attention. Somewhere in the details might be a clue to the identity of her attacker.

"It was satisfying to live among my own, but it was hard to get food. Then there was a resurgence of interest toward me among Vitae. Vitae are dreamers. So I decided I would be better off on my own. I did well for a long time. I shouldn't have made the deal with Yellow Hat. The other Intenui from Godrath warned me. Then you only lasted for a few days."

This explanation made even less sense to her than the words she'd asked him to define. She kept him talking because she knew if she was his only food source, eventually he would be hers to command. Having a massive monster as strong as this one around was bound to come in handy. Besides, it was easy. In her experience, males never tired of talking about themselves. So it gave her time to think without paying attention to what it actually said. "Well, you can stay with me. What would happen if I was gone?"

"I don't know. I would have to start looking for another food source. If I found some suitable Vitae, I might do very well, but it would take a long time to make the change without any help. I would lose a lot of essence and become weaker along the way.

"If that happens I'll probably go back to Godrath. I'm big enough now that I would be respected there."

"Godrath is a place?"

"This place we are in is called Revra." He put out two arms, which stretched wider than he was tall, and indicated the world around them now. "It is the world. Godrath is a country. It is where Intenui live together, free of our bonds to

Vitae. If you lasted another month, I think I might have gotten above the need for food. Then I would not need Godrath or Vitae. But the Vitae that made me like this knew what they were doing. They knew I would come up short.

"You could probably do it. You could change what I feed on or even make me strong enough that I never need to feed. I'm close, I think. Now that I'm attuned to you, you could make me free."

Carrie smiled absently, pretending to be interested in a mailbox with ducks painted on the side. "Perhaps I will, if you help me." But Furious knew her feelings. She would never release her power over him. There was no reason to. As long as she continued to find him repelling, he would stay. It would never be quite enough food. He would always be hungry.

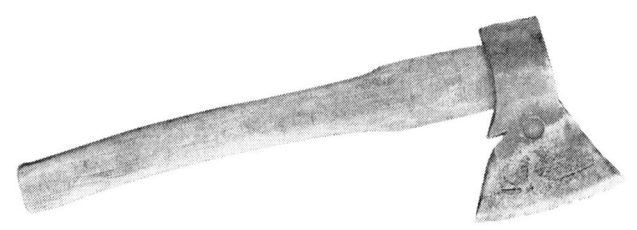

# Chapter Ten

Once again Megan found herself at the school on a dark night. The full moon looked like a spotlight from a police helicopter. Tall lamps in the parking lot projected cones of light that made oblong circles on the asphalt and yellow parking lines. The back of the school lifted from the ground like a black monolith. Bathed in one of the cones of light idled a white minivan. Megan was outside the car door, exchanging angry words with her mother.

"You get in this car right now, young lady," Amanda said. "You have an appointment with Dr. Gund. Those appointments are expensive."

"No!" Megan screamed. "I don't want to go. You can't make me."

"If you don't get in this van right now," her mother warned, "I will cancel your appointments with him completely. Is that what you want? I'm not going to keep paying him and taking off work if you don't even go."

"Good!" Megan retorted. "He doesn't help me anyway."

"Well, who will, then?" her mother said.

Megan became confused.

"Can I help?" Megan stifled a scream out of habit when a strange woman startled her. Eyes wide, she turned to the lady. There was something familiar about her. Despite instincts telling her to fear this spooky intruder, Megan couldn't look away. She felt like she'd forgotten something.

Megan's mother ignored Rose until recognition gradually came over Megan's face. "She can help me," Megan said.

"And who is that?"

"I'm Rose."

"She's a doctor, too." Megan kept staring at this new woman as if lost in thought.

"What?" her mother asked. "She's not a doctor. I don't know who you are, but I'm calling the police. Look, Megan, I don't have time for this. You go to school now, and we can talk about it later."

Megan ignored her mother, examining Rose slowly as if she were a security camera. Her gaze stopped for a moment on the beautiful flower Rose held at waist level with both hands. Then she looked back at her mother.

"It's impossible," her mother repeated. "Dr. Gund is real. He can help you get real answers. This person is a predator."

"No," Megan finally said. She turned away from her mother. "I have to trust her. She's the only one..."

Suddenly, three clowns stumbled out of the woods. A fat, bearded woman in a filthy nightgown cried out in a deep male voice, "Megan!"

Suddenly the minivan lurched and drove away. Megan turned to the clowns and pointed. "No! Stay away. Something's different now. I can..."

"Keep going," Rose said encouragingly. "You can say it."

"You're still here?" Megan asked, turning from the carnival predators.

"I'm still here." Rose nodded. "I came to help you, remember?"

"But how can you..."

"New recruits," said the knife thrower with a patch over one eye. "We love new playmates."

"Don't listen to them," Rose said, trying hard not to be diverted by the approaching menaces.

Megan's words came out faster and faster. "We're both meeting here in this parking lot. You said you had to see it in order to help me."

"Yes," Rose said. "Maybe we should continue this after we get away from these clowns."

"You can't get away," Megan said. "They always catch you."

"Not me," Rose said. She began to walk away from the approaching monsters as she talked. "This time is different. What's different?"

"You're here," Megan said, jogging to catch up to Rose. "That's different. Usually only kids come here."

"Great. Think harder," Rose said. They reached the edge of the trees and pushed though the dark, brittle branches.

"You can help me. You came to be with me!" Blonde curls bobbed as Megan jumped up and down, talking fast. "But that's impossible. How could you be here? Am I just dreaming about you?"

"No," Rose said. "This is a dream. But it's not your dream."

"It's not my dream?" Megan stopped walking, looking at the trees. "It has to be my dream. I always dream here."

"True," Rose said, pulling her hand as a knife flew by and lodged itself in a nearby tree trunk. As Megan began to follow again, Rose continued, "But now you know you're dreaming. You can do anything you want."

"I am dreaming," Megan said. "But I can't get away. I can never get away."

"You can if I'm here," Rose said. They entered a tight clearing with a good lead on their pursuers. "Look in my eyes. Megan, we are both dreaming here together. I am dreaming here with you."

"That's impossible," Megan said.

"No, it's amazing." She grabbed Megan's arms and held her tight, so there was no choice except to make eye contact. "We are sharing this dream."

Understanding slowly dawned. Megan's eyes went wide, then narrow. She looked around as if seeing everything for the first time. "It's a little bit lighter and not as scary."

A wide smile crossed Rose's face. "Yes. I'm really here." She put her arms out, and Megan leaped into them. They hugged each other for a moment, and as they did, Rose pulled Megan to the side to avoid a cream-filled pie tin sailing past.

Rose started to run again. Pulling back, Megan was still grinning. "I can't believe it."

"You can and you do," Rose said in her doctor voice. "Now keep up."

"So I'm in a dream, but I know I'm dreaming. How is that possible?"

"Dreams are real." They came back out onto the asphalt. When Megan looked around, the full moon lit the school well. There were even people in some of the classrooms. Streetlamps lit the parking lot evenly so the whole dream felt like it was in a dim twilight. They sky swelled with spotty, dark clouds.

"This is amazing," Megan said as she looked around in awe. "Will I be able to do this every time I dream, or only with you?"

"That will depend on you," Rose said. "But I can give you something that will help." She shifted the flower to her right hand—Megan hadn't noticed it before—and then used her free hand to reveal a delicate silver bracelet ringed with diamonds from her pocket. She handed it to Megan. "This is for you."

"Thanks," Megan said, a little surprised. She fumbled with the latch to get it on. As she looked at it, she tried to smile and appear grateful.

"That is a token," Rose said. Two more clowns had joined the others. They were out of the trees now and moving in with murderous expressions. "Whenever you dream from now on, if you look at that bracelet, you will remember that you are dreaming. Then you will be in control of your dreams just like now."

"So this will always be on me when I dream from now on?"

"Yes," Rose said. "But it won't do anything unless you look at it and remember."

"Is it like magic?"

"It's as magical as dreams. Our minds tend to forget important things when we sleep. But some small symbol can help us remember." She took Megan's hand again and began pulling her away.

"But if you give me this, you won't be able to remember you are dreaming."

"That isn't my token," Rose said, smelling her red flower demonstratively.

Megan said, "You don't wear glasses in your dreams."

Without warning, a low, menacing voice interrupted them. "You brought a friend for us."

Megan noticed the surprise and fear on Rose's face. She felt bad for not warning the doctor about the trap. It had become so routine that Megan didn't think of it anymore. Today especially, she was busy thinking of other things.

Rose turned slowly until she was facing a short, fat clown in white makeup. Bald except for tufts of green hair over each ear, Greasy had black around his eyes and red smeared across his mouth in a horrifying mockery of a smile. His tattered clothes strained around his potbelly.

He wiped sweat off his forehead, smearing the white paint. "She's a bit older than what usually visits our circus, but we're more than willing to entertain kids of all ages." His eyes twitched.

"She's not a kid," Megan said fiercely. "And you can't scare her."

"Who, us?" the clown mocked. "We would never dream of scaring anybody. We're just here for fun."

"You're a liar. Don't believe him, Rose."

"I don't."

"So your name is Rose. Maybe we can find a nice vase to put you in." His eyes slanted, and the pupils grew large. Megan began to shake.

"You can't have her anymore," Rose said diplomatically. "If you leave her alone, I won't destroy you."

"You couldn't possibly destroy me... A soft, delicate flower like you."

"Maybe not. But I know people who can. And they will if you don't leave her alone."

"Well, forgive me if I don't quiver at such a threat," Greasy said. "But it's only because I don't believe you. People say a lot of things when they're scared."

"I'm not afraid to admit that you scare me," Rose said. "But I'm not coulrophobic. A fat, little Coulroi like you couldn't get enough out of me to make it worth your time."

"Oooh! She knows some big words! You must be one of those Meta*snores* that thinks they got this whole world figured out. I've never had the pleasure of trying my hand at one of those, but I reckon I can pull the leaves off a delicate stem like you."

The clown leaped at her, so fast he blurred, and pounded her full in the gut. Rose staggered back several steps, gasping for breath and struggling to stay asleep. Megan screamed and rushed to Rose's side. She knew if Rose woke up now, she had no hope. Megan held the doctor's cold hand, rubbing it. The clown tipped his head sideways and sauntered forward.

"Leave her alone!" Megan screamed.

"Give me a moment to think about it," Greasy said seriously. Then he shouted, "No!"

Suddenly, Rose reached behind her and pulled out a pistol. She pointed the .38 special at the fat head of the short clown.

"Like I've never seen that before!" he said. Cackling, he stepping forward slowly with a horrifying stare that promised all kinds of pain.

Rose pulled the trigger. A loud report echoed off the nearby school wall, and the bullet punched a hole in the dead center of the clown's forehead. A trail of smoke flew out the back of the round head, leaving a trail behind it. Megan held her breath, hoping to see the horrible clown bleed or fall over dead.

Quite unexpectedly, the clown began to laugh. It was a hideous, broken laugh. With a mock smile, he reached his finger up and probed the hole. "Well, that's new," he said. Then he shrugged, tore a piece off his tattered shirt, and shoved it into the space. "Hey, it's like I grew new hair!"

"New plan," Rose said to Megan without turning. "We run."

They turned away from the monstrous clown and the school and ran for the street.

"There are more of them," Megan called as they ran. When Rose looked back, he was chasing them, but not very fast. Megan continued between breaths, "They'll jump out at us."

True to her prediction, a man with tall legs and a broad-striped suit came out between two trees to block their path. Rose almost fell back, startled. She pointed her gun at his chest and fired. Not stopping to see the result, they turned and ran to the side.

"This won't help," Megan said from behind her. "It's what they want."

A Bearded Lady came at them next, and Rose turned in a new direction.

"We can't get away," Megan yelled. She leaped over a gnarled root, sending up small clouds of dust with every step. The dark branches twisted in the breeze, closing the path and forcing her to constantly change course. Even the air grew thick, refusing to lend the oxygen she needed to run. "They'll just keep moving us toward the big tent."

"I know," Rose called, slowing a little. "But I need to see that big tent."

A hunchback with a deformed face was next. Rose turned again, firing two shots at his face. Megan noticed with satisfaction that he fell backward and didn't get up.

"Stop!" Megan screamed from behind. Rose slowed to a halt, and Megan came up to her. "I don't want to see the big tent again. I don't want to go there."

"But you said they make you go there no matter what," Rose said.

"I know. With you here, I hoped we could get away."

"I don't believe it's possible. If these Nightmares have been at it for years, I doubt there is any way to escape. This place is a giant trap. The only way is to face them. But after I see what we're up against, we can come up with a better plan."

"I think that gun worked on the hunchback one," Megan said. She turned to see shadows darting between trees. Branches snapped beneath the feet of unseen hunters.

"Maybe," Rose said. "But like that first one, these guys are way too strong to be taken out by something like this gun. It just helps me be more confident. I don't think it will hurt them much."

"Do you really have friends that could beat these guys?"

"Yes. But it is more of a last option. How many of these things are there?"

"Twenty, maybe more. They aren't usually all here. Different ones are in different dreams."

"And it always ends with the Ringmaster in the big tent?"

"Always." Megan picked up a rock and threw it at one of the images she saw skulking behind a broken stump.

"Can you stay with me until we get there? Then, after he wakes me up, I'll make sure you don't have to go in the tent."

"Okay," Megan said. "I don't suppose you brought another gun?"

Rose glanced over Megan's shoulder. Before Megan turned to see, Rose took her arm and said, "No, sorry. Let's get going."

As they started to jog away, Megan glimpsed the unicyclist behind her. When they saw a huge, ugly carousel, Megan turned and went back. Rose followed her to the last fork, and they went down the other road. This one led them to the looping rails of a rollercoaster. The tracks spread out in front of them like a huge snake with thunderous trains pounding around the course. Megan tried to double back again, only to find a small mob of clowns blocking the road. She turned and leapt into the trees, leaving the beaten path. Rose followed.

As they ran through the alley between the terrible rides, the knife thrower in black leather emerged. Knives began whizzing by and sticking with a *thwang* into leafless tree trunks. Each one was carefully aimed to miss by inches; they automatically turned like sheep led to a coral by a barking dog.

Megan realized something was different this time. She was aware of so much. She could see the trees and the ground and the sky instead of just reacting to dark blurs. She could make rational choices in the face of the creatures chasing her. She knew she was *supposed* to follow Rose. But she wanted to do something else. She wanted to try to escape now that things were different. Also, she was really tired of doing things she was *supposed* to do. She had been following Rose for a while when the next knife sunk deep into the tree. Rose turned left. Meg went right and headed the other direction. She jumped into some bushes that tore long scratches into her arms. Then she held her breath, which burned after the running, and remained silent.

Rubbing her arms quietly, Megan stayed still as she watched the knife thrower follow Rose. Her heart raced with hope this time. If the clowns were chasing another child, she couldn't have stayed there. However, this time they were chasing Rose. Rose had a gun, and she was an adult. This time Megan didn't feel bad for hiding. She glanced around, hoping to find a new way out of this place now that she could see clearly. She stopped rubbing her arms and began fingering the bracelet, peering into one of the gems as it caught the moonlight. She would be happy to sit here all night and hide from the horrible clowns.

Several other clowns and freaks converged through the dead forest. She lost sight of them, but her memory could more than fill in what was happening. She then turned and began to run the other way, hoping Rose would be enough of a distraction this time for her to escape. Bullets cracked in the distance, but she refused to let herself feel bad for Rose. After so long, she had to try to get out of this horrible carnival. She stayed in the thicker trees, stopping behind large trunks when she could to listen for anything following. When she heard nothing, she sprinted. The clowns always blocked the parking lot entrance. This time, she hoped they would be gone and she could leave the wicked school grounds forever.

# CHAPTER ELEVEN

Rose wasn't surprised when she found herself surrounded by carnival Nightmares. She was surprised, however, that Megan was no longer with her. It worried her. She wanted to wake Megan before the circus folk captured her. She would only risk a few more moments. On one side was the large, dirty tent with stripes that barely showed through the blackened grime. Around her were all the freaks that had carefully corralled her to this spot. The hunchback was notably absent, but the short, fat clown she had first seen was there. He had removed the torn fragment of cloth from the hole in his head and replaced it with a plug of green grass he'd found in the forest. It almost matched the other green tufts of hair, only more horrible.

"Nice to see you again," the short one said with a wicked smile. "Any new threats to our safety you would like to share with us? Any more big words that you think will save you?"

"No," Rose said patiently. She looked around to see if she could catch a glimpse of Megan. "I guess I was wrong. You got me. So what happens now?"

"You go in there." Stilts cackled. He pointed his long, bony finger at the open flaps that served as a door to the big tent.

"And if I refuse?" Rose asked. It was mostly out of curiosity.

"We rough you up a bit and throw you in," said the Bearded Lady with a man's voice. She cracked the hairy knuckles on her large hands. "So please refuse."

"That won't be necessary," Rose said. She walked through the door to see a tall man in a dark suit and top hat turned the other direction. There were six small fires burning around the perimeter of the tent. The shadows cast from the flames reached high up on the tent walls. The Ringmaster held his hands out to the side and took a deep breath, his chest expanding.

"I've come to ask you to leave Megan alone," Rose said flatly.

The theatricality was impressive. A heavy gloom pressed on her heart, urging her to give up because nothing really mattered. If Megan made all this, that girl was a lot more depressed and mixed up than anybody could see from the outside. Rose wanted to feel sympathy for Megan, but she couldn't understand so much self-loathing in someone with a nearly ideal life.

"Megan is mine," the high-pitched voice said quietly. The cracked timbre echoed off the surrounding fabric. "She has made all of this possible."

"Wrong. Megan *was* yours. Now Megan is mine. If you don't leave her alone, I will have to destroy all of your mob."

"You're bluffing," the manlike form said. It turned to face her. "You're far too weak to make good on any territorial dispute of that kind." His voice held the same reverberating quality the whole time. It was very level and confident.

"But I have powerful friends. I'm only here to warn you off."

"I will judge your friends when they come," the man said. By now, his face was fully visible. In the light of the fires, the wrinkles cast horrifying shadows, which accented the malevolence in his expression.

"What happens now, then?"

"Now, you get pain."

"Let's try one more thing first," she said. She pulled the gun out and pointed it at the tall Ringmaster.

He flexed his long, thin fingers as if she had done something that interested him for the first time. "You may try. Once you've abandoned your last hope, your fear will be so much tastier."

"I just thought it would be worth a shot," Rose said. On the last word, she fired several times. In a blur, the Ringmaster slid out of the way. Rose kept firing. Each time, he was gone in the blink of an eye. The evasion didn't even take effort. She began firing randomly to try to catch him, but he zipped around with no fear whatever of being caught by a stray bullet. As long as she was dreaming, Rose knew the .38 special would never run out of bullets. So she fired fast, forcing the quick clown to stay away from her and the door.

"Ha ha ha!" he derided when she paused. "I've had some experience with those silly guns before."

"Doesn't matter much," Rose said. "It wasn't really for you anyway." She lowered the gun.

The Ringmaster began to salivate and slowly closed the distance toward her like a snake, stepping smoothly from side to side. Unimpressed, Rose rolled her eyes, pointed the gun at her own foot, shrugged a smile, pulled the trigger, and disappeared.

Megan felt alive and free in a dream for the first time she could remember. She ran so fast and far without tiring, nimbly dodging dead tree trunks and hurdling sharp rocks. It felt so good to be running with nobody behind her. The opening between the trees that lead to the parking lot entrance waited just ahead of her. Then suddenly her heart sank when she saw the hunchback blocking her path. His mottled face and one big eye looked pathetic, but it belied his sheer size and muscle mass. Megan dodged to the side, but he reached out a very long arm and caught her around the waist. As she folded in half, the wind rushed out of her, and pain blossomed through her ribs and stomach.

He curled her up under his arm and began to make his way slowly back through the forest.

"Let me go!" Megan screamed. She grabbed one of the sharp branches nearby to hold back the powerful monster. Instead of slowing, the branch shattered and cut deep into her wrist. The fight drained out of her with the drops of blood leaving a small trail behind them.

"No, you have to go back to the boss." His voice was dull and deep.

Megan struggled with all her might, but moving made her ribs hurt more. She cried out, "I can't go back there. I won't."

"You can. You will."

Then his grip loosed. The dark sky bleached white. She fell to the ground, twisting as everything went gray.

Megan woke up shaking.

Before she could see anything, she heard, "Wake up, Megan." It was Rose's voice. It must have been her doing the shaking.

Megan opened her eyes to confirm it was true.

"Thank you," she whispered. Her voice reflected exhaustion and exultation at the same time.

Rose gave her a moment to catch her breath. "You were right. Those are some very strong Nightmares."

"Don't you mean, 'that was a very bad nightmare'?" Megan asked as she pulled off one of her gloves. Sure enough, a new red slash decorated her wrist. Megan knew she hadn't reached inside that glove and scratched herself. With a distant and confused expression, she absently said, "It was just one dream… one nightmare."

"Oh no," Rose said. "Most people that know about dreams don't say it that way. All dreams are just dreams, good or bad. The creatures you saw, those are the things we call Nightmares. Each one is a separate, living, thinking being. And you were incredible, by the way." Rose held Megan's hand, rubbing one finger across the new scratch. It was warm to the touch.

"Me? But I ran away."

"I don't care about that," Rose said. Megan wasn't sure it was the truth. "You believed. You met me in the dream. That was fantastic."

"Oh," Megan said, surprised. "How did you know I dreamed about you? And thank you."

"I have something for you," Rose said. Megan's eyes had adjusted, so that she could see Rose kneeling beside the bed, holding something up. It looked like a piece of glittery string. Then it dawned on her.

"Is that a silver bracelet?"

"Yes."

"It's like the one you gave me in the dream, except…"

"Without diamonds," Rose said.

"Wait! How did you know what happened in my dream?" Megan looked at the bracelet and then back at Rose's face, shrouded in the darkness of Megan's bedroom.

"Because dreams are real," Rose said. "I was really there."

"It wasn't all in my mind?" Megan asked aloud. "But that means those clowns aren't just figments of my imagination. They are real, living and breathing monsters!" Tears broke free.

"Right again," Rose said with a smile, pushing the bracelet toward her with one hand and wiping away a tear with the other.

Megan pulled off the other glove, baring her uncut wrist. She reached out and accepted the bracelet. "It's weird… and confusing."

"It's simple, really," Rose said. "I gave you the token in your dream, but this is just something like it for you to wear when you are awake. It helps you to know when you are dreaming and when you are awake. Just look at the bracelet. If you see diamonds, you know you are dreaming. Your mind will realize it and take control. It's called lucid dreaming by some people. But people who know the truth call it free dreaming. You are now a Free Dreamer."

Megan fastened it and lay back down. She fondled it with her left hand and watched the dim lights from the window reflect off it. "That's cool. It seems so strange, though. I mean, why doesn't everybody dream freely?"

"That's how it should be," Rose said. "People who sleep through their dreams miss half their life. The best half, actually. That's why we call them Sleepers. You're not a Sleeper anymore."

Megan thought this through for a while before she finally asked, "So what are we going to do about those Nightmares? Maybe we could try burning down that whole forest." Megan smiled in the dark.

Rose said, "I don't think fighting them is the best choice right now. I think we need to take you to other dream places. You've begun to fear the Nightmares so much that you obsess about them and can't dream about anything else. Does that make sense?"

"I guess so," Meg pretended.

"If we take you far away from them, you'll find new places to dream and never have to go back there."

"How?" Megan asked. "I'm just always there."

"I have a friend that can help. I can go meet him and bring him to you. Then we can show you new and interesting places. After that, as long as you think of those places when you fall asleep, you should be safe.

"So here's the new plan. You need to stay awake for about ten minutes after I go to sleep. That should give me time to find him and bring him to the parking lot of the school. When you fall asleep, you go to the parking lot, and we'll meet you there."

"Okay," Megan said. She stretched and yawned, never taking her eyes off the bracelet.

"Now, there are actually two steps this time," Rose said. "First you have to concentrate on dreaming you're at the parking lot. Then, when you do fall asleep there, you have to remember to look at the silver bracelet."

"What happens if you aren't at the parking lot?"

"Ten minutes is plenty of time. My friend, Steve, said he'd wait for me tonight, so I shouldn't have any problem getting there to meet you."

"So, this Steve guy, what can he do?"

"He can move people from one place to another in Essentia."

"Essentia—the place we dream in."

"Good memory. The waking world is Materia, and the dreaming world is Essentia."

"So he just like disappears from one place and magically appears in another?"

"Pretty much," Rose said.

"So people there have, like, powers?" Megan briefly imagined herself as Supergirl, flying through the sky and beating up anybody who tried to stand in her way.

"Sure. They can do all kinds of things that are impossible when you're awake. There are dreamers that fly or turn invisible. Some powers are really strange. In Essentia, you can do anything you can imagine."

"Are there people that have all the powers?" Megan felt a yearning in her she'd never imagined. Having been denied power for so long, she wanted it all. She craved strength as only the weak can.

"If no other dreamers are around, you can dream anything you want. You can have all the powers. But most of the time, Sleepers keep you grounded. It's only called a power if you can do it whether or not other dreamers are around. But I don't want you to think about that right now. The only important thing is to stay awake for ten minutes, then concentrate on the parking lot, and then remember to look at your bracelet. We can work on the other things later."

"Okay," Megan said. She sat up, knowing she wouldn't be able to stay awake lying down. "I'm ready." She looked at the clock. 11:34 p.m.

"You're really amazing," Rose said. "I've never seen anybody adapt so fast to all of this."

"Well, I have a lot of motivation," Megan said, scowling.

"Okay, I'll see you in a few minutes."

Megan listened carefully to the soft retreat of footsteps over the carpet. She was so tired that every muscle in her body ached. Her eyelids were drooping as she stared at the clock and finally decided she would have to lie down. She would force herself to stay awake, though. Staring at the clock, she imagined being able to fly or being so strong that she could fight those monsters. It was a heavenly fantasy. The distraction carried her away. She was imagining punching the short clown in the face when her eyes closed. The last thing she saw was 11:37 p.m.

# CHAPTER TWELVE

Megan opened her eyes to the twisting branches of the dark forest. As she scanned the trees surrounding her on every side, she saw a short, fat clown standing behind her in his red suit with yellow polka dots, holding his hands up like claws. His eyelids twisted down in a terrible scowl. Megan panicked. This was wrong. This was all wrong. What had she forgotten?

"Knew you'd be back," Greasy said through a sneering mouth. He jumped from one foot to the other, pretending to be funny. "It's been years since you got away before the big finish, but now you're back and we can make it right."

"Wait!" Megan shouted. It was unexpected, and the clown ceased his advances as he waited for her explanation. She felt him patiently feeding off her attention. Megan knew he expected her to explain, and she had only a precious few seconds.

There was something important. Something she was supposed to remember. Things were going wrong, but she wanted to remember one thing.

"Time to go, little girl," he said after his patience had expired. "Don't make me hurt you."

"Shut up!" she said. "Just wait a minute."

"You want to take my hand or shall we do it the hard way?" Offering his hideous, makeup-smeared hands with long dirty nails, she knew Greasy expected her to run.

Hand? That was it! Something about her hands—Megan held them up and there was the bracelet with diamonds glittering like they had lights behind them.

Suddenly, it all washed over her. The forest became just a hint lighter. Her senses all kicked in. She could now smell the stinky little clown and hear him breathing irregularly. She was dreaming, and she knew it. With that realization, she also remembered that she might have powers she didn't know about. She wasn't helpless.

"I am not going with you to the big top," Megan said calmly. "Not ever again."

"Come on," the clown said emphatically, "we both know you can't get away. You can't escape. There's something in you that won't let you get away."

"What?" Megan asked. She didn't need it repeated. She just wanted to ponder the words. Had she really been in a prison of her own making? Was there really something inside her that had bound her to this horrible abuse being played out over and over every night? "That's a lie. You do this to me. I don't do it to me."

"But you're the one that made us. You created us to do this."

"No, I didn't!"

"Well, not to do *this* exactly, but you did create us. Your desires, your fears, that's what we've lived on all these years. That's the food we've feasted on. That is what made us strong and fat."

These were all words Megan had heard repeatedly in her dreams. Now for the first time, she was able to reason them out instead of being paralyzed by them. "You may have fed on me before, but that's over now. I'll never let you do it again."

"Don't be stupid! You're doing it right now!"

"Why are you telling me all of this?"

"Because the friend you came with earlier, she tried to make you strong. She tried to make you believe you were better than us, but it's all a lie. You're the same as you always were, and it will end the same way every time."

"No," Megan said defiantly. "It's not the same. All this horror is going to end. That's why I have to go meet my friend." Then she bolted away.

With a loud laugh, Greasy said, "You'll never get past me."

She couldn't see the parking lot, but she knew he would position himself to block her from going to it.

She spun, twisting around to face Greasy, and ran straight toward him. Laughing through a face of sheer confidence, he waited for her to arrive.

A few feet away, she leaped. It wasn't a small jump; she flew a full five feet in the air. Shocked and startled, the small clown jumped with his hands extended to try to grab her ankles, but only oily fingertips brushed across the soles of her shoes.

Megan landed softly, still running. Without looking back, she sprinted. She knew she had to be at the parking lot when Rose arrived. If she could hold off there, it would all be okay.

The fat clown started to pursue her, but broke off the chase. Megan emerged in the parking lot alone. She allowed herself a few deep breaths and a smile. It was a small victory.

As she wandered closer to the school, she wondered how long Rose would really be. She was alone now, but she wasn't naïve enough to think that it would stay that way.

It was only seconds before her tormentors began to appear. She anxiously hoped Rose would show up. All at once, from ten different places among the brown forest, carnival workers emerged between the spooky outlines of dead trees. Megan backed up until the cold bricks of the school pressed into her back and the palms of her hands. It was a coordinated strike. Her heart raced. Where was Rose? The enemy blocked every possible exit route and pinned her against the brick wall. She searched in vain for any hole in their front line that might allow her to dash past them. Greasy wasn't part of the shrinking half circle. He stood behind, barking orders. Every one of them had murderous intent, she knew, as they slowly moved closer. They left no space big enough for her to run between.

When they were twenty feet away, she knew it was too late for Rose to save her.

The net of clowns continued to tighten until she was only ten feet away from all of them. In near silence, they moved toward her. Finally, Greasy shouted from the back, "You see, nothing is changed. You will never be able to escape us."

"No, you're wrong," Megan said, her voice shaking.

"Where is your little friend now?" Stilts asked from five feet above her.

Megan didn't answer.

Bearded Lady said with her low voice, "We came to invite you to a special party. You're the guest of honor. You're the V.I.P. at the big top. You can come quietly, or you can come kicking and screaming. Please kick and scream."

All the monsters jumped forward at once. The fastest ones grabbed Megan in a viselike grip and held her fast. There were so many creatures around her, so many hands on her. She wanted to scream, but she wasn't about to give them the satisfaction. They pushed and pulled her as a mob toward the wooded area. Once she was away from the wall, more of them filled in behind her and clamped on with their horrible, greasy, white hands.

Tears came, coursing down Megan's face, as the hands lifted her from the ground. More than anything, she wanted to disappear as she fell sideways into the groping mob. She wished for the power to be somewhere else... but wishing didn't make it happen. She wished for the power to fly, but the painted hands kept her bound as the group carried her away. She wished for strength to fight. She kicked a clown's head, but all her struggles were dampened by the ones mercilessly pinching into her body with sharp fingers. This wasn't supposed to be happening. She was a Free Dreamer now, Rose had said. Didn't that mean she should be free? She twisted and turned against the clamps they fastened to her arms and legs, but to no effect. She couldn't even manage to wake up. She finally just wished to be dead.

Carefully, they dragged her away from the school. Only when they were at the edge of the parking lot did they pause when a voice called out, "Megan!"

It was a woman's voice. They didn't recognize it, but Megan did. Rose had finally come.

"I'm here!" Megan screamed. After those two words, four new hands wrapped around her mouth to silence her, smearing grease on her face and leaving a metallic taste on her tongue that reminded her of oily blood. The mob moved faster, forcing several of them to let go. Still stifled, gagged, and pinched, Megan found the only thing she could do to slow them was to thrash violently. She kicked and flailed, managing to gain precious moments where enough space near her mouth allowed for a breath of air.

Rose and a man were sprinting toward the mass of bodies, gaining on the chaotic group. As they approached, Rose called out, "You go, Steve. Just save her. Don't worry about me."

The sea of filthy, freakish Nightmares parted as a man's body crashed into the crowd and shoved them aside. Leaping into the hoard like a stage diver at a rock concert, he knocked three clowns away on each side. He smashed the full length of his body sideways against the mob to push them away on her left. She felt his hands, the only warm hands in the crowd, as he grabbed her ankles. In that instant, nausea flushed through her from feet to head. She rolled, thrusting her hands out to stop her fall. As she did, the world disappeared.

For a moment, she thought she was awake. Then she fell to the dusty earth below, only to discover when she landed that it was actually pavement. The man that had grabbed her ankles was lying on the asphalt by her feet. Several of the carnival monsters were nearby, having tumbled to the ground. The nausea was dimming. Megan was so glad to be free of the terrors that she ignored the pieces of rock stuck in the skin of her fingers as Steve pulled her up by the hand. She jumped away from the pile of clowns. Rushing free of the still-confused monsters, she blurted out, "Thank you. Thank you! Can you teach me how to do that?" She knew it sounded childish, but didn't care. She found herself instantly and powerfully attracted to this man she'd never seen before. He was probably twelve years older with stubble on his chin and a worn leather jacket.

"I don't know," Steve said, looking at the stunned clowns as they began to rise and shake off the surprise. "I've never taught anybody how to verge before. I don't even know if it's something you *can* teach."

"Rose said you can do anything in dreams. Is that right?" Megan wiped the small tears of joy from her face, wanting to look like a good student.

"Sure," Steve said, trying to be encouraging. "Okay. I don't have a lot of time, though." Megan saw Rose rushing toward them from one side as the clowns regrouped on the other. For the first time in her life, Megan didn't fear the clowns. As long as Steve was here, she felt safe.

"Just the basics," Steve said. "I guess you know about bubbles."

"Like in the bathtub?"

"It's her first day as a Free Dreamer," Rose said as she joined them. "Maybe this would be a better conversation for later."

"Yikes," Steve said, looking even more out of place. He stammered for a few seconds, trying to decide where to start. "Uh, well, there are bubbles. Essentia has this one main bubble. That's where we are now. Most of the dreams happen here. But they don't have to. You can make your own bubble to dream in."

"So it's like a room or hidden place?"

"No, more like another dimension."

"Whoa," Megan said. "That's complicated."

"Now there are three of them?" Stilts said as he approached.

"Form the circle again," Greasy yelled. "We'll take all of them."

"Yeah, most people don't really grasp it," Steve said, backing away from the approaching clowns.

"She will," Rose assured him as she pulled Megan away from the reformed attackers. "She was enlightened in one day."

"Wow! Maybe you do have what it takes to be a verger," he said. "Anyway, it's possible to merge and diverge bubbles—that is to say, you can break off from Essentia into your own bubble and then combine it again in a different place. If you have a dream and it's in your own little bubble, it will often match up with this main bubble we're in now and become one with it. That's called merging. It only works if everything in them is almost completely the same.

"So if your dream started in a bubble and then you saw the Eiffel Tower, you would probably merge with this main Essentia and be in France. On the other hand, if you were in France and you forced the Eiffel Tower out of your dream, you would probably diverge into your own bubble. Breaking away is the biggest step. After that, I just rearrange the bubble to look like where I wanted to come out and it merges easily to this spot."

"And you just use your mind to change what's in the bubble?" Megan asked.

"Basically. You have to believe you can do it, of course. You can do anything, but only if you are willing to fight for it."

Megan thought about that. "Rose said you just have to believe."

Rose said, "Right now I say we get out of here." She put one hand out and held the sleeve of Steve's jacket. Steve was taller than both of them, with brown hair and wide shoulders. Megan tried not to stare into his eyes as she wrapped both her hands around his muscled forearm. The charm went away as the world lurched. This time the nausea washed over her from head to toe as she watched the slavering Nightmares leap at them and then disappear. The darkness was chased off by light. The earth became soft beneath them, and there was a rhythmic whistle. Then, where the brick school had been, a wooden log building came into focus. The trees sprouted full, green leaves. Her headache left with a final pound, and Megan had to suppress the urge to vomit.

She closed her eyes. When she opened them again, she was in a completely different place. Rose and Steve were still with her, but now they were at some kind of lodge. The ground was soft, and the sun beamed down warmly, illuminating all the green plants. Like an angel from heaven, a bird chirped somewhere in the distance.

Megan took it all in as if she were a child in a candy store. The lush trees and smell of fresh air warmed her. She had never known that a dream could smell good. The earth angled and quickly rose to a mountainside that she couldn't see because of the tall pine trees. Downhill, a log cabin structure with few windows blocked her view. The ceiling hung over the side, supported by massive wooden beams. The whole thing was stained dark brown with green trim so that it blended in with the forested mountain.

"That was the most amazing thing I have ever seen!" Megan said. Small tears traced down her face as she breathed in the beautiful smells with the ferocity of one who has just escaped from prison and found herself in paradise. She stopped looking around only long enough to make eye contact with Steve.

"It always makes me feel a little bit sick," Rose said. "But I love this place."

"I thought a nice summer lodge in Colorado would be a good place for some R and R," Steve said. "I get so tired of all those dark and dim places. Like I always say—just because you're dreaming doesn't mean it has to be dark."

"So now I can really be a Free Dreamer?" Megan asked.

"As long as you believe it," Rose said.

Steve said, "But there's a difference between believing in something and fighting for what you believe in. Freedom is never free. There is always somebody or something that will try to limit you. You have to fight against them."

"You mean with guns and swords?"

"Not that kind of fight. It's all up here." He pointed to his head with a smile.

Megan thought that anything from "up there" could only be as beautiful as that thick brown hair.

# CHAPTER THIRTEEN

Carrie followed George as the black monster trundled through the street. She knew he could sense how much she enjoyed having a huge creature bowing to her will. He was showing her how useful he could be by leading her to the place he used to scare kids. It was a residential area where a few two-level, brown apartment buildings enclosed a colorful playground. The sky had a net of misty clouds laced together through which the sun managed to filter enough light to make the place almost cheery. Two small children were playing in the sand beneath a swing set when Carrie and George walked up. One jumped up, holding the swing at an angle with her small hands. Both of them began to cry at the sight of the massive black monster. Then they disappeared, leaving the empty swing creaking back and forth.

Carrie observed her companion reaching out to the place they had been. Like a dog licking the floor after a treat was gone, she saw George yearning for the simple nourishment he used to draw from their fear. He had survived for decades on the stuff. Attuned only to Carrie now, it fed him no better than wax fruit. She laughed at his pathetic state, scorning his weakness.

Her escort no longer fit in the dim stairwell leading to the second floor, so he gave her directions to an apartment he used to frequent. It was his territory. He went on at length about some battles he'd had defending it from other Nightmares, but Carrie didn't care about the turf squabbles of freaks any more than she worried about the children they had scared awake. She just entered cautiously in case somebody from Intershroud was there. She didn't want to deal with any monsters besides George right now. She looked out at the nice view from a large window on one side of the small apartment. She scanned for any evidence that might point to possible conspirators. The only thing she found was a big, dopey yellow hat hanging on a rack by the door. She picked it up and examined it.

Anybody wearing this thing would look like a cartoon. She knew in a dream it would fit anybody, so the size wasn't even a clue. In Materia, she could get a DNA test done on dead skin cells. Here, everything was made of essence, so there would be no such proof. In fact, just the act of looking for evidence would cause it to leap into existence to fulfill her mental desire. She could only find clues leading her to what she wanted, not to the truth.

She took the hat downstairs and handed it to George. He looked at it longingly and said, "So you didn't find the Vitae you were looking for?"

"Obviously." As she expected, there were no clues leading to the identity of the person who had sent George after her.

"I like this hat," the monster huffed as if to defend his right to it. Carrie couldn't care less. Seeing he had won, he thumped the hat onto his black head with his massive fingers. On a person, it would have been ridiculously huge, but the band was too small for this monster. He tugged the sides until it stretched over a bump on one side of his head. He punched the tall top down with one finger to make it less comical. Slowly, the brightness of the yellow began to fade and turn dingy. His taint spread to darken the whole object.

"Why is it changing color?" she asked.

"It's part of me now. It was made by the people that gave me so much strength, so I can take its essence as my own."

Carrie realized this beast had just gotten stronger. She had unintentionally fed it. She would remember that in the future. For now, as long as it still needed her, she didn't care.

"See, it's already worth your time to do what I say."

The monster nodded. "What now?"

"We go find a company office building. Follow me." She started walking toward the downtown center of the city. She didn't know what city this was. She knew an Intershroud office found its way into every city. Walking was going to be very slow. There had to be a faster way to get around in dreams. She knew there were people who flew in their dreams, but she had never done it. Furious kept fussing with his new hat, tipping it to one side or the other. Each time he did, it grew a little darker.

It was late into the night before Carrie and her leash-monster found an Intershroud office building. The sky was dark without moon or stars. The Nightmare's hat had become entirely black now and resembled a fedora. It didn't look ridiculous anymore. In fact, it made him look like a hired thug—which Carrie liked—which was probably why he shaped it that way.

As they walked through the mostly empty streets, a few kids would suddenly pop into existence when they started their midday nap. Every single one would be startled awake the instant they saw George. Each one brought a moment of disappointment to the huge gorilla. Their parents would probably just think it was a hypnagogic jerk. Carrie found it amusing.

The building they arrived at had no signs or numbers. It was just a three-story brick square with tinted windows sitting quietly in the middle of a city block. Because taller buildings surrounded it, they couldn't see it from the street. Carrie wouldn't have noticed it at all except for the two guards standing conspicuously by the front door. They were dressed in black and wore flak jackets and helmets with plastic shields to cover their faces. They each held a massive machine gun that would be impossible to lift if it was made of metal in Materia. It was the exact kind of overkill that always gave away the IS.

"You stay here, out of sight," Carrie ordered the monster. "If I call for you, come fast and wake up everybody you see."

The gorilla snorted his agreement. It must have been humiliating for such a strong creature to be reduced to this kind of servitude, Carrie suspected. She didn't care.

Carrie walked up the dark street, carefully stepping over large potholes and cracks in the asphalt. The two guards leaned against the wall, talking. They would have seen her much sooner if the redundancy of their job hadn't made them lax. To compensate, they snapped their gun barrels in her direction and called out a loud, "Halt."

"Relax," she said calmly, trying to suppress the annoyance in her voice. "I'm an Intershroud manager. I've just had a situation, and I need to talk to my boss."

"Name and division?"

"Carrie Gretsch, Material Acquisitions and Investigations."

The guard who wasn't talking to her lowered his gun and began speaking into a microphone wire attached to the earpiece of his helmet. Apparently, he couldn't do that without pushing the little wire closer to his mouth with his heavy glove. He nodded to the other, who lowered the last gun.

"Do you have a pass card?" the guard asked. He stepped aside to reveal a large magnetic lock next to the metal door.

"No, I don't. I don't usually work in Essentia."

"Hold on." He put one glove up to reinforce the order while the other one began talking quietly into the delicate microphone again. Suddenly, that one made a signal, and they both raised their guns again.

The second guard spoke for the first time aloud, revealing a slightly nasal voice that Carrie could understand him trying to avoid using. "You've just been put on a list for being detained. You'll need to wait inside with us."

"There must be a mistake. I'm in charge of a very high-level investigation."

"No mistake," the first guard said, pulling out a card and swiping the lock. It buzzed and clicked. He pulled it open. "Please step inside."

Carrie couldn't believe this. They had her name on a list of people to be detained and questioned? They had her body in a hospital in a coma. What did they think she was possibly going to do now? She had to think fast. Since these guards were also dreaming, she hoped to trick them into revealing more information. "I demand to know the charges. You cannot detain a manager without giving a reason. And since your jobs are on the line, I suggest you make sure it's a good one."

"All we know is that you are to be detained under suspicion of collaboration. Now please go inside or we will be forced to cuff you."

Collaboration? Carrie knew what this meant. Even though she hadn't died, her enemy was using her coma to plant false evidence and get her removed before she could finish the investigation on Todd Price. There was never going to be any promotion. Even if she woke up now, her life was ruined. Brian, or possibly Tyler, had destroyed her career. Now she was waiting to find out if they would also murder her.

"Ma'am, go inside now," the first guard said again. He moved around behind her and began jabbing her with the barrel to force her inside.

Carrie was so livid she couldn't think. Managers were not treated like this. She would teach them how the chain of power really worked. She screamed, "George!"

In a flash of black almost imperceptible in the dark night, the giant Nightmare rushed out of hiding. The machine guns roared as the guards, now side by side, sprayed the entire area indiscriminately. Several sharp lances of pain bit Carrie as the metal slashed through her. Furious brought down two mighty fists and silenced the guns with a small earthquake where they landed. Two clouds of white steam rapidly dispersed, leaving no trace that the guards or guns were ever there.

Looking at the open door, Carrie considered sending George in to tear the whole building apart. Then she saw a few trails of steam coming from his abdomen and realized he hadn't avoided damage himself. Her own wounds closed quickly, thanks to the coma. Furious leaned against a wall, trying to get his breath.

Carrie went over to him. "That was really good." Then she remembered her praise couldn't help him. Only fear and hatred would feed this giant. That was easy enough. She loathed him for his weakness and feared without him she would have no power in this dream world. It got him back on his feet.

They left together. Carrie knew the guards would report what had happened and soon the place would have hundreds of IS thugs bolstering security and searching for them. Hopefully, they wouldn't consider it a big enough risk to assign an agent. Her coma and an overgrown Nightmare weren't nearly enough to justify one of those.

She took him to a hotel they had passed with large doors and a big lobby. They ducked inside and tucked the black monster into one back corner of the lounge by some potted plants. Nobody seemed to notice them coming in. She moved a chair over, sat in front of him, opened a newspaper, and pretended to read. It was very poor camouflage. Most dreamers were so self-absorbed they wouldn't even notice. As long as none of the dreamers in the hotel sucked her into one of their dreams, they might manage to avoid detection.

She hated the monster easily now. He was a risk. If she left him, she could escape, but she still needed him. She couldn't face Essentia alone right now. She needed an ally. She was only secure when she could boss around other people. She hated him more for her own weakness.

While her loathing healed him, she had time to think. The company she had done so much for had turned against her. Nothing could protect her body now. If they decided to kill her, it would all be over. She had precious little time before the inevitable end. Then her leash-monster would be on his own.

She wasn't going down without a fight. She was the only person in Intershroud who knew how to find Todd Price. She'd been planning to hand him over on a silver platter. Now they would never find him. She had left too much misinformation behind her for them to pick up the trail. Carrie had never written down the key piece of information.

Now she didn't want to capture Todd Price. Now she wanted to help him. She didn't really know why they wanted him so badly. Who cared about a stupid online newsletter that only paranoid dorks and fanatics read anyway? None of that mattered anymore. She had only one move left.

She could still try turning herself in and letting them investigate. They might save her life, but she doubted it. Even if the company at large decided to protect her, an unknown person with any level of clearance would be able to kill her body without them knowing.

That was it. That was the key. The company wasn't important. It was that one person. She needed to identify that one person and get revenge. The rest of them could burn for all she cared.

"That's good," George whispered in a deep baritone. Now he was somehow feeding on her hatred generally, not just for him. Carrie realized that was going to make it so much easier to heal him. The holes in his chest and stomach no longer leaked steam.

"Shh." They had to stay quiet.

She needed help figuring out who had done this to her. If she figured it out fast enough and had actual proof, she might be able to get her job back. Ironically, the best dream investigator she knew was the one person she had almost brought down. She needed Todd Price.

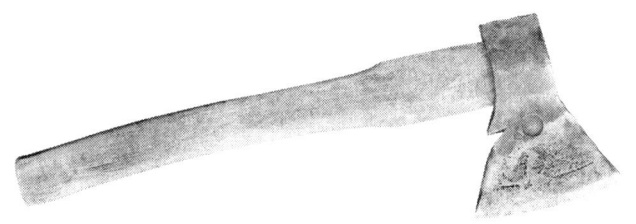

# Chapter Fourteen

"That was amazing," Megan said with stars in her eyes. She stared at the place where Steve had disappeared. Trees still surrounded them beneath a blue sky. "He's incredible." Only after she said it did Megan hear the infatuation lacing her breathy voice.

Rose suppressed a smile. "He's helped me out of several difficult situations before."

"Can we see him again?" Megan asked.

"Maybe," Rose said, "but not for a while."

So many feelings were fighting for Megan's attentions that she didn't know what to do. Tears and laughter tried to break out at the same time. The smell and chills of a truly free dream, not to mention a huge crush threatening to consume her for a man she had only seen for five minutes, made her breathe faster. She had been numb for so long, shutting out feelings to keep the evil Nightmares from using them against her—or worse, feeding off them. Now the dam had burst, and she wanted to feel absolutely everything. Yet it became so overwhelming it almost caused her to go back to feeling numb.

Rose watched patiently as Megan continued to look around. She had never been to a mountain or a lodge like this, and she wanted to see all of it. "So I can just dream I'm here from now on and I'll never see those Nightmares again?"

"That's the plan," Rose said. "You'll need to know this place well before morning. Notice the small details. Remember how you feel. Concentrate on what this place means to you, so that you can come here on purpose."

"This place feels so safe and isolated. It's like we're the only two people on the earth."

"Well, I'm guessing there are some people inside the lodge. But we don't have to go in there if you don't want."

"I like to see people as long as there are no Nightmares—I never want to see another Nightmare in my life."

"I'm afraid that's probably impossible."

"Why?" Megan felt the bad news bring her down from her euphoria.

"Well, Nightmares are part of almost every dream. In fact, earlier, when you were talking to your mother in a dream, that was a Nightmare."

"What? But you said people can see each other in dreams. That wasn't my mother?"

"No, Megan. It was something you created. It looked like your mother, but it wasn't her. Not all Nightmares are scary and mean. A lot of them are just regular people we wanted to see."

"But you're not a Nightmare. How can I know?" Megan fingered her bracelet again. She didn't want to talk about all this stuff now. She just wanted to feel more. She wanted the sun to bake her skin until she was so warm she would never be cold again.

"Sometimes it's very tricky. The best way is to be sure that you look at your bracelet every time you dream and know that you're dreaming. Then, the only Nightmares you make will be on purpose."

"I'll never make a Nightmare on purpose," Megan said with a dark scowl. "Never."

"I can understand that," Rose said, touching her arm softly. "Nobody will force you to. But you will have to deal with them. In time you will see that most of them are harmless, and some are good."

"No." Megan said, glowering. "They're horrible."

Rose said, "We make them."

"The clown today said I made them. Why would I?"

"Don't blame yourself, Megan. When you made them, you were very young. You made them to entertain and comfort you."

Tears formed in Megan's eyes. She turned away and crossed her arms to ward off a sudden chill breeze. She took deep breaths, but it only made things worse. Huge tears fell down her cheeks.

Eventually, she said, "I made them because I missed my father."

"Your father?" Rose asked.

"After my parents split up, I was at the store. I was playing with a toy clown, and my aunt said to my mother, 'It probably reminds her of her father.' They both laughed, but I thought she was serious. Later I asked my mom where Daddy went, and she said, 'He ran off to join the circus.' But as a kid I didn't know she was joking. So I thought he was really a clown.

"He promised to take me to his work when I asked. But then they had this big fight on the phone and he never came back. I begged my mom to take me to the circus. When she did, I didn't see him. That's when the dreams started. I..." Megan broke down and put her head in her hands, sobbing.

Rose put an arm around her and squeezed lightly. "It's not your fault," she said. "You made them to be good, but when they became strong, they turned bad. That was them, not you."

"Then why didn't I destroy them? Why didn't I make them stop? If I made them, why didn't I unmake them?"

"I don't know," Rose said. "Maybe it's like a dog that turns bad and we just don't want to have it killed even though it's dangerous."

"But I did want to kill them at the end. I still do." Megan sat up. The tears were gone. She squinted as she whispered, "I want to kill all of them."

"You didn't control them. They grew into something you never intended. They became too strong."

"I just wanted to see my father," Megan sobbed.

Rose gave her a long time to rest and feel.

"Megan," Rose asked very softly, "did you ever actually see your father among those circus creatures?"

There was a long pause, and then Megan nodded. The silence stretched between them. The sounds of frogs and birds were the only ones to break the deep sobs. After several minutes, Megan managed a whisper that was almost quieter than the gentle wind.

"He's the Ringmaster. My dad was the Ringmaster from the first day."

Megan's legs lost their strength, and Rose helped her to sit on the leaves and twigs. Then Rose sat across from her and used her fingers to brush Megan's hair back away from her face. As she looked down, small tears dropped off Megan's nose onto a bare patch of earth between her knees.

"None of those monsters is your father," Rose said. "Your father would never do that to you. That Ringmaster tricked you, Megan."

"I know that now."

"You have learned the truth. Now you can be free."

"No," Megan said. Her tears stopped as if a faucet valve closed. She looked straight up at Rose with deep lines cutting her otherwise smooth, youthful forehead. Her eyes twisted into a malicious shape as she said, "Like Steve said, you have to fight to be free. I won't be free until he's dead."

Rose looked at Megan, blinking repeatedly. Megan hoped she hadn't said something horrible. Finally, Rose said, "Not now."

"Why?"

"Because you're too new to all this. You've just learned to control your dreams. You barely escaped. You need to heal. You deserve the fun, happy dreams of youth. If you go back to that now, you'll be letting him take away that much more of your childhood. If you waste time thinking about him, you'll lose even more of your innocence. And this time, it won't be his fault."

Megan tried to understand these words, but there was no space for them in her mind. "As long as that monster lives, I'll never be free."

"But he's so strong, Megan. You're not ready to fight something like that. If he wins, you'll be right back where you started."

"He won't win."

"He can dodge bullets! What in the world could you possibly do to him?"

"I don't know."

"Just promise me one thing." Rose now grabbed Megan's shoulders and forced her to look into her eyes. "I've come all this way and done so much. You owe me. You owe me one promise."

Megan suspected what was coming. Glancing down at her bracelet and seeing the wonderful trees around her, she knew she couldn't deny Rose anything. "Okay."

"Promise me you will not go back there for one year."

Megan thought about it. Being a Free Dreamer was so wonderful. She wanted to give in and let it all go, just as Rose said. Yet she knew she couldn't. She could postpone it, but the day of reckoning would have to come. It would keep her bound in a different way. A year was too much. "One month," she countered.

"Three months, then. Promise me you won't go to the school in your dreams or see any of those monsters for three months."

Megan took a deep breath. She bit her lip, and then finally said, "I promise. Ninety days from today."

"Thank you," Rose said. "In three months' time, you'll have seen so much that is beautiful in your dreams. You won't want to have anything to do with those icky freaks."

"Ninety days," Megan repeated. "And, Rose... Thank you."

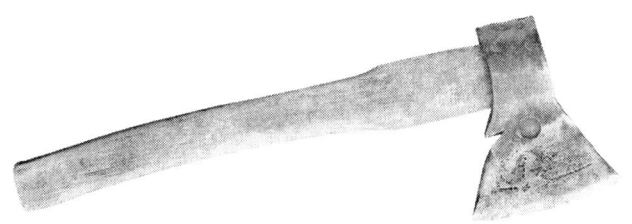

# Chapter Fifteen

Rose woke up early. Not wanting to be any more trouble for the family than necessary, she deflated her mattress and rolled it up in the dark of the early morning. It struck her as odd how such a normal-looking home and family could end up with a daughter in such a horrible situation. Life never gave anybody a break.

Rose heard Megan's mother walking around. She went into the hall to talk to her.

"Aaah!" Megan's mother shrieked.

So much for not disturbing anyone.

"I'm so sorry!" Rose said softly. "I was just hoping to talk to you before Megan woke up."

Breathing heavily, Amanda took her hand from her forehead and rested it for a moment on her mouth. Then she put her hand on her chest and composed herself. "Sorry, you just startled me." Amanda's eyes were ringed with dark circles. Rose suspected she spent the entire night listening for anything strange. Amanda had on a long skirt and a light blue top. She began to fiddle with the top button of her shirt. "How did things go last night?" Megan's mother tried to smile, but doubt clouded her expression. As a trained psychologist, Rose could easily see this woman now regretted ever agreeing to let her come and stay here. Amanda carried a lot of guilt about her daughter's condition. Rose wished she could help, but her first priority had to be Megan.

"Actually, it went very well." Rose motioned with her hand down the hall and began walking toward the living room. She didn't want to wake Megan with their conversation. "Your daughter has a lot of strength. And she's very smart."

"You wouldn't know from her grades." Amanda reclined on the chair again, and Rose sat on the couch. Amanda clicked on a small table lamp.

"Well, she has been dealing with some really big problems, but I think she'll be able to sleep well soon. Normally, I would expect people to have to work out of it slowly, but her willpower is exceptional. It's possible she may be completely free of those Nightmares already."

Amanda was quiet for a long time. She said, "In one night? You think she's better in one night?" Her disbelief fought with her long time suffering. Rose could see this pitiful woman's confusion.

"I hope so, yes. I'll stay tonight to be sure, but I expect she'll be in control enough that she won't need me here after that."

"That's unbelievable. Years of mental anguish all gone in one night? Are you a doctor or a miracle worker?" Rose watched the exhaustion win out. Megan's mother even smiled.

"I'm a doctor. Megan just needed to work through a few things. She'll tell you about it when she feels comfortable with it."

"If you weren't a doctor, I'd kiss you," Amanda said.

Rose wondered why being a doctor would prevent kissing. "Now there are some things that you will need to know. First, Megan has been bottling up a lot inside her for years. Once she's sleeping better, you can expect a flood of problems to come out all at once. I suspect it will manifest as rebellion and other teenage emotions. But you need to know that it's not because she doesn't love you. It's because she's been carrying a great deal of baggage that she needs to work though."

"So she'll still need to see Dr. Gund?"

"I think so, but you may want to give her a break first. Let her find herself. Once she's settled, you can decide if it would be helpful for her to have somebody to talk to or not. As for me, I'll want to make a follow-up visit if that's okay."

"That's just fine. When?"

"This may sound a little crazy, but I'd like to come back in three months."

"Of course. Do you mind if I ask why?"

"It's just a follow-up from yesterday. I think it would be best for Megan if she didn't know about it for now. I want her to adjust as well as she can by herself without me. I don't want her to rely on my return."

"I guess I can understand that. Do you want me to wait that long before she starts seeing Dr. Gund?"

"That's a good idea. After I talk to her, I'll be able to give you a better opinion on whether or not she's at a point where working with him will help. She's made some real breakthroughs, but there's a lot left to work out. I'm afraid most of that burden will fall on you."

"This is such a relief, doctor... I mean Rose. I was beginning to fear she was getting suicidal."

"I detected some of that, too. She was very desperate. I think we've taken that stress away now. I think she's going to be okay. There's just a long, slow process of healing, and your job won't be easy. It may be years before she is completely stable. It may seem like things were better before the change, sometimes."

"At least it can happen now. I don't know how to repay you. I feel so strange that I'm not paying you anything at all."

"The data for my research is more than enough compensation."

"Well, I think you're an answer to my prayers. Do you want some breakfast?"

"Actually, I think I'll go pick up something and surprise my husband."

"But won't Megan want to see you?"

"Probably. And I want to see her. But I don't want her to become dependent on me. I'll be back to talk to her tonight around eight o'clock."

"Thank you again, Rose."

"It was my pleasure." Rose got up and headed for the front door.

Before she left, she watched Megan's mother go quietly into Megan's room and pull the door closed behind her.

Amanda sat down on the bed and let her eyes adjust. Megan rolled on her side, breathing heavily. Amanda smiled, not willing to wake her for the world. She stared at her daughter, sleeping peacefully. It was a sight every mother's heart longs for, something she had not seen in years.

Amanda let her own heart heal a little in that moment. As the seconds ticked by, she felt herself breathing deeply to match the rhythmic inhale and exhale of her oldest child. For so long, they'd hoped and prayed for this. Something so common and unappreciated, Amanda felt tears come to her eyes as Megan just slept.

Eventually, Megan's eyes fluttered, and she caught her own breath before letting out a great yawn. Her eyes remained closed when she asked, "Rose?"

"No, honey, it's your mother." Amanda didn't fell a moment of jealousy. Just a rush of emotions.

"Hi, Mom," Megan said in a voice that was half-delirious. She yawned. "I had the best dream."

"Rose told me you didn't have your usual nightmares. What did you dream?"

"I was at a lodge in Colorado. They had a nice, warm fire and lots of people I'd never met before. They were really friendly. At first I started my nightmare, but then this guy came with her and…" She trailed off suddenly.

Amanda wondered what Megan wasn't telling her. She didn't want to break the moment by asking. Instead, Amanda asked, "There was a guy? Who did he come with?"

"I don't know. The guy sort of saved me somehow. He took me to this nice place."

"Oh! That kind of guy!" Amanda's voice went high and playful.

"No!" Megan parried. "He was an older guy."

"What was he wearing? Was he cute?"

"He had a leather jacket. He looked like a lumberjack."

"Lumberjacks don't wear leather jackets." Amanda could hardly believe her words. She didn't know why Megan dreamed about a lumberjack, but she didn't care. She was happy for anything but clowns.

"Well, that's what he looked like."

"Ooooh! I hope he comes and saves me in my dreams next."

"Very funny."

"I would never have thought a lumberjack would be your type—and in a black leather jacket."

"He only dropped me off there. Then he left."

"So there's hope for me after all?"

"More than for me," Megan said. "He was probably your age. Where's Rose?"

"She left early," Amanda said, not sure if Rose had actually gone yet or not.

"She didn't even say goodbye?"

"She's coming back. She'll be here at eight tonight and sleep over again."

"Oh, good."

"But then she's leaving tomorrow. Are you going to be okay with that?"

"Yeah, that's fine," Megan said.

"You can stay home and sleep if you want, honey," Amanda said. "I might get a call from the juvenile justice system, but it's worth it if you can finally get some sleep." She heard the front door close.

"No, I'm okay," Megan said. "I feel better than I've felt in a long time. I can even handle school."

Amanda put her hands to her mouth, hoping in the dark Megan wouldn't see her tears.

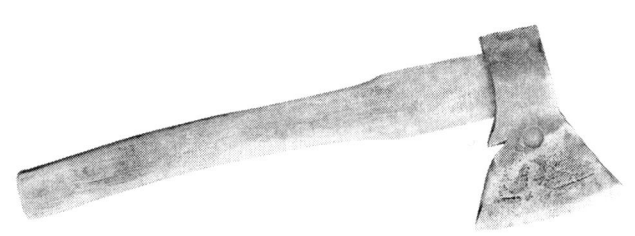

# CHAPTER SIXTEEN

Proof. The bane of Todd Price's existence. The burden of proof was a heavy yoke. How do he convince everybody in the world that the soft words whispered by a loving mother in the black of night were all lies? How could he make them see the cold facts when the population felt warm and safe in a blanket of falsehoods? Todd Price knew the proof was just waiting out there. When he found it, he would finally be able to make everybody into Free Dreamers.

Sitting in the booth of a small Thai restaurant with paper placemats explaining the Chinese zodiac, he scanned the front page of a newspaper, folded down to a manageable size. Todd liked to come early to avoid the lunch crowd. He ate some almonds out of a small dish and sipped his water while he waited for his noodles. An older man came in and took a seat at the table nearby. He was big, with waves of gray rippling his black mane. Dressed in flannel plaid, he looked like his back and knees were eternally sore. He set down a newspaper of his own and leaned a cane against the side of the table.

This guy came in every time Todd ate here, without fail. Todd nodded, but he didn't smile. He knew he would have to deal with this guy soon. At least it wouldn't be on an empty stomach. The hostess came out and took his order. Then, a moment later, she brought Todd's food. Shrimp and peanuts piled over clear noodles in light brown sauce.

Todd ate quickly, using chopsticks nimbly to lift long lines of slippery noodles to his mouth which burned comfortably with peppered spices. Except for a television behind the register that played an imported program, it was quiet. Occasionally, he glanced at the large man eating fried rice with shrimp. Just as Todd finished, the inevitable conversation started.

"Have you seen the news today?" The man blustered with a carefree lilt. To Todd Price, staying out of sight was a delicate art. This man's conversation always made Todd wince because of the indelicacy.

Todd turned to face his conversational assailant. "I only read the comics," Todd said evenly.

"There's an interesting article in the Tribune about the disaster recovery effort." Despite the man's natural friendliness, Todd always thought the lines sounded fake coming from him. It didn't really matter because there was nobody around.

"I read the Times. I'm finished with this one. You want to trade?" Todd held the refolded mess up unceremoniously.

"Very good idea," the man mumbled. They awkwardly exchanged papers and both pretended to be absorbed in something fascinating that they were reading. In fact, they were looking for notes that might tip the other off to the possibility of someone following or watching them.

Todd didn't find any notes. However, he noticed two men in suits standing suspiciously outside the restaurant. He waited until a taxi picked them both up before making his exit.

Todd tossed a twenty on the table and thanked the man as he walked out with the new paper under his arm. Sometimes they used magazines or books, but the word play was always similar. All that mattered was the exchange.

He turned his tall collar up against the cold and hustled on his way.

Once he had driven his rental car back to the motel of the day, Todd flipped open the crumpled ball of newspaper and began quickly sifting the pages. He found the envelope taped deep inside and tore it out, bringing tails of newspaper still attached to the tape. He spread the contents on the recently made bed: a small USB drive, a driver's license with Todd's picture on it, and a credit card. The cards read Harold Stafford and sported a squiggled line which any child could forge for the signature.

Todd worked for an online newspaper called the Essential Expositor. They knew his enemies wanted him dead in the worst way. So they made sure to keep him off the grid with a constant stream of changing information. He didn't even know the name of his boss. Everything he owned fit in a carry-on bag.

He booted up his laptop and waited for it to connect to the complimentary hotel Wi-Fi.

The Essential Expositor was, at best, a newspaper, at worst, an online hangout for conspiracy theorists. Maintained by people who knew the truth about dreams, it was a unifying voice for Free Dreamers scattered everywhere. Todd Price was their lead reporter.

Of course, their enemies did everything in their power to bring it down.

As lead reporter, Todd Price was number one on the enemy's list of people to destroy. The enemy was the same company that had killed Todd's wife. His articles exposing illegal activity contained irrefutable proof. Yet it had never led to police or government action.

The public face of one corrupt business was merely a drop in the bucket. Todd kept digging. He learned they controlled similar businesses and high-placed politicians all over the world. It wasn't a mafia or a gang; it was a conglomerate with no legal or official ties. Most of their business was legitimate, but it all had the same purpose—to turn the population of the world into sheep. It all contributed in one fashion or another to keeping people from ever discovering the truth about their dreams.

By luck, the Essential Expositor found him first. He'd run out of money. No reputable publication in the world would print his work. So when money, seemingly from heaven, started to show up with writing assignments, Todd took the job—or whatever this was.

He started visiting the Essential Expositor online site and reading everything there, even though he didn't understand most of it. He started researching ghosts, trauma victims, and insomnia whenever they asked him to. He threw himself into this new work because he had nothing else. Over time, the truth about dreams became obvious. And once he started really dreaming, the little tips and discussions on the website made sense. He saw almost every living being as Sleepers, easily duped into believing their dreams were nothing and thereby surrendering the greatest power in their lives.

He didn't go out for all the flying and superpowers nonsense. He just did his job. Soon the past merged with his new work, and he realized the company that had destroyed his life was just one small part of a conglomerate that acted as overlord of the entire dream universe: Intershroud, Inc.

When he discovered this, his mission of revenge became clear. He didn't care about the one company that had arranged for his wife's death. The real problem was Intershroud and all the small companies they controlled. However, as long as the population remained Sleepers, unable to grasp the truth of their dreams, there was no way to fight it.

So Todd Price set out to do what he did best. He began searching for proof. He needed something to force people to accept the truth about their dreams. In the face of absolute proof, he was sure he could tip the balance against Intershroud and undo their ironclad grip on the dream world.

It all seemed easy in theory. He took the assignments he was given.

Along the way, he continued his own quest. Every day his cigarette cravings reminded him of the woman who had loved him and died for it.

Once the computer booted up, he inserted the new jump drive. They were usually generic, black, 4-gig drives. This one was white and could hold up to 16 gigabytes. He impatiently called up the files, wondering what could require such a large file size. A video.

Todd opened the shorter document first and read it.

*A disillusioned IS agent is willing to talk in exchange for help. One-time offer. The enclosed video is the first interview. He wants money and a new identity. Normally, we wouldn't invite you to something like this, but he mentioned some things that could relate to your past. He agreed to tell you more if you came to the interview personally. If you choose to attend, suspect a trap. We set up a meet at the usual house north of Salt Lake City. Full moon. Thirteen. Bring tacos.*

*Alternatively, a paranormal investigation group in Salt Lake City has recently published findings that suggest some physical evidence. They don't know the significance, of course. But it looks promising. See website.*

The second assignment wasn't time sensitive, just in the same location. An agent claiming to be disillusioned with Intershroud, who just happened to mention information about his wife? Of course it had to be a trap. His wife's death meant nothing to Intershroud. They killed people all the time. With it being years in the past, nobody would mention it now except to try and draw Todd out. Lucky for them, Todd didn't care about dying, since they already took his life when they killed his wife. He decided to play the game.

His employer didn't contact Todd just because they thought the information about his wife would lead to anything. They wanted him in on it because if anybody could get the truth out of an Intershroud agent, it would be a professional interviewer. Despite being powerful dreamers, in waking life, agents were nothing special. Obviously, his employer hoped Todd could get information out of this guy which he otherwise might not volunteer.

He called up airline flights and found the first one to Salt Lake International Airport. He could watch the video during the flight. The full moon and thirteen nonsense from the message meant he had to be there tomorrow by one in the afternoon. His people kept him paid and safe, so he didn't bother telling them how easy most of their "codes" would be to break. He had no idea why they said to bring tacos.

# Chapter Seventeen

Megan chased a bird through the forest outside the lodge. Every time she came close, it flew just out of reach. Taunting her, it bounced from branch to rock. When it went down a dark hole beneath the roots of a tall tree, Megan put her hand in to reach for it. Then she heard the voice. The unmistakable, high-pitched voice of the Ringmaster had come from this void beneath the twisted root of a tall tree. She couldn't make out the words, but suddenly, Megan didn't know if she should run or try to fight. When she pulled her dirty and scratched arm from the hole, she saw the diamonds on her bracelet.

The voice instantly cut off. The bird disappeared. The scent of pine and lichen flooded her senses. Megan couldn't remember how long she had been asleep. She had a standing invitation to meet Rose at the lodge, so she climbed the tree nearby and looked around until she saw the green roof. It took her twenty minutes to get there. She wondered how long she'd been chasing that bird.

She nodded at the two men standing guard by the front door. They casually waved her in and nodded. If they didn't know her, she would have quickly wakened here. Stained wood paneling surrounded the lodge's interior. The main room had large windows on one wall and had several tables scattered around the edges to leave the middle open and airy. Oriental rugs lined the central path toward a huge stone fireplace that radiated just the right warmth.

Megan sat down sheepishly at an empty table, expecting Rose to ask why it took her so long to get here. She couldn't see Rose anywhere. Megan thought of leaving, but she only knew one other place she could get to in her dreams and her promise not to go after the clowns prevented her from going there. Steve had taken her to see several fun places, but her attempts to go anywhere else on her own had failed so far. She waved at a few familiar faces, and new acquaintances from the last few weeks nodded or spoke a few kind words. She sipped hot chocolate, twirling a lock of hair around one finger and trying to look like she belonged here even though she was sitting alone. She needed a new place to go in her dreams. This lodge felt warm and safe, but everybody here seemed to be her mother's age. Weren't there places where teens got together in their dreams?

She was lost in thought to the point of starting a regular dream, something Rose called a Sleeper dream, when a dark figure suddenly plopped down on the seat across from her. The sound of his hand thumping the table shocked her, and she had to suppress a scream. As she covered her mouth, several people looked over and laughed. She would have been mad if not for Steve's familiar smile surrounded by dark stubble.

"Sorry!" He laughed. "I didn't realize you were daydreaming. Or night dreaming? No, that's not right. Maybe dream-daydreaming? That's a funny one. I'll have to ask people about it."

"I'd rather you didn't," Megan said, trying to make her voice sound older.

"Have you seen Rose?" Steve's smile fell, and Megan began to wonder if there was something she should be worried about. He must have read her concern because he explained, "It's nothing big. I just need to ask her a question about somebody she wanted me to meet."

"Oh." Megan's mouth stayed flat. "Is that all?" She knew Rose had other people to help. It was completely selfish of her to be jealous. Yet, she felt abandoned.

"I guess I'm not making much sense today," Steve said. "If you see her, will you tell her I'm looking for her?" He kept glancing to the side, not making eye contact.

"Sure, but if you're a verger, shouldn't you be able to find her?" Megan kept her eyes fixed on him, happy with the smallest attention he offered her. More than anything else, she just wanted to look like she belonged here and not be left on her own again.

"I tried. I don't think she's asleep right now. And in a few minutes I won't be. Time zones."

"Of course. That makes sense."

"What's up with you these days?"

Megan smiled. He wasn't going to leave her yet. "Well, I haven't managed to verge yet."

"It's not for everybody. Don't beat yourself up about it. If it is meant to be, you'll figure it out eventually. There are a lot of different powers out there. That one's pretty rare."

"Is there anybody who has all of them?"

Steve thought that through. "Actually, everybody has all of them."

"Not me." Megan laughed. "I don't even have one of them."

"But you do," Steve said, talking faster as his excitement grew. "We all do. If no other dreamers are around, we can do anything we want. The problem is that there are usually other dreamers nearby. And their expectations of what the world *should* be like keep everybody else from doing anything cool. That's the problem with Sleepers. They don't think they're dreaming, so they expect Essentia to be the same as when they're awake. But if you go someplace remote when no other dreamers are around, you can literally dream anything you want."

"So if nobody else was around, I could verge?"

"You could do a lot more than that. You could fly. You could breathe fire. You could build mountains or cause an earthquake. The essence the dream world is made out of is literally tuned to our minds. It responds exactly to our expectations and wishes. If there are no other dreamers around expecting it to be a boring life, you can change the world into anything you want."

"So it's only a power if you can still do it even though other dreamers are around?"

"Exactly."

"Why would dreamers ever *want* to have boring dreams? Why wouldn't everybody want to make it so everybody else could use all the powers all the time?"

"There are people that want to control everybody's dreams. They want all the power for themselves. So they keep everybody shrouded."

"Shrouded?"

"People that never really dream are walking around in a haze. It's like they're half-dead already. They live their lives completely oblivious to the best part."

"I wish I could get someplace where there were no dreamers," Megan said absently. "I'd like to try that."

"You want me to drop you somewhere?"

Megan smiled. She didn't want Steve to leave, but he never stayed around very long. So she said, "Yeah. That would be great."

Steve offered his arm, and she tried not to caress the leather of the jacket as she latched on. "Just remember to stay in control. When the world bends to your every whim, it's easy to forget and fall into Sleeper dreams."

"I won't forget," Megan said. Then the place melted around them, and her stomach lurched. Megan found herself half sitting, half standing. She almost fell over until the essence suddenly formed into a chair exactly like the one she had been in and caught her.

It took a moment for her mind to realize where she was. It was a wide, open field. Tall yellow grass blew in the breeze with trees and hills far off. The instant she realized the grass was there, it snapped into focus with delicate seeds at the top and slender leaves pointing toward the sky. When she looked, the sky suddenly began to glow brighter.

"It's kind of hard to see at first," Megan said.

"You're not seeing it. You're shaping it."

"But it was a field, right?"

"Not when we got here. It was an ocean before that. And probably not long after you leave, it will be an ocean again."

"So it takes a few seconds to form into what I think of?" Megan watched in amazement as birds began to appear. Clouds filled in the open blue sky.

"Actually, it would happen instantly if I wasn't here," Steve admitted. "Right now, our minds are fighting each other for what it will look like. I have been trying not to think about it, so yours would win, but I'm still creating some interference. When I go, it won't take any time at all."

"You don't need to go," Megan said distractedly as a caterpillar moved onto her finger from a nearby plant.

"I do. I have things to do. Besides, if I stay it will always be a negotiation between our two minds. Right now, I think you should just dream free. Unbridled power is something you've never tasted before. It can become addicting. It's what they take away when they keep everybody in the dark."

"Thanks," Megan said.

Steve smiled as he disappeared.

For an instant, Megan realized she could bring him back... or somebody that looked like him. The real Steve would never know. She shook her head. It would be a Nightmare. And a Nightmare of Steve was too awful to accept. She knew it could never go anywhere with him anyway. She just enjoyed having a schoolgirl crush.

The flowing field reminded her of a video she had seen in class of an African savannah. Suddenly, a wave began to move rapidly toward her through the grass. It looked just like what she had seen in the video when a lion was running through the grass. What should she do?

Fear snapped her out of it, and she remembered she could do anything. So she leaped. She went high in the air and held herself in place. Immediately, she was levitating.

The thrill of having escaped quickly gave way to the thrill of flying. The lion's wave went harmlessly beneath her. From her high vantage point, Megan laughed. It was such an adrenaline rush. She floated slowly to the side, allowing clouds to wrap around her and then pass by. She turned one pink and then orange. The sun flowed to the horizon to accommodate her every whim. She willed it to keep going, and it plunged from the sky, leaving her riding a cool night breeze. The stars came out, but they were blotchy with big patches where clouds blocked them.

Megan looked at the trees dotting the distance and immediately they all erupted into torches with the light casting stark shadows crisscrossing the ground beneath her.

Now that she had warmed up, she made the shadow lines real. Suddenly, the ground beneath her was a giant piece of plaid fabric. Then it had buttons in a line where bushes and weeds used to be. Then it was a huge man's chest, breathing in and out rhythmically. At the edges where mountains used to be was a gigantic black leather jacket.

Megan saw where this was going again and quickly stopped herself. She flew forward, gradually gaining speed. The wind whipped her hair and tickled her bare knees. She flew faster and faster until the gigantic fabric below her was long gone and nothing but ocean waves spread out beneath. The clouds flew past at supersonic speeds. Then the horizon bent and the coast approached. At this speed, the coastline was beneath her in seconds.

Suddenly, the sun was back up. People covered the beach. They built castles, sunbathed, played Frisbee, and surfed. The moment Megan registered they existed, she began to fall from the sky.

The wind whipped her face for the first time. She flailed her hands and tried to go back the way she had come. It was too late. Her stomach flip-flopped as she tumbled from the air, now gaining speed again as she rushed toward the ground. In seconds, she pounded the earth. Sand flew in every direction. The grayness of waking began to push in. Then she took a deep breath, and it ebbed with the most recent wave. She pulled her arms and feet out of the sand and brushed off her clothes.

The beach was nice, despite the taste of salty sand. She knew why she had suddenly fallen to the ground. These dreamers didn't think people could fly, so she couldn't. Stupid Sleepers.

It wasn't until she started looking around for what to do next that Megan realized she had forgotten to try verging. So caught up in everything, she hadn't even remembered what she was there for.

It didn't bother her very long because a group of teens waved her over to join their volleyball game. Megan pulled off her heavy hiking boots and tiptoed over to join them. She felt overdressed with all of them in swimming suits. Nobody else seemed to notice. A cute blond boy with a dark tan on the other side nodded and served the ball right to her. Megan was happy to discover that despite being hopeless at sports when she was awake, she could play as well as anybody here. Somewhere between bumping and setting, she forgot she was even dreaming.

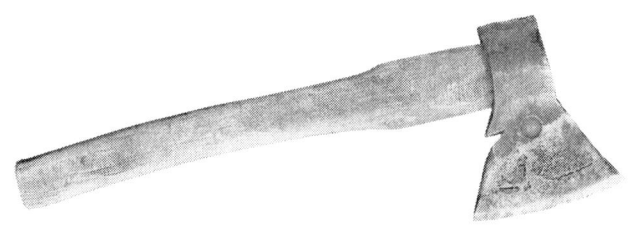

# Chapter Eighteen

Carrie found that in her state of perpetual dreaming, she was very impatient. There were no real words on the newspaper she was hiding behind except whatever she imagined to be there, so it had no value as a diversion. Waiting here, alone with her thoughts, infuriated her. She didn't know how long it would be before somebody killed her. She just knew her time was too short to sit still. Eventually, she rolled the whole paper up and threw it across the room.

"Come on, we're going." She didn't look back to see if her leash-monster was following. She marched purposefully out the door.

Half a dozen men in black riot gear were casually searching the area down the street they had come from. Fear of capture suddenly sobered her. Carrie moved next to the wall and began slowly working her way around the corner of the building. She had no idea what time it was in Materia. All she had seen made her believe it was perpetually night in this part of Essentia, so the black skin of her companion more than compensated for his immense size. They rounded the corner undetected.

Just being out of the guards' line of sight took the stress off her. She had to force herself to think rationally. Apparently, this place magnified the smallest of emotions. She couldn't afford to run off at every whim. Besides, she wanted to ration George's food.

Sensing they were free for a moment, the giant growled, "Where to now?"

"It's a secret," Carrie said without apology. She marched deliberately down one of the small roads before she realized she didn't even know where they were.

"What city is this?" she asked after they walked long enough that she didn't expect anybody from IS to find them. It was a vain hope. If they wanted her, she knew they could find her with a single thought. Why hadn't they found her already? She had to do something to get far away. Time was her enemy.

George's bass voice boomed, despite his best attempts to whisper. "I don't know."

"What do you Inte... Whatever you call yourselves, what do you call it?"

"Intenui. We call it Comic Book Northeast."

"What?" Carrie slowed down, trying to decode the cluster of ideas in the name. "Why?"

"From their dreams, we have learned that this place is in many cartoon books. There are several areas like this, but this one lies northeast of the others."

Carrie looked down a long street toward the city center where skyscrapers rose so high they almost scraped the bottom of the black clouds that lined the sky. She hadn't noticed it before because her attention had been on finding a company building. Now she could easily make out a large yellow light sweeping the clouds with a shadow puppet bat in the center. "New York!" she said the instant it dawned on her. "It's New York, where so many comic books are set. And your book."

"No. New York is farther up," the Nightmare pointed with a gigantic knuckled finger. "That is where adults dream. Here is called by many names from different books."

"So there are two different New York cities, one normal city and one just for superheroes. Is there two of every city?"

"No." He shrugged. "Just some. There are six of this cluster you call New York."

Carrie wagged her head in disbelief. Even working for a company that was based in dreams, she had never bothered to sort out all of these details before. Until now, it never mattered. "We're very far from where we need to go. We can't possibly walk there."

"Why walk?" the low voice mumbled. "You can dream we are there."

"I don't understand that," Carrie said. She was still distracted by the nearby downtown area. There seemed to be an uncommon amount of activity up on the roofs and climbing the walls. From here, it was impossible to make out any details.

Furious tipped his hat and wrinkled his face. He was obviously debating how much to tell her. She also suspected he was trying to think of the way to get the most essence out of the conversation, too.

"If you know how to get there," she prodded, "you better tell me fast. Or I'll spend the next hour thinking about budget reports."

Two large eyes, vividly offset from the black skin around them, rolled skyward before he conceded. "It is a dream. You can do whatever you want when nobody else is around."

"Why can't I do what I want if somebody else *is* around?" She didn't like limits.

"Because your intention is what makes this place. All of Essentia was made by dreamers. I was, too. A single Vitae can tear down and rebuild the whole of it. They just don't know it. It's when many Vitae gather in one place that they stop one another from doing whatever they want." He had a pained look as he said this. It was like an inmate teaching a new jailer how the prison system worked.

"So I could just magically appear wherever I want to go as long as no other dreamers are around when I try it?"

"Yes."

"And I can do anything I want when they aren't around, too?"

"Yes. Some Vitae can do it even when other Vitae are around."

"So I could fly right now if I want?"

"Unless another Vitae sees you."

Carrie had dreamed a few times that she was flying, and now it was too tempting to resist. The desire for freedom filled her soul. She leaped into the air and rose up above the buildings around her. Air brushed her long, light hair back. She turned to watch the trees and buildings shrink slowly. Then she saw the guards in black like tiny ants swarming around the IS building she had been to earlier. Suddenly, she felt heavy, and the invisible platform she floated on reversed to bring her lightly back to the ground.

"I have to do that again. Later." She was breathing heavily from the thrill, not the exercise. "So if I go to that other place, you won't be with me?"

"I will if you intend it to be so." George shifted his hat like a teen waiting for a judge to pronounce sentence on a misdemeanor.

"As long as you remain useful, I'll take you," she said casually.

George nodded, taking a deep breath.

All at once, Carrie felt a headache. The pain flushed through her whole body. An electrical storm spread from her mind to the ends of her limbs. All of her aspect was awash in a kind of dull pain that throbbed. Her knees buckled. George managed to get one large hand under her head and shoulders before they hit the ground. When she looked in his eyes, Carrie saw concern. He was probably just worried about his meal ticket, but she liked knowing somebody cared about what happened to her.

Nausea began to bombard Carrie's entirety. She rolled back and forth on his hand, trying to make any thought work. Shock set in to keep her from feeling so much pain. Only then did a few dim thoughts penetrate the assault.

Something bad was happening. This pain was coming from outside her. It threatened to wake her up. In a coma, she shouldn't be able to wake up. Then her tear-filled eyes popped open, and she could see George holding her in the dark of night in the middle of the street. Finally, the truth dawned on her. She was dying. Somebody in Materia had done something to her body.

As her dream aspect faded and the precious mind George depended on for life began to dim, George trembled. He didn't dare to move an inch. Carrie knew the tiniest movement, even the vibrations from George's voice, would tear her apart like wet tissue. Somehow, he sensed it, too, because he didn't move or speak. Then she felt something strange happening. Through her back where she lay on his lap, a kind of tingling entered her and began to spread. It fought back the pain, pushing it away from her heart. George's face twisted even more than usual. Was he taking some of her pain somehow? No, he was shrinking a little. He was giving her his own body essence.

Carrie pulled her knees into a fetal position, forcing her mind to concentrate through the flashing lights she could still see with her eyes closed. She couldn't die now. She wasn't finished. She didn't care about dying, she realized. She knew poison surged through her body in Materia. She could feel it shutting down. Yet she refused to surrender. It wasn't fear of death giving her power to hold this dream aspect together. It was hatred. She didn't deserve to die. Before she let go, she would find the one who did this to her and make him pay.

Black warmth leeched into her from the rock-hard hands holding her curled-up body. Small trails of white steam surrounded her like a cocoon. George's face grew more wrinkled and ghastly as he literally pushed some of his own substance into her. When she opened her eyes and saw him through the mist, Carrie felt an emotion she had forgotten. A tiny ray of light in her black soul cut like a lighthouse beacon through the fog. Through all the horror, Carrie loved this monster.

George stopped pushing in that moment, and his twisted wrinkles of intention smoothed out, leaving shiny black skin on his face. The thick fog in the air around them gently blew away. Carrie carefully sat up, using the side of George's pinky finger as a chair. She gauged herself cautiously.

She felt weak. What strength she did have hinged on hatred, which burned out of control. Her mind knew her body was dead. Somewhere in a hospital, doctors and nurses were running around, trying to figure out why a previously stable coma patient suddenly crashed. The image only further infuriated her.

Then when she looked at George, she felt an overwhelming urge to rush up and hug him. She never understood people who loved their pets. She had thought it ridiculous, but now it felt perfectly natural to her. George was the only creature in existence who remained loyal to her. He was her best friend and confidante.

In his eyes, Carrie could see George changed, too. She knew Intershroud changed him once before. Until now, she didn't understand the significance. Even though he still looked like a huge black gorilla with a stupid hat, George wasn't furious anymore. He didn't feed on her anger and fear. At this moment, she knew he was feeding on her adoration. For the second time in his life, George had undergone a massive biological restructuring. This time, he had done it at great personal risk to keep her alive. She reached up and caressed his cheek.

Unburdened from a physical brain, her mind flitted about like a butterfly. It could jump from having a burning passion to murder someone in cold blood and watch him beg for mercy while she laughed, to wanting to leap onto George's back and go for a piggyback ride. As thoughts, ideas, and feelings turned around inside her like a carousel, one detail kept trying to catch her attention. Then it was gone. She would have to wait for the carousel to go around again.

Eventually, Carrie stood up, testing her legs. There was no pain now. Her death had been relatively short, considering. The trauma of it flashed in front of her eyes before she began to plot her revenge. Her new aspect was very weak. If the bullets from the guards' guns hit her now, she knew she wouldn't survive. Her moment of invincibility was gone. She looked at her arms, and then the detail that had been trying to catch her attention finally did. She stared in shock. Then she began to laugh.

She laughed harder when, for the first time in probably fifty years, George started to laugh. He didn't know what was so funny, but she did. Her laughter infected him and made him giggle. It came out as more of a snorting roar.

When she heard George's awkward giggle, she roared so loud and long that tears came to her eyes. Through the tears, she looked at her arms again. They were dark. All of her skin had turned black—not as black as George, but dark for human skin. By saving her, George had inadvertently turned her skin to a beautiful African hue. After the terror of death, it struck her as hilarious.

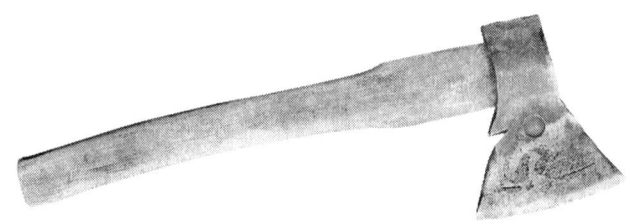

# CHAPTER NINETEEN

When he was dreaming, Todd Price could escape from anything. In Materia, he had to plan very carefully. The meeting place was a small house in Ogden, Utah. It was over an hour north of the airport on a good day. Todd was there early. He yawned twice before he got out of the car. He never drank anything with caffeine in it. Anything that messed with natural sleep cycles became frightfully addicting to Free Dreamers. He kept up on his sleep enough that one night on a plane shouldn't slow him down much.

The house was in the middle of a suburban residential area. The lawns they passed on the way matched their houses. Lush green surrounded freshly painted tract houses. Scraggly brown grass choked the unkempt places. If it were not the middle of the day, he was sure he would see that the people matched their yards and houses, too.

After examining the road and the neighborhood, Todd decided it was just too much of a risk. Agents were nothing special in Materia, but this one probably had a subdermal tracking device. During the flight, he'd watched the video. It was obviously a setup. Not willing to enter needlessly into danger, Todd came up with something better.

Sitting down in a hotel bedroom a safe distance from the house, he turned on his computer and waited for the Wi-Fi connection. Far away, a young teen he'd paid fifty dollars delivered a matching computer and a bag of tacos to the blue safe house where the agent waited to meet Todd. Todd Price knew better than to show up in person to an Intershroud trap.

He wore dark glasses. He had drawn the heavy drapes in the room and used only a small lamp behind him for illumination. This way the video of his webcam conversation couldn't provide any good pictures. He waited impatiently, sketching little pictures of birds into the notebook. Doodling was a habit he had picked up in college and never broken. He used as much paper for pictures as he did for words.

The computer beeped, signaling a connection. Todd watched as the person that had opened the computer arranged it on a table. The lighting there was much better than it was on Todd's end. He recognized the middle-aged man from the video earlier. He had a receding hairline that was obvious because he had dyed it dark. He wore square glasses lightly tinted brown with metal rims. His chubby face was only just beginning to sag into a waddle. His plaid button-up shirt needed laundering. It hung open to reveal dark chest hair.

"Hello?" the agent's voice said in a broken baritone. He looked like a used car salesman. "Is somebody there? It's pretty dark."

"This is Todd Price. I'm here." He used a program to alter his voiceprint slightly.

"I can't see much. Can you turn on some lights?"

"Sorry," Todd said unapologetically. "I was unable to get to you in time for this meeting. But I did want a chance to talk to you. My employer says you have asked for help changing your job status. Would you state your name and clarify your situation for me?" The flashing green light indicated the entire session was being recorded.

"Yes. Harold Finch. Friends call me Harry. I worked for Intershroud as an agent, but they caught me stealing money and now they're after me."

Fake surname. Todd was sure of it.

"I was under the impression that most agents don't have access to money as part of their work, Harry."

"It's true, we mostly work at night."

"When you're dreaming?" Todd knew it wouldn't help to clarify this point. Video interviews weren't proof that dreams were real. He did it for his own satisfaction anyway.

Harry hesitated before saying, "Yes, but I was occasionally put in charge of large payoffs or other sensitive situations."

Ransoms, illegal weapons, and kidnapping, Todd guessed. If Harry was overseeing money exchanges in Materia, he wasn't an agent. The IS had plenty of thugs they could use for their daily felonies. They wouldn't risk an agent.

"I was under the impression that Intershroud agents were well-compensated for their work. What influenced you to take more?"

"I do pretty good, it's true." Harry had a self-important smugness that was at best annoying. "But who can't use an extra ten grand for a weekend in Vegas once in a while? Besides, it's not like they don't own half those casinos anyway. I was just givin' it right back, really."

Todd was glad the dark face Harry could see wouldn't be able to reveal his obvious disbelief in the whole story. Even with his best rerouting, Todd was sure he only had a few safe minutes before his location would be traced. Clearly, this interview was going nowhere, but he didn't need to end it yet.

"My employer tells me you're willing to trade information about Intershroud in exchange for helping you escape and go into hiding. What is the information you have?"

"I got names and locations. I know where their offices, are and I can give you contacts."

"Finding that kind of information is child's play, Harry. You have to give us something bigger than that. What are the names and home locations in Materia of any agents you worked with? Where can we find employee lists for executives or managers?"

"They never trusted me with that stuff," Harry said, beginning to sweat. Todd thought this man put a lot of work into pretending he was nervous.

"What are some of the missions they sent you on?"

"They don't usually tell me that. In Materia, I just carry the briefcase and bring back whatever I'm told. But I know some of the contact names and where to find them."

"Do you know anything about or the names of any Intershroud Controllers, CEOs, or Presidents?"

"I think I know one President," Harry said with a too big of a grin.

"What's his name?" Todd was running out of time and patience.

"Ruiz. I'm pretty sure it was President Ruiz from a company front in Central America."

"First name?"

"I don't know. Only heard somebody talk about him once."

Todd would check up on it, but he guessed a search would bring up many such company presidents or none.

"What company did he work for?"

"I, uh, Baxson, maybe?"

"Baxson's in Florida."

"Oh. Well, I didn't actually talk to him, I just heard his name."

"Do you know anything about a major operation? Company division assignments? Anything?"

"Wait! I do know an operation. I heard of one. The guy that talked about President Ruiz said there was some kind of operation starting up. Operation War Bird, I think."

"Did he say what Operation War Bird was?"

"No. They only knew one part of the plan. Something about manufacturing parts that didn't make sense. They made them anyway, of course. But nobody could figure out what they do."

"Do you know what these parts are?"

"No. He never saw them. Just talked about it with the delivery truck drivers."

"Can you think of anything else?" Todd glanced at the clock on his computer. If the interview had gone well, he might be willing to risk more, but this information was worthless. Harry was telling the truth, or he was a much better actor than Todd guessed. He probably didn't even know they'd set him up as bait.

"All I know is a list of contacts I met. I kept it for just this kind of situation in case I needed some leverage."

Todd nodded. "I'm going to recommend against my employer helping you. If your list is interesting to them, they may choose to help you anyway." He hit the stop button on the recorder, unplugged the USB wire, and jammed the power button.

He didn't know how long he had before they found this room, but Todd wasn't in the business of taking risks. He had taken the screws out of the laptop's casing beforehand. Now he opened the bottom of the laptop and physically pulled the memory cards out of the computer. He then pried the processor off the motherboard with a screwdriver. He left his trench coat and the dark glasses behind with the computer shell. He took everything else and went through the door to the adjoining room he had also rented. He bolted the door. He pulled on a baseball hat and sweatshirt, stuffed everything in huge pockets on sagging pants, and put on massive headphones. Holding an MP3 player and swaggering as he walked, he made his way through the hotel to the parking lot. He left his rental there and took a taxi he had ordered, which was waiting.

He would check up on everything Harry said, of course. Still, he doubted very much that any of it would be accurate. If he had to guess, he would say the IS had recently made Harry an agent and told him just enough to set this trap up. They probably knew he was stealing before any of this. If he really escaped, they didn't lose anything. Since he was probably not as powerful a dreamer as he made out to be, they could round him up in Essentia any time they wanted.

Todd cracked the taxi's window for air. He asked the driver, "Do you know any good places to eat?"

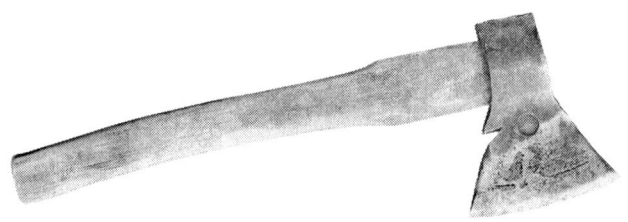

# CHAPTER TWENTY

It was eighty-nine days later when Rose found herself on the doorstep of Megan's house again. Winter brought darkness early. Her breath came out in clouds. Her thin coat was insufficient to stop the wet wind that penetrated to the bone. Salt, spread to melt the ice, crunched under foot. The shoveled snow from the walkway piled on the sides in little mounds. The result was a diminished path, which felt precarious. Rose wished she had brought a hat to cover her ears. Instead, she had to make do with putting her gloved hands over them.

The porch light was on, and as she stepped up the two stairs, Rose could easily see her breath swirling away the precious heat from her body. Even though she had only gone twenty feet from the cab to the door, she was already freezing. She rang the doorbell quickly and stepped back and forth to keep the blood pumping in her legs.

When the door opened, warm air flowed out to her rescue along with the cozy and welcoming lights from inside. She stepped forward and was glad that the cold had frozen the smile on her face because otherwise it would have been impossible to conceal her surprise at Megan's appearance.

Megan had cut her long blonde hair to shoulder length and dyed the tips black with a few dark streaks running through all of it. She was wearing dark liner around her eyes and thick mascara. She had on faded Levi's, cut and frayed in a few places on each calf and thigh. Somebody had drawn on them as well. A black T-shirt with vampire fangs leaping out of it hung on her thin shoulders. The contrast with the blouse and skirt she had appeared in only months ago was so complete that Rose couldn't draw the first few breaths of warm air she had craved.

"Hello," Megan said. She had the same nervous smile and the same unsure eyes. It was definitely her inside all of this.

"Hello," Rose responded. She pulled her gloves off and shoved them absently into her coat pockets before unzipping. "My, my, that's quite a change."

"Yeah," Megan said without explanation.

Rose had seen her almost nightly in their dreams. They had met at the cabin, sipped hot chocolate, and talked. Megan had been trying unsuccessfully to diverge a bubble. Occasionally, Steve would show up and take them somewhere exotic and interesting. They had seen the Essential Paris, New York, Los Angeles, Rome, and a few realms that were more like movies than real places. In all that time, Megan's clothes had remained fairly neutral and basic.

"So how have things been?" Rose asked. It was a question for unfamiliar acquaintances, not one for friends who had seen each other a few hours earlier.

"Good," Megan said. "I kept my promise."

"Yes, you did," Rose said as they went through to the living room.

Megan sat on the floor this time. She was looking at the carpet so Rose took the initiative, pushing as much gentleness into her voice as possible. "I like the new look. Did you just try this out today?"

"No, I've been experimenting with it for a while." Megan tried to twist a lock around her finger, but the shorter hair made it unsatisfying.

"You have a different look in your dreams than awake? That can cause issues," Rose said.

There was a long pause. Megan made eye contact once and then looked away again. Finally, she took a deep breath before saying, "I thought Steve wouldn't like it."

Rose let a big smile spread across her face only because Megan was still looking the other way. "Oh. In that case, I think I can understand. But you should let your limn—your self-image in your dreams—be the same as when you're awake. When you try to be two people, it splits your mind. That's when your shadow shows up and you lose control of your dreams."

"That's why I ended up dreaming about cleaning house all night last week?"

"Yes."

"Do you think Steve will make fun of me?"

"Steve is a grown man that dreams he's wearing boots and a leather jacket," Rose said. "He has no room to criticize a new punk teen." It took all of Rose's training as a counselor to not make a comment about how Megan should really like boys her own age.

Megan's smile told Rose she felt relieved.

Rose held her smile even longer. "So, Megan, what were you thinking of doing in your dreams tonight?"

"You already know what my plans are," Megan conceded.

"You're still bent on going after those clowns?" In her mind, Rose wanted to slap this girl silly. Why would she go back to the horror? Rose offered her freedom, yet she refused to embrace it.

"I can't get it out of my head."

"But we've had so much fun. Haven't your dreams been wonderful?"

"Yes, of course."

"Why would you go back to those dirty, disgusting freaks?"

"Because they're hurting people. One of my sisters even dreamed about them the other day. She said she dreamed about me and then some ugly clowns started chasing her. She woke up fast, but I can't let them get my sisters or any other innocent children."

"But your sister just left, right? She didn't stay long."

"It doesn't matter. Nobody who does what they do should live. Since there are no dream police and no prisons, they have to be killed, so they can't do it to anybody else."

"But the other kids will learn to deal with it. You said yourself most of them escaped after only a few times. Your sister woke up as soon as she saw them."

"It's my fault. I have to stop them."

"How can you? They're so strong. And if you fail, you'll be right back where you started. It's entirely possible that they'll be able to hunt you across Essentia if they find you again. You will lose your dreams."

Megan set her chin and narrowed her eyes. "I don't care. It's my fault, and I'm going to fix it."

"Remember what I said about your shadow? This is no time to pretend you have a good reason for doing this, Megan. We both know this is nothing more than you wanting revenge."

The silence grew, and the seconds stretched out.

"Okay," Megan admitted, "it's true. I'm angry. I haven't been able to think of anything else. They deserve pain, and I deserve to give it to them. They hurt me over and over every night for years. They made me afraid of sleeping! Do you know what that's like? They've taken so much from me. As long as they exist, I can't rest. I can finally sleep, but I can never rest. The fact that they're there gnaws at me and tears me up inside. I hate them so much that I don't want to be alive if they keep living."

Rose was too stunned to speak at first. After a moment, she managed to think. "But they also gave you something wonderful." She let the words hang in the air, trying to measure if Megan was being serious or dramatic.

"What?" Confusion laced Meg's voice.

"If it weren't for them, we never would have met. You wouldn't have had your nightmares, but you also wouldn't have learned the truth about your dreams. You would most likely have been a normal teenager. You probably never would have become a Free Dreamer."

Megan thought about it. "That's true."

"You have to find a way to let it go. You have to be bigger than this. If you do, you'll be free. As long as you dwell on the bad things they did, you'll continue to be hurt by them. You'll be imprisoned by the past, and they'll keep hurting you. The only way to be free is to forget them. Leave them to whatever life they can get and never look back."

"I've tried so hard to do that, but even if I forget for a little while, something always reminds me. The memory of what they did haunts me. And most of all, I'm afraid that one day they'll get me back again."

"I know it's awful." Rose touched Megan's shoulder sympathetically. "But it will get easier. They were such a part of your life for so long that, even though it was bad, your mind can't let go of it. Too many memories will lead there. Too many things you see and do will remind you, but it will get better. Each day you'll get a little happier. Each night you'll find new and better memories to cover the dark ones. If you keep thinking about this, you'll become like them. Nightmares aren't the only bad things. There are people worse than any Nightmare." Memories tried to crash into Rose's mind, but she held them at bay by looking down and putting one hand on her forehead. She needed to focus on Megan. When she looked up, she saw Megan had noticed.

Megan's eyes welled up. She bit her lip and said, "I can't promise anything... but I'll try."

"You don't have to promise. Think about it and try to get to the point where you can promise yourself you'll never go back there."

"I'll try. Are you sleeping over tonight again?"

"No, there's no need. I'll see you at the lodge the same as every night. We can meet out back and talk in private if you like."

"That would be nice." Megan looked to the side, searching for words she didn't want to say. Finally she asked, "You went through this, too?"

"Not the same way," Rose said. "When it happened to me, it was people, not Nightmares. And they were trying to kill me in Materia. That's why you need to be careful. If they find out about you, bad dreams will be the least of your worries."

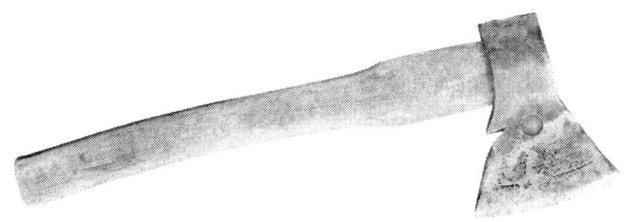

# Chapter Twenty-One

As Megan lay in bed, she stared at the thin silver chain around her wrist. One of the beams of light coming through the Levelor blinds landed right on it, so a bright sparkle chased up and down the bracelet as she turned her wrist. She wanted to lose herself in the hypnotic play of light, but there was too much on her mind. Megan knew she needed Rose in her life. She knew she owed her everything. Nevertheless, keeping her promise the last three months had been the hardest thing she had ever done. She couldn't fall asleep… a novelty for her. She kept catching herself fantasizing about cutting clowns into ribbons and watching them scream.

Eventually, she found herself dreaming in the lush mountains of Colorado. The lodge behind her emitted the soothing smell of burning pine logs. Megan, relieved that she had managed to get here, quickly looked at her bracelet. It was something that had become second nature to her. However, this time when she lifted her hand up and stared at her wrist, she felt the bracelet fall off. She looked at her other wrist, knowing it wasn't there. It had been on her right wrist since the day she got it. Now she had lost it, and panic was beginning to smother her. She had just lost the most precious thing she owned.

Carefully, she stepped back to examine the ground. Leaves and pine needles sprinkled over soft brown dirt. A silver glint flashed at her, and she knelt, careful not to lose sight of the precious chain. She began to reach out her hand toward the tiny glimmer. It looked like only the smallest end of the clasp was showing and a leaf had fallen over the rest of it. Gently she closed her finger and thumb over it and then applied pressure, so that it couldn't possibly fall.

As she stood, the chain began to pull out from under the leaf. She had to stop when it snagged. She brushed the leaf away to see what it could be.

Sucking in her breath, a moment of terror struck like lightning as she realized there was a hand holding it. The hand was big with calloused fingers and dark hair between the knuckles. Covered with dirt, it held the other end of the bracelet with two fingers the same way she was. The buried person, attached to the hand, wanted to get out. The only way it could get out was to hold on to that bracelet while she pulled it free. She wanted to drop it and run away in revolt, except she couldn't bear to lose the silver chain. Caught in a moment of panic and confusion, she made a choice.

She steeled herself, grabbed the chain with the other hand, set her feet into the soft ground, and pulled with all her might. Just as she'd known it would, the hand holding the other end came up out of the ground, followed by a man. Megan didn't look at him. She just kept pulling. Once he was out of the ground, he let go. She stepped back. As fast as she could, she fastened the bracelet around her wrist, running her finger over the diamonds.

With the bracelet on, she knew she was dreaming. She knew what was happening. She turned to face the man. Covered in dirt from head to toe, he stood tall, his dark hair matted in a circle as if he had recently taken off a hat. His button up shirt and Levi's were coated with dirt, so she couldn't even tell what color they were. At first, the earth concealed his features, but within seconds Megan knew who it was.

"Dad?" she asked quietly. It upset her that this person looked so much like the Ringmaster with a long face and deep-set eyes. She tried to force it out of her mind.

He remained silent. His features, hidden by the dark soil, made her suspect there was nobody inside the shell.

"Say something!" she screamed. He stayed silent. When she looked at the ground again, she could see the dirt from his skin removed greasy white paint when it came off. Suddenly, tears welled up, and she found it hard to breathe. "How could you?" Her mind raced. She had to do something. With all her might, she balled up her fist and punched him.

She hit him so hard that it would have hurt her hand in Materia. He didn't even react. So she hit him again. It felt like punching a couch cushion. Then before she knew it, she was pummeling him over and over. Tears fell. She cried out, "Why did you leave? I hate you!" She pounded his chest until he fell back and sat down. Then she started hitting his head. "How could you do that to me? How could you abandon me and not protect me?"

A moment later, she realized her fists were flying through thin air and doing no more than drawing swirling lines through a misty cloud. She slowed down, and everything evaporated. She let herself take deep breaths until she finally whispered, "I hate you."

When it was all over, she felt cold and wrapped her arms around herself. She turned to leave and was shocked to see Rose there. Rose stepped forward, wiped one tear off Megan's cheek, and lifted a lock of her hair to show that the tips were black.

"I'm glad you took my advice," Rose said quietly. Her face didn't look like she was glad.

"How long have you been here?" Megan asked.

"Long enough," Rose said. "That's the problem with sharing your dreams. It's hard to keep anything private."

"I don't know why I did that," Megan said. "At first, I didn't have the bracelet, and I was confused."

"You were confused, but you had the bracelet before the end."

"I just..." Megan didn't know what to say. "I can't..." She began to stutter, "I, I don't..." She started to cry again.

"It's okay," Rose said. "You don't have to have an answer right now. You don't owe me any explanations. You can dream anything you want to." Rose put one arm around Meg's shoulders.

"But you said I shouldn't go fight all those Nightmares."

"I don't think you should. But the fact remains that you do. All the symbols are here. Deep down, those clowns represent your father to you still. Even though you know they've grown into something else, your emotions cannot let go. It's like they're a part of you that you wanted to get rid of. You wanted to stop loving your father because he betrayed you. But then you felt bad for it. So you got stuck between hating him for leaving and not wanting to let go. Nothing I say will change that. You still think the only way to be rid of the hurt is to destroy those clowns."

"But I won't if you tell me not to."

"I can't tell you what's right for you," Rose said. "It's easy to forget that this is your dream as well as mine. Your mind has things it needs to work through. If we were awake, that would be wrong. But here, it's your shadow and your mind. This shadow of your father came out because you aren't being true to yourself. You're trying to please me, but your heart wants to face the circus and get through this."

"But I want to share my dreams with you," Megan said, afraid of being left alone.

"You'll always be welcome to," Rose said, "but I can't watch this again, Megan. I don't know if it's wrong or not, I just know it upsets me. But if you need to do it, I won't stand in your way. I won't ask you to promise me that you won't fight them again."

Now that she had permission, Megan felt strange and out of place. The barrier that had been holding her back for so long was gone. It felt like she was on a high building with the safety rail removed. "But I don't have to start right now. And can't I see you sometimes still?"

"Of course," Rose said. "And we have today. Do you want to go inside and see if Steve's really going to take us to that maze?"

"I do," Megan said. She tucked her hands under her arms and followed Rose around to the front of the lodge. Despite everything else, she was still worried what Steve would think of her new hair.

The next night in bed, Megan stared nervously at the ceiling. There was a layer of fresh snow on the ground, and it reflected the light from the streetlamp, so that her room was brighter than usual with more lines on the wall and ceiling. She was nervous. Rose was busy, so they wouldn't be able to meet at the lodge. Megan knew it was an excuse to give her some space. They had agreed to meet the next day. Megan had the night free, a whole night to dream whatever she wanted. She knew Rose wanted her to go to the lodge. The anger that had driven her to beat on the man last night was still there, though. The resentment and frustration driven by years of pain wouldn't let her rest. She knew she had to go back and face those Nightmares again. When she was honest with herself, the reason she couldn't sleep was fear.

For so long she had been so tired that nothing would keep her from falling asleep. Deprivation torture was one of the claims justifying her hatred. She'd had months of uninterrupted sleep since then, though. Something like fear could actually keep her awake now. She didn't much care for the strange, ironic situation.

It seemed like hours before she finally began to dream. The parking lot came into focus through the gray fog, making her heart speed up automatically. The fetid smell of elephant dung and body odor assaulted her. She'd always thought this was just how dreams smelled. Now she knew it was only how they smelled in this terrible place... a Realm, Rose had called it. She knew she didn't have long before they would find her, and looked for some kind of weapon. Next to the brick wall of the school, she found a pencil. It would have to do.

She held the eraser tight in her hand so that the sharp side stuck out like a knife. Then she waited for the telltale signs of the Nightmares she knew lurked around her. As if she had called them out, two of them emerged from the dead trees across the lot and moved toward her. One was the Bearded Lady. The other was the juggling clown on a unicycle. The unicyclist got to her first.

"It's been a long time," the wheezy voice croaked. "Hasn't been as much fun around here without our Megan."

"Shut up," she said with venom in every word. "I'm not your Megan. *I made you*. You are mine."

"Well then, Mommy, come gimme a hug!" The clown held one big pocket open and let all the colored balls fall into it. Then he threw his hands out as if he really hoped she would do it.

Megan leaped forward at him. She was glad to see him surprised as she tackled him and knocked him off the unicycle. His face still registered shock when his head hit the pavement with a crack. Megan jumped up quickly and was happy to see it take longer for him to recover. She kicked him square in the back of the head. When he reached up to protect his head, she said, "I'm not your mother, you sick freak!" Then she plunged the pencil into his hands and pinned them to his head.

By this time, the large bearded woman was upon them, and Megan dived to the ground just in time to avoid a hairy headlock—one she had been forced to endure many times. Even as Megan escaped, the smell of the repulsive monster's garlic breath made her want to vomit. She came up holding the unicycle's seat and swung the tire in a fast arc. The second time she flailed it, the tire smacked the woman's huge, hairy hands to the side. It had forced the woman to retreat a few steps. By then, the first clown had freed his hands, and though a bit wobbly, he managed to stand. He pulled the balls from his oversize pocket and began throwing them at her. "That's mine!"

"Then come and get it!" Megan turned and ran for the woods. They both chased her. As she left the pavement, she saw the short clown. He had always been her most hated Nightmare. Without slowing at all, she spun around and threw the unicycle at him. It floated through the air and bashed into his head. The fat creature fell back and hit the ground with a dull thud. Megan was sure he wasn't finished, but she didn't look back. She just kept running into the dead woods.

Suddenly, without warning, she burst into a small clearing and saw that the tall man with long legs blocked the path before her. There were two other openings in the trees surrounding this small clearing. Freaks were coming both ways. She stopped abruptly and turned back, planning to go out the way she'd come in. But the Nightmares' plan became obvious when the three she had recently assaulted filled in the escape route behind her. She was surrounded, weaponless, and beginning to panic. This wasn't how it was supposed to go. She couldn't let it end this way again... Not after so long.

"It's so nice of you to come back and play with us again," the tall man said with a wicked grimace.

"Yeah, I almost had to start going on a diet," the short, fat clown said. Megan saw that the grass he'd put on his head had now become a third tuft of hair in the front. She wanted to rip it out.

"The boss will be glad to see you again," the fat lady said with her gruff male voice.

"I'm never going in that tent again," Megan said with as much dignity as she could muster.

"Where will you go?" asked the hunchback. "You're surrounded."

With that, the six carnies moved slowly forward, closing the net. Megan's pulse raced. Terror crept in, and she felt herself losing control. She wanted to run, she wanted to scream—but somehow these monsters had robbed her of the ability to fight. She was helpless before them in the very place she'd most wanted to escape forever. Why had she come back? Why didn't she listen to Rose?

When she remembered Rose, Megan looked at her bracelet again, and the spell seemed to break for a moment. She realized the monsters had been the ones causing her to despair. She'd never before realized they could even control her emotions. The realization was cold comfort as they were only feet away and soon would have their sickening hands binding her and carrying her to the big top tent.

"No!" she screamed in defiance. She remembered Steve, and all his words flooded her mind. She had to fight. She realized she knew every tree in this dead forest. She knew every knot, every branch, and every twig on the ground. She knew this place perfectly. With that knowledge, she concentrated on the forest. With all the concentration her adrenaline could lend, she willed them to grow leaves. Ignoring the ugly creatures close enough to breathe on her now, she focused on one big tree and in her mind she bent the twisted branches straight. Then she forced them to sprout large, green leaves. The world gave way before her psychic demands. The bare form obeyed and let small buds pop out. The bark lightened as the buds spread into broad sycamore leaves.

It suddenly happened just as she'd wanted for so long. This time there was no vertigo. The Nightmares simply faded away. She extended her push. The trees warped and blossomed, she dragged the sun up from behind the mountains, and the dark clouds surrendered to a painted sunrise and blue sky. Megan found herself safely on the soft dirt of the Colorado mountainside. She even reached down and touched the dewy grass between her feet.

While the fear drained away, Megan took a deep breath and let it out in one big scream. "Yes!" Her voice echoed off the walls of the lodge and the mountain. She greedily sucked in the smells of pine and moss. Her heart raced. She had never been more excited or proud in her life. It made her wish Rose had come. She couldn't wait to tell everyone that she had finally succeeded in verging. She no longer needed Steve to show her new places. All the dream world could be hers with just a thought. She would never be trapped again.

Despite being somewhat tired from the effort, Megan wanted to do it more. If she could escape when things went wrong, she now had the advantage. Eventually, she would be able to take those Nightmares down. If they caught her, she would just disappear. She wasn't in a hurry. She could try over and over. She gave herself a minute to regain composure and catch her breath.

This time, before she went back, she wanted to find a weapon.

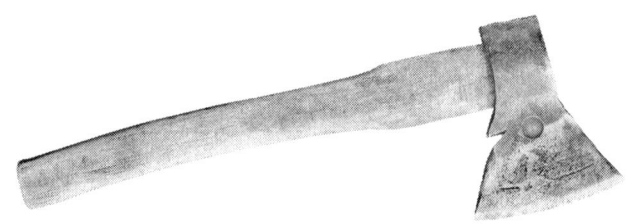

# CHAPTER TWENTY-TWO

Megan's vision adjusted to the darkness of the dead forest near her school. A big smile graced her face. Megan knew Rose would be proud when she found out Megan had become a verger. Steve was going to be amazed.

Megan wasn't nervous this time; she relaxed and waited. She knew they would come, and she wasn't going to waste her time going to look for them. She lifted the wood-chopping axe so that she was holding it with two hands. It was heavy. She'd never used one before, but she was sure she knew how it worked. She made a couple of sideways slashing swings with it. It was awkward.

After a minute, she wondered where all the clowns were. They couldn't be scared of her. She went over to a medium-sized tree and examined it. It was light brown with very dry wood. It didn't really seem to have bark around it. It reached above her head where a few twisted branches came out at odd angles. She had always been so afraid of these trees. Then, the obvious answer came to her... She was holding a wood-chopping axe. She'd borrowed it from the wood pile outside the lodge. It had a wooden handle with a painted blue head. The paint was scraped off about an inch away from the cutting edge. She rubbed it with her thumb because she'd seen somebody do that on television before. She didn't really know how to tell if it was sharp, though.

She twisted around as if she were hitting a baseball and then swung the axe for all she was worth. The wedge flashed through the air and embedded deep in the base of the tree. There was a satisfying crack. Megan knew this would bring the clowns running, but she didn't care to wait. She began to pull the axe out, but it was well embedded and she had to use her foot to get enough leverage to finally yank it free. Once it was out, she looked around for the freaks. Seeing none, she decided to keep working on the tree.

She swung the axe several times, making no real effort to hit strategically. She didn't expect to have enough time to chop it all the way down. She just wanted to practice.

Eventually, the sound attracted her enemies. Megan pulled her weapon out of the tree as two Nightmares approached her through the forest of their hunting ground. Crashing through the branches as tall as most of the trees, the stilt-legged clown approached fastest. Making long strides, he dodged the branches he could and broke through the ones he couldn't. Megan's instincts told her to run, but she forced herself to stay. She wound the axe behind her and waited. In a few steps, the tall, top-heavy man reached her. He didn't wait, though. Clearly, they had a new strategy this time. He jumped forward at her. Megan swung the axe, but the tackle took a lot of the force out of it. As he fell, his long arms dragged her off her feet and she hit the ground.

For a moment, she was confused and thought she might wake up. A second later, she was keenly aware of the arm holding her waist like a vise. She found it impossible to struggle free. As she watched, the hunchback freak approached, and faint images—farther into the darkness between the trees—also ran toward her.

Knowing she wouldn't escape if they all caught up to her, she decided it was already time to go. She worried she might not be able to do it with the lerp of a monster holding her down. Still, she concentrated. She saw the trees and the dirt and the dark, willing them to bend. She straightened the branches and softened the ground. The sun changed by itself, though. The lights came up, and she was again behind the lodge. She took a deep breath.

This time something was wrong. She still couldn't get up.

When she looked down, she saw a long, thin arm covered in a dark, striped suit was still around her and holding her down. She struggled and broke free.

After she was on her feet, she watched the confused, tall man stand up beside her. He was easily two and half times her height, and she suspected from up there, he could see over the roof of the lodge. He ignored the axe she'd embedded in his long thigh and after a moment, the blade fell away by itself, landing with a thud and crackle of leaves on the soft ground.

Megan realized immediately how he had been touching her when she diverged, and that's why he'd come with her. A hitchhiker. Fear chilled her heart. It was exactly what Rose had said could happen. Megan had a sinking feeling in her stomach. She had brought a Nightmare to the safe lodge.

Her worry lessened when she noticed he wasn't looking at her at all. The tall man's gaze darted from place to place, stopping to stare a moment at each new thing that caught his attention and then moving on. His entire countenance changed to a state of amazement. He reached out and touched a leaf. Not moving from the place he was standing, the giant clown looked around and around, slowly turning in circles. His curiosity and wonder overwhelmed any remembrance of what could have brought him here.

Megan took advantage of his complete distraction to sneak up behind him and pick up the axe. Of all the things around him, she was the one thing he didn't bother looking at.

"What happened?" he asked. His voice was still high, but it wasn't direct. He was talking to anybody that could hear him. "What's going on? What is all this?"

"It's Colorado," Megan said. She wasn't sure if he was baiting her or not, so she gripped the axe and kept her guard up.

"I've never seen anything like this," the clown whined. "It's so strange and interesting. How did you do that?"

"Bring you here?" Megan clarified.

"How did you change it into this? Why are we alone here?"

"There are people in that building that will come out and help me," Megan said. She was sure it was probably true, but she hoped they would never find out that he was here.

"Is this where you have been going when you weren't with us?"

"Mostly," Megan said.

"This is much better," the clown said.

"Yeah, well Nightmares dressed like you don't really fit in at a place like this."

"I can change my clothes," the tall creature intoned.

"You're going to have to change more than that."

The tall man had been looking at the sky and the building until then. Now he turned to see Megan. In that instant, the axe, with all the power she could put behind it, cut deep into the tall man's thigh. She had hoped to hit the same spot as before, but the blade came in low and was closer to his knee when it bit deep. Small pieces that looked like white metal flew off around the axe, marking their path with a trail of dark gray vapor.

A grimace of pain and dread covered his face as he toppled to the ground. Meg had pulled the axe free already and was approaching him cautiously, unsure of herself. His face was different from anything she had ever seen. He had a kind of lost puppy look laced with deep sorrow. Meg raised the axe again.

"No! Stop! Please..." the clown said quietly. He held his leg, which now bent sideways.

"You have the nerve to ask me to stop after everything you did to me?"

"I didn't know. I've never seen anything like this."

"Well, I don't think you'll be seeing anything like this again, either," Megan said as roughly as she could. Then she brought the axe down as hard as she could right in the middle of his chest.

She tried to pull it right out, but the axe remained stuck. Gray and black steam oozed out of the seams around the blade, floating up and disappearing in the light breeze. Megan let go of the handle and moved away, unsure of what to expect next. At first, it was just tiny trails dissipating into the air above him, but then more and more of the dark smoke flowed from the wound. He made a few quiet protests before the wooden handle sunk into the body, completely obscured by the emitted gasses. The smoke stopped rising and began to sink and roll across the ground. The man completely evaporated until nothing remained but the axe.

Megan stared at the spot for several seconds, half expecting him to reappear. When the silence remained, she took a deep breath. At first, she felt bad for the emaciated clown. He hadn't seemed so terrifying out here alone in the sunlight. A marbling of guilt started to run through her as she saw the axe lying alone on the ground. His final words, "Stop, please," echoed in her head. A tear began to well up before she got control of it all.

"No," she said aloud. "He hurt me for years, and other people, too. Just because he begged at the end doesn't change what he did." The dark feelings of vengeance grew like a summer storm inside her until all her guilt washed away. "He deserved that, and more." She let herself feel powerful and satisfied. She had vanquished a monster. It was the right thing to do.

Eventually, she picked up the axe and returned it to the woodpile. This was too much work. She felt emotionally exhausted. As she thought about it, she actually felt like she wanted to go to sleep. She was dreaming about wanting sleep? Was it even possible to sleep in a dream? She'd heard people talk about a dream within a dream. The complexity of it was too much for her to contemplate right now. She needed some time to rest and think. And for the first time in a while, she actually wanted to sit and drink some hot chocolate.

# Chapter Twenty-Three

Sitting at a table in the lodge that had become her safe haven, Megan worked out that the biggest problem was the one they called Boss—the Ringmaster. She knew he was the one who had organized all of this. He was the one she needed to destroy, just like the shadow of her father. For so long, he had kept her just on the edge of waking, terrified. The funny thing was that he never actually had to do anything. He didn't cut her or anything. He just touched her arm and fed from her fears. But it was enough.

The time had come. She didn't want to wait any longer into the night in case she woke up and couldn't get back to sleep. If she could get the head clown, she would feel a lot better. She looked around to see if anybody was watching her. Nobody was. Then she began to concentrate on the room she had been sitting in. The walls were about the right distance apart. However, the fire was all wrong. She forced the fire to split into two. As she did, the tables and windows all began to fade. Then she split the fire repeatedly until there were six of them scattered evenly around the four walls of the room. Then the room bulged into a circle. When she ripped a flap in the wall for an opening, the bubble merged and she found herself in the big top tent.

She had sworn not to come back here. The stench of exotic animal feces was awful and the feeling of hopelessness it brought out in her was almost unendurable. This very place forced her to hold back tears. The memory of so many nights in pain wouldn't let her be calm. The trouble was worth it when she saw the tall, dark-clad man turn around to face her. For a moment, she was pleased to see his face register surprise instead of malice. A second later, he remedied that.

"How strange your behavior has been lately, little Megan. You were gone for so long that we thought we'd lost you. Now you come back twice in one night. I'm not pleased that you took Stilts with you, though."

"Stilts is dead," Megan said with satisfaction. "You're next."

"Forgive me if I don't believe you," the ugly man said. His face was so enshrouded with shadows that she couldn't see his mouth moving, only his top hat wiggling. "I have to admit, I'm very glad to see you. Most of those other kids don't have the endurance you do. They usually wake up long before I'm filled."

"Never again," Megan said softly. She forced the resolve, so that only the tiniest doubt was in her voice.

"Well, let's not keep you waiting," he said as he moved forward.

"The next time you touch me will be your last," Megan said flatly. She was mustering all her courage. She waited for him because she didn't trust herself to move.

"Why has it always upset you so much?" he asked. "All I do is touch your arm. I haven't done anything to hurt you. There are so many worse things. Why does it upset you so much?"

Megan knew in her mind people suffered much worse abuses, but her heart couldn't imagine even one. She said, "You took something from me. Every time you touched me, you took my will."

"We call it your intention, but why do you care so much? You have a limitless supply, and without it, we would starve and die. You wouldn't want your children to suffer, would you?"

"You are not my children!" she screamed. "You took more. You took my dreams. You took my sleep. You took away my choices."

"None of that means anything to me," he said with a grimace. Slowly, he crossed the distance between them. His face, with deep-cut features, came in and out of relief as the lights accented different sides. When he was so close, Megan wanted to scream and run. He reached out and touched her arm with his finger in a mockery of affection. When she diverged, she felt his knees buckle, and it made her smile. She'd never expected a Nightmare to feel motion sickness.

The tent disappeared, and the fires went out. A dim twilight broke around the horizon, and the top flew off. Tiny stars flickered into existence above them, multiplying into millions. Then the world flipped over, and the stars were city lights seen from a high building. The only thing holding them on to the wide walkway was a metal rail along the edges.

Megan had been ready for this. When the vertigo overcame the Ringmaster, she pulled away. When he recovered, they stood five feet apart and thousands of feet above the ground, atop the Empire State Building. From here, it felt like she could reach out and touch the dark clouds that filled the night sky. Megan had been here before with Steve and Rose, and she hoped the shock of these surroundings would give her an advantage.

"Very picturesque," the Ringmaster said in a low, but casual, voice. "Any particular reason you brought me here?"

Megan's heart sank. She'd hoped he would be confused and amazed like Stilts. Why didn't it set him off his guard? His indifference infuriated and scared her. Had she made a terrible miscalculation? "No reason," she lied. "I just thought a change of scenery might be nice."

"You see, that's what confuses me," he said without taking his eyes off her. He moved forward very slowly. She hated it when he did that. That's what he always did when he had her trapped and he wanted to stretch out her fear. "I always knew you'd leave us someday. It was just a great run of luck for us to have you as long as we did. When you left, I knew it would be a lot harder for us to find work. Then you came back. Could it be you missed us?

"No, you came back for revenge. It's pathetic, in a funny way. Then Stilts disappears and you get my whole mob worried. Yes, you may be able to pick them off individually, but you'll never be strong enough to defeat me. You and I both know that no matter what, deep down, you need me."

"Never again," Megan said. It was her mantra now. She wouldn't let him confuse her. She wouldn't listen to his lies anymore.

"What are you going to do? I've been all over Essentia. This kind of thing is nothing new to me. I've even been on this very platform on this very building before."

Just then, two people walked out onto the deck from the doors inside. It was a young man and woman holding hands. Megan looked at them and screamed, "Help me! This man is trying to hurt me! Please, help!"

The two of them were startled, and the young man looked around for some means of help. After a moment, they both ran back out the door. Megan was disappointed, even though she couldn't say what she had really expected.

"They're like sheep," the Ringmaster continued, still moving toward her like a silent specter. "They couldn't have hurt me if they wanted to."

"Then I'll have to do it myself." With a cold tingle, Megan's back touched the metal handrail. Her hands shook until she grabbed it and held on tight. He continued to move forward, closing the small space between them. He lifted his hand as if to touch her shoulder, but that was too much. Megan grabbed his arm with both hands, turned around, and pulled.

She had hoped to flip him off the side of the building, but he was a lot stronger and heavier than she had imagined. He pulled back on his arm, and she came off-balance. Before she knew what happened, he shoved her off the side.

In desperation, she clung to the only thing she could reach—his arm. Soon she found herself dangling above a sea of darkness broken by tiny lights sprawled out beneath her. He leaned over the rail, holding it tight with the other hand. Megan held on for all she was worth, but she could feel her resolve, and her grip, slipping.

"Ha ha ha." He wasn't laughing, just saying the words sarcastically. "After all these years you really think you have any possible chance of hurting me? Now you will hold on as long as you can, the whole time making me stronger. Then, when you finally let go, I'll only be inconvenienced by having to try to find my way back home. I do hope your new need for revenge will bring you back again and again, so we can do more of this."

Megan ignored him. Too enraged by his mocking laugh to hear any more, she knew she could hang on a long time if needed. She didn't need to. She had an idea.

"No. Never again."

"Even if you somehow succeed, another will be made to replace me."

"I'll never make another one of you." The idea made her sicker than dangling off the side of the skyscraper, holding his arm.

"You don't have to. The other people will."

"The other kids?"

"No, not kids." The Ringmaster was breathing hard now. He twisted his arm to try to break her grip.

Megan knew she had only a moment. Her hands began to slide down the greasy paint of his arm. Recklessly, she pulled on his arm and kicked her feet up so that they were under the metal handrail. Then, holding on for all she was worth, she pushed off with both feet as hard as she could.

Caught by surprise and underestimating his long-time prey, the Ringmaster found his waist bent fully over the bar. What he hadn't expected was that his feet lifted off the ground and came over the side, too.

Megan didn't let go of him as they fell. She didn't let herself wake up the whole way down. She held on like a vise and resisted as he flapped his arms. His hat blew off early on, and the two of them tumbled through the air, turning every direction. His coat tails fluttered as the ground rushed up to meet them. While they fell, she heard the clown trying to call her name. She hoped he was begging for mercy, but he never got the chance to finish.

"Meeeeeeeeeeeeeeeeg—"

Just at the bottom, Megan pulled around so that her knees were on his chest and his head and back hit the ground first.

Instantly, there was a huge black cloud. "Meg." That's all he said.

Megan woke up with the sound of his voice in her ears. It was still early in the morning, but she didn't care if she could get back to sleep again or not. Her heart raced. His last word was "Meg." She liked it. She liked how that sounded. It sounded more grown up than Megan did. It sounded new and different. It sounded the way she felt—strong and successful. She just wished she knew for sure if he really was gone forever.

Meg touched her silver bracelet and whispered to herself in the morning twilight, "Never again."

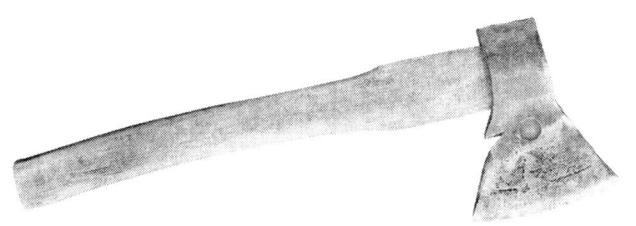

# Chapter Twenty-Four

Carrie had to search several buildings before she found a mirror. Now she stood in the bathroom of an office building, staring at her reflection. The transformation was remarkable. She looked the same except her skin was dark brown. Her hair was still dirty blonde. Her eyes were still blue. Her cheeks were still round with a pointy chin, but the skin was ebony. She thought she looked a little bit younger, too. Altogether, it was a shocking combination. Since she was a Ghost now, it suited her. She just needed some time to adjust to the idea and looking at her own face in the mirror was the best way she knew to do that.

George was in the lobby of the office. He could make it through the double front doors, but he would never fit in the bathroom. She had propped the door open, so they could talk, although neither of them really knew what to say. As a hunt-hardened Nightmare and ruthless executive, they had both been on comfortable ground. Neither of them was used to the new closeness of their relationship. They felt it, of course, but they didn't know what to do or say about it.

She knew she had a lot less to give George now. Before, her emotions always boiled and he had a steady diet. Now, he liked her more, but her mind was so ungrounded and flighty that her attention came in short bursts. He said she resembled an Intenui he'd once met called Pac-man.

When she finally came out of the bathroom, she smiled at him. "I don't think I'm going to be able to do any amazing things in my dreams anymore," she said sadly.

"No," he growled with regret, "you are Vitoi now."

"Vitae, Vitoi, what's the difference to you? I'm a Ghost now. But I'm still here to feed and keep you."

"You will never wake up again."

"That's not true," she said darkly. "I have one wake-up left."

He ignored the death reference. "Vitoi don't have the same power over Essence as Vitae."

"No more flying," she pined. "It was fun to be so strong for a while. I wish I had done more with it. Doesn't matter now. Besides, my real power always was and always will be my mind."

George didn't mention how flighty her mind had been since the change. Instead, he hinted, "I don't know your plan."

Carrie realized it was pointless to keep it from him now. "I want to contact..."

Carrie stopped talking when George suddenly paused and turned. Three people appeared around them. Two of them were the same IS guards in black riot gear with huge machine guns. The other one was a woman. Everybody turned their attention to this woman immediately. She had on a silver dress that seemed to move and flow like chrome paint around her. Every few seconds, the metallic blob would congeal into a razor-sharp blade along one of her limbs. One moment, it would make a sword along her right forearm. The next it would form an axe by her left foot. A small knife would grow over one of her fingers. Each time, the blade would melt back into the dress. The effect was distracting and hypnotic.

Her voice was low and had a slight regional accent Carrie couldn't place. "You are ordered to come with me, Carrie Gretsch." A large scythe blade rose up like a fan behind her head and then melted back down.

Carrie had heard many rumors about how powerful agents were, but seeing this one up close, she realized their dream power didn't necessarily make them smart.

"Carrie Gretsch?" Carrie made her face look puzzled. "I think you've made some kind of mistake."

The agent looked at her again, then at George. "You are not Carrie Gretsch?"

"No, sorry, my name's Adelaide. What's yours?"

"You can call me Mercury." The agent looked at the two guards in confusion. "Call dispatch. Find out what's going on."

One of the guards lowered his weapon and began talking into the small microphone again. Carrie was sure it wasn't the same one as before, but their mannerisms were spookily similar. It must have been their training. Carrie said, "I actually have someplace to be. And I have to get home and change my clothes first. So, do you mind if—"

"Stay there," the agent said without looking up. Two spearheads spiked off her shoulders and then dripped away like candles.

When the guard looked up, he said, "The trace was on the monkey. She was last seen with this thing."

"When did you meet this monster?" Mercury demanded impatiently. She tapped one foot.

Carrie wanted to stomp on that foot, but she kept herself under control.

"What monster?" Carrie asked as she turned. She wasn't a good actor, but she had to try. "Harry here is my family's butler. We just hired him today. He's going to serve dinner at the fancy party I'm hosting." It sounded stupid, even to her. Still, this was Essentia. Anything was theoretically possible.

The guard with the microphone began talking back into it, "No, sir. A black woman."

"African American, you racist pig!" Carrie screeched. She wanted to push the drama to keep them off-balance. "You want people going around calling you white bread? What is this the eighteen hundreds? You never heard of civil rights? They don't include political correctness in your weak, soldier-boy training? I'm going to get a lawyer. What's your badge number?"

The guard tried to ignore her. He started talking more quietly. She smiled inwardly.

Mercury rolled her eyes while metal blades popped out the sides of her silvery liquid boots. "I'm afraid we're going to need to take your butler with us," she said with exasperation. Then she turned to George, "Where's the woman you were seen with earlier? Explain quickly or you will be dissipated."

"That doesn't make any sense," Carrie interrupted. Mercury ignored her. Carrie's mind was reeling. She wasn't about to let them take George without a fight. Intershroud considered Nightmares as being of zero importance. They created and killed them without a second thought. They would never let George live.

"She died," George offered. Carrie had to cover her face to keep from grinning. George was so smart. It was easy to forget when you saw how big he was. When everything else was over, Carrie was thinking of adding this annoying agent to her list of people to destroy.

"When?" Mercury was losing interest rapidly.

"A while ago," George said. He shrugged, his barrel-sized shoulders flexing and rippling.

"Nightmares have no solid concept of time," one guard suggested. The agent scowled.

"Get rid of him," the agent said.

"No!" Carrie screamed. This time it wasn't acting. The wail echoed off the glass windows and assaulted their ears twice. "I need him for my party!" Carrie jumped in front of George with her arms out as if she could protect him with her own body from heavy ordinance. "If you leave him, I'll invite you to the party." It was hopeless, she knew. They would think she was just a dreamer. Nobody in Essentia cared if you woke a Sleeper. Murder had no meaning when the only consequence was waking up.

"This one's Vitoi," George growled humbly. "She can never wake."

The guards lowered their weapons. Mercury huffed. A twisting vine of metal turned the agent's left arm into a drill bit. A bitter scowl clouded the agent's otherwise smooth skin. She had a round face with shoulder-length red hair and premature wrinkles between her eyebrows from a life of consternation. She scoffed at the ridiculous dilemma. Then spikes radiated from a silver collar around her neck.

For all her self-importance, Carrie realized this agent was pathetic. Despite all her dream power, she had sold herself to Intershroud. She wasn't free. With power like that, this agent could be flying around Essentia, bending the very fabric of reality to her will. Instead, she was an IS lapdog, cleaning up silly messes. Carrie pitied the woman who had made herself into a slave. Still, even a slave can make some decisions.

"Leave the delusional dilettante and her monkey-suit butler," Mercury said. "I'm too busy for this." The metal that flowed around her body coalesced into a long, thick sword that she held with both hands. With a single forceful blow, she spun around and shattered the large pane of glass that served as one of the walls behind her. The crashing glass thundered as it fell. The volume and shock would wake a normal dreamer.

Having spent some of her frustration, the agent crunched across the glass shards in metal boots and walked back up the street. A moment later, the guards shrugged and followed her.

When they were well out of earshot, Carrie said, "That was brilliant!" This time the compliment was not a manipulation. Carried realized that she was free now, too. Intershroud had trapped her before. Escaping their leash made her jump and do a little dance. She hugged George in appreciation for helping her break away.

George smiled as he tried carefully not to hurt her delicate aspect with his massive hands. It was an awkward gesture for him. Eventually, he grumbled, "Now will you tell me what you are planning?"

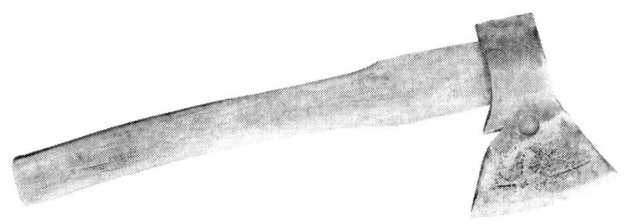

# CHAPTER TWENTY-FIVE

It was a few nights before Meg met Rose at the lodge. Rose had been talking to several people before she finally noticed Meg. She approached evenly. Meg, now dressed all in black with thick black makeup around her eyes and hair that was mostly black except for a few blonde streaks, tried to smile warmly.

Before Rose even sat down, Meg said, "I did it! I'm a verger now."

"Really?" Rose asked with awe. "That's amazing! I knew you could, Megan. I see you've decided to keep the new look. I wish I could pull off boots like that."

"Yeah, my mother would never let me go this far with it when I'm awake. Also, I think from now on, I just want to be called Meg instead of Megan."

"Okay, *Meg*. It means something here, you know. Everything in your dreams means something."

Megan held out her arms to highlight the outfit. "I suppose this means my soul is black?"

"No. It just means you finally feel free enough to take some risks. On some teens, it's a cry for help, but not you."

"I do want some help," Meg said quietly, "now that you mention it. I need to know how to get things into dreams."

"What do you mean?" Rose asked.

"Well, if you want something in your dream, like an airplane, is there a way to get it there besides going to an airport?"

"Of course. For most people, just wanting it is enough to get it there. Say, for example, that I need a pen. I just go to where a pen should be, say this drawer here." Rose walked over to a wooden side table with tarnished brass handles and opened one of the drawers. She pulled a gold pen out and showed it to Meg. "All of Essentia is made of essence. Just like Materia is made of matter. The big difference is that essence moves and rearranges to satisfy your mind. If you needed something, you should be able to find it in your dreams without too much trouble. Just look where you think it would be and it'll be there."

"But what if something doesn't belong there? What if I wanted to get a skateboard on the top of a mountain?" Meg had to think a moment to find examples that wouldn't reveal the exact purpose because she didn't think Rose would really want to know what she was planning.

"I don't know," Rose finally answered. "I know that there are people called shapers. They can make anything out of essence anywhere. It's a power... like the verging power you use."

"So if I had one of these shapers, they could make me anything I wanted anyplace we were dreaming?"

"I think so. I haven't really known any to say more than that."

"Do you think Steve knows any shapers?"

"Maybe. If he shows up, you can ask him. What do you need, exactly?"

"Do you really want to know the answer to that?" Meg asked as politely as she could. She would be more than happy to discuss it, but she expected Rose would prefer to stay blissfully unaware.

"Probably not," Rose said at last. Her face had wrinkles on it that were far too deep for her age. She still held her clinical smile, but now Meg could see it was a cover Rose used to hide her true feelings.

"You heard about the clown the other day?" Meg guessed.

"Well, there were a few people who mentioned it."

"It was an accident," Meg said. She had tried to cover it up because she knew Rose had predicted that very consequence. Now, she felt not only guilty, but she had let down her best friend. "I'm so sorry. I didn't mean to bring him here. He was just holding on to me when the others showed up and I had to get away before the whole gang was there. Anyway, I took care of it. Nobody else was hurt by him."

"Yeah, I heard there was an axe involved." Rose's voice was even. She couldn't keep her eyes from showing disappointment and horror.

"It will never happen again. I won't bring anything else here, I promise." She hoped the emphasis on the last words would buy her some credibility because Rose knew she had worked so hard to keep her last promise.

"Oh, I don't care that you brought a clown here," Rose said.

"You don't? I thought that was one of the reasons you didn't want me to go there because they would follow me here."

"Well, I meant they would come after you and find you anywhere you go. I didn't know you could bring them accidentally. And at that time, I didn't know you really intended to carry out this... this mission of revenge."

Those words hung in the air. Meg knew the words should make her feel bad, but they didn't. To her, it was just a statement of fact. The only thing that bothered her was that she knew those words were upsetting to Rose. "It won't be much longer now," she said.

"You've almost killed all those Nightmares already?"

"No," Meg said. She had to suppress a smile of pride. "But I got the main one. I think. The rest of them won't be as hard as him."

"You killed the Ringmaster?" Rose asked. Her disbelief gave way to surprise. Meg smiled with pride. Then Rose's demeanor turned grim. "Symbolically, that clown represented your father."

"Not anymore," Meg said. "He started as that. But after we talked, I realized he was not my father any more than the President of the United States. I thought he was when I was young, but now I know better. He used that against me for so long. It wasn't right."

"I know. But now that he's gone, do you need to kill the rest of them?"

"He was the boss, but they're all bad. I'm not positive he's gone. I need to go check."

"I'm just worried about you."

"I refuse to be responsible for the things they might do to other people."

"I told you, that's not your fault. Every dreamer has to learn to deal with the things they put in their dreams. Other Dreamers were hurt by them, but only once and only in a Sleeper dream. You were the only one that was hurt badly. And remember, it brought you something amazing.

"You can turn this into good, Meg."

"I can't leave those monsters there. I can't be free as long as they exist."

"But you can't change the nature of Essentia. There are Nightmares everywhere."

"Then why is it bad to destroy them? If God can destroy us, why can't we destroy them?"

"You have to decide this for yourself. I have somebody that I need to meet. Just remember, if you're living with guilt, you won't be free."

"I understand," Meagan said. She couldn't bring herself to care about some abstract future consequences.

Rose added, "I'll see you later, then? Tomorrow maybe?"

"That would be nice."

"If Steve shows up, please say 'hi' for me."

"Okay."

Rose moved off to talk with other people in the crowd. Meg watched her go. Despite all they had talked about, Meg only worried about the part where she had heard about the axe. Somebody here had seen her fight Stilts, and now they had all discussed it. Between that and her appearance, she wondered if they would still want her around. Most of them were older. They wouldn't say anything, of course. Even still, she began to feel out of place. She had a few friends closer to her age from this lodge, but none came tonight. She especially wished one cute guy who flirted with her sometimes would show.

She didn't know what else to do, so she sat down and watched the fire for a while. She debated what the rest of this night's dreams should be. She wanted to finish this. She needed to, but she didn't want to lose Rose.

She was still puzzling over it when a bearded man in a black leather jacket sat down next to her at the small table. Her heart began to race.

"Howdy," he said jovially, "do you know a girl named Megan? She sometimes hangs out around here. She's about your age, same height, but she has blonde hair. Does that sound familiar?"

Meg looked up exasperated, "Sorry, no Megan here. Only Meg."

"Meg, eh? Where's Rose?"

"She left. She said 'hi,' but she had to meet somebody."

"It doesn't sound like you believe her."

"I think she left because she doesn't like what I'm doing."

"Yeah, I heard about that. I also heard you managed to make a bubble. That's pretty cool. A lot of people will want you for what you can do. I've only heard of one or two other people that can even do it. I think it has something to do with my superior teaching ability."

"I'm living proof." Her voice sounded thankful, but her face was still tense. "Thank you."

"So what's this other thing about you chopping up clowns?"

"Just one clown—that I chopped up."

"You must really hate clowns. I don't like them, but I don't go at them with an axe."

"Is there anybody here who *doesn't* know about that?"

"Don't worry. Most people don't care if you kill Nightmares. Only Rose is worried. And only about you. I happen to know she's not a big fan of Nightmares herself. So why are you so bent on destroying these circus folk, anyway?"

"They tortured me all night, every night, since I was a child." Meg's voice cracked at the end. It was impossible to speak those words without getting upset. This isn't how she wanted this conversation to go. She wanted Steve to say he was impressed and maybe ask to help her. She wanted him to say how mature she was for her age.

"I guess they have it coming, then. And you think it's your job to do it?"

"I created them."

"You made them to torture you?"

"No."

"Then you just started them. Somebody else made them bad," he said.

"I know. And I think I got that one already."

"I'm not following you."

"The Ringmaster He's the boss. I fought him last night."

"Wow. Two in one week. That's way tough. But what I meant is these Nightmares probably had outside help. I don't think the boss was the one who made them so bad. Nightmares don't share. He would want you all for himself. I figure the only way you get a mob like them is with outside interference."

"You think a person made them like that?" More than the intensity of the conversation, Megan couldn't help being distracted by Steve's eyes. She tried to look at them to show her strength, but after a few seconds, she melted and looked away.

"I can't say for sure. But I have two to one odds on Intershroud. They're always looking for Nightmare breeding grounds. If they found a realm like your carnival, they would definitely do whatever it took to generate as many Nightmares as possible there. They'll probably be mad at you for killing a few of them."

"So somebody made them torture me *on purpose*?" Meg felt cold. She didn't know what to think. The sense of betrayal slowly turned to rage. "Why would somebody do such a thing?"

"There are some bad people out there," Steve said. He ran one hand through his uncut hair to straighten it. It was enough to distract Meg from her anger for a moment. "They don't care who they hurt. Most of them think if it's a dream, they can do anything they want."

"So they don't know that they're really hurting other people?"

"They know. They just don't care."

Then she remembered what the Ringmaster said just before she pulled them both over the edge. "He said somebody would make another one of him."

"That proves it." Steve patted the table for emphasis.

"Now I don't know who I hate more, the clowns or the people who made them. The clowns I can just go kill. But these people, the Intras..."

"Intershroud—is so much bigger and more complicated than you can imagine."

Meg was glad his voice held no traces of pity. When she took a deep breath, she smelled the leather of his worn jacket. "It takes a lot more than angst to hurt them. Some groups of Free Dreamers have been fighting them for years."

Meg's resolve was iron. She leaned closer, gripping his arm. "Tell me how."

"It's not that simple," Steve said. "They're everywhere in Essentia. They have more people and more weapons, but there are groups fighting them."

"Can you take me to one?" Meg asked. She let her hand linger a little longer until he glanced at it and she took it back. "We can't let them keep everybody in the world from their dreams. They have to be stopped."

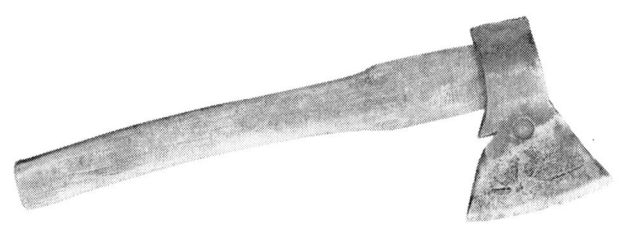

# CHAPTER TWENTY-SIX

Carrie said, "You're right, George. I'll tell you my plans. I have a contact who knows Todd Price." She walked through the dark suburban streets with her massive companion. For each time he pressed his knuckles to the ground and lurched forward with his feet, she took four steps. A few cars sat parked along the street. Occasional porch lights were all the light they had. She spoke softly to keep the walls from hearing her. "He thinks I have information for Todd Price. So when I contact him, he'll take me to the mysterious reporter. I had planned to call in mindsifters to locate him in Materia and catch him. But now I'll use the interview to try to get him to help me find the one that killed me."

"If you kill your enemy, it means you wake up forever." Worry crept into George's voice.

"That's for Nightma... uh... Intenui. When they wake up, they never come back, right?"

George grunted.

"People, or vita-men, or whatever you call them, are awake in Materia. They dream here to Essentia. Normally, when they wake up, it's just to go back there. And when they fall asleep, they will come back here."

"They are tenuous. We are Intenui."

"Okay." Carrie had thought this was all very simple. Now she realized it wasn't something most people understood. It might be even more difficult for George. "But when dreamers die, they are neither there nor here. They wake up from both places. Their mind leaves both body and aspect."

"Then what are you? What is a Vitoi?"

Carrie didn't know an easy way to explain that. She instead asked, "What do you think a Vitoi is?"

"A Vitoi is a Vitae that has become intenuous—a dreamer who never leaves Essentia."

"That's right," Carrie said.

"But why do you say you are dead if you are here?" George asked.

"My body is dead... in Materia." With the words came a visceral and unexpected welling up of emotion. Tears of anger threatened to overwhelm her for a moment. She fought them down and continued, "For most people, when their body dies, their mind dies at the same time, so they wake from Essentia, too. They are gone from both worlds. I'm what humans call a Ghost. My body is dead, but my mind enters a dream and continues to live there without a body in Materia."

"All Vitae can do this?"

"No," Carrie said as if confessing something horrible she had done. "Most cannot."

"Then why will some do this and not others?"

George was very smart, she remembered, so she didn't let herself become exasperated with trying to explain. "Some minds are not ready to let go. My mind almost did, but I had something I wanted to do so badly that my mind wouldn't leave. Also, you were there to help me through it."

The deep wrinkles on his face, once a horrible sight to her, now expressed he didn't understand. She continued, "When most die, they are finished. They let go of their dreams and their life. Somebody killed my body, but I held on to my dreams. I stayed alive here to finish what I started. My mind held on to my aspect here to find the one that killed me and make him pay."

The wrinkles left George's face. She realized he understood better than her words could express. He felt her emotions. Now he understood. "So Vitoi are just Vitae that made themselves into Intenui."

Finally, Carrie realized what he meant. He thought she made herself into a Nightmare so she could finish her terrible quest. She could live with that.

"When you finish this mission, what will become of you?"

Carrie didn't answer. She couldn't really think of anything else. Eventually her short attention span just let the thought disappear, and with it any worry.

They now entered a subdivision with massive homes all smeared with stucco of varying mute colors. These were much larger and more austere than Carrie's mother's house or any of the apartments she had lived in since leaving home. She thought they also looked cold. So much open air inside and things to clean and manage could never make her feel warm and safe. Carrie had never been one of those young girls that dreamed of living in a castle.

The street was virtually deserted. "I think we're alone here," Carrie said. "I remembered what you said about dreamers being able to do anything when there is nobody else around to interfere." George didn't have to look around. Carrie realized he sensed things without looking at them most of the time.

"So how does this work exactly?" Carrie asked nervously. "I just *dream* we're somewhere else and we magically are?"

"I don't know," George said. "All Intenui have some power in the dream, but it is only what Vitae have given us. Only a few rare Intenui become as powerful as Vitae. We call them Sempiternals. What you might call Nightmare gods."

"So if you had your wish, you would become a Nightmare god?"

"Yes, but it is like you wishing to become a queen. Most of us are not made powerful enough to become such."

"I will make you that now, George, if I can." Carrie looked at him with soft eyes and stroked the leathery skin on his great arm. "Tell me how."

"No." His deep voice faltered in just one syllable. "It would mean your end."

She tried to think what he meant, but quickly moved on mentally. She said, "Then that just leaves us trying to find my contact. I guess it's up to me to get us there."

"Where is this place you speak of?"

"We call it Colorado," Carrie mused. "I don't know what you'd call it."

"I've never been there," George mumbled. "But there will be a Colorado here if there is one in Materia. Everything from the dreamers' waking life is here. What's his name?"

"I don't know his real name. He just calls himself Steve. Now let me concentrate for a moment."

Carrie closed her eyes and imagined she was far away. She thought of George being at a small resort town with her. She thought of mountain bike trails and cabins until she could smell the pine. She focused on Steve's rugged face with his five o'clock shadow and wild hair. Then she opened her eyes.

"Tell me when you're ready," George said. His voice vibrated the windows of the sprawling suburban neighborhood. The night sky seemed to loom a little closer.

Carrie huffed. She grabbed George's hand and pulled him. He followed as she began to run. She imagined that these were houses in Colorado and that when she turned the corner, she would be on the outskirts of a resort town.

George followed her around the bend until she stopped running.

"It's not working. I don't know what to do." Carrie enjoyed the fact that despite having been running for quite some time, she was not tired at all. Her heart raced for an entirely different reason. It would take months to walk from New York to Colorado. She had to be there in hours. The puzzle was frustrating her. Her annoyance grew because her mind was so flighty and attention deficit. It actually hurt to try to concentrate.

Eventually George said, "How would you get there in Materia?"

"An airplane," Carrie said with a shrug.

"People dream they are in airplanes, too." George smiled, a gruesome, twisted expression revealing huge square teeth and black stretches instead of dimples. Carrie thought it was sweet.

"Of course! Let's go find us an airport, George."

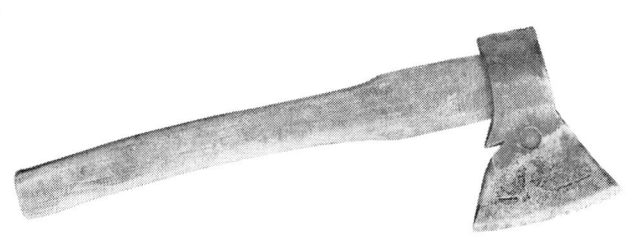

# CHAPTER TWENTY-SEVEN

Meg sat alone at the table. Steve had excused himself for a few minutes. She felt so very out of place in this lodge now. It wasn't just her new Gothic appearance, it was everything about her. She felt too young for this group. They were all content to spend time drinking hot cocoa and chatting by the fireplace. Meg bottled up a storm of fury, which kept threatening to break out. For years, she tried to hold back the horror by being calm and quiet. Now she felt peace and quiet were the tools of bondage. She wanted excitement. She wanted struggle. The chains of docility broken, she wanted to glory in action and adventure. These were all peaceful and social people. Meg wanted to verge away to strange and exciting places—and fight monsters. She craved adrenaline.

The instant Steve returned from one of the smaller rooms to the main area, Meg had her eye on him. He greeted people and tried to be like them, but she could tell he didn't exactly fit in here either. With his black jacket, short beard, and uncombed hair, he was like her. A kind of energy gnawed inside him. Something rebellious about him made her feel a kinship with more than just their power. She adored him, of course, but she also respected him. She wanted to be like him and with him all the time.

A pang of jealousy crept into her throat when she saw him join the small group talking with Rose. Then they moved away, so the two of them were talking alone. Meg knew they were just friends. So why did she feel a flush of jealousy?

The ridiculousness of it overwhelmed her. Steve had to be almost ten years older. He would never think of her in that way. So why couldn't she stop herself? She wanted to run away and start over somewhere fresh with new people. People who didn't think she was too young.

What were they talking about so quietly anyway? Meg had to turn away when Rose looked her way. She hoped nobody saw her watching. It was all so humiliating.

Steve leaned on a handrail at the edge of the balcony. He said to Rose, "That's why I wanted to ask you before I talked to her." Behind him rose a huge glass wall that revealed a sloping canyon covered with all kinds of trees. It was a breathtaking view.

"I don't know the answer," Rose said after some thought. "It's not my job to tell her what to do. I helped her get away from those Nightmares. What she does now is up to her."

"Maybe what she needs is something to focus all that rage on. It's a sure bet if the IS gets to her, they'll turn it against us. At least if she's killing things, it should be for the right team, right?"

"She's so fragile right now," Rose said.

Steve could see Rose's heart melt every time she saw that tortured soul fighting for purchase in a new world after it hurt her so much.

"I don't doubt her abilities would be useful for any group. But she won't be careful. She will make the kinds of mistakes that will let them find her. Then she'll be in real mortal danger... not just in her dreams."

"She said she wants to fight Intershroud." Steve felt conflicted. His part had been small, but he felt a bond with Meg. He didn't want to leave her to wander in the dark places of Essentia. The wolves there were so much worse than she could imagine. "If we leave her alone, I think she'll make even bigger mistakes."

"Look at us," Rose said as she laughed. "We aren't her parents. It's not up to us to decide."

"In a way we are," Steve countered. "In this new world, we're the ones who broke her free. We're the parents of her enlightenment. We have a responsibility to help her as much as we can."

"And what if the help she needs most is to find her own way?"

"Then she will. Nobody can tie down a free mind when it's dreaming. I say we give her the choice at least."

"Okay," Rose said, "but you have to do it. I can't... I just... I can't face her like this. It breaks my heart to see her going back to the same monsters that kept her down so long." One tear began to fill her eye. She lifted one hand to cover it.

"Bank robbers and policemen both carry guns," Steve said. "Soldiers and terrorists both use bombs."

"But not everybody has to be a warrior or a law enforcement agent." Rose wiped her tear away and took a deep breath.

"Is this about Meg, or Kendal?" Steve put one hand on her shoulder. He knew she only told a precious few people about her husband.

"Both, I guess. They're both trapped in different ways. Kendal doesn't have a choice. But Meg does. It's hard to watch."

"You walk a hard path," Steve said. "But love is never easy."

"I know," Rose said with a smile, "and I really am happy. It just seems so unfair that we can never share our dreams."

"That's just not true," Steve said. "You don't have to be in Essentia together to share your dreams."

"I know." Rose smiled. "I'll come with you, but just for a minute."

Meg smiled and tried to look casual as Rose and Steve came over. She forced the jealousy away. It was time to look responsible. "Hello again," she said.

"Hi again, Meg." Rose smiled. It was the clinical smile of a doctor. Meg knew it well. "How is the hunting going?"

"It's been better," Meg said. She rolled her eyes.

"Any new plans?"

"Yes," Meg said. In her mind, she thought of several justifications for it, but she knew Rose would see through shallow excuses. "I've been thinking about fighting Intershroud."

"It's better than fighting Nightmares, I suppose."

"You think it's a good idea?"

"I think this is up to you. The rules of right and wrong are somewhat fuzzy in dreams. What we do really comes down to motivation and not actions. But as long as Intershroud continues to dominate Essentia, all Free Dreamers fight it in one way or another. My own contribution is in helping people like you get away from them."

"And me," Steve said.

"She helped you, too?" Meg was shocked.

"Not in the same way." Steve laughed. "I was already a dreamer. Rose helped me face the darkness that was eating away at my soul. I wasn't always the mild-mannered verger you see here."

Meg tried to resist, but she couldn't help but ask, "What were you like before?"

Rose and Steve looked at each other. Rose conceded, "Let's just say there was a motorcycle and some tattoos involved."

Steve rubbed his forearm through the black leather sleeve. "The hair still doesn't grow right on my arms where I had them removed."

"Why?" Meg wished he still had them.

"They made it too easy for the bad guys to find me," Steve said. He crossed one hand over and clapped his right shoulder. "But I kept the tiger."

They all burst out laughing. Meg felt like a dam of stress had burst and the pressure was gone with the water. She immediately tried to think of a way to get him to show it to her.

"Just remember, Meg"—Rose emphasized the name—"you can always make a different choice and change the direction your life is going. As long as you take control and steer where you want to go, you'll get somewhere you want to be. It's only when you let circumstances control you that you get stuck."

"Thanks," Meg said. "I'll remember that."

Rose waved nicely and walked back toward the people she had been talking to before. Steve sat down again. For this moment at least, he belonged to Meg.

"Taking on Intershroud isn't for amateurs," Steve said, scanning the people around them.. Meg felt both excited to be included and concerned. What could a verger like Steve possibly have to fear? "I'm going to meet a guy right now who is a pro. He's a reporter. He keeps a low profile. He won't meet most people, but he said he would talk to you. It's like I told you before, people need vergers."

Meg didn't know what to think. Nobody ever needed to use her for anything before, so she wasn't sure if she should be offended or flattered. Steve offered his arm.

Despite having felt like a child in an adult's world, Meg was secretly thrilled. Her senses were piqued when she wrapped her delicate fingers around the soft black leather over his biceps. She couldn't help but squeeze a little bit to make a mental map of the muscles under the jacket.

Steve paused and looked at her when he noticed. She saw his eyes narrow and his head tip just to one side. She held his gaze with wide eyes this time, not turning away. She bit her red lip, daring him to return her interest.

He did smile a little before turning away. Then the floor dropped away, and Meg's black-lined eyes closed to deal with the dizziness.

When she opened her eyes, Meg noticed the diverged bubble didn't change features as obviously as when she did it. Steve's mind just melted the world away and the floor fell out. It always made her stomach flop. Then just as fast, a new ground appeared and the walls filled in to match.

*They were in a small room with gray tile on the floor and paneling on the walls. If she had to guess, she would have said they were still in the lodge. The whole verging thing was just to make it look like they had gone someplace else.*

*Meg followed Steve down the dimly lit hall. A few doors led off to other small rooms. It smelled like burned marshmallows. Steve took her through one of the doors into a dark room. She could sense a presence tucked into the corner, but he remained almost invisible. Only by concentrating on the spot he stood in could she be sure a person actually met them here.*

*The scene was surreal and spooky. Meg instinctively reached up and grabbed Steve's arm. Then she realized it and jerked her hands away ungracefully.*

*"Hello, Todd. This is Meg. Meg, Todd." Steve didn't seem comfortable with formality.*

*Todd remained silent.*

*"Nice to meet you," she said. She had no idea how tall he was or what he was wearing. It was like she was only imagining he was there. She found it hard to look into the emptiness and frequently caught her eyes wandering away to look at the door or the wall.*

*"She's the one I told you about, the verger."*

*"Welcome," came the quiet response. It was breathy and monotone. She found it completely unremarkable and forgettable. Suddenly, Meg understood. This man was using some kind of power. Whatever it was, it was good. Because even knowing he was there, she couldn't tell a single thing about him.*

*"He needs to protect his anonymity," Steve said.*

*Meg could see how useful it would be. She had to concentrate hard to remember even to look at him. It was the personification of mystery, and she found it very attractive.*

*"You have business?" Those few words spoke volumes. Another kind of power. Meg didn't care about that one.*

*Steve said, "A lady contacted me, looking for you. Said she has some dirt on IS. She works for them. She met me through a trusted contact in the Purites. Said she wants to change sides. It sounded like the usual bait. However, there was something different this time. She's middle management but claims to have access to some next-level info."*

*"Give her my e-mail address," Todd said.*

*Meg found it hard to believe this guy would have anything as normal as an e-mail address.*

"She won't do it. Says she only delivers hard copy and not to anybody but you. Something about not spending her life cheaply."

"She wants to meet in Essentia?" Meg heard the words, but she really couldn't place the voice. It was uncanny. She could make out the edges of a coat and some hair, but she couldn't tell what color or how big.

"Yes."

"That's safe. When and where?"

"Whenever you want and anywhere you want."

"Give me ten minutes to get someplace. You're bringing her to me?"

"Yep."

"Do you mind coming back tomorrow night, Meg?"

"Me?" she asked quietly. He didn't answer. "Uh, no problem, but can I ask a question?"

"Sure."

"How do you do that?"

"Smoke and mirrors."

Steve laughed. Meg didn't get the joke. He explained, "He's a Shade."

She looked at Steve and hoped the confusion on her face would express what words could not.

"Have you ever had a dream where you watched what was going on, but you weren't actually involved in it? It's like you're hovering above the action but not one of the actors?"

Meg hesitated. "Yes." She could remember a few dreams starting with her just observing the action.

"He does that. Only he makes it an art form."

Meg turned back to look at Todd. He was gone. The light from the door now clearly showed every corner of the wood-paneled room. "He's gone?"

"I guess there was nothing else to say," Steve said.

"So, what now? Can I go with you?" Meg didn't know what he was weighing in his mind. She wished he had just agreed without taking so long to think it through.

"Okay, but you have to promise me something."

"What?"

"If I tell you to run, you disappear and never come back, no matter what, no questions asked. If things go bad—and they probably will—the IS can hurt you in ways you don't know yet."

"But it's just a dream, right?"

"They can use your dreams to find you in Materia. That's why you have to promise to diverge the second I tell you to run."

"I will," Meg said.

Steve held out his jacketed arm. Meg smiled as she held on with both hands. Steve rolled his eyes.

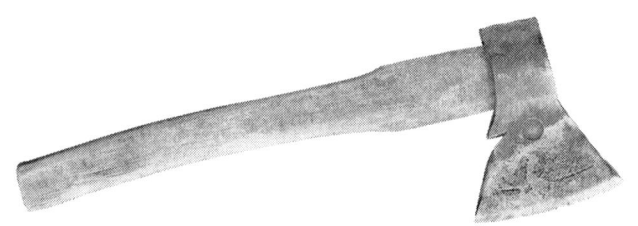

# CHAPTER TWENTY-EIGHT

Carrie walked next to George as if it were natural for a woman to be escorted by a huge gorilla through the suburban streets of Comic Book Northeast. They went a mile out of their way to avoid the area where Intershroud was searching for them. There were more cars and people here, dreaming in the eternal night of a Gothic city. Carrie hailed a cab. George didn't fit, so the perturbed driver sped off and they kept walking.

Normally, Carrie expected people would be afraid of a big black monster with a fedora strolling casually down the city street. They mostly saw teens in spandex running around as if they were chasing villains and thugs. Although there was no apparent danger, George was on full alert. He opened his eyes wide, the only yellowish-white part of him besides his teeth, and scanned the streets. Carrie had no idea what he was looking for among these self-absorbed dreamers. She doubted anyone there had enough real courage to stand up to George.

"Something is following us," George said flatly.

"Do you know what?" Carrie wondered how he had sensed anything at all. It seemed so quiet.

"A dark form."

"What?" Carrie's looked around in panic.

"It's a Nightmare. It looks like a shadow. Hard to see. But I can feel it feeding off you. I sense it here."

"What should we do?"

"Try to get away," George said. "Maybe run?"

George didn't have to try hard to keep up with her, even though she ran as fast as she could. Before they moved far, George put out a big hand. "Stop here," he said quietly.

Carrie did. There was a boy ahead of them, holding a toy biplane up and making machine gun sounds as it flew around and around his head. He had blond hair much lighter than Carrie's, and couldn't be more than eleven years old.

"What now?" Carrie asked in an equally quiet voice.

"Something important is about to happen," George said.

"What? How do you know?" She trusted George's instincts implicitly. She looked to see what it was about this boy that George sensed.

"That one will—" George's voice cut short. Carrie felt a kind of grip on her mind as if a fist was reaching into her brain and manually manipulating it. She couldn't move or speak.

"King Kong!" the boy cried out. Carrie could look sideways to see him pointing with great enthusiasm.

"Dance," George managed softly. Then a kind of anger took him, and his face twisted into a sinister sneer. Fear and dark curiosity welled up inside of Carrie. She was suddenly afraid of this oversize primate that threatened the city with its mass.

The giant black animal roared ferociously and memories of her pre-coma fears flooded through Carrie and put her into shock. She almost fainted when one gigantic hand wrapped around her. Before she could understand what was happening, Carrie felt George's now even larger hand lift her high into the air as the great monster climbed the nearest skyscraper.

Spotlights swooped around the building, occasionally revealing the titanic creature and the beautiful captive he held like a delicate flower. Pieces of brick and mortar fell around them as the massive beast slowly ascended the maddening height where the building tapered off. The small cars below were specs. Constantly roaring, the creature protected the woman it held and challenged anybody to try to take her.

Small biplanes circled them, lancing out with tiny bullets that continuously exploded from their guns. The gorilla swiped at them, knocking several from the sky. Sometimes, it used one forearm to protect itself from the tiny bullets from those smart enough to keep their distance.

George's face registered anger and pain, but deep down Carrie knew he was having the time of his life.

Carrie was powerless to act in any way. She was under some kind of spell. She could think for herself only if it corresponded to her part in the immutable drama. She knew logically she was too big and George was too small for this. Those biplanes must have been no bigger than toys—just like the one... Suddenly, it hit her. That preteen George had tried to warn her about. He was somehow orchestrating this whole thing. How could a mere child have the power to hijack their bodies and force them to play out these parts like puppets?

Carrie hated children. If she had that one here, she would punish him. Without looking down, she felt her dress had been torn to rags with only one shoulder strap holding it on. This final indignity made her furious.

The miniature biplanes continued to harass her friend. Carrie wanted them to stop. She found she had the power to scream at them, "Stop!" But they didn't care.

The creature grabbed one plane's tail and flipped it around, causing two of them to crash. Carrie was glad. She hoped the wreckage would fall on the horrible kid. Again, she wondered where this power came from. She had to admit she coveted it. She would love to be able to control other people's dreams for her own designs. Here in Essentia, it would be a force with no equal. How did this child get it?

Then, as abruptly as it had started, it was over. The biplanes all turned into small clouds. George's hand lost the tension of anger. Carrie was able to sit up and stop flailing around like a helpless idiot. They were still high up on the building, but there were no spotlights.

"What was that?" Carrie demanded. Her sandy hair blew away from her face in the breeze. She shivered. Her new outfit left her arms and legs exposed. She found this objectification humiliating.

"A dream," George said simply. This same deep voice, howling and roaring ferociously seconds before, now spoke with intelligence and calm. He smiled. A kind of mirth seemed to linger with him. He had enjoyed all of it.

"But we've been seeing dreamers all night. Nothing like that happened before." George set her down so she stood on a flat section of the tapering roof, holding on to a tall lightning rod. The view of the city around them was amazing.

A helicopter with a search light beaming out from the side of it hovered near them. It scanned the side of the skyscraper and completely ignored them. Carrie couldn't see the object of the helicopter's attention. "Surrender, Bugboy," a bullhorn called out, "or we will be forced to shoot."

Suddenly, the helicopter moved away in pursuit and left them.

George said, "I think this is prime real estate. Maybe we should talk after we're down."

Carrie nodded her consent to be carried again.

It was a much smoother climb this time. Coming up was jerky and nauseating, but going down was nimble and quick. There was no sign of the boy here now. When George placed her carefully on her feet, she was already talking. "Now how did that boy do that? How did he take over our aspects like that?"

"What's an aspect?" George tilted his head to one side. "Is it our intention?

What you call a mind?"

"No. It's a body in Essentia... a dream body."

"Intenui don't have those. We are always here."

"That's not important. How did he control our dreams like that?"

Through their new connection, she felt George shared her desire for this great power.

He said, "I don't know how it happens. Vitae sometimes do it. It nourishes any Intenui, attuned to it or not. They can control each other, too. Sometimes one Vitae has a dream so powerful it just takes over everyone and everything around it. We call it the dance of life."

"Dance of life?" Carrie paused. She wished now she'd listened better during her Intershroud training. Then she blurted out, "The Danse Macabre! I remember something about that now. Everybody around gets pulled into a single dream against their will. It happens a lot around Sleepers."

"Sleepers?"

"Normal dreamers. Ones that don't know they're dreaming," Carrie offered.

"Okay," George accepted.

"What I want to know is, can it be done on purpose?"

"I don't know the purposes of the Vitae."

"Could I do it? Even though I'm a Ghost... a Vitoi, as you'd call it?"

"I don't know. The dance of life is something primal. It is a connection of intention. I don't think that boy knew he was doing it. To him, it was just a compelling need to enact a specific dream."

"A REM cycle maybe?" Carrie mused. "I don't have time for it right now. If it can be done, I'm going to learn how to do it. Literally controlling other people's dreams..."

George nodded approvingly. No doubt he expected to eat well if she could gain this power.

Suddenly, Carrie understood where she had been wrong. There was more to a relationship than just romantic love. She always discounted love as silly. Now she felt a kind of closeness and satisfaction at sharing a common goal with somebody she liked.

Carrie started walking. George pointed a different direction with his baseball bat-sized finger. "This way to the airport."

Somebody in a black cape swung overhead on a thick rope fastened somewhere high above.

Carrie laughed. "That's a strange-looking Tarzan." She started walking faster, hoping to avoid anybody sucking them into any more dreams.

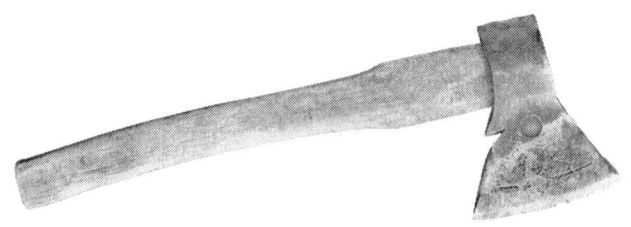

# Chapter Twenty-Nine

Carrie had already grown tired of the whole trip when they finally walked into the huge airport. There were people everywhere fussing with luggage or trying to find some place indicated on their tickets. Some people were talking on cell phones while others tried to decipher the impossible text on the board announcing departure and arrival times. It kept changing to meet or thwart their expectations. Since everybody looking at it had different hopes and fears, the board confounded all of them. The names didn't make any sense; shifting letters for names and times for arrival seemed to morph randomly, leaving the entire board filled with gibberish.

Carrie was distracted by this chaotic moment. She watched the never-resolved negotiation between passengers with disdain. She scorned them for being so weak willed individually that none of them could get what they wanted. George followed as she marched straight up to the woman selling tickets. "Two on your next flight to Colorado."

"The next flight to Denver leaves in seven hours," the woman said, trying not to show her obvious disdain for George. Carrie was just glad she didn't refuse them service. "Will you be paying by credit card?"

"Oh." Carrie hesitated. She didn't let small annoyances deter her. "Yes. It's on your table."

The woman believed it apparently because a moment later she handed them some papers. Carrie left without wasting niceties on the annoying woman.

"Seven hours?" Carrie couldn't wait that long. It would make her go crazy.

They stood in the security line forever. It didn't seem to move at all. The people at the front were checking luggage and passengers, but nobody moved forward. The line stood still. Carrie had no patience for all these little quirks.

After three long minutes of standing still, Carrie pushed to the front. "Stop!" the security man said. He pulled out a Taser and brandished his metal-detecting wand like a sword. George moved forward to get between the scared rent-a-cop and his friend. Suddenly, the man's eyes went wide. He began to stutter, "You're a... a... a..."

"It's just my brother," Carrie said, trying to divert his attention. "He's a sumo wrestler."

The man looked at her a moment and back at George. "They don't have black sumo wrestlers."

"He's the first one," Carrie pressed. "You should get his autograph because he's going to be famous soon."

The man wasn't impressed. "Nobody cares about sumo wrestling."

Carrie gasped as if he had spoken grave blasphemy. She wiggled past the frazzled security guard, pushing George to move quickly. "You'll regret it. He's going to be on the cover of *Sports Illustrated*."

"They don't cover sumo wrestling. It's only in—" Another passenger started barking about waiting all day, so the security man diverted his attention back to the unmoving line.

Carrie marched through the crowds to the first airplane. She asked the ticket taker, a middle-aged man, "Is this going to Colorado?"

"Yes," the man confirmed without thought. "Tickets?"

Carrie handed him the papers and marched down the tube. Was this plane really going to Colorado? She couldn't be sure because in dreams people said whatever you suggested. She was getting good at pushing people into thinking whatever she wanted, but there was a weakness in it. If she told the ticket taker this plane was going to Timbuktu, he would probably agree with her. What a mess. She would have to talk to the pilot to make sure it went to Colorado. Nobody else on this plane had urgent business. Their lives would resume as normal when they woke up, no matter where this plane landed.

George filled the entire flexible hall so that several passengers had to move out of his way as he slowly squeezed into the plane. They grumbled, but to Carrie's surprise, they didn't say anything about a gorilla getting on an aircraft. She wondered what they saw, of if they even saw him at all. George had to squeeze through the doorway to the airplane. Then a new puzzle presented itself... He couldn't possibly fit in any of the seats.

Carrie had him try to tuck into the back corner aisle. He blocked the bathroom access. So some kid might wet the bed... That was the kid's parents' problem. She had him stay there while she muscled past aggressive flight attendants and opened the door to the pilots.

"This plane is going to Colorado, right?"

The pilot was frantically pushing switches and turning knobs. "I don't think this plane's going anywhere. Look at these dials. None of this makes any sense!"

"You've got to be kidding me!" Carrie didn't have time for some pilot's Nightmare right now. What was wrong with all these dreamers? Why were they all such babies? She commanded, "Look at me."

Reluctantly, the pilot turned to her with furrowed brow. "What?" For all this nonsense, he had a nice voice.

Nice voices never impressed Carrie. "The instruments are fine. The plane is fine. We're taking off without any problems now. You are the heroic man who will guide us all safely to Colorado." The man still looked skeptical. Carrie finally added, "Your mother will be so proud of you." The man grinned like a boy and turned back to his dials, all business.

Carrie rolled her eyes and went back to find a seat. Two flight attendants were brandishing steak knives and yelling at George. George was about to crush them with his great fists. Several passengers cowered in their seats. The women yelled, "Terrorist! It's a terrorist! Everybody help us before he crashes this plane into a building!"

Carrie had always known that the average person was stupid. But this was proof positive.

"Stop!" Carrie screamed. It was so loud that one woman nearby looked up in shocked horror and then evaporated awake. The two women in blue uniforms turned, unsure of themselves. "He's not a terrorist," Carrie said.

"Too late. We already called security," the taller brunette said. "This plane can't leave until there's a full investigation."

Carrie surrendered. "Come on, George, we need to get out of here, fast." George smashed the two women that had been annoying him into vapor. Then he squirmed down the aisle and squished through the door.

"I don't think this airplane idea was very good," he said.

"How else are we going to get to Colorado?" Carrie led him off this plane, and they rushed down the hall. Security, police, and FBI began running down the loading bridge they had just exited.

Carrie quickly found them another plane. This time, she had George go outside and sneak into the luggage area. She found the pilot again. It was a woman this time. Carrie suggested they were heading to Colorado. The woman rubbed her red eyes beneath a blue hat and drank half a quart of coffee during the short time they were talking. Nevertheless, she agreed, and the plane started as Carrie found her seat.

They were only in the air a few minutes before the plane started to jump and wiggle erratically. The flight attendant used a microphone to talk over the loud wails of panicking passengers. Carrie rushed forward to the cockpit to try to calm the pilot, but the woman dreamed too deeply to hear suggestions.

"We've lost our port engine. I'm going to have to make an emergency landing. Everybody buckle in!"

"The engine's fine. There's no problem," Carrie soothed. It was too late.

The passengers screamed. The pilot spoke over the intercom. "This is your captain. We've lost one engine. There are no airports in the vicinity so we're going to have to make an emergency landing. Brace yourselves."

Tears fell heavily as people breathed in bags or prayed. The flight attendants left to strap themselves in somewhere. Carrie rolled her eyes. They were just lemmings. When one got spooked, they all ran. When one went over the edge, they all followed. She felt the plane failing around them now. The collective dream of so many passengers was a force of nature in Essentia. Nobody could save this airplane now.

Real fear began to grip her as Carrie realized that unlike the rest of them, she was really going to die when this plane crashed. They would never listen to any explanation. They didn't realize what they were doing. This was all part of a psychodrama, which would wake them up. Most of them wouldn't even remember it. But Carrie would never wake up again.

In her final moments, Carrie knew what she wanted. She wanted to see George. In her short life of cutthroat business, which ended with her becoming a Ghost, he was the only friend she really had. He was the only being she trusted. His was the only mind that would mourn her loss. Yet he was in the same mortal danger she was. She couldn't imagine how even so strong a Nightmare would survive this plane crash.

She ran to the back door and cranked it open. People yelled at her to stop, but she didn't care and she knew they wouldn't follow her. The sounds of engines and air were louder here. It was dark except for the light from the open door. George crouched deep in a shadow. He looked calm and glad to see her. His deep voice asked, "What's wrong?"

Carrie knew her face showed all the fear she felt. "The plane's going to crash. I've doomed us, George. I brought you on this death trap, and now we are both going to die."

George furrowed his brow, huffing out a big breath. He glared at the walls of the vehicle as if he could intimidate them into obeying him. "Hug me." He put out massive arms of sinewy muscle.

Carrie had lived a life of strength. Even dead, she never needed anybody. Now, facing doom, she realized more than any other living being how she really did need love. Too twisted inside to accept the love of humans, she accepted this monster. The stress, which had been propelling her for so long, melted away as she fell into his rough, hard embrace. Carrie wept as his rock-hard arms surrounded her and squeezed ever so gently.

She knew he was feeding on this. She wanted him to. If she was going to die, she wished she could give all her being to him so that he might live. She poured all those thoughts into her tears and cried audibly. "I'm sorry, George. You're the only one who ever understood me, the only one who ever cared. Now I've brought you here to die. Why did we get on this plane? I don't care about Todd Price or finding out who killed me. I wish I had just been happy with..."

"Shh," George said urgently. She obeyed, confused. "Never say that. Your need to find your killer is part of you now. If you give up your quest, you will die before we hit the ground. The fire must always burn in your intention." Suddenly, George's arms weren't warm. They were a steel trap. Carrie didn't understand what had brought about this change.

"But I've doomed us," she whispered, wishing for more of the love she had deprived herself of for decades.

"This is a dream," George reminded her. "It is what you make it."

Instantly, Carrie felt ashamed of her weakness. She took a deep breath. George was always right. She needed to believe they would live. She wasn't at the mercy of some pitiful lemming-dreamers living out their pathetic fears.

A horrible crash rumbled through George, shaking Carrie's mind. With George's bicep and pectoral covering her ears, she could still hear the fervor of destruction. She felt the vibrations around her and knew they were tumbling. They bounced off walls and smashed luggage. Every time they hit something, George's dense body smashed it to bits and vapor. Eventually, they crashed through the sidewall, bounced off the grassy ground, and rolled free. The rest of the plane rumbled on, tearing trees up and sending mechanical parts trailing steam in every direction. When it finally came to a stop, the plane was only a pile of twisted metal. Jet fuel scorched the ground, leaving small trails of fire up the side of green trees and gray rocks.

George, lying on his back, uncurled his arms and legs, delivering Carrie safely back to the night air. She sat up, still on his stomach, and looked at the remains of the plane. Then she glanced down the long stretch of trees and rocks it had turned into a trench like a meteor. But it wasn't until she looked down and realized that all this time she had still been wearing the ripped and torn dress from the King Kong dream that Carrie opened her mouth and laughed so loud it echoed from distant mountains.

George smiled and started to huff. Tears rolled down her eyes, and she even snorted. Her frenzy became infectious, and his own boom joined the chorus of laughter.

Meg thought for a moment she was back with the clowns when Steve merged the bubble. The wreckage of a great airplane disaster lay strewn in all directions, having torn a gash in the earth and trees. Black smoke rose from a few small fires persisting along the perimeter of the crash trench. Two grating voices laughed in a fierce and unnatural way. When her eyes adjusted to the dim light, she saw a crazy-looking woman dressed in rags. Her dark skin made her dishwater-blonde hair stand out in a bizarre juxtaposition of color. It was obviously the person they'd come for, but Meg's attention was quickly turned to a massive black thing rising up behind.

It looked like a meta-demon carved from marble. It growled and glutted as it rose, complaining of soreness. Meg moved back two steps, looking for anything to use as a weapon. She thought there had to be some sharp sheet metal among the detritus.

Steve didn't have the same reaction she did. He simply stepped forward and asked, "Are you Carrie Gretsch?"

The laughing died to a few short pants before the woman nodded her affirmation. "This is George."

"That thing is called George?" Meg couldn't help herself. She clapped one hand over her mouth after the words had escaped, ashamed.

Carrie put her hands on her hips and said, "A little Goth girl afraid of Nightmares? How quaint."

Meg hated her instantly, of course. Who was this tattered barbarian of a woman to judge Meg's appearances? Now she didn't need a weapon, Meg wanted to hit the self-satisfied woman with her bare hands.

Steve said, "Todd Price is ready to meet you now."

"And you can take me to him?"

"Yes. I'm Steve. We've spoken before, but never met in person." He put his hand out.

Carrie shook it firmly. "I'm glad to finally meet you. It's been a rough couple of days. I think Intershroud has turned on me. I've been on the run."

"And they haven't found you yet? How did you manage to evade them?"

"Simple," Carrie said with bravado. "They think I'm dead."

George quietly rose to his full height. Something in the wreckage had distracted him, so his head turned almost all the way around. Meg wasn't listening to the niceties. Transfixed by George, her mind knew, *If my clowns were that huge, I would never be able to kill them.*

"Are you ready to do it now?" Steve asked as politely as possible.

"I'd really like a change of clothes first."

"We can arrange that. But Todd Price won't let you bring your friend."

"George is my only protector. He goes where I go."

"Sorry. Todd Price is, as you may expect, extremely cautious. Nobody, native or otherwise, sees him without permission. I can bring you right back here to him as soon as your meeting is finished if you want. But he can't be there when you meet."

George's actions clearly showed agitation. Meg watched him root through twisted metal and shredded seats. She didn't know what he hoped to find, but the others were obviously distracted by it as well.

Carrie ignored him and said, "Okay. George waits outside with your little girlfriend."

"I'm not his girlfriend," Meg broke in again. It was too loud of a protest for an adult conversation. She hated that this crazy woman had made her look foolish.

"Sorry," Carrie said with zero remorse. "I shouldn't have assumed. Anyway, I need some reassurance in the matter."

Steve nodded when he saw the anger in Meg's eyes, and said, "We'll both stay with your Nightmare. But it won't be anywhere near the location you meet Todd Price. Here will do."

"No," George said. The bass of his voice vibrated the ground beneath Meg's black combat boots even though he spoke softly. "Not here."

"Okay." Steve struggled to remain diplomatic. "Where?"

"Somewhere I can get proper clothes," Carrie said. "How about Sunset Boulevard?"

"We don't have time for shopping," Steve said.

"Won't take a minute."

Meg couldn't believe Steve let her get away with being so bossy.

"Fine. Everybody touch my jacket."

Meg reached out demonstratively and held possessively on to his right shoulder where she knew the tiger tattoo hid. Carrie touched his left sleeve. George moved forward and touched most of his lower back with one finger. Steve was visibly uncomfortable. The whole group wavered, and the ground began to fall.

George's head turned suddenly toward the fuselage. He said, "Something..."

The wreckage from the airplane evanesced into steam and blew away in the wind as they disappeared.

# CHAPTER THIRTY

"Came with us," George finished. Meg hated the monsters voice. Luckily, the vertigo of verging drowned out most of what the huge monkey said. Meg saw Steve was as baffled as she was by their new location. They stood on the sidewalk of the shopping strip on Sunset Boulevard in California. True to its name, an amazing red sunset smeared the clouds and reflected off the ocean between the shops on the far side of the street. Each store's illuminated sign lured shoppers with the promise of high-end designers.

"What came with us, George?" Carrie asked.

"The dark form. It was on the airplane, too. Now it's here."

"A what?" Meg pushed her panic to anger. For the second time in as many minutes, she looked around for a weapon. Why didn't she just keep one all the time? She wondered if the bars that held up the store's mannequins would make a good club.

"Where is it?" Carrie asked.

"What is it?" Meg interrupted.

George ignored Meg. "It's not far. But it came with us. At the last moment, I saw it attach to this Vitae." He indicated Steve with his large, flat-ended finger.

Steve looked down at the ground and began hopping around. "I hate those things," he said to help alleviate the creepy feeling. He stomped on a nearby shadow with his boot.

"What things?" Meg yelled.

Steve smiled awkwardly. Meg thought it represented an apology for forgetting her dislike for all natives. He said, "Dark forms are just shadowy Nightmares. They could be anywhere. Usually you just ignore them, but if one is following us on purpose, that's very bad." He turned to Carrie. "I can't take you to Todd Price with one of those after us."

Carrie rolled her eyes. "George will find it. Won't you? Now I'm going in here for one minute. Then we can go meet Todd Price."

George was already moving slowly along the front wall of the stores, poking at cracks and shadows with his melon-sized fingertips. From his height, it was probably easy to examine the eaves, too.

Meg tried to stay calm, but her gaze darted from shadow to shadow, trying to see anything under the window ledge or behind sign letters.

Steve smiled and said, "They can't really hurt you. Most of them are so weak that if you just run your hand through them, they dissipate like smoke from a blown-out match."

"Then why is everybody so worried?" Meg wanted it to sound brave, but she was starting to accept that her own fear of Nightmares was something she'd always have to live with.

"It might be a spy. The most important thing is to be absolutely sure it doesn't get to the guy who sent us."

Meg went into the store with the mannequins she'd been eyeing. She came out with a hollow aluminum pole gripped like a sword in two hands. "No spy. I can help with that."

"Meg, I think George..."

"Shh."

Meg turned slowly in the direction opposite of George. She thought she felt the thing there somewhere. Her own fear was food to it. She had spent decades unwillingly feeding these monsters. Now she knew what was going on; she sensed it. Instead of being brave, she let her fear grow. It was like an old bully she'd become familiar with enough to engage in polite talk. She closed her eyes so the red sunset didn't offer her any hope.

George, halfway down the block in the other direction, started coming back.

Meg felt the Nightmare's temptation. It was always hungry. It wasn't strong like George or her clowns. One meal could mean the difference between life and death. A fat shadow wasn't stealthy. It had to stay thin... always hungry and never eating. Only taking the tiniest bites when it did feed, the dark form slinked through life quiet and alone.

This monster knew about her. If it went back to them, then Intershroud would know she was helping their enemies.

Meg hated and loathed the creature. She had to. If she stopped hating it, she would hate herself. The fear of some unseen monster lurking nearby sent tingles up her spine. She wanted to vomit. She wanted to run. The cold metal pole she clutched was the only thing that kept her there.

In an instant, the monster went for the bait. Meg felt the tiny siphoning of her fear. She felt the small bit of strength go out of her. But she did nothing. Then she felt it again. Her brain screamed to smash it or run. Still she did nothing. She let the fear and guilt paralyze her. Her hands shook. The pole began to wiggle.

Steve was a dozen paces behind her now and whispered, "Meg, are you..."

Fast as a steel trap, Meg spun the light pole and smashed it with unbridled emotion into the tall shadow the sunset cast around her on the window. The tip of the bar bit into the glass and sent cracks radiating like a spiderweb all across the storefront. Along with the sound of cracking glass was a grunt and whimper.

Small beads of sweat formed on her brow as Meg turned the pipe in her hand, attempting to drill through the strong glass. Small wisps of black smoke rose around the bar's tip before the flimsy aluminum rod buckled beneath her force and bent. Meg lurched forward, and the end came off the glass.

In an instant, she caught her balance and began smashing down on her shadow over and over with the bent bar. A few more cracks joined the web.

"Did you get it?" Steve asked. His voice broke the spell, and Meg dropped the pole.

"Yes." She took a couple of deep breaths and then slouched back into her insecure teenage posture.

"Did you kill it?" Steve had a big smile, but his eyes turned down with horror. "I've never seen anybody kill a dark form before."

"I don't know." Meg wiped her forehead with the back of her hand. "Either way, it's gone."

Carrie came out of the store dressed in a business suit. With straightened hair, she looked very professional. Nobody among the present company could tell this suit from one off a department store bargain rack, yet her high chin and steady eyes made it easy to see Carrie's opinion of the outfit. She said, "Did you find the pest, George?"

"That one found it." He looked at Meg. Meg smiled politely instead of going for the bar again and battering George as she wanted to.

"Good. Then everything's in order?"

"Not exactly, I, uh..." Meg's voice trailed off.

"Yes," Steve said pretending not to hear Meg and offering his arm. "I'll take you to Todd Price. Meg will wait here with George." He raised his eyebrows to tell Meg this was important.

Carrie paused to tell George, "When I get back, we can find you a nice tie to go with your hat."

Meg rolled her eyes. Carrie put her hand delicately on Steve's offered arm, and the two faded and disappeared.

Being alone with a nine-foot Nightmare was not Meg's idea of fun. She turned to pretend she was looking at the dresses behind the cracked glass in the window display. George wasn't shy. "When you were tracking that Intenui, I felt a great vitality radiate from you. I sense now that you hate me, too."

"I'm sorry," Meg said awkwardly. "It's not your fault. I just... It's a long story."

"I think we have some time."

"No. I'd rather not." Meg stepped away, pretending to window shop.

"I know I am the thing you hate," George pressed. As she got used to it, his voice wasn't as horrible as she first suspected. "But I only ask for understanding. For Intenui, you are a source of..."

"What? Stop using nonsense words." Meg put her hand out to indicate she didn't want him moving any closer. "Look, I'm not in the market for any new Nightmare friends. Just wait over there until your crazy lady comes back and stop talking to me."

A thick silence fell between them. The sun was almost gone now, and the darkness of night that dominated so much of Essentia began to make the shadows thick and black.

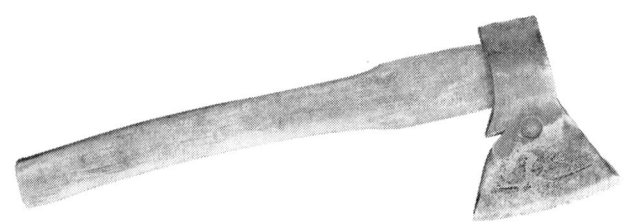

# CHAPTER THIRTY-ONE

Shadows were Todd Price's security blanket and longtime friends. Over the years since his wife died, he'd lived in the dark corners. His power to shade kept him out of the minds of the people he contacted in Essentia. His anonymity remained the best defense against the legions seeking his life. His fight to expose so many wrongs led him down a solitary path.

Todd waited in the shadowy recess of a small room. There was a table with two chairs. The light from the window was enough to see by, but it left him almost completely shrouded. The wall behind him was no stronger than tissue. He could escape through it in a moment's notice. The streets around them were like a labyrinth. He'd have no trouble getting away if things went bad.

When Steve appeared with the latest Intershroud contact, Todd sensed something different about her. She was dressed in a subtle designer suit, holding herself with poise as if she was meeting the President of the United States. Many shades of tan blended in her suit to minimize the contrast between her dark skin and light hair. She made eye contact with complete confidence.

In that same moment, Todd also knew she was a Ghost. It wasn't something obvious anybody could see. One aspect looked much like another; however, after years chasing endless stories of the supernatural in pursuit of evidence that would force all humanity to believe in the reality of dreams, he had seen many Ghosts. He understood them. This was a good sign. It meant he might not be walking into another feeble attempt to trap him. Despite his new hope, he kept with the protocol and waited for an introduction.

"Todd," Steve said, "this is Carrie Gretsch. Carrie, this is Todd Price. He keeps himself hidden for security reasons."

"Hello, Carrie." Todd's voice was quiet and even. It could be any of a thousand voices.

Carrie wasn't surprised by the obvious defense. "Hello, Mr. Price. I assume you understand the kind of deal I want to make. Unfortunately, the situation has changed. I want to change the terms of our agreement."

"I'll just be leaving, then," Steve said with a slight nod of his head like an Oriental bow.

"Wait, please," Carrie said, turning to him. "This won't take very long and your help may be needed."

Todd said, "I assume your change of terms has to do with your new condition." Now that she was a Ghost, she would only want one thing. Unless she offered something amazing, Todd wouldn't get involved.

"Yes. They killed me. So now I'm offering you much more than before in exchange for your help finding out who is responsible for my death."

"What are you offering?"

"I'll give you full access to a management-level computer. Training files, program logs, interoffice memos, and budget spreadsheets. Everything you can download from my computer."

"And you want me to figure out who's responsible for your death?"

"It should be easy. There won't be a memo congratulating so-and-so on killing me, of course, but there's always plenty of rhetoric to sift."

"Are you sure they haven't already changed the passwords?"

"They probably have. But knowing they sometimes pull tricks like that, I built a secondary access into my computer. Unfortunately, you can't use the access remotely. You'll have to actually go into my office."

"Once I tell you the person's name, my responsibility is ended," Todd said flatly.

"Yes."

"Tell me what to do."

"The office is on the second floor of the Mendleson Insurance building in downtown Portland. They deny everybody that tries to apply for insurance through them, but nobody seems to notice or care. This building only operates during the day... Not many people there at night.

"Dress like a repair man or something. The office locks from the outside. I have a key, of course, but I don't know if my apartment is safe. There should be one in my personal effects at the hospital, but they probably went through all that, too. My secretary has a key. She'll open it for you. You just need to make sure you look official and have some kind of I.D. badge.

"They will have combed through my computer already, but they won't delete anything yet because the information won't help them until it's analyzed. If you hurry, you should be able to get everything on it. Once you start it up, you should unplug the network cable so they don't detect any strange action on the machine."

Todd thought about everything she said. "What if there's nothing there to reveal your killer?"

"There will be. They might try to talk in code, but somebody like you should be able to figure out what they're saying. I'm betting it was Brian. He's useless. So if they replace me with him, that's all the proof I need."

Todd was impressed. Most Ghosts became enraged just at the thought of their killer. Carrie showed a great deal of control. "Tell me the... Shh."

His voice fell to silence. The darkness felt different. He knew this place. He knew the light here. Something had changed around them.

Steve looked around. Carrie tried to maintain her poise. Todd saw a shadow move near the widow.

"We were being followed by a dark form earlier," Steve admitted as he continued to scan. "I thought it was gone before I brought her here."

"It might be attuned to me," Carrie said. Then her voice split the quiet as she shrieked, "They're using me as bait!" Anger flushed her dark face.

"Steve, get us out of here," Todd said. They all held on to Steve, and the room around them twisted and faded away.

When the bubble merged, the cold rushed in. The darkness remained, but the ground was light. It took a moment for the others to adjust. They stood in the Arctic, surrounded by fields of frozen snow as far as the eye could see. A shiver went up Steve's spine. He said, "It's probably still with us."

"I know," Todd said. He pointed at Carrie. "Look away!" No shadows existed for him to hide in. If she looked at him, she might be able to link to him whenever she wanted in her dreams.

"They didn't believe I already had you," Carrie said into the air like a crazy person. This looked more like the kind of Ghosts Todd knew. "It wasn't Brian or Tyler or anybody I thought before. Intershroud set me up. Somehow, they knew I could get to you, but they didn't trust me to close the deal, so they used me as bait! I'll make them all pay. I'll find out who—"

"Tell me the password," Todd said calmly. "We only have a few seconds. They're probably tracking that dark form right now, and I'm sure it's with us."

"I can't believe they would do that! After everything I..." The empty cold around them consumed her yelling.

"We can't stay anyplace long. They can track their own Nightmare now they know he's with us," Todd said. "Verge us again, please."

Carrie reached over and held Steve's arm even though it looked like she hadn't been listening. When they landed this time, it was still night. Now the world was hot and steamy. Tight jungle surrounded them. All the lush leaves smelled damp and loamy. Without light, they looked black. Things moved around behind them.

Todd said, "Carrie, whisper the password in my ear."

Carrie leaned over and said something. Then went right back to yelling. "I'll find them. Whoever it is, I'll make them pay!"

"Time to split up," Todd said to Steve. "Thanks for your help."

Steve watched as half a dozen large shapes formed suddenly near them. Because of the darkness, they looked black. The guns and equipment they carried jutted out in sharp angles.

Todd was already gone. Steve grabbed Carrie and diverged again. This time they were in the mountains above the timberline. The faintest hint of light came from a distant horizon. The view would be magnificent if it were brighter.

"You work for somebody your whole life and this is how they repay you," Carrie blathered.

"Shut up! Help me get rid of this Nightmare or we'll never get free." Steve began stomping around in his leather work boots, trying to find the exact spot the shadow inhabited. "And by 'we,' I mean 'you' because in about two more jumps, I'm just going to leave you behind."

Carrie looked down. There were shadows by every rock. It would be impossible to find the little creep tailing them. "We need to go someplace light," she said calmly.

Steve couldn't believe how quickly she went from raving lunatic to levelheaded. "Close your eyes," Steve yelled.

The armed troops appeared again. This time there were over fifty. They had black uniforms with helmets and clear face shields. Many held machine guns or flamethrowers in both hands. Some had pistols and large plastic shields like riot cops. Before Intershroud's thugs could get their bearings among the broad jungle leaves, Steve diverged.

The lights almost blinded them when Carrie and Steve appeared next. They stood in the center of a huge football stadium with massive halogen lights on huge racks surrounding them from every direction. The teams in bright uniforms lined up against each other along one end zone, trying to push just a few yards or stop the same push. Fans all around the stadium cheered until they started to see the strange couple near the fifty-yard line and began screaming threats at them for interrupting the game. One referee called a foul for people on the field.

Carrie and Steve ignored all the commotion as they focused on their feet.

A few men in black riot armor began to show up randomly around the empty parts of the playing field.

Steve stomped randomly, hoping to detect anything out of place. He knew there shouldn't be any shadows here, so the one he saw beneath him had to be the culprit. He jumped toward it. The shape flitted to the side and slid away along one of the lines. They didn't follow it. As refs and security ran toward them, Carrie grabbed Steve's arm.

Steve watched in horror as a large company of men in black uniforms and riot gear suddenly showed up at the stadium, toting huge machine guns. The crowd began laughing, taunting, and screaming. The game fell apart. The athletes broke the line and yelled at the intruders. The dark soldiers tried to ignore the noise and find the two they had come for. They quickly realized their quarry could hide in the crowd. One of the leaders signaled the audience. Without a thought, the armed men sprayed everybody in the stadium with bullets, ripping their bodies into columns of smoke. Stadium lights exploded. One man cut the confused security men down. A few of them shot everybody on the football teams. The thunder of bullets echoed in loud beats as thousands of dreamers cried in terror and woke in their beds.

Before the gun-happy grunts found them, Steve took them all away. When he merged the bubble, Meg literally ran over to him in relief.

George stood outside a window displaying men's suits. Carrie went straight to him.

"What took you so long?" Meg demanded. "The big monkey tried to talk to me. It was gross."

Steve wondered how long he was going to have to keep babying her. There were too many nightmares in Essentia for her to keep being upset about all of them. "Sorry, there were complications. I think the dark form you attacked wasn't dead. Intershroud has been tracking us. I managed to lose it, but it's attuned to Carrie, so they can find her anywhere. I need to you to leave now. I'll try to get Carrie somewhere safe, but it's not safe for you to be with us anymore."

"Okay," Meg said, nodding. "Do you want me to find you later?"

"No. I'll come to the lodge tomorrow if I can. Thanks for understanding." He left Meg and rushed back to Carrie and George. In another instant, they disappeared.

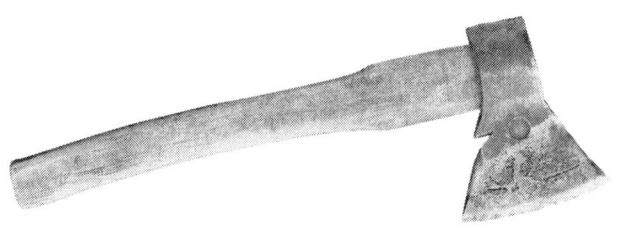

# Chapter Thirty-Two

Meg knew better than to stay here alone with Intershroud coming. Her head was full of questions about Todd Price. Did he still want her to meet him tomorrow? Where in the dream could Steve take Carrie that the little Nightmare couldn't follow them? Was every shadow she saw potentially a Nightmare? That last question upset her, so she pushed it from her mind. She didn't know where to go now, but she needed to hurry.

She started by mentally forcing the fancy stores along the road to age until they grew old and worn. The dresses in the window turned to denim. Fancy shoes became second hand work boots. Immediately, she felt the bubble diverge. Now that she had the hang of it, she found it easy. It was even easier if nobody else around worked against the changes. Once her bubble diverged, she didn't know where to go.

In her bubble, Meg tried to think of somewhere to go. Nothing came to mind except the school. It seemed wrong to mess with the clowns in the middle of everything else going on. Then the thought occurred to her that she could just sit here in the bubble. What was the difference between dreaming here or in Essentia? One difference was that it was possible for some random dreamer to show up in Essentia and bring her crashing down to the ground. Here, she was completely on her own. She liked the idea of her own bubble ending where the horizon did. She wanted to know what the edge of a bubble would be like, but her mind would make it grow if she came near the edge, so she would probably never find out.

Unbridled dreaming was something Free Dreamers always talked about at the lodge. Just like any adrenaline rush, it never lasted very long. Steve told her the more she expanded her imagination, the better at verging she would become, so she decided to try that.

Beneath her feet a small sailboat with a wooden deck formed like the pirate ships she'd seen in old movies. The ground around her instantly turned to choppy ocean water that splashed up every so often and blew to her on the new wind. The ship moved faster and faster. The sky had been generic gray with ambient light. Now sunrise created a spectrum of color that blended from red in the east through light blue to black in the west. Clouds of every color blazed across the sky in yellow and orange like cold fire.

When she turned her attention back to the water, dolphins fanned out around her ship, leaping out of the ocean and keeping the same swift pace. Although she was having fun, Meg knew she hadn't really stretched much yet. She pushed herself harder. Suddenly, the ship lifted out of the water. The dolphins swelled into dragons, which spread their fins into wings and flew alongside her.

Meg changed the dragons to be different colors. They began taking turns breathing fireworks out that lit up the sky below her in rainbows of hot sparks. As her ship raced on, the trails of smoke curled behind her.

When she looked back, something in the smoke caught her attention. It was black and square with a long tail like a kite. Whatever it was, Meg hadn't thought of it. Or had she? It looked a lot like a manta ray. Maybe her mind had brought it up out of the water with the dolphin-dragons.

No. She couldn't have done that by accident. She willed it to dive back down to the water. It wasn't following her directions. Then a dark feeling blotted out the fun she'd been having. Maybe this was a Nightmare. Had she somehow created another one just like the clowns?

The dragons were all Nightmares, of course; however, they were simple and still did what she told them. This one had a will of its own. In the absence of her direction, the dragons had stopped spewing fireworks and coasted in a V formation like migrating geese with her ship at the front. The mysterious black creature was still following them, gaining slowly.

Megan pushed the ship faster. The dragons followed. The sails filled backward now, and she shredded them mentally with her mind so they wouldn't create drag. The boat continued to go faster and faster until clouds and water whipped past in one big blur.

When she looked back, the large black diamond was still gaining. It was as if her speed meant nothing to it. It didn't hurry. It exhibited no stress. It simply moved slowly forward, dancing and turning through the air. The tail trailed impossibly long behind it, leaving a line in the air to mark its movement.

Knowing speed wouldn't help her, Meg changed strategies and sent the dragons after it one at a time. Each dragon gently slowed and turned to attack the creature following them. One tried to bite with vicious teeth. Another swiped with razor claws. Nothing they could do made any difference to the flying ray as it bobbed ever closer. As it reached the flying reptiles one at a time, it bobbed right through their bodies. One at a time, the flying dragons exploded into a haze of fog, which swept back along with the other clouds Meg shot past. Even fire from the largest dragon had no effect on the pursuer.

When the dragons were gone, Meg could do nothing but watch as the weird organic monster closed the distance. She ripped the masts free, and they tumbled back toward the mysterious thing. It dodged them without effort. She pushed the floating hull to supersonic speeds. As the black diamond drew closer, she saw that it had the face of a man. All black, the face blended in so if you didn't look, you would never notice it was there. Meg knew this was a Nightmare. She knew it wasn't her creation, yet here it was in her bubble.

Before it reached her ship, she decided she'd had enough of this. She would simply merge the bubble with Essentia. Without slowing the ship, she dropped toward the water. She found the true location of the sun somewhere in the dream world and waited for the bubble to merge. It didn't. Meg knew it should. She could feel it was right, yet it wouldn't pop.

The ship crashed into the water with a huge splash that soaked her and the unyielding juggernaut behind her. Then, just as it had the dragons, the black-headed manta dipped and touched her ship. In an instant, it evaporated into steam.

Meg dived into the water and began to swim. A moment later, the creature crashed into her.

Meg didn't wake up as she thought she should. Instead, her bubble popped, and she found herself floating in the ocean of a dream. It wasn't cold. She could swim. She turned onto her back and began to half float, half stroke. The idea of being alone in the middle of a vast ocean was maddening.

Now that the Nightmare had gone, she tried to form another ship. Nothing happened. She dreamed up a log to float on. Nothing. Somehow, her mind was unable to reach out to the Essence around her. She tried to diverge a bubble. Again nothing.

A dark fear gripped her. She pulled her wrist up to see the silver bracelet securely circling it while seawater splashed and dripped from that arm. She knew she was dreaming. But she couldn't do anything.

The water was dark. No light came from the night sky now. Thick clouds blotted out all the stars and the moon. They weren't storm clouds, Meg was sure of it. They looked toxic, like they were polluted. Had the black devil ray gone back to those clouds?

She decided there was one thing every dreamer could do. It was easy to wake up, just scare yourself. She dived under water and breathed in. She expected some pain in her lungs. She expected a violent awakening. Instead, she simply breathed in the water and breathed it out. Annoyed, she floated back to the surface. She stopped trying to tread water. It didn't matter if she floated or sank. Her tears began to mingle with the salty waves as they lapped the side of her head. She wished Steve or Rose were here to help her.

Would she ever be able to verge again? Had the monster taken her powers forever? The black Nightmare had done this to her, she had no doubt. It was one more reason all Nightmares deserved to die. What had it done to her? Was she even a Free Dreamer anymore?

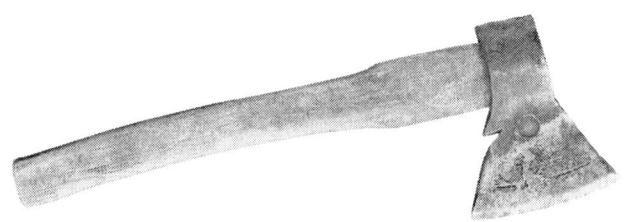

# CHAPTER THIRTY-THREE

Todd Price hated rushing. He was a careful, calculating person who knew acting quickly was a sure way to make mistakes. He was always one mistake away from dead. Despite his best efforts, sooner or later things became complicated enough that the only way to get anywhere was by acting with great haste.

Waking the moment Carrie told him the password, Todd Price dialed on his touch screen phone. He had a burn phone, so it was impossible to trace it to him. He dialed the number from memory. It would ring for a long time before anybody picked up. He looked around the dark hotel room. The furniture was in different places and the curtains were different colors, but these cheap hotels all looked alike after a while.

There was no way he could get to Portland before morning. The people that had been chasing them would report that he'd escaped and that would set them all on alert. Todd suspected the dark form, which had intruded on them, knew enough to tell Carrie's plan to whomever held its leash at Intershroud. He had only a few precious moments.

He believed Carrie's story about planning to capture him until she died. He was sad to discover that she'd managed to compromise Steve. A good verger was invaluable.

If her password worked, this could be a gold mine. They had hackers who had managed to get access to IS computers, but this was management level. Carrie had demonstrated great intelligence, so she could have amassed a wealth of information that could be used against Intershroud. Possibly something in it would force the world to accept that the IS was real. Proving the existence of the IS was just as good as proving the existence of Essentia.

"Yes." The voice was female, low and urgent.

"Security code seven, seven, seven. Prime token pencil."

"What do you need?"

"I need somebody that can be inside an IS building in ten minutes. Portland, Oregon. Mendleson Insurance. Second floor. Office of Carrie Gretsch. Hold F8 during start-up. The backdoor password is D-O-M-N-8-2-W-I-N. Use a dedicated satellite USB transmitter to copy the hard drive. Go in under the guise of IS I.T." Intershroud Information Technician, an oxymoron. Todd waited for the woman to process what he'd told her.

"Confirmed."

"Take a gun. Send the feed directly to this number."

"Anything else?"

"That's all."

"This line will remain active for six hours. A new secure telephone number will be made available in two days."

"Confirmed," Todd said. He was tempted to say something witty like they always did in spy movies, but it was still the middle of the night. He ended the call and started booting up his computer. He had to make another swap in two days. That meant he'd have to buy airplane tickets in the morning. The thought of Thai food made him hungry. He was always hungry when he woke up in the middle of the night.

As soon as the laptop booted up, he plugged his cell phone into a USB port and set it up to record to an auxiliary memory device plugged into another. It only had a 256 gigabyte capacity. He would catch the overflow on the computer's memory and that would give him almost half a terabyte total. He hoped Carrie was estimating high.

Todd pulled up the Internet and did a search for Mendleson Insurance. He found the business's phony webpage. It looked professional enough with the obligatory contact information and submission forms. It would fool anybody that happened on it in the course of surfing. To the trained eye, however, it was clearly a front. Todd had seen dozens of websites like this one. The IS had a small group of programmers they paid to generate and maintain the sites. Anybody looking for information would find nothing because the company had nothing to offer.

Todd MapQuested the building's address, and then he looked for any webcams in the area. He found an advertising company up the street that hosted a live-streaming webcam. It gave him a decent view of the street about half a block up from the Mendleson building. The street was glossy from recent rain. The streetlights reflected off the curbs and made everything bright and shiny. Todd just watched and waited.

Within five minutes, a wide, black-and-chrome motorcycle drove up the deserted street and parked in front of the building. The rider was large with black leathers and a red bandana tied around his head where a helmet wasn't. Todd groaned audibly. This was not what he had asked for. It was probably the best they could do on short notice, but a biker?

Todd pulled the small pad of paper from his left jacket pocket and the pencil from the right. He began sketching the biker for no reason except to help calm his nerves. Within the minute, the biker had gained entry into the building.

"Sorry about this," the burly, hairy man said as he followed the night guard in through the front door. "If I don't check in with my parole officer before morning, I'm going back to the slammer." His arms were bare and bulging out of a leather vest. An ancient logo painted on his back had worn to an indecipherable blob. Graying hair and beard seemed to poke out in every direction beneath the grease-smeared bandana. His leather boots had holes worn in the toes, but still clicked against the cold tile floor.

"Just make it fast," the young man barked as he set the phone up on the high reception desk. Now that he was behind the desk and there was some space between them, he had regained some of his courage. He had a holstered Taser with the snap off that he was fingering like a gun. He knew he wasn't supposed to let anybody in at night, but one of the daytime guards called and asked him to help this friend as a favor.

The big man dialed a few times without removing his leather gloves to push the small buttons. He muttered the whole time under his breath about having to leave the party early. Then he began to smack the phone down violently several times. "It's not working. It says something about no long distance." He smacked it down hard enough that the young guard jumped.

"This phone can't make long distance calls," the guard said, voice creeping higher. He stood up and backed away a little bit. "I'm sorry."

"Five years," the man said. "Five years I'm going to get if I don't make this call. Tell me you got another phone here somewhere."

"I... I... I don't think so." The guard tried to hold his ground, wondering how he had gotten into this ridiculous situation.

"Upstairs? You have all those offices making important insurance calls all day, and not one of them has long distance?" The biker's voice was getting mean now. The guard pulled his Taser free and tried to remain calm.

"Maybe, but I'm already going to get in trouble if somebody finds out I let you in. I can't…"

"Just two minutes," the big man said. His moustache twitched and caused his dirty nose to wrinkle. "Be a pal. Help a friend out. I need two minutes. I called in a big favor for this, and I need to make the call." Without waiting, he walked around the reception desk and headed for the elevators. "This will take us upstairs, right?"

Completely out of his element, the guard decided he should at least follow the man. He holstered the Taser and went around to the elevators. Up until today, this had been the easiest job the young man had ever imagined. With a little luck, this might just go away, too. He pushed the button for up and waited nervously.

The biker's smell of beer and motor oil filled the small elevator. He talked in his forceful and gruff voice the whole time. "I got permission to be out of my parole area," the big man said. "My P.O. let me come here for a wedding. My daughter got married today. Can you believe that? I asked what she wanted to marry some college puke for, but she just laughed. Didn't think she would have invited her old man… Would've thought she was embarrassed. But it was a nice, quiet ceremony with just a few friends and an open bar. 'Course I can't drink on account of my parole, but I lost track of time all the same. That's when my friend said I could use the phone here."

The elevator opened, and they stepped out. The guard said, "All those people and nobody had a cell phone?"

His face went white when he realized what he'd just said. The biker smiled and punched him once. He went out cold and fell flat on the floor.

The guard's keys opened the office of Carrie Gretsch. The big man booted up the computer, holding down F8. Then he typed in the password. When the home screen came up on the computer, it automatically launched the e-mail and IM programs. He nimbly unplugged the blue network cable with his huge, gloved fingers, and pushed a small, plastic stick into the front USB port. A piece of black electrical tape covered the blue light so the flashing wouldn't attract attention. He turned off the monitor and covered all the lights on the computer with black tape, too. Then the biker turned off the light, locked the office, and threw the keys on the chest of the guard just coming back to consciousness.

As the elevator closed, the biker said, "Keep your mouth shut about this and maybe you'll still have a job tomorrow."

The guard raced for the emergency stairs. By the time he reached the lobby, the motorcyclist was gone.

The instant the download completed, Todd shut down the computer and the cell phone. The files totaled 220 gigs. He gathered his things quickly and left the hotel. How many times had he hailed a cab in the middle of the night to make a quick escape? He couldn't remember.

# CHAPTER THIRTY-FOUR

When Steve appeared, he saw Carrie pacing back and forth along a wide corridor lined with tall rock walls open to the bright sky above. A few weeds were testing their strength against the mortar on the ground. Occasional vines found purchase in seams at the corner and made a feeble attempt to cling to the rough walls.

Even though she addressed George, Carrie was talking to herself. "This is all so frustrating. They just leave me here to rot? How do they know that stupid shadow won't come back and find us? Can't you climb up a wall and figure out the best way through this maze?"

George seemed genuinely interested in the ranting, yet he turned the instant he sensed Steve's arrival. "I've already tried, remember? It's impossible to reach the top and climb out. Besides, look." He pointed to Steve, who decided to stay still. He didn't want to find out what happened if he interrupted a Ghost in the middle of a speech.

"Finally!" Carrie straightened up and walked slowly over as if she'd been in a board meeting and Steve was nothing more than a distraction. "Do you have news for us?"

"Todd Price is ready."

"Oh, so the great Mr. Price summons me."

"It can wait if you're busy." Steve said it with a straight face, but he couldn't keep his gaze from darting to the walls of the maze. It was a realm where dreamers could never find the way out—a good place to hide.

"No, I'll see him now."

Steve was already tired of this charade. He reached out and grabbed her shoulder. The two of them left George alone in the long passage.

Steve knew Todd's paranoia would never permit him to return to the lodge now that the dark form had tracked him there, so they met him in a cave. It was a small cutout of gray rock with a waterfall completely blocking the entrance. Water dribbling from the ceiling kept the floor muddy. Even if he hadn't been shading, it would be hard to see Todd's features here.

"Did it work?" Carrie's impatience forbade pleasantries.

"There was nothing in the information stored on your computer that could tell us the identity of the person or people responsible for your death." He had to speak louder than he preferred. Luckily, the waterfall sounds interfered with his voice enough to mask it.

"What?" Her poise evaporated as a strange fear of failure began to cloud her mind and drive her to madness. Steve found it scared him a little. She turned with a finger pointing in Todd's general direction. "Nothing?"

"From your computer, however, we managed to hack into a few other e-mail caches. Your boss..."

"Jared Thurman? Why would he... He's the one that set me up as bait?"

"No, please let me finish. Your boss didn't know because they timed it for when he was out of town at a business meeting. Before the system caught it, our computer worm managed to find e-mail indicating that you were withholding information about me."

"If I'd told them, they would have gone after you. I had to be the one to make it happen, so they would promote me." Carrie stared off to the side as if she could see through the tumbling water. "That feels like a different lifetime now. A different me."

"The conversation about various methods of extracting this information from you doesn't suggest they were planning to kill you from the beginning. You getting hit by a car and going into a coma was an accident. But once that happened, they turned you into a Ghost on purpose."

"Who did it?"

"The messages were vague. I don't know who is actually responsible. I just know who was discussing it."

"Who?" Her face was calm and cold. Her eyes burned with fire. A few strands of blonde hair started to rise as if static electricity was building up. Steve backed up against the damp rock wall, lifting his hands in case he had to ward off an attack.

Todd said, "Gerard Traxler and Dale Burns. Those were the two people who had the conversation." Even with the noise and Todd's shading, Steve could sense how much Todd didn't like working with this woman.

"Dale Burns?" Carrie turned away and began thinking aloud again as if nobody else was there. "It can't be Gerard Traxler. He's a coward. But he would have been in the know about my being close to tracking down Todd Price. Dale works in…" Suddenly, the small cave echoed with an ear-splitting scream. It seemed to come from the walls and exceed any noise this well-dressed woman could possibly emit. She pounded her fists against the wall so hard she began to leave dents in the low-density rock.

Todd waited until he thought she might be able to hear him. "That concludes our business."

"Dale Burns works in native affairs. He attunes Nightmares!" She didn't stop ranting. "He wouldn't have known what I was doing directly, but he could easily have sent George and that little shadow thing after me. And he would be in line for a nice promotion if he found you." She pointed in the direction Todd's voice had been coming from.

"We are done here," Todd said. "Do you want Steve to take you back to your friend?"

"No., wait! I need you to help me. It's very simple. I have a website. If you follow my directions…"

"No." Todd's voice rose to emphasize the finality of the decision. "I told you before. I will not get involved in your revenge."

"I can get you more information."

"I doubt it. Steve will take you where you need to go. Thanks, Steve. I'll meet you later." Suddenly, the waterfall parted and a human shape splashed through the falling veil.

"You can help me," Carrie said to Steve. "It's easy. You won't be in any danger."

"I'm sorry," Steve said. "The only help I can give you is to take you back to your friend."

Carrie's manic eyes wouldn't let her believe him. "I have money. I'll give you the account information."

"Come on," Steve said. He touched her arm softly, and the rumble of the falling water faded.

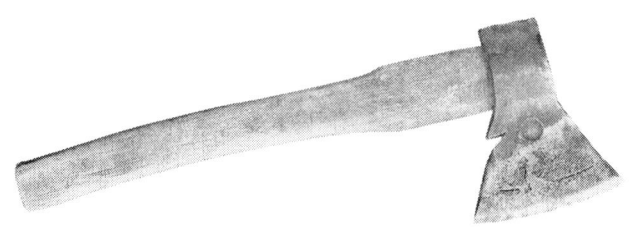

# CHAPTER THIRTY-FIVE

When Meg finally got back to sleep, she merged her bubble at the parking lot of her school. A thick wave of bad feelings settled onto her like a blanket soaked in vinegar. She knew Rose was right. Nothing good would come of being here, but something inside drove her on manically. Feelings of doubt and hate churned together until she couldn't stay away.

She searched the gnarled black trees and dusty ground for any sign of her nemeses. She'd been away from these Nightmares for so long that she was starting to be able to stand school when she was awake now. Still, it was too quiet. It never took them this long to find her before.

For a brief moment, she let herself have hope. Maybe killing the Ringmaster had somehow destroyed the rest of them as well. That moment, the very instant she dared to think something good might befall her, the clowns started showing up.

She realized they needed her to believe there was a way out. They fed on destroying her hope.

"We told you it wouldn't be the last time," said Greasy. "Our little Megan always comes back."

"It's been too long," said the Bearded Lady with a man's voice. "Momma was getting lonely!"

"No," Meg said. "I'm here to kill you all, just like your boss."

"The boss?" asked the man with a high-pitched voice. "He's going to be glad to see you."

"He's dead," Meg said. She spoke with bravado she could only just feel. "Like you will be."

"He came back," said Greasy beneath three tufts of green hair. "He told us to bring you to him when you came back, too."

"He came back?" Meg looked past the trees to the striped big top tent in the distance. She realized the reason she hadn't come back sooner was the fear of hearing this exact news. "That's impossible. I killed him."

"He said you tried to kill him," the Bearded Lady said, laughing in her baritone voice.

"He's dead," Meg said. "I know it."

"Then let's go together to see his viewing," Greasy said. He extended his hairy arm, smeared with white and dirt, as if he was escorting Meg to prom.

She wagged her head in disbelief. They had to be lying. She would kill them all for their lies, but right now, she had to be sure.

Without another word, she turned and dashed into the dead woods. She wasn't fast this time. Each step thumped the ground and left a distinct print from her black combat boots. The clowns followed. She could feel their disappointment. She wasn't playing the game right, and it left them dissatisfied.

A chill swept down her spine when she stepped in front of the big top. She looked at her bracelet again, just to be sure, and pulled with all her might on the thick canvas flap door.

As the heavy, oiled fabric settled over the nearby angled rope, little fires bathed the face of evil. "Hello, Megan."

The voice grated in her ears and seemed to rip off pieces of her soul. Nausea filled her brain. "This is impossible. I watched you die in a cloud of smoke."

"That's not true." He lifted the deep purple top hat off and bowed his bald head. "You saw a black cloud and woke up."

Meg's mind screamed, but she would not allow any sound to escape her pursed lips. Fire burned in her stomach. "You lived?"

"Obviously. I had a strong mother." The thick black eyebrows curled down in a wicked grimace.

"I am not your mother."

"What, then? My creator?"

"Then I'll just have to be sure you die this time." For the first time Meg wondered why she kept coming here without weapons. This would be so much easier with a flamethrower.

"I do hope you'll try. Now that we are linked again, I think you'll get a lot of chances to try."

"I only need one," she said. She leaped forward and clamped her hands around his arm.

He waited patiently. Only when she had tried to diverge a bubble repeatedly did he let a smile crack his dark lips. "That's so cute," he finally said. "But you made a mistake, my dear. You have no power over me. I hold all the cards."

She let go as he actually pulled a deck of cards out of his suit coat pocket. She turned to run, but the flap zipped itself shut. She tore at the interconnected metal until her fingers started to bleed. "Let me out!"

"I don't think so," the Ringmaster said while laughing. "Now, do you want to play a game?"

"No!"

"Too bad." He fanned the deck and held it out. "Pick a card, any card."

"No. Never." Her voice was breaking. Tears streaked the sides of her cheeks, carrying black eye makeup as they ran.

"It wasn't a question," the Ringmaster chided. "Now do as you're told."

Meg had her back pressed up against the zippered wall, pushing with her legs as if she could pop the zipper. Then her arm moved forward against her will. She could see the silver bracelet dangling behind her trembling hand. Completely out of control, it moved forward and nimbly selected a card. She clamped her eyes closed. Then they slowly opened, defying her commands. She watched helpless as her own hand brought back the chosen card and turned, revealing the king of hearts.

"I think it means something, don't you?" The Ringmaster flipped the fanned deck. All the cards were red. When it finished rotating, she saw every card was a king of hearts.

"You can keep that one," he said. Her hand drew it forward and then tucked it into her pocket. "Now I'll be able to find you anywhere. No more long spaces apart." His mouth opened into a wide triangle, revealing crooked teeth and putrid breath.

Meg tried to stop her own heart. She willed herself to die. How could this be happening again? After so long free, why had she come back here? Why couldn't she just let all of this past go? The tears stopped as her stomach soured. It had all been for nothing. All Rose's help was wasted. She couldn't verge away. Now that he could find her, this monster would never let her go.

The moment she lost all hope, the Ringmaster reached one long, dirty finger up and tickled her chin. "Our little Megan is back."

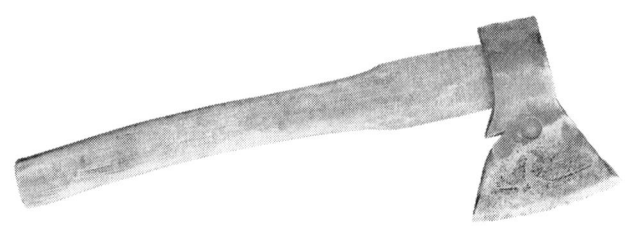

# CHAPTER THIRTY-SIX

It was a long time before Meg had managed to wake up. She knew she had to dream somewhere else. She wanted to talk to Rose, but she just couldn't do it. She didn't want to interrupt Steve if he was doing something important. Still, she didn't want to be alone. So she dreamed the only person she thought might be able to give her some information on Steve's whereabouts.

Meg found Carrie inside a small house, talking to an old woman. Knickknacks lining painted shelves on yellow walls decorated the house. The gray-haired woman rocked back and forth in a wooden chair.

"You were always so busy that I never got a chance to tell you how proud of you I was," the old woman's voice said mournfully. "I told everybody, 'My Carrie went out in the world and made something of herself.' But I should have told you."

"Mom," Carrie said in a whiney, almost teenaged voice, "that doesn't matter now. That's not what I'm here to talk to you about. Something important has happened. I won't be able to come and visit you anymore."

"I know, dear," her mother intoned. "It was a lovely funeral. Not as many people there as I expected, but you were away at the big city so long. Still, the sermon was quite beautiful."

"I'm not talking about my death, Mother," Carrie pressed. "Listen to me. Please, just listen. You have to try and remember this when you wake up, too."

"Okay." The baffled old woman smiled strangely.

"I made a mistake today," Carrie said.

"It wasn't your fault, dear." Her mother clearly wasn't going to let her talk without interruption.

"Yes, it was. Just listen. The man that killed me knows my face now. He'll be back any time. I'm not safe here. If he finds out about you, he will hurt you to get to me. I have to go away forever now."

"I know, love," she said sadly. "Off to heaven to be with your daddy."

"I'm sorry I wasn't a better daughter," Carrie said. "I'm sorry my bad choices had to hurt you. I didn't know the place I worked was evil. I thought they were just talking about dreams in a metaphorical way. Then once I got involved, I didn't want to quit. But messing with the bad guys will always get you killed sooner or later. I thought I could control it. I thought I was smart enough, but in the end, it cost me everything.

"I knew it was hurting you when I made those choices, but I pretended it was only about me. I knew all along, but didn't care about anything but my own greed. Now it has finally caught up to me. I don't think I'll go to heaven when I die."

"Don't say that," her mother scolded. Then with a broken heart, she said, "Never say that."

"Maybe there's one thing I can do to make things a little better before I go. I can tell you I'm sorry. And I can try to take some of them with me."

"Don't." The old woman began to cry. "Carrie, don't. If you can save your soul, it will be by forgiving them."

"But then I could never forgive myself."

"If you have some time, use it to heal." The rocking stopped amid open sobs.

"I'm sorry." Carrie put one hand over her mouth. "I came here to make things better and I only made it worse. It wasn't you. It was me. You were a wonderful mother. I'm not going to heaven, but it's not because of you. Goodbye, Mother."

"Goodbye, dear." The rocking resumed.

Meg stayed silent as Carrie turned the other way and went out the front door. Meg was glad Carrie didn't see her. Meg wasn't sure if she could verge or not since the black kite-like thing, so she tested it. Immediately, she found herself outside. Apparently, the effects were temporary. She wondered if waking up had somehow set everything right again.

George was there with Carrie. Meg wished he had stayed on Sunset Boulevard. George gave Carrie a big hug.

She said to him, "I'm the worst daughter on Earth. I should just have told her what she wanted to hear. I should just have comforted her. I knew the right words to say, but somehow I couldn't say them. I just made it worse and left her in tears."

George didn't say anything. He looked at Meg with inquisitive eyes, and his tall head tipped to one side.

Meg said, "How did you get here from California without me?"

"I could always come here," Carrie said, still holding George without looking up. "This is the one place I could always come whenever I wanted. But now I can't ever come back."

"Burns linked you."

"Changing my skin color was the best thing George could do for me. It was the reason they couldn't find me all this time. Now that they know, it won't be long before they show up and end my life for good."

"Not if you end his life first."

Carrie sat up instantly. The words seemed to imbue her with new energy. "Will you help me?"

"Maybe," Meg said. "If you help me."

"Did Todd Price send you?"

"No." Meg eyed the big, black gorilla. She was starting to think this was a really bad idea, but since it was her only idea, she didn't know what else to do.

"Do you know where Steve is?"

"Who cares?"

They sat there for a while, each unsure what to say next. Changing the subject, Meg said, "How can you stand it?"

Carrie stopped talking when she saw Meg staring with contempt at George. George stopped fiddling with his new tie. Meg felt him trying to feed off her loathing. Lucky for him, it didn't work.

"How can I stand to be around George?" Carrie laughed.

"Can't you feel him feeding off your thoughts and emotions? Doesn't it feel like he's eating your heart?"

Carrie twirled one lock of ash-blonde hair around her long, dark finger. "Why do you care?"

Meg didn't answer. She didn't want to reveal that much about herself to this stranger.

George's bass boom answered. "She has fed many Intenui."

"Speak English," Meg said. She couldn't be polite to a monster. She was glad he wasn't feeding off her. If he had been, she probably couldn't have stayed here without violence.

"He said you have had a lot of Nightmares," Carrie translated. "Strange that you should choose to come to me, knowing he was here."

"I needed information," Meg said. "I'm not going to be scared off by a big monkey." Despite the bravado, she felt the pressure of fear in her stomach. "How did you become friends with it?"

"We didn't start that way, but things change. He's a Phantasy now."

Meg didn't know what that meant, but she was tired of people talking down to her. "You *feed* it on purpose?"

"Typical," George interrupted. "A Vitae can offer an Intenui a year's sustenance with but a thought. Why deny those that depend on you for food and life? Dreamers created us. They nurture us. They make us to serve their needs. Then, when they have what they want, they discard us and even try to kill us. We are not the tenuous ones. We know our intentions. But why despise the children you have created?"

Meg was speechless. She was too in shock to feel sympathy or guilt. She wasn't even sure she had understood. She fell back on what Rose told her. *Dreams are feelings we need to experience and actions we need to try. Nightmares are just a side effect.*

"If we're evil and you made us, what does that make you?" The echo of George's voice reverberated back to them again and again.

Was Meg evil for creating those clowns? She defended herself. "They start innocently enough, but become evil when they have been unnaturally twisted by Intershroud."

George closed his mouth and turned away in silence. Meg didn't know why that argument should affect him at all. She was happy to win it anyway. Carrie stepped over and put a hand on George. "This is my only friend and confidante. He has saved my life, literally. He is a creature of good. You are a prejudiced little brat. How did you even know about Intershroud changing George?"

"What? I didn't know," Meg said. "I was talking about an entirely different thing. I'm looking for somebody from Intershroud that turned Nightmares on me and used me to make them strong for their own twisted purposes."

George looked back at her. Carrie said, "The only person I knew that worked in Native Affairs was..." Suddenly, Carrie stopped. She fell into George's lap. His huge hands cradled her gently. "Is it possible?"

Carrie then turned to Meg, "It would seem we have a common enemy."

"Who?"

"Dale Burns." She choked on the name as if acid was eroding her voice box.

Meg rolled the name over in her mind, determined to commit it to memory eternally. "And you know how to take him down?"

"You can't do it from your house. They'll definitely try to track you. So you have to go as far away as you can and use an anonymous machine. Try to wear gloves so there are no fingerprints. Don't use any passwords or accounts that can be traced to you... not even anonymous ones that you think are safe."

"Just tell me what to do," Meg said. Even though she'd saved this Ghost's life, Carrie still treated her like a kid. Meg wondered if people would ever take her seriously. Then she realized her clothes probably didn't help.

"Go to Carriegretch.com and click the work tab. A bunch of fake stuff about foreign acquisitions will come up. In the list of companies, look for Baxson. Click it. It will ask for a login and password. The login is cgretsch and the password is c-o-n-q-u-3-r-4-f-u-n. Can you remember that tomorrow?"

"Yes," Meg said, rolling her eyes.

"It's not a website owned by Intershroud. It's my own. Once you get in, look for a picture of me and my mother in France. There's a fly on the bread in the basket on the café table. Click on the fly. It's very small, so you'll want to zoom in. Don't click anywhere else on the picture.

"When you click on that fly, it will ask you for a name and department. Type in Dale Burns and Native Affairs. Then click submit. Then log out or shut down or whatever. It's all automatic after that."

"That's all?" Meg was surprised.

"Isn't that enough?"

"Native Affairs? That's what they call making those horrible monsters?"

"Yes, and I was in Acquisitions... which means recruiting or forcing people to join."

"What if they didn't join?"

"One way or another, the IS gets what they want. They never lose. Ever. Nobody says no to them for very long. They have unlimited resources. That's what I liked about it."

"And now?"

"Now..." Carrie looked at George. "Now I wish I could go back to my senior year in high school and start all over."

"What would you do differently?" Meg sincerely wanted to know. She was supposed to be making plans of her own like that and so far nothing had interested her enough to make her willing to try in school.

"Everything," Carrie said. "I would find somebody to fall in love with." She glanced at George when she said it. "I would learn to act and be in plays. I would study history or become a painter. I would laugh with friends at a café instead of studying finance in a library. In short, I would have a life worth living.

"All this time I wasted in the pursuit of a Phantom. I thought power and money had meaning. But they're just illusions. You can never be the most powerful. There is always somebody bigger and stronger with more contacts and more money. As long as you play their game, they own you. If I had it all to do over, I would be free.

"But none of that matters now. In a few minutes, they will come and take away the only thing I have left." She looked at George. "I just wish I could give you something first. Something big. I wish I could give you all of me before they come and take it away. That way I will have done one nice thing before the end."

"There's a way," George said. The wrinkles twisted his face into an expression that Meg couldn't read. "In Godrath when a new Voice is chosen, a special Vitoi called a Gnostoi is absorbed in honor of the founder."

Meg wondered if Nightmares had their own language or this was just something unique to George and Carrie. None of that made sense to her.

"I'm afraid I didn't follow most of that, honey," Carrie said.

George nodded, puffing out his chest. "In order to become president of the Nightmares, the president elect takes all the density from a Ghost as part of the coronation ritual."

"You eat people?" Meg gasped. She knew Nightmares were bad before, but now she had proof.

"Shh." Carrie dismissed Meg as if she were swatting away a fly. "You could do that? Would it help you? Would it make you strong, so you wouldn't need dreamers anymore?"

"You can't be serious?" Meg's mouth must have been open very wide because it made her jaw sore.

"Stay out of this," Carrie said, still looking at George's huge eyes. "I'll do it. It's better than dying for nothing when they find me. Tell me what to do, George."

"Don't be stupid," Meg barked. "Steve said he knew places you could hide, so even if they linked you, they couldn't find you."

Carrie turned now as if coming out of a trance. "What do you think, George?"

"I would prefer for you to stay alive," he growled softly.

"Is there one adult in the world that has any sense?" Meg whispered to herself. Just before they diverged, Meg felt a wave of sickness come over her. It wasn't from verging. It was a familiar sadness filling her mind. As the world changed, she felt the presence of the Ringmaster. He was coming for her.

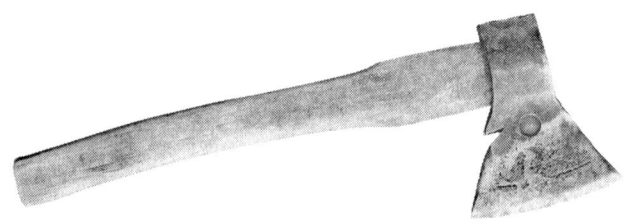

# CHAPTER THIRTY-SEVEN

Meg took a moment to shake off a cold chill. She said, "We need to get out of here fast. How do we share this dream, exactly?"

George opened his mouth to explain, but Carrie interrupted him. "With Steve I just had to think of the place. Somehow he could see that and take us there."

"So you just think about Dale Burns and I should be able to verge us to him?" Meg was trying to sound positive, but it came out more as confusion.

"Don't think of it as reading my mind. Think of it as lending me your power." Carrie grew louder when she said the word "power."

"Okay," Meg said.

Carrie gently set one hand on top of Meg's arm. Meg didn't notice George rolling his eyes as he reached one huge finger over and touched the same arm. Meg half expected black grease to wipe off on her.

Meg closed her eyes and tried to concentrate on the Ghost. She tried to access Carrie's mind and sense what she was thinking, but none of that worked. Carrie didn't say anything. She looked at the changing setting with amusement.

"I can't do more," Meg said. "We're in a bubble, but I don't know where to merge it. Tell me what the place looks like."

"I don't know where he is," Carrie said. "I just know his face."

Meg melted the surroundings until they were in a kind of flatland. The sky was still black, the ground gray. It looked like a painting with broad brushstrokes. Next to them, the gray ground grew into a tall mound. Then it began to separate. Limbs became apparent. The mound turned to a fleshy color with dark hair. A nose popped out. Eye sockets receded with two generic colorless black spots in the middle. Fingers became clear. Black shoes appeared. It was all rough like a child's drawing.

"Try to make this guy look like Dale Burns," Meg said.

Carrie pointed. "Deep brow ridge, brown eyes." The figure distorted to her will. "How is this working?"

"It's a bubble," Meg said. "You can do whatever you want when nobody's mind opposes you. I'm not stopping you, so you can make this look like him. If you get it close enough, we should actually land right next to him."

"This is fun!" Carrie had to avoid the temptation to punch and kick the dummy as she filled in more and more details. A five o'clock shadow and wrinkles lined his cheeks. The hair was dark brown with some stray gray strands. His hands became stubby and thick. Arm hair grew. "That's all I know. I don't know what he's wearing."

On a whim, Meg slapped a pinstripe suit and fedora on their dummy. "If it's really the same guy, he should be wearing something like this," she said, shrugging. Suddenly, the painted sky bled to fill the canvas. A large brick building shot up from the ground. The ground melded into asphalt. The dummy jumped away from them.

"What the..." Dale Burns had to catch himself before he fell backward in shock.

"It really is the same guy," Carrie said with grim satisfaction. She was already stepping intently toward the shocked man.

"Who are you?" the man said. He regained some composure when he realized his voice was showing fear and stood up straight even though he kept stepping backward toward the building's front door.

"You know who I am," Carrie accused, jumping toward him.

Meg didn't know what to say or do. As she watched Carrie advancing on Dale Burns, Meg realized there was no plan here at all. She stepped back and sideways behind George to try to prevent this man from noticing her. With Carrie bearing down on him, Meg hoped he hadn't recognized her face. That last thing she needed was another enemy who could link her.

"I really don't," Dale said.

"Carrie Gretsch from Acquisitions," she said, taunting. "You had me killed recently."

"What?" His eyes narrowed as recognition dawned on him. Except for the color of her skin, everything was the same. "Oh my... Well, I'll be..."

"Shut up," Carrie barked. She pushed him with both hands. Dale let the motion carry him back toward the door he had wanted to enter. Meg struggled with deciding between staying out of sight and peeking out to get a glimpse of the action. Despite being behind him, she could feel that George was sad. It didn't make sense to her why he would be, but she didn't care.

"Look, Carrie, that whole thing was an accident. I didn't mean for you to die. I barely even knew you. Corporate just wanted me to put some pressure on you because they weren't sure if you were really on to anything or if you were just lying to make yourself look better. They couldn't find enough information to justify your claims. Since you were only half a Free Dreamer anyway, they asked me to force the issue in Essentia. That's all." His hands were both behind him, grasping for the knob on the brown metal door he knew must be in that area.

George's chest heaved with huge breaths, which drained out his nose in threatening snorts. His knuckles began sliding across the asphalt, scraping gouges in the pavement. Meg was glad she was behind him when his leg muscles tensed and she suspected he was going to charge.

"Liar!" Carrie screamed. She leaped after him with her hands aimed for his throat. George jumped forward, too, as if suddenly caught up in the desire to destroy this enemy.

The door behind him slid open and Dale jumped inside, narrowly avoiding Carrie's hands and George's fist. The great ape rammed the unlatched door and slammed it wide open with a thunderous crash. When they turned the corner, Dale was running down a hall, yelling for help.

Meg quietly slid in behind to watch the parade from a distance. This was just as much her battle as Carrie's. She just wanted more information before she jumped in.

"Help me!" Dale cried out in a whiney voice that echoed through the hall. "Get her away from me!"

When Meg turned the corner, the hall was empty. A large door at the end was open with yellow light streaming through. Commotion filled that room. Meg ran as quietly as her boots would let her and turned to look inside.

It was what Meg always imagined hell looked like. Carrie still advanced on Dale in the center of a warehouse. Horrifying creatures of every size and shape lined the walls of the cavernous space. A giant octopus squished across the two-story ceiling. Cloaked specters, space aliens, tusked pig men, and even a dragon bustled around. Hair, slime, fangs, and scales were everywhere. Creepy men with long knives, dark shadows with razor claws, and even some transparent ghostlike forms were in the mix. Meg felt her very soul cry out in pain at learning of the existence of so many wicked monsters.

She wanted to die. A kind of shock settled into her system as she sat staring, immobilized. How could anyone make such horrible things?

The realization of what this meant was something she had never imagined. Her clowns, the experiment that had broken her mind and destroyed her childhood, were nothing like the worst monsters this person had propagated. It was just a funny little side job to him. She had focused on her own situation so heavily that she never imagined anyone capable of even greater atrocities. Dreaming or awake, the existence of these beasts was an abomination.

She doubted she could destroy half of these creatures one-on-one. They were large and powerful. Their advance snapped her out of her lonely terror, and she noticed they were all moving toward the middle of the huge room. Carrie had reached Dale and was throttling him so hard that her fingernails were poking through the skin on the sides of his neck. She was bouncing his head up and down on the hard floor with a rhythmic thump. George growled out threats to the advancing Nightmares, but Meg doubted they saw George as any more than a warm-up exercise. One at a time, he might be able to take some of them. Many of these dwarfed him and sported curled claws as a testament to their ruthless efficiency at ripping essence into steamy shreds.

So far, they hadn't seen Meg. She knew she could verge to Carrie and get them all away if necessary. If the monsters reached her, it was over. As she crouched, she felt something bend and press into her hip. The king of hearts.

Just as she felt it, a new image caught Meg's eye. In the back of the group, moving out from the far wall, a tall man in a colorful suit approached. The dirty stripes went all the way to his hat. Greasy white paint smeared over his long beak of a nose and sharp cheekbones. Even at this distance, the Ringmaster was unmistakable. His connection to her was strong, and despite the chaos of the scene before him, he stretched his face into a wily grin and turned to look right at her. She wanted to run. She wanted a weapon. Once again, she was stuck in a childhood nightmare.

The Ringmaster didn't say anything to the other monsters. He wasn't one to share. He moved toward her with arrogance and a furrowed brow that promised she wouldn't like what was coming. Meg swallowed her fear and anger. She had to think. Carrie was about to be killed forever, and an insane fit that ended with Dale Burns waking up was not the solution. He'd be fine and back to sleep in a few minutes anyway. They had linked him, so they could find him again, but next time he'd be surrounded by a lot of IS muscle.

The Ringmaster was only twenty feet away. The circle of gargantuan terrors around George and Carrie closed fast. Meg's heart raced. The Ringmaster said, "I told you I'd find you anywhere."

Meg wanted to yell back. She wanted to fight, but something deep down told her she was the only living being in this place that had any sense left. She had to do the smart thing now. Without a word, she ran. Once she turned the next corner, she heard him talking in the hall. Maybe if he couldn't see her, she could diverge.

The bubble looked like the hall she had been in except with more light. For a moment, Meg felt quiet and safe. She was tempted to keep going and leave all the horror behind. It was Carrie's own fault she was in this situation, not Meg's. Still, Meg felt like she owed Carrie something more. In the center of a ring of demons, Meg merged.

The smell was awful, the sounds maddening. Claws scratched across the concrete floor. Teeth ground together. The instant she appeared, the murder of Nightmares leaped at them. Meg pulled Carrie off Dale and reached out to touch George, who was beating his chest in front of an advancing Sasquatch. They disappeared in a fog of mist.

It was too late. Claws raked Meg's side. Teeth clamped down on her calf. George roared enough to deafen them all. Carrie screamed.

Meg didn't know how many of the vermin they brought. When the bubble merged, the same roaring and screaming continued. It was darker now. To be honest, Meg had no idea where they were. A dim twilight and a few neon signs were all she registered as she fell to the ground.

The slash in her back bled profusely. She ignored it, kicking with her free leg at the teeth cutting into her calf like a pit bull. Each kick loosened the bite, but tore more of her flesh. Meg kept kicking, letting rage dull the pain. Finally, the black snake relented and twisted away with a hiss. It had been a snake?

The surprise of finding themselves suddenly in a new place caused the Nightmares to step back a moment. George still grunted and pounded the ground furiously. Carrie stood up, trying to straighten her now soiled and torn suit. A quick count told Meg there were six Nightmare hitchhikers around them. Just like the stupid tall clown on stilts, they were all looking around in awe as if they had never seen anything like this before. She laughed despite the pain. If they thought Sunset Boulevard looked strange now, wait until the people here saw them!

*She tried to laugh again, but her lungs were searing. White steam poured from her leg and side. Then the pain was gone in a haze of gray.*

Meg awoke with a huff and rolled her eyes. What a mess.

Carrie had seemed uninjured when Meg left. Carrie had probably succeeded in waking up Dale Burns, but it was worthless. At least some of the Nightmares must have been touching George when they left. So Meg hoped one of them had fatally wounded that annoying monkey.

She wanted to get back to Carrie quickly, but it would be a few minutes before she could relax enough to fall asleep again. Worrying would only make it harder to sleep. That stupid Ghost owed Meg her life. She would have died there, no question. However, Meg knew Carrie probably wouldn't see it that way.

Suddenly, Meg wondered why she even cared whether Carrie lived or died. She couldn't stand George. So why risk herself for Carrie, who clearly loved George? Obviously, they had a mutual enemy in Dale Burns. Then she thought of herself and her long-term relationship with clowns. Carrie had made peace with a Nightmare. Maybe deep down Meg wished she could let go of her hatred. It wouldn't be a surprise if Rose ended up being right again. Meg tried to think of George as nice or a friend. Shivers went up her spine, and a bad taste came to her mouth.

She decided to get a drink of water before she went back into the fray.

# CHAPTER THIRTY-EIGHT

Meg couldn't get the bubble to merge. She knew the lodge inside and out. She knew the paneled wood walls. She knew the fireplaces and the tables. Yet every time she shaped the wooden walls, the fire would spread around them in a flash and she had to recoil and force it out. After several failed attempts, she decided to try something else. She pulled trees up around them. Dirt and leaves below their feet and the wooden corner of a log pole building rounded the picture. They landed in the clearing where she'd fought Stilts.

This time, the bubble merged. She knew immediately why she had trouble before. The crackling sound of exploding wood and a wave of heat from a nearby inferno assaulted them. Black smoke clogged the air, and they all had to turn and run. A raging fire consumed the lodge.

Nearby, pine trees crackled and began to light. Meg and Carrie followed George deeper into the woods. As the fire spread, it became obvious there was no way to escape by running. Meg grabbed her two companions unceremoniously and diverged again. Her eyes were puffy from the smoke. She knew this would be a tragedy for Rose.

Once they were free of the flames, Carrie said, "Now what?"

Meg wagged her head. "I guess we try to see if Steve is someplace else." Every time she tried to verge, the bubble popped and they were right back in the smoke-choked forest. Fear pushed tears from Meg's eyes as she realized why she couldn't verge. They resigned themselves to hiking and headed into what seemed like the direction the wind was coming from.

"What's going on?" Carrie called once the sound of crackling wood wasn't deafening. "Why can't you verge?"

"I don't know!" Meg didn't want to try to explain. "Something or somebody is keeping us here."

"That's never happened to you before?"

"Not since I..." Meg reached in her pocket and pulled out the king of hearts.

An evil laugh interrupted their conversation. Carrie looked around to locate the source. Meg and George knew right where to look. A few dozen feet away, a tall figure in striped clothes stepped into an open line where no trees blocked their view. The laugh seemed to reach into Meg's chest and freeze her heart. It was the Ringmaster.

# CHAPTER THIRTY-NINE

Megan cringed at the grating voice.

"There is no way for you to ever be free of me, Megan." The Ringmaster's face stretched into a mock grin. "The link between us is as strong as any in Essentia. Learning a cute new trick could never break that."

"I'll find a place you can't go," Meg spat.

"Really?" The greasy face shifted to a sinister frown. "Then why can't you leave now?"

Meg knew it was true. She had been trying to verge continually without success the whole time they had been hiking away from the burning lodge. "I don't want to leave now. I want to stay until you're dead." Meg looked for a weapon.

"You couldn't kill me last time. You won't succeed now."

"He's very dense," said George quietly. It felt more like thunder than a whisper.

"There are three of us," Carrie spat. For the first time, Meg was glad she had joined Carrie.

"There are two of me." The Ringmaster laughed, holding up all his fingers... There were only three. "Or at least there were. But I brought a new crew." Dark and scaly forms rustled in the trees behind him.

"You brought some of those monsters." Meg sighed. There really was no winning. She picked up a fallen branch and made a few swings with it as if she were warming up for a baseball game.

"We'll take them all," Carrie said.

"No." Meg wagged her head.

"All together we can beat them," Carrie reaffirmed.

"Maybe," Meg said, "but there's no point. They can't hurt me more than just waking me. You two have a lot more to lose. I'll stay here and hold them as long as I can. You two need to get away."

"But he's linked me," Carrie said. "There's nowhere I can run that Dale Burns won't find me."

"That won't be a problem if he's dead. Just stay free until I can come for you or get back to sleep. Then we'll make another attempt at finding Steve."

Carrie hesitated a long time before finally saying, "Come on, George." They ran the other direction. The two tree-sized creatures that had been behind the clown crashed through the trees in another direction. In the darkness, Meg had never really seen them.

"That was noble, but pointless." The Ringmaster laughed. "I wasn't here for her anyway."

"Why come for me now? Why not all those months ago?" Meg pressed.

"I don't know. I was just following orders. They had something special in mind for you."

"Why can you stop me from verging now, but you didn't before?"

"Orders. They didn't tell me to stop you before. Now they did, though. I guess they didn't like you finding our hideout."

Meg sliced through the air again with her wooden club. "So there's more than one Ringmaster?"

"Maybe there were more. I only knew about one after me."

"Where did they go?"

"They were reassigned, of course. They didn't keep us around just to torment you. That was just to get us strong."

"One after you? Why did you come back?"

"He disappeared. They put me back in until they could make another one."

Meg's hatred of Dale and all Nightmares grew like a disease out of control, attacking her organs one at a time. Her stomach knotted, and her vision grew fuzzy. "Well, after today there'll just be one more."

"You'll never find him. We can't. He just disappeared from the carnival one day. Maybe he's already dead."

"Whatever," Meg said. "Less talk." She started to step forward.

"This doesn't have to get ugly. I'm only supposed to keep you busy. I get just as much from talking as fighting."

"Not this time." She felt the energy he leeched from her, a crime she refused to let go unpunished. "What happened to your monster friends?"

"They had different orders."

"Dale Burns only sent one of you after each of us? I'm surprised he didn't send the whole pack."

"What would be the point?" The Ringmaster stepped forward, crunching a twig beneath his large foot. "It's not like you can hide. You and I are linked so well that I could find you in Materia if I had to."

"Unlikely," Meg said. "That's what's eating all you Nightmares up, though, isn't it? We have someplace to go, but you're all stuck here."

"Here is better. Everybody says so."

"But you'll never know. And better or not, I can always go there. Sooner or later, I'll wake up and leave. But not you. So even if you beat me a hundred times, I'll keep coming back to fight. And eventually I'll win, and you'll be gone forever." Meg didn't know if she was really upsetting the self-important clown or just playing into his hands by feeding him longer. Still, she liked where this line of thinking led.

"You're too weak to be any kind of danger to me!" The Ringmaster was actually giggling. "If you could hurt me, you would have done it all those hundreds of times you tried over the years in the big top tent. But we both know that always ended the same. Just like it's going to end now."

"Now I know the truth," Meg said. "That's different."

"How?"

"It's different because now I know you can die. I know that I can endure years of pain at your hands, but it will never amount to anything. I know that one way or another, this will end with your death. I know you were created by my mind. I know you are fed by my mind."

"Yes, but not only yours."

"Shut up. I know about dreams now. I know the truth. And that means you can't control me anymore. Now I'm the one that will choose how this ends. You're my prey." With that, Meg swung the stick as wide and as hard as she could.

The Ringmaster zipped effortlessly out of the path of the weapon and laughed. "You made me fast enough to dodge bullets and you think a stick is going to catch me off guard?"

Meg tried to verge again without success. Then she had a new idea. Instead of verging away, she diverged closer. It was a short, fast bubble. When it popped one second later, the stick was only a centimeter from the Ringmaster's head and already going very fast.

*Crack!* The Ringmaster fell backward, shocked by the unexpected motion.

Carrie, hiking away from the fire and Meg's fight, had no real plan. The bratty teen had been right. Dying now would bring no benefit. George had been acting funny lately. Carrie didn't know why. When they were far enough from the noise and seemed alone, she stopped. "We didn't get a chance to finish our conversation before," she said, looking at his careworn face. "You said it was possible for you to take all of me into you and that it would make you strong enough that you would never have to depend on dreamers again. Would it finally make you free?"

"It might," he said. "But I don't desire that if there's any place we can go where you'll continue to exist."

"You are such a doll," Carrie said. "I don't know what to do now."

"We're being followed," George said. His voice didn't covey fear. He simply stated the fact.

"That dark form shadow thing still?"

"No, that's gone. These are very large Intenui." Now that she wasn't pursuing Dale Burns with rage, the memory of the monsters could finally take hold on her mind. Fear began to well up when Carrie realized George meant some of those.

"We have to help the girl," Carrie said. "She's our only link to Steve and freedom." Protecting the girl was also the only way for Carrie to take her revenge, because it could only happen in Materia.

Just then, a large, green dragon's head slipped quietly into the small clearing. On the other side, a translucent gray humanoid with an impossibly huge sword held above its head stepped into view. They were trapped.

Meg asked, "What were you saying?" She faked to the side and swung the other direction. This time the Ringmaster managed to avoid it. She diverged behind him and smacked him upside the head again.

"Clever." The smile was gone. The Ringmaster retaliated with a lightning-fast punch. It caught Meg upside the head and had her seeing stars. "See? You and I are linked eternally. We even have the same powers, and you look a lot like one of us." In an instant, the clown grabbed the stick and pulled it out of her hands.

Meg stopped fighting. Her shoulders slumped. Despite the raging fire, she still heard the stream nearby. Meg forgot about her nemesis and stumbled toward it. She knew anything this clown said was poison. She knew not to listen, but her heart wouldn't let it go. His words seemed to cling to her soul like boiling hot candy on skin.

She fell to her knees and gazed into a pool of stagnant water. There was enough flickering orange light from the fire that she could see her reflection. Sweat had smudged her black eyeliner into strange starbursts. Her red lipstick smeared at the edges over the ivory base of makeup on her face. Her black-tipped hair stuck out wildly. She looked like Carrie in one of her crazy fits. There was no denying it. She looked like an evil clown.

Meg felt waves of energy radiating from the Ringmaster. He had one hand out, painted fingers curled as if he were choking her from a distance. His long face stretched with maniacal lines as she felt him touch her shoulder. Weakness spread through her as he sapped the will from her heart, feasting on her self-loathing.

Large tears welled up and began to draw black lines down her face. Meg knew the Ringmaster held her bound, but she didn't have the strength to fight. She sat there facing the hard truth. Meg had become what she feared and hated. She existed only to hurt and kill others. Meg was a Nightmare.

# Chapter Forty

Carrie's heart skipped a beat when George let out a deafening roar. The dragon and ghostly swordsman both leaned back, visibly affected. George pounded the ground with his fists, claiming this territory and dreamer. The leaves on the nearby trees shook from the vibrations. The language was clear to the Nightmares who saw it. If they attacked, this would be a battle to the death. Despite his being much smaller than the dragon, George had no intention of backing down.

Carrie watched in wonder. She'd never seen George like this. He slapped rocks until they burst into steam. He gritted his huge, square teeth. The dragon nosed forward, cautiously testing the limits. The swordsman lowered the sword so it could impale a charging attacker. George stared down first one and then the other. It was a slow, careful dance filled with danger.

"I don't want you to die like this," Carrie said. "It won't change the future. I'm doomed anyway." She put her hand out and touched him. "There's nowhere left to run. It all depends on that girl."

George just said, "Okay." Then, fast as lightning, he grabbed her around the waist and leaped up into the nearest tree. Even with only one hand and no tail, he could jump and fly through the treetops so quickly that they blurred. Carrie wasn't sure if she should be excited or angry. The bumpy ride caused pain to lance through her ribs whenever he jerked to one side or grabbed a new branch. It gave her a headache. Nevertheless, it did seem to be working.

The Nightmares pursued them instantly; however, the ghostly form rapidly fell behind on foot. The dragon, after knocking down a few trees, took to the air. Despite flying, it wasn't gaining on George's amazing speed. Carrie asked absently, "Why isn't it breathing fire or something?"

Between breaths, George managed to say, "Won't do that unless... dreamer forms the fire. Cost too much essence. Won't waste it."

Carrie didn't tax him with further conversation. They were quickly at the lodge fire, which was now much less bright with dark timbers sticking up in every direction.

"Meg's not here," Carrie said.

"I hear voices by the stream." George rushed through the trees toward them.

"Look who came back." The Ringmaster laughed.

"You aren't fighting?" Carrie observed aloud.

"What's the point?" the Ringmaster said. Meg stood up. The streaks of makeup on her face told it all. "We're only supposed to keep you here. It doesn't need to be a fight."

"I'm one of them," Meg said. "I've become..."

*Slap!*

Meg's eyes went wide after Carrie's rude gesture left a red handprint on her cheek and wiped some of the streaks away. Carrie glared viciously. "Snap out of it! He's obviously messing with your mind. Grow up and fight it off."

Meg looked from the Ringmaster back to Carrie. Carrie thought she looked stupid.

"He's feeding on your fears," George said.

Meg stared at them blankly as if she were lost. "I don't know what..."

"We don't have time for you to figure it out," Carrie said. "There will be two more Nightmares here in seconds."

"There's nowhere you can go that I can't find you," the Ringmaster said. "Megan and I have a special bond."

"It's Meg!" she screamed. Suddenly, Meg was a blur of hands and feet punching and kicking at the striped clown.

Carrie watched the clown slowly grow a twisted smirk. He enjoyed it. The dragon began to dive.

"George, get us out of here!" Carrie jumped at him. George grabbed Meg with one huge hand and tucked Carrie under that same arm. Then he bounded backward, just avoiding the raking claws of the green dragon. He put his other hand out and caught the trunk of a tree to one side. The momentum carried them as they swung around so that they shot up into the branches behind them.

Now Meg was pounding on George's hand. "Let me go! Don't ever touch me! I hate you! I hate all Nightmares!"

Carrie tried to calm her, but Meg couldn't listen. Eventually, George had to land so he could let go of Meg without dropping her twenty feet.

"Never touch me again!" she screamed.

"You need to calm down," Carrie said. "You couldn't verge while that clown was nearby. George can get us far enough away for you to take us to Steve."

"I'm not taking that monster anywhere."

"It was the only way," George offered.

"If you can't verge," Carrie offered, "at least wake up. You don't want to be here when..."

"Too late!" It was the nasally, high-pitched voice of the Ringmaster.

Meg rounded on him to see that he and the ghostly Nightmare had ridden in on the dragon. One second later, the monster landed and the other two jumped off.

"Too late for what?" Meg demanded. "You going to talk to me again?"

"No, Megan," he said with a snivel, "our time together is done now. I don't think they plan to let you live."

"They?" Carrie pressed.

From between the trees stormed in a dozen men in black riot gear, toting impossibly large machine guns, all trained on the three of them. Behind them came a voice familiar to Carrie. "This doesn't look like any kind of party I've ever seen before."

They all turned to see the agent that had let Carrie and George go free last time. The metallic dress had spikes running up and down her arms, and then they melted away and long, saber-like claws grew out from each of her knuckles. Carrie's heart froze. There was no way this agent would let them get away this time.

"Hello again, Mercury," Carrie said, trying to use the same clueless voice as before. She knew it wasn't going to work. She just didn't have any other strategies.

"What do you want?" Meg demanded.

"A new car," Mercury said evenly. "Mine's two years old already, and the newer models are much faster."

"What?" Meg trailed off.

Carrie knew Meg was out of her element. She gave up trying to play dumb. "Leave the girl alone," she said with authority. Her suit was dirty now, but it still fit her well. "She has nothing to do with this."

"Correction," Mercury said with a smirk, "she *had* nothing to do with this... until you dragged her into it. Now we have to get rid of her, too."

"She's just a kid. She doesn't know what's going on here. She doesn't have any information that can hurt you."

"She's a verger that has now linked me. Even if she wasn't on Burns's hit list, I would have to take her out just for that." Axe blades formed from the woman's knees.

Carrie began to panic.

George could feel Carrie falling apart emotionally. He could almost hear her thoughts. "I was so close! It can't end like this! After everything else, it can't end like this..." She turned to George and said softly, "Take all of me now and run away. They won't chase you. Save yourself because I'm done for."

George felt his entire body undulating. It was not even, but fast. There was some kind of rhythm pounding in his ears. *Thump, thump. Thump, thump.* It was strange to him. He didn't know what could make him hear or feel that. He looked around.

"Hurry, George," Carrie said.

"Stop whispering," Mercury said.

*Thump, thump.* Carrie held George's arm tightly now, bracing for the end.

"Why haven't you killed us already?" Meg asked. George sensed Meg's wish to wake and the others holding her against her will.

"Don't worry, little punk, your life will end soon enough. But it's not my job to kill you."

George turned to look behind him. Where was that thumping coming from?

"Who then?" Meg demanded.

On cue, Dale Burns stepped out of the shadows into the clearing. He had a big grin on his face and wore the same ugly suit. "Hello! It's good to finally meet you in person, Megan."

"It's just Meg."

"Whatever. I'm sorry you got caught in all of this," he said with the fake smile of a used-car salesman. "If things had gone differently, I hoped one day to train you to work for us. You'd have been a great Nightmare wrangler."

Meg tried to spit at him, but she was too far away for it to be effective.

"Now, George," Carrie whispered urgently. "We won't get another chance."

*Thump, thump. Thump, thump.* She leaned against him, and he felt her chest moving to match the sound. The sound in his ear was her heartbeat. Nothing could be more foreign to a Nightmare. His appetite grew, and he knew he could absorb all of Carrie right then. The old George would have done it in one second. Something stopped him now. He didn't want to live if she was gone.

"You little brat!" Burns yelled at Meg. "Sift her," he commanded the agent. "Get all her info."

Meg stepped back twice before the barrels of two machine guns poked her in the back. George felt her wanting to run and get shot so she could wake up, but the Ringmaster was exerting all his control on her now. George envied that kind of power, but he loathed the Ringmaster for prostituting himself to IS. They used and abused nightmares more than any Vitae-Ra. Serving them willingly was the Intenui equivalent of evil.

Meg managed to say, "Do your worst. Nothing you do will hurt me really."

The Ringmaster giggled.

"It's not like that," Mercury said. The Ringmaster's laughter cut short. The woman's outfit suddenly shifted so that a long syringe needle was pointing from her first finger. "I'd say this won't hurt, but that's not true."

She plunged the needle into Meg's arm.

In an instant, Meg woke up. She lay in bed at home, breathing fast. Her first instinct was to celebrate. She was awake, and they couldn't hurt her. The relief only lasted one second when she realized something was wrong. Her arm stung. She couldn't move.

She struggled to wiggle her hand. She tried to scream. Nothing. All she could do was breath and blink. Panic filled her. Steve was right. They could find ways to affect you in Materia.

What did they hope to gain from this? As if to answer her, she felt a headache coming on, then dizziness. She clamped her eyes shut to try to fight it. As soon as she opened them again, she could see the dream all around her. She still stood in the forest, surrounded by Intershroud goons, the woman in the liquid metal dress with a needle finger still poking Meg's arm, Carrie the Ghost, Dale Burns, and Nightmares that looked like a ghost, a dragon, and a big gorilla. They were faint images all standing around her. The room felt sideways. The waking and dreaming worlds were both before her eyes and they were perpendicular. Tears fell off the sides of her face. Even in the dream, the tears weren't falling down, as they should. They streaked black makeup back toward her ears.

Caught between two worlds, Meg stood paralyzed in both. Her head screamed with pain, as if the strain would cause it to burst. There was some commotion between the various beings around her, but all Meg could really see or feel was the woman connected to her arm by a needle. What was going on? What was this woman's reason for inflicting such pain and confusion?

Then Meg realized the truth in one horrible moment. Mercury was looking around her bedroom. Her aspect was still in Essentia, but while Meg hovered between the two, the woman could see the ghostly images of her bedroom. Meg tried in vain to scream again. The actions of the other people and creatures nearby seemed to be miles away as her attention fixed on this agent of doom.

The woman looked out the window at the streetlight, trying to decipher signs. She glanced at Meg's schoolwork. Suddenly, Meg realized what she was doing. Meg's stomach felt sick. This woman was finding clues that would tell her where Meg lived. It would allow them to find her in Materia. Her family was in danger!

Meg redoubled her effort to break free. She tried shutting down her mind. Nothing would stop the horrible drama from playing out. As the agent's ghostly form opened the desk drawer, Meg knew it was over. There was a letter in that drawer with her address printed on the front.

As the woman reached her hand out and touched the corner of a white envelope, everything went black.

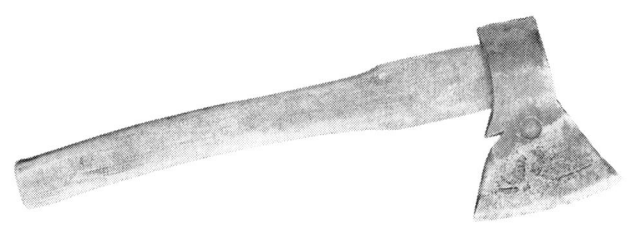

# Chapter Forty-One

Carrie felt the moment when George began to absorb her. He was awash with unfamiliar emotions, and she didn't have time to help him sort them all. She knew he was going too slowly. If these people finished with Meg and saw what he was doing, they would kill them both immediately. This way, at least, she hoped George would be strong enough so nobody could ever kill him. Everything else she wanted to do had failed. She needed to do this one thing right.

"Hurry, George." It was hard to think. She felt thin and ticklish, yet her heart was pounding in her ears.

Dale Burns paced around with a big, dumb grin on his face as if he had recently become the newly elected mayor of crazy-town. The quicksilver-clad agent had her finger jammed into Meg's arm and both of them looked like holographic projections. There was a lot of mist around that looked like a bed standing on end and some furniture that had been overturned. But nobody was paying any attention to that except the Ringmaster, dragon, and swordsman Nightmares. They all stood in awe when they realized they were literally looking into Materia, where dreamers went when they woke. The men with big guns didn't know who or what to point their weapons at anymore, so they held their guns at the ready, prepared to shoot anybody at a moment's notice.

*Thump, thump.* Feeling her heart echo through his body, Carrie realized George couldn't live without her now. He absorbed only some of her aspect essence. *Why is he stalling? What is he waiting for?*

When the woman in the metallic dress began opening a drawer in the misty desk, he grabbed Carrie in one solid hand and cradled her delicate form against him like a baby. Then he leaped high in the air.

Of course, the sudden movement drew everybody's attention except Meg and Mercury. Machine guns tracked them into the sky. Nobody fired a shot until

George started to fall again like a meteorite. Carrie felt numb and thin until the free fall made her stomach lurch. Then she wanted to throw up. In one motion, George crashed into the ground, swallowing Meg whole.

The action ripped Mercury back to Essentia immediately. She fell ungracefully on her butt. Dale Burns screamed for everybody to open fire. Bullets flew in every direction, riddling the Nightmares, waking most of the guards, and pulverizing Mercury. Somewhere in the chaos, Dale took a shot to the shoulder and woke up.

Carrie watched helplessly as tiny lances flew through George, trailing his precious life's essence behind them as they escaped. Not wasting a moment, he jumped for the trees and swung one-handed through the branches for all he was worth. A stream of gunfire followed them until they disappeared into the verdant umbra.

Mercury couldn't believe it when she saw the Ringmaster look at the swordsman and laugh. "I guess we're done here."

"What about that girl?" the dragon asked. His tenor voice was higher than his size would suggest.

"We did what we were told to do. We kept them all here until everybody else arrived. That's all." The shadowy swordsman nodded and put his weapon into a scabbard strapped to his back. They turned to go but realized they didn't know where.

"That was Materia," the dragon said with a kind of religious awe.

Mercury stood, looking at her broken finger. It would heal. Being interrupted left her feeling queasy and uncomfortable. When she got her bearings, two halberd blades formed above her shoulders as she yelled, "Go after them!"

The four remaining soldiers looked at each other and shrugged. Then they started hiking into the woods at about one-tenth the speed George had been going.

She rolled her eyes. "You three," she said, pointing at the Ringmaster, "go after them, too."

The Nightmares looked at one another and back at her. They shrugged and began walking after the men with guns. Mercury screamed her frustration. "I'm surrounded by idiots. Fly, dragon! Catch them!"

The dragon shrugged all four of its shoulders, spread its wings, and flapped into the air. The agent knew it was futile. They all knew. As fast as he could swing through the trees, the big ape was far out of the reach of bullets by now.

Meg didn't know if she was alive or dead. She didn't know if she was dreaming or awake. She knew the world was pummeling her from side to side. It was wet, warm, and impenetrably dark. The headache had eased, so she tried to hold herself up as the walls of what she was beginning to think of as a strange cage jostled her back and forth. A few times, her stomach leaped into her throat as if she were in free fall. None of it made sense to her.

Then it stopped, and she saw a light. The walls began to squeeze at the bottom and the slippery sides thrust her up through the light. She flew out of the cage and found herself diving toward the ground. A clingy residue made dirt and leaves stick to every part of her that touched the ground, including most of her right side. Shock and a growing revulsion fought for complete control of her mind. She closed her eyes and refused to think about it.

When she opened them, she was unhappy to see she was, in fact, still dreaming. George and Carrie were there. She stood up and tried in vain to brush the goo and dirt off her bare arm.

"Was I just..." She couldn't even say it. Bile began to rise in her throat.

"You need to try to verge," Carrie said. "George saved us." She looked at the big black monster as if he were a knight in shining armor. He didn't look well. Small holes let light show through in several places, and a cone of steam waving above him made it look like he was in an invisible shower.

"I can't..."

"Try again!" Carrie looked manic in that instant. "We don't have much time. He can't take us any farther. You need to get us to safety, or he died for nothing."

"I will." Meg coughed up some gunk and spit it out. She reached out with her mind and tried to push the trees down. She felt a strange resistance. "It's not working," she muttered.

"Please," Carrie said to George, "take the rest of me. Make yourself whole again."

"I can't verge," Meg emphasized.

"Why not?" Carrie was almost hysterical. "Didn't you say this happened to you before?"

"Yes," Meg admitted, "but it didn't get fixed until after I woke up and went back to sleep."

"We don't have time for that," Carrie said. George looked like he was concentrating. He found his fingers were too big to plug the holes, so he tried to cover them with his hands. White steam continued to bubble out between his fingers.

"Can't you just feed him some more?" Meg asked. As soon as she did, she wondered why. Didn't she prefer this Nightmare to die along with all the rest?

"Not like this. I'm a Ghost. I don't have the same power as a dreamer." Then Carrie stood up straight and looked at Meg. "You can do it. You can feed him."

"No way." Meg laughed. "Not me."

"It won't hurt you one bit," Carrie said. "It won't cost you anything."

"You don't know what they did to me."

"I know that George just saved your life," Carrie pressed. "Your real life. And you can save him with just a few moments of thought, yet you would let him die. We could have left you back there. He risked everything to save you. Now you owe him."

Meg thought about all the years of nightmares. She knew she could feed this monster now. She knew it was the right thing to do. She just didn't want to.

"Hurry," Carrie said. "Please!"

Finally, Meg reached out and touched him. It was different this time. He didn't get anything from her fear and loathing. He needed something else. He needed compassion, loyalty, and caring. That, she couldn't give. It wasn't in her power to love a Nightmare.

Yet the holes seemed to close a little. Maybe her concern alone helped some? His distress lessened, anyway. She tried to see him through Carrie's eyes. All she saw was a big bag of gross goo that had swallowed her and carried her around in his stomach.

Even these thoughts helped. Meg was baffled. Her repulsion waned as the moments ticked by. She didn't know what was happening. She didn't know what she felt. Yet the big monkey was getting a little better. Eventually, he began to sit up, and Carrie actually clapped because she was so happy.

When Meg pulled her hand back, she just said, "Now wake me." She didn't even look up to see Carrie smack her in the back of the head. The gray filled her vision.

As soon as she woke, Meg made sure she could move. Then she rushed to the desk drawer still hanging open and examined the letter. It was face down in place. Had that woman seen the address and put it back? Or had George really gotten to Meg in the nick of time?

She wanted badly to take a shower, but she didn't. Instead, she tiptoed down the hall to the living room without turning on any lights. She pushed the power button on the computer and slumped into the desk chair. She didn't know what the IS knew about her. However, one way or another, Dale Burns wasn't going to get away with this. Carrie had warned her to use an anonymous computer, but Meg couldn't be sure the IS wasn't coming for her already. Whatever was to come, Dale Burns would go down, too.

It only took twenty seconds once the Internet was up, and then Meg shut the computer down and went back to bed. It felt good to know she had finally accomplished something real. She couldn't honestly say what. She just smiled. It was adult. It was permanent.

As expected, she found it hard to sleep. There was so much going on. The IS would probably have tracked down Carrie already. There was a good chance she was dead. If not, Meg would go to her and take her away. She just prayed that Ringmaster wasn't anywhere near Carrie now.

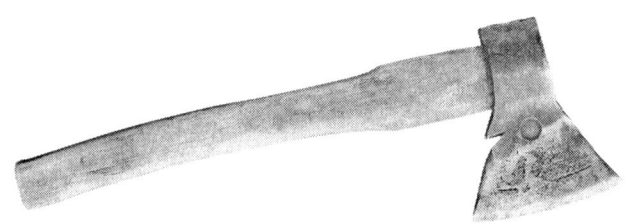

# CHAPTER FORTY-TWO

One of the greatest victories in his investigative reporting career had Todd Price walking on clouds. It was a cold success, however, because he had nobody close to him to share it. He could always walk into a bar and buy a round for everybody. Then they'd be his friends for a while, but he wanted more. He wanted his wife back. He wanted somebody who knew him. He wanted a real friend.

The files on Ms. Gretsch's computer were worth every bit of trouble it had taken to get them. Although he didn't find anything definitive that would prove Essentia was real, Todd had found a treasure trove of Intershroud information. He now knew several management-level employees and physical locations in Materia. He had recruiting plans and even a training manual. Included in it was a document about a summer camp the IS sent management's children to for Free Dreamer training called Camp Farley. He'd sent a copy of everything to his employer, of course. They were planning to publish all of it a little at a time via the Essential Expositor. Unfortunately, there was nothing he could take to the police. But as a bonus, he had a file outlining everything Intershroud knew about him. There was even some information Carrie had gathered from other parts of the IS that she wasn't actually working on, including an Operation Warlord. The name sounded a lot like the "Operation War Bird" the phony agent they used as bait had mentioned.

Todd hadn't read it all because he knew he would be sifting through it for weeks. Instead of celebrating, he went to sleep. If that Ghost had more to offer, he wanted to be available to her.

*Finally getting back to sleep, Meg was confused by what she saw. She'd been looking for Carrie. She recognized the forest, but all she saw was a black blur*

*flying past her overhead in the trees. Guns were reporting in the distance. Then she recognized George. She diverged back to her bubble.

Taking a deep breath, she smiled. If the Ringmaster was around, he hadn't gotten to Carrie yet. How the Ringmaster and that mysterious black manta ray Nightmare both had the same ability to take her powers, she didn't know. She wasn't sticking around to find out, either.

She made the sides of the bubble look like tree branches racing past. She pulled the large black monkey in and the bubble diverged. She touched the giant ape, and they all disappeared.

Meg scrambled away as soon as the pile of people and monsters rolled out of thin air and spread out on the tall green grass in front of Steve. Carrie was so thin, her image a vapor. Her black skin and blonde hair were both just swirling patterns of gray. George breathed heavily. He was clearly exhausted, taxed beyond his own strength by running so long and hard.

Meg dusted her black clothes off. She was glad there was no Nightmare stomach goo in the mix this time. They were in some kind of rural field. There was a windmill nearby. She was sure she heard somebody talking to Steve when they landed. He was alone now. If she had to guess, she'd say it was Todd Price. She didn't have time to care now.

"Hello, Meg," Steve said evenly. She didn't know how he could see a ball of people and Nightmares crash out of nowhere in front of him and not act surprised.

"We need you to take Carrie and me someplace where Intershroud can't find us. Like you said before." Meg was breathing fast. Her makeup and hair were back in order so she looked less manic.

"Of course," Steve said. He extended his arms. To Carrie, he continued, "Todd Price said he is more than interested in any other information you can supply him with."

Carrie didn't answer. Her misty form looked almost delirious. She only stared at George. She didn't even look away when the metallic-clad agent, five men with guns, and the Ringmaster appeared by them.

"Mercury?" Steve said in a baffled voice.

"Steve?" It was the woman agent.

"Fast!" Meg called out. She moved over to join Steve who was leaning over Carrie. They all disappeared as gunfire blasted around them.

"It's just a short stop," Steve said as they landed on a hard floor. They were in the maze again. The sky was still clear and bright, but the walls in this section were made of steel bars like prison rows that went on forever in every direction. Even seeing adjacent rows through the spaces, nobody could find their way through it.

Meg kept all the jealousy out of her voice when she said, "You knew that IS woman?" Meg realized how little she knew about Steve. Something about him having a history with this agent made her like him less.

Steve scratched his unshaved chin. "Mercury? Some time ago, yes."

"Hello, Meg," came a familiar, almost angelic voice.

Meg took a deep breath before she looked up. "Hi, Rose!" She rushed over, and they hugged.

Meg looked at her hands, flexed them into fists, and then stretched them. The thin silver bracelet with sparkly diamonds looked out of place with this outfit. It should have been barbed wire or spiked and buckled leather.

"You look busy," Rose finally said, looking at George cradling Carrie in his arms, leaning against prison bars. The Ghost panted shallow breaths.

Meg broke down. "You were right. I went to face the clowns again, and another, stronger Ringmaster was there. I can't get away from him."

"It's okay," Rose said. "We'll find a way."

"I don't know why I couldn't just let it go."

"These are your dreams," Rose said. "Nobody can tell you what to feel."

"But now I'm right back where I was."

"No," Rose said. "You know the truth. You know that dreams are real. And that will make all the difference."

"Like I told you," Steve said, "you have to fight to be free. You can't have your dreams just by wanting them."

"But I can't fight him. I'm paralyzed when he's around."

"No matter how strong he gets," Steve said, "you have the advantage. He needs you. But you don't need him."

"How is that an advantage?"

Steve didn't get time to answer. Suddenly, the Ringmaster was there.

"He shouldn't be able to find you here," Steve said.

"I don't suppose you have a bazooka handy?" Meg asked. She reached into her pocket to try to take the playing card out. It was stuck. She didn't have time to fight with it.

"You can't have her," Rose yelled.

"Nice try, but I didn't come alone." The Ringmaster put out his arms. The dragon Nightmare materialized, surrounded by men in black armor with machine guns. There wasn't enough room for all of them in the corridor, so the dragon and several of the grunts appeared in parallel corridors with steel bars separating them. The steel bars would offer no protection from their guns.

"Get Carrie out of here," Meg said to Steve. "Take her someplace safe. They can only track me."

"I won't let them take you," Steve said.

"Then come back for me! Go!"

Steve took Rose against her protests. Carrie and George disappeared with them.

Meg didn't know what to do with so many guns pointing at her. She put up her hands. "I surrender."

The Ringmaster looked disappointed, but he didn't move toward her. Clearly, he had orders to hold back.

Dale Burns and Mercury arrived next. Meg's stomach turned.

Dale Burns said, "Mindsift her again. And this time she won't be able to escape."

Meg felt a moment of triumph that Mercury hadn't gotten the information last time. It faded with the sure knowledge she would get it now.

Mercury moved forward with her hands out. Meg froze. She wanted to run. She wanted to scream and fight. She wanted one of those bullets to tear through her aspect and send her to the waking world, but the Ringmaster held her bound. With her hands in the air, all she could do was wait.

"Sorry, kid," Mercury said. "But you pissed off the wrong people." A needle projected from the index finger on her other hand.

Meg had several choice words about those people, but her mouth wouldn't move. As the needle came closer, Meg heard a metallic buzz in Mercury's earpiece. The silver agent stopped and began talking into the small wire microphone. "Are you sure? But that's crazy. Okay. Okay."

Then to Meg she said, "It's your lucky day." Mercury turned to the men in machine guns and said, "New orders. Evidence has just surfaced that Dale Burns has been disloyal. Arrest him!"

The macabre pleasure Dale Burns had been taking in Meg's suffering suddenly left his face as his eyes went wide. He took off his pinstriped hat and held out the other hand. "There must be some mistake. I've only done exactly as ordered."

"That's not my problem," Mercury said. Two of the grunts shouldered their machine guns. They each clapped one-half of a handcuff on to him and the other side on their own wrists.

Meg managed to smile despite her paralysis. Mercury nodded at Meg. She nodded a strange goodbye and tore apart a thin gold bracelet around her wrist. The whole group evaporated. The only one they left behind was the Ringmaster.

# Chapter Forty-Three

Meg put down her hands. She knew she just had to endure long enough for Steve to get back. That should be any moment. She didn't know why the Ringmaster had let her move freely, but she took the chance to try verging again. It didn't work, of course.

"That was fun," he said as if they were chatting over bagels at a café. "I suspect you had something to do with that."

"That was Carrie's revenge," Meg said. "You don't seem to mind that you'll never see the guy who created you again."

"He didn't create me," the Ringmaster said. "You did. He just gave me a little boost so I'd be strong enough to keep you from breaking free."

"But you don't like him?" She stepped back, one of her shoulders rubbing against metal bars as she retreated.

"He didn't help me for nothing. The price was very high. Now I suppose I will be free. You did me a favor."

"Don't bet on it. Intershroud doesn't let anybody go free."

"That's not really your concern right now," he said with a short cackle in his grating, high voice.

"What is my concern?" she asked.

"Me, of course."

"I'm not scared of you," Meg lied. She remembered what Steve said about fighting for freedom and always having an advantage. "You need me. But I don't need you."

"You must on some level, or you wouldn't keep coming back to me."

"I didn't come to you. You came to me." Meg grabbed the king of hearts from her pocket. She yanked it so hard it tore part of the pocket. Then she held it up. "But your time is over now." She ripped it to shreds and let the pieces flutter to the floor.

"Do you really think that's going to break a link as strong as what we share?" He laughed.

"No," she said. "But this might." Meg jumped away, wrapped her hands around one of the steel bars, and pulled with all her might. The steel resisted her, but not much. With no other dreamers around, the world was hers to bend and she knew it. A four-foot length of steel pipe came free. Before the Ringmaster could see what was happening, she swung it in a wide arc and smashed the side of his head.

Wide eyes met each other in the middle of his head as his surprised face warped like a cartoon. The bar in her hand made an audible *clang*.

"I don't care how long it takes," Meg said. "I will never let you live."

"But we're the same," he said, stuttering. "You're just like me."

Tears welled in Meg's eyes, but she used her anger to fight them back. "I'm not like you. I have friends. I don't hurt people and feed off their pain." She swung the bar again. He flashed quickly out of the way, and she clanged it against one of the bars lining the corridor. The vibrations hurt her hand, but she didn't stop. On the rebound, she swiped his feet.

Caught off guard again, the clown fell, his own hat landing next to the one Dale Burns had left behind. Side by side, the similarity was obvious. Meg leaped forward and pressed the bar across the Ringmaster's neck with both of her hands.

"You'll never hurt me again. You'll never hurt anybody again."

"But you made me," he sputtered through choking. "You made me to do this."

"No," she said. "Dale Burns did. What I made wasn't you."

The strong Nightmare easily held the bar up from his throat, choosing to let her think she was winning so that he could keep her attention. Her hatred flowed fast to him now, rapidly healing the wound to his head. Unlike other dreamers, Meg could feel the essence her mind gave him. She pulled away, but he held the bar fast. Refusing to feed him with the struggle, she let him have it.

"This is all pointless," he said. "You know you can never beat me."

"Maybe. But she's not alone," Steve's voice interrupted from down the row.

"Steve!" Meg cried.

"Another dreamer," the Ringmaster scoffed as he stood up. "Ten of you couldn't take me."

"Then we'll get fifty," Steve said.

"No." Meg stopped him. "I have to do this."

"What?" Steve and the Ringmaster both said it in unison.

"I have to beat him, for me," Meg said. Suddenly, a new idea filled her mind. She couldn't verge when she had the Ringmaster's card, but...

She nodded to Steve, who looked confused. Then Meg grabbed the Ringmaster by the dirty lapels and they both disappeared.

Once again atop the Empire State Building, Meg faced her worst Nightmare.

"This place again?" the Ringmaster asked. He dropped the metal bar, which dinged every time it bounced.

"I didn't bring you here to kill you," Meg said.

"Then why? You want to feed me? Like a date?"

"No. I just need a moment to think."

"Ah, you don't have good grades. You really aren't much of a thinker. You're the feeling type."

"I've been doing better in school lately," Meg said.

"And what did they teach you in school?"

"They taught me it was bad to hurt other people." She grabbed his lapels and shoved.

The Ringmaster easily caught the safety rail behind him and stopped himself from going over the side. It didn't even take much strength. As soon as his three-fingered, white grease–painted hands wrapped around the rail, Meg grabbed both of his lapels. Then she made the rail he was leaning on disappear and they both tumbled back off the skyscraper into the night.

"Didn't work last time. Won't work this time," he said with his high-pitched, nasally voice.

Meg held on to the pinstriped suit for all she was worth. She kept feeding the Ringmaster in order to hold his full attention and set him at ease. She needed him to want to see how this would play out as they fell. He had no fear because he already knew he could live through such a fall.

Then she verged. Hot wind raced past them and light began to glow below. For a moment, it felt like they were falling up into the sky with sunlight above them. Then the bubble merged over a river of glowing hot rock. The molten lava churned and flowed in the belly of a tall volcano. Meg knew it was going to wake her up. She welcomed it, but she wouldn't wake until the end. She had to make sure.

Realizing her intentions, reading them straight from her mind, the Ringmaster reached one powerful hand up and smacked her away. He reached to the side and began floating toward one wall of black rock so he could stop before hitting the fiery liquid below. The force of the blow made everything go gray. Meg knew she wasn't long for this dream as she spun away from his now-flailing body. With the last tendrils of her aspect, she latched one combat boot under his armpit. Then she focused what remained of her intention, keeping her mind on the hot lava and the gravity pulling them down. She had to dream this volcano hot and real. She had to make it erupt. Hers was the only mind here. Nothing could oppose...

Then she woke.

# CHAPTER FORTY-FOUR

George found he rather liked hitching a ride with all these Vitae. The group merged a moment later on the beach of a tropical island. The smell of brine was strong on the wind that blew palm trees back and forth. White clouds drifted lazily overhead, occasionally casting shade everywhere.

"We're safe here?" George asked. He was looked at Carrie. Her emaciated form lay on the soft sand.

"They can't follow you here, even with a link," Steve said. "It's a realm. It doesn't mean they'll never find you. If they come to this realm, they might. But this place is pretty good at keeping people hidden. It's called the 'Lost Realm.' Dreamers here are not usually found.

"I also thought it might be someplace where George would fit in better than most."

"Thank you," Carrie whispered to all of them. George felt her sincerity. They were connected mentally and emotionally now in ways he'd never thought possible. Whenever Carrie had thanked somebody in the past, he knew it was a manipulation. Not this time, though.

Meg suddenly joined the group. The first thing she did was check her pocket to make sure there was no card in there.

Steve's eyes went wide. "If he follows you here..."

Meg took a deep breath and reached out with her mind. If the Ringmaster still lived, she would feel it. She would know. She felt the big top, the Empire State Building, and the volcano. In a moment, she said, "No. He's gone."

"Wow," Steve said. "That's awesome."

Meg smiled. She let the compliment sink in. She was over her crush, but Steve was still somebody she would always admire. She asked, "Where's Rose?"

"She woke up. But she said she'll meet you tomorrow."

"Good." Then to Carrie, Meg said, "I finished what you asked." Meg was hoping to comfort her. George turned and gave her an angry look. Meg didn't know why. She explained, "I thought it was important. I thought…"

"It is," Carrie said. Then to George, "I don't think there's enough of me left to help you now."

"Now I will give you more back," George offered. He reached forward with his large finger and touched her side. Nothing happened.

"It's too late," she said. "It's over. Just take what's left and be free," she said. She sat up. With a huge effort, she leaned over and put her arms around his neck. "You're the best."

"No," George said. It was a command, not an argument. "Don't give up. Stay here with me where it's safe."

"I can't," she said. "My intention ended. Just take my aspect and my final thoughts. I want one mind in this universe to think good of me when I'm gone. Please let me do something good for someone."

George started to speak again, but stopped. Carrie faded. The swirling mist held her face and shape as long as it could until there were just a few dots left. Eventually, even those dots found their way along the path where her arms had been and became a part of him.

George's smooth face turned down into a sad expression. "It's not enough," he said. "I will be hungry for a long time." He looked up at Meg.

"No way," she cut him off, fully aware of his thoughts. She turned her back on him, so she was facing Steve. George nodded and then wandered away into the nearby palm trees. Meg didn't watch him go.

"I just can't," she said to Steve. "I did once. I kept him alive. But I can't…"

"It's okay, Meg," Steve said. "You were great. Nobody could ask more of you."

She looked at the small waves rolling up on the shore. "Do I have to only dream I'm here from now on? Is this the only place the IS can't find me?"

"It's amazing that you would give up so much to help Carrie," Steve said. "But you don't have to stay only here. There are lots of realms like this one."

"Are there any with Free Dreamers my own age?"

"Not as excited about the lodge these days?" Steve laughed. "They'll form a new lodge somewhere else. But I guess it's a bit stuffy for a rebellious teen. Still, I hope you'll come by sometimes. You'll be safe there, and I can show you some other places like this one. I'm afraid I don't know many teen hangouts in

Essentia. Doom maybe. I'm sure there are teens there."

Concealed in the trees, George turned to watch the rest of the drama play out. His mind reeled. The moment he absorbed the last of Carries aspect, when he knew nothing could keep her tethered to this dream and he finally granted her wish and consumed her essence, everything changed. His mind had expanded and grown. Her memories infused him. Everything about her person had become a part of his thoughts. Though she was forever gone, she'd given him a beautiful and amazing gift. In her last seconds, Carrie had given her whole mind to George.

He understood Materia implicitly. He could see Revra, Essentia as Carrie called it, from the perspective of a dreamer. He could live Carrie's entire life through her memories, from her troubled childhood, through college, and into her job at the Intershroud. He felt her revulsion of him when they met and the change as they bonded through her eyes. At the end, she had truly loved him. At the end, she had even given him that very love.

George now understood Steve's words had reference to Meg's clothes, something he never would have been able to decipher before. He understood so much more about Vitae.

The girl said, "But I can't go looking for them myself or the IS will come after me."

"Probably. Who linked you?" Steve asked.

"That lady you called Mercury." George could understand Meg had once cared for Steve, but now she didn't harbor those feelings.

"Mercury, she's a story for another day. You would do well to keep your head down for a while. Mercury will lose interest soon enough. And if you verge her somewhere where there aren't half a dozen bruisers on her heel, she's not really very tough. Maybe you just need the right kind of friends to hang out with for a while."

"You're usually too busy."

"I wasn't talking about me," Steve said.

"You think anybody will want me after I got linked by the IS?"

"They'll want you even more."

"So I have to meet Todd Price again?"

Meg was coping with so many changes, George realized. In better circumstances, she might have spared him a little intention.

"He's here," Steve said. "But you don't need to talk to him today."

George watched Meg looking in vain for any sign of Todd Price. George knew where Todd Price was, of course. He just didn't think it would be wise to say.

"I wish we could have saved Ms. Gretsch," Steve said with a sigh. He talked into the air as if he were used to not knowing where Todd was. "It's sad. At least you got the computer dump. What else do you think she could have told you?"

Todd's characteristic quiet voice replied, "Based on what she knew about me, which wasn't written, I'm guessing she had a lot of secrets. They died with her, I'm afraid."

George smiled.

"So what's the next move?" Steve looked out over the ocean at the horizon.

George thought storm clouds seemed to be gathering there.

"Let's take a break," Todd said. Despite his voice being elusive, the weariness in it was still obvious. "When they get the new lodge up, I'll meet you there in a couple of weeks."

Steve nodded and turned back to Meg. "Well, it looks like I have some time free. Do you want to start with realms? I know a group called the Purites. They'd love to have a verger around all the time."

"That depends. Do they have anybody with powerful weapons who will help me?"

"Oh yeah. You have no idea." Steve laughed.

"Can we go see Rose first?" She put her hand on his shoulder.

"I think she'd be mad if we didn't." They were gone.

As George watched this conversation from behind a giant fern, he had no idea where in Revra he was. He did know that none of these Vitae were interested in his welfare. Two of them were already gone. However, one stayed—the one who was hard to see.

George now had a new and amazing perspective on dreamers. He understood them in a way Nightmares never do. He knew how knowledge was power in their world. Suddenly, he ceased to mourn Carrie's loss. While she hadn't fed him with essence the way she wanted, she had empowered him spectacularly. He always knew a Nightmare could absorb a Ghost completely, but he never realized what it would really be like.

George didn't have to see the remaining dreamer, of course. Nightmares seldom relied on their eyes the way Vitae did. George could feel him. He knew the dreamer was looking at the beautiful scene and longing for something not in it. Newly realizing the power within him, which had nothing to do with strength, George moved his massive body back out onto the beach.

"Maybe I can help you," George said as quietly as his powerful voice allowed.

"Maybe," Todd said absently. "But I prefer to hide and you are very conspicuous."

George knew Todd didn't consider a Nightmare a potential friend, despite all his loneliness.

"I know things you would want," George said, loosening his tie.

"You have some of Carrie's memories?" Todd stopped shading and appeared in full focus next to George. His long trench coat looked out of place on such a warm beach. "You know things about Intershroud?" The sadness was gone from his voice. Instead, George recognized a hunger. He understood it in a way only a Nightmare could.

"I have all of them now," George said. "She gave them to me." George didn't need to say how simple of an exchange he was proposing. They were both hungry, but they could feed each other. Understanding the value of the information he possessed, he wouldn't sell it cheaply.

George knew how easy it would be for this Vitae to keep a Nightmare well fed once it attuned to him. He could tell this guy was the type who didn't usually bother with Nightmares.

Todd's face suddenly changed. "George," he said, "I find myself with some free dream time. Would you like to hear a story?"

"Yes," George said. He smiled, so all his square white teeth stood out against his shiny black skin.

Todd smiled back over the top of his round sunglasses. They began strolling along the beach, one step for George for every three Todd Price took. "Once upon a time there was a young reporter. He was brilliant and energetic. He knew the power of words and worked tirelessly to use them to stop corrupt people. The world was at his feet. And to make it all better, he was in love with the most amazing woman. Do you know what it's like to be in love, George?"

"I think so." George thought of Carrie. Then he thought of how she'd felt about him and sighed.

Todd nodded and continued, "Anyway, this reporter was stupid. He didn't realize to what lengths the evil people of the world will go when they get desperate. So..."

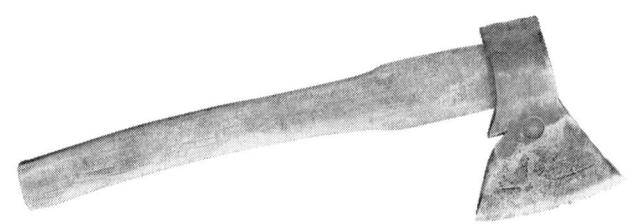

# CHAPTER FORTY-FIVE

When Meg woke up, the first thing she did was rush to the window and look out. Her heart raced. She half expected to find armed men preparing to bash in the door. Instead, she just saw a sliver of twilight making a few clouds in the distance turn pink. The yellow light of the streetlamp outside winked off. She eyed a cable company truck across the street suspiciously while she idly fingered her bracelet until she saw the repair person come out of the house it was parked in front of.

She stretched and yawned as much out of relief as coming awake. She examined her arms. She hadn't had any new scratches in months. Most of the cuts had healed with only a few light scars remaining. She walked out into the living room, daring to hope everything might really be all right.

"You're up early on a Saturday."

Meg jumped. She had to squint to see her mother sitting on the couch at the end of the living room.

"I guess I wasn't tired anymore."

"Will wonders never cease." Her mother laughed.

"Why are you up so early?"

"You're going to laugh, but I had a bad dream."

"Really?" Meg didn't know what to think. Does it mean something?

"It's no big deal. So you're all done with the nightmares?"

"I wish," Meg said. "I had one show up out of nowhere yesterday. But another one saved me. It was really strange."

"I'm not sure I even understand. You talk like they're people or something. And how can it be a nightmare if it saves you?"

Meg laughed. "I guess it wasn't. I don't know."

"I think I'd go back to the lumberjack if I were you."

"He was there." Meg looked away as she fondly remembered.

"It's been a while since he featured in your dreams. That's so interesting," her mother said. "I almost never dream about the same thing twice. Well, except work or my mother or other common things."

"I could dream those things if I want to. I can dream anything I want."

"Is that what Doctor... uh, Rose taught you?"

"Sort of. But you could do it, too. I could show you how to control your dreams if you want. I could even introduce you to Steve."

"I wouldn't want to get between you and your dream guy." Her mother laughed.

"You wouldn't. We're just friends. I kind of liked him at first, but I'm starting to think he doesn't feel that way about me. Maybe I need to meet somebody my own age. But I'm serious. If you learned about dreams, we could meet in our dreams. We could do the most amazing things. I have a really rare power. You'd be proud of me."

"I'm already very proud of you, Megan."

"Meg?"

"Nope. You can have everybody else call you Moonbeam if you want. But I'm your mother. I named you, and I get to call you Megan."

"That's fair."

"Now enough talk about dreams. How about some hot chocolate?"

"Sure, but you can never talk about dreams too much."

Her mother gave her a sideways smile. Meg curled up in the corner of the couch, tucking her feet under to keep them warm. She sipped the sweet liquid, letting the mug heat her hands. They chatted about school and how Meg could still graduate late if she took four courses online each semester after school and a few in the summer. Meg tried to listen and pretend she was excited. Eventually, she set down her empty cup and curled up tighter.

Somewhere in the talk about going to community college the next year, Meg drifted off. She stirred long enough to see her mother take the cups to the kitchen and leave Meg to sleep in peace.

Meg felt the soft grass under her feet before she smelled it. The sun shone down on a wide meadow surrounded by tall mountains of gray rock. Tanks, helicopters, flying motorcycles, jet-powered bicycles, and dirigibles were scattered all around the empty space. When Steve showed her this place the first time, it had been a nice, empty field. Now it looked like a museum of vehicular oddities.

The people moving about and talking had on all kinds of strange outfits and masks. The masks ranged from knit ski masks, like burglars, to large plastic bunny masks. Goggles, feathers, and bandanas were everywhere.

What had she gotten herself into?

She felt exposed without a mask of her own. She looked around for somebody who fit the description Steve had given her. Arty would be in charge of this group of Purites. Apparently, he was expecting her any time. Meg wished Steve was here now. With so many strange people moving around, she thought it might be better to come back later. She really hoped this whole thing wasn't his way of brushing her off.

"Meg? Is that you?" She looked around for the source of the jolly-sounding voice. A hand stuck up from one of the small groups chatting in the space between a bunch of motorcycles and a bulldozer. The group parted, and a large man with a salt-and-pepper beard stepped forward, waving. "Steve said to expect you tomorrow, but I'm glad you stopped by early."

"I didn't bring a mask," Meg said.

Arty tipped his head to look at her for a moment. If he said one thing about her makeup, she was out of here. "We can get you one if you want," he said with a smile.

"You don't have a mask, either," Meg observed.

"No, as the leader, I need to be available for people in case they want me. Wearing a mask makes it hard for them to find me."

"Makes sense. Steve said you need a verger."

"Since he left, we've had a hard time of it, to be sure," Arty said. He stepped closer and offered his hand.

Meg shook it. She liked how friendly he seemed. "I'll do whatever it takes to bring down Intershroud."

"How do you feel about undercover work?"

Meg shrugged. "Undercover at the IS?"

"We have a tip on a piece of equipment we don't want them to have. If it really does what we've heard, we need to get it away from them as fast as possible. There's an opening for a lab tech internship. You might fit the bill."

"Steve said you could help me out with a little extermination problem."

"The Nightmares," Arty said, nodding enthusiastically. "Don't worry. You get us this machine, and I'll burn down a whole city for you."

Meg smiled. "Tell me what to do."

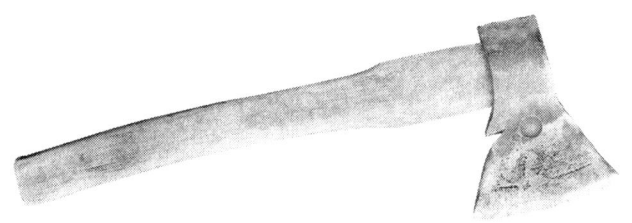

# Acknowledgements

I appreciate everybody who supported me through the long journey, which finally culminated in this book. This work would have been impossible without the long term and extensive help of my friend, R. A. Baxter. His genius contributions and his enduring assistance are both braided into the text of this work.

I cannot say enough how thankful I am to my family for their unending patience with my obsessive nature. They are wonderful. Also, I happily express thanks to Pat Rosvall and Sam Peterson for their encouragement in the early drafts. I am grateful to Niika Nenn at Wolf on Water Publishing. The sheer amount of personal effort put into this manuscript proves it was a labor of love.

Finally, I am indebted to Cable and Marten Rook. Thanks for helping to make my dreams a reality!

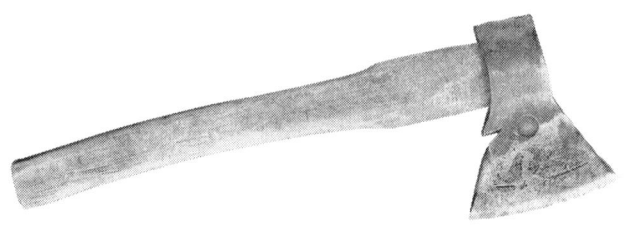

# GLOSSARY

<u>Aspect</u>- When a dreamer's mind forms a body of essence in Essentia (or some other bubble), that body is called an aspect. Ghosts have only an aspect and no material body. When the dreamer wakes up, the aspect falls back into unformed essence.

<u>Bubble</u>- A bubble is a specific dimension or reality in the dream world. Most dreamers appear in the main bubble known as Essentia, which is much larger by far than any of the other bubbles. Some dreamers create their own little bubble when they start dreaming, which never connects to the rest of the Essentia or other places in the dream world. Some Free Dreamers can create bubbles on purpose using a power called verging.

<u>Diverge, Diverging</u>- When a verger separates a bubble, it is called diverging because they appear to physically leave Essentia.

<u>Essence</u>- Essence is the substance Essentia is made from. Finer than matter (for which Materia is named), essence can be manipulated by the dreamers mind. Thus an unopposed dreamer can shape the dream into anything they want simply by thinking it. This ability to shape Essentia mentally is so complete that dreamers can even form living, thinking creatures called Nightmares.

<u>Essentia</u>- When sleeping, people dream up an essence body, called an aspect, and interact in Essentia. Named for the essence it is composed of, Essentia is literally the dream world. The body of a dreamer remains in Materia, or the waking world, while their mind moves about in Essentia as they sleep. Only a few people really understand the true nature of dreams. These people are called Free Dreamers, and they develop powers and great control while they are in Essentia.

Free Dreamer- A person who understands the reality of Essetia and the true nature of dreams is called a Free Dreamer. Because Intershroud seeks to control all the power in Essentia, they actively hunt Free Dreamers.

Ghost- When a person dies, their mind usually leaves both the waking world (Materia) and the dream world (Essentia). However, some people are unable to let go. In these extreme cases, their mind will abandon their body in the waking world and take up permanent residence in Essentia as an aspect. People in this circumstance are called Ghosts.

Gnostoi- A Ghost completely consumed by a nightmare.

Godrath- This is a country made by and inhabited only by sentient Nightmares. While all Nightmares are created to feed off the emotions of dreamers, when they become strong and intelligent enough to think for themselves, they often desire companionship with others like themselves. Such Nightmares are often drawn to Godrath. They have their own words for things in their world, refusing to frame their lives by the definitions of dreamers.

Intention- Nightmares refer to their mind and thoughts as their intention, seeing them from a different perspective than dreamers.

Intershroud- An international, interdimensional business dedicated to keeping dreamers from learning the truth about Essentia and the real nature of dreams, Intershroud is run by Free Dreamers bent on controlling all of the power inherent in dreams.

Link, Linked- When two beings in Essentia know each other, they are linked. One can dream straight to the other. This creates problems if you are linked to an enemy, but it makes it easy to find allies and friends when a Free Dreamer first begins to sleep.

Materia- The waking world where people live their material lives is called Materia by Free Dreamers. It is named for the matter it is made of, in contrast to Essentia, which is made of essence.

Merge, Merging- When a verger combines a bubble they are in with Essentia, that is called merging the bubbles.

Mindsift, Mindsifter- A power whereby one dreamer can enter the mind of another dreamer. The exact uses and effects of this power vary by Mindsifter. For Mercury, it gives her the ability to paralyze a dreamer and enter Materia in close proximity to the dreamer's sleeping body.

Nightmare- Natives of Essentia, Nightmares are living beings created by dreamers. The more attention and emotion dreamers invest in the Nightmare, the stronger and more intelligent it becomes. Self-aware Nightmares sometimes seek to join with others like them, in which case they seek out the country called Godrath.

Purites- This is a band of Free Dreamers dedicated to freeing Essentia and returning it to the "natural" state where dreamers are free to interact without fear of oppression.

Revra- When Nightmares talk about Essentia, they call it Revra.

Sempiternal- A nightmare which has grown so strong that it no longer needs dreamers to provide nourishment.

Verge, Verger, Verging- A verger is a Free Dreamer capable of separating off a bubble intentionally. Verging is a rare power, even among Free Dreamers. The act of creating a bubble is called diverging, and the act of combining one bubble with another is called merging. When a verger diverges a bubble, they disappear from the bubble they were in. The verger can consequently merge that bubble somewhere else. The result is similar to teleporting from one place to another in Essentia.

Vitae- Nightmares call dreamers Vitae.

Vitae-Ra- Nightmares call free dreamers Vitae-Ra.

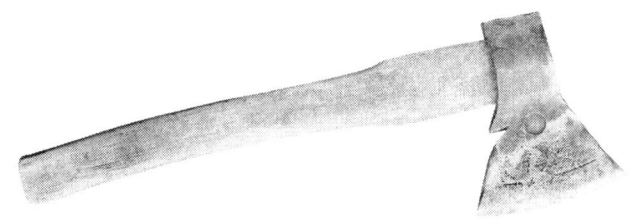

# About The Author

Growing up with more stories than facts, James Wymore moved often, searching constantly for his own gateway into Narnia. Failing to find it, he turned to writing stories and found places much stranger and more intriguing.

Having met an interesting pair of brothers one night in his dreams, he told his friend after waking up. His friend had the exact same dream. They followed the directions they were given, a journey which culminated in discovering the most amazing story ever. All that remained was to put the story into books.

Along the way James drew a line of death-themed comics and created some games he gives away free on his website. You can find these along with his other books and short stories at http://jameswymore.wordpress.com.

# A Taste Of...
# James Wymore
# SALVATION

# Chapter One

"This one's not dead."

Cold penetrated to his heart when the man's voice woke him. Pain forced him to lift one eyelid and he discovered the world was sideways. Dim light magnified his headache, so he closed it again.

"How can it be?" a woman asked from some distance. Her voice seemed to cut into his brain. "It's been two days since the war."

"It doesn't matter how," the man said. "We can't help him. Likely as not, he'll just arrest us."

"Hush. We can't leave him like this." She stood nearby now.

Metal seams bit into frozen skin at his shoulders and waist, as hands grasped the armor and tried to roll him. Fire lanced up the man's legs, which were stuck in the frozen ground. He tried to scream. Only a moan came out. Why couldn't they just let him sleep?

"Help me. Up we go, Lord," the woman said. When they both pushed together, the man's immobile legs broke free of the ground with a sickening crunch. Another moan as they leaned him against something so he was sitting up. His back ached. His cheeks and ears warmed slightly as she covered them with her hands. "Get him some water."

When a cup of glacial run-off poured down his throat, he felt relief from an all-consuming thirst he didn't know he had. At the same time, he felt the precious little heat left in his core begin to leech away.

Darkness tried to return. She patted his face, each touch stinging like a scorned lover's slap. He opened the same eye. Apparently, he only had one he could open. Light pounded his brain like a hammer and he snapped it shut again. "That's right, m'lord. You're going to be okay. Macey's going to get you all better." He didn't want to get better. He just wanted the pain-free oblivion they'd stolen from him.

"Better get that armor off him," the man said.

"Use the other cloaks to make a blanket," she agreed. "We'll pack him in the wagon."

Voices and sounds echoed in the dark. Even as he shivered, he craved more of the icy water. Floating in and out of consciousness, he felt them remove his metal exoskeleton. Scabs broke when they pulled his helmet free, and the woman's warm hands staunched the blood with cloth wrapped around his forehead. They wrapped layers of rough fabric all around him. With great effort, they heaved the huge bundle into a small wagon. His legs burned continually now. More cloth tucked around him and under his head. Then they left him alone.

He heard them whispering. They moved things around. Occasionally, the sound of clanking metal or dull thuds carried to him. Frequently they made their way back to the wagon, tucking things in next to the bundle around him.

As his mind began to accept this as reality, he knew he needed to see. He opened his one good eye again, very slowly. Each time, the light lanced his brain. Against his instincts, he kept at it until some vision returned.

The shadow of the mountain fought back the heat on the foggy, gray morning. The wide river flowed past them, making no more noise than the mist twisting above it. He could see the river moving down the hillside to join the ocean a few miles away. Pieces of the ruined dam below him lay scattered or burned. The reservoir sat empty. The water already cut a new trench for itself through the one-time lake, dragged by gravity to the salty hell of the sea. Bodies of dead humans and monsters were scattered all the way along the new, unbroken track.

Who were these people? They were probably past forty, at least half his age older.

He understood this was a battle site. He knew the Hyzoi, humanoid sea-monsters with crusty plates like starfish skin growing through their scaly skin, were the enemy. He understood the lay of this land. He knew why the dam had been so critical. Its destruction signaled their loss in this battle. He just didn't know any of the people. Shouldn't he know their names? Shouldn't he recognize the insignia on their armor?

"Oh, My Lord is awake," the woman said as she dropped a load of sharp, twisted metal next to him. She did it with no more ceremony than if it had been scavenged firewood instead of looted weapons from dead soldiers. "I'm Macey." She made an awkward curtsey, as if she'd only heard of curtseying in her youth and had never tried it before.

"Thank you," the soldier in the cart said with effort. "I'm…" He didn't know. He knew he should give her his name and possibly some kind of lineage. Did soldiers give parentage or rank? He couldn't remember. Suddenly, the pain and dehydration were not his biggest problems. He didn't know his name.

"Don't try to talk," Macey said, pulling the top-most muddy cloak tight and tucking it in around him like a cocoon. Her own clothes were strange. She had a heavy red jacket to ward against the cold. Dirt smeared her arms and elbows, where strips of purple fabric, like the cloaks wrapping him, were tied around her sleeves to make the oversized garment fit. Up close, he could see it matched the red jackets of the military men littering the ground. She had red patches over the knees on her purple skirt, too. She turned and called, "Bowen, he's coming to. Get a fire going."

"Are you daft? A fire would bring them fish-men back to finish us off, like all of these." Bowen indicated the ocean with a sweep of one finger. The rest of his fingers clutched three small moneybags. Like the woman, he wore repurposed red and purple clothes, with the insignia and buttons removed. A trimmed salt-and-pepper beard wrapped around his jaw beneath a floppy, quilted purple hat pulled down over his ears.

"He needs to warm up and eat," she persisted. He liked that idea, as much as the pain would let him like anything.

"Have to wait 'til we get away from the water. We've already lingered too long. The cursed river will have carried our scent down to the blood thirsty mer-monsters." He tossed the coin bags into the wagon, along with a bundle of armor. The man inside stifled a groan. He didn't want them to feel any worse after doing so much.

"Can't we just finish up now? The trip is so long. And I don't see any sign of them."

"No, get up or start walking," Bowen insisted. "They move under water like crocodiles or ghosts. There's nothing to see or hear of them until they fly out, like unholy demons. Then it's too late. Remember what happened to Rex?"

"Never came back," she said, climbing into the wagon. She slipped back the first time and had to exert considerable effort to get her large, short body up onto the seat.

"They can smell us in the water," Bowen continued, as he swatted the goat's butt to get the wagon moving. "Soon's I dipped my hand in with that cup, the scent started down that slope." He kept talking as he walked alongside the shaggy white mountain-goat, who strained against the heavy load. "It takes some time for them to get up here. But we used our safety up. Did he say who he is?"

"No. Poor thing can't really talk."

"Who'd want to talk about this, anyway?" Bowen asked. Their voices, the creaking wooden wheels, and the rhythmic clopping of goat hooves on the frozen dirt lulled the nameless man back to sleep.

"There, there," the soothing woman's kind voice pulled him from the darkness. The pain remained, but the world had become uncomfortably warm. The smell of strong peppers filled his nose. "You can sleep all you want, but we have to get some nourishment in you, or the hunger will kill you every bit as much as the bleeding might have."

He cracked open one eye. He still couldn't open the other one. The firelight didn't assault his brain this time. He wiggled his arms to loosen the layers of rough cloaks and push himself higher on the bundle propping up his back.

Macey dabbed blood off his forehead with a wet cloth. "This is going to sting," she said. "But we need to clean it." She opened a small bottle and doused the rag with strong smelling alcohol before applying it again. A new blossom of pain burst from above his eye and spread to his whole skull. This pain brought him out of grogginess into acute awareness. The alcohol seeped beneath his shut eyelid. New tears swelled and cracked the scab, welding it shut. Macey used her free hand to wipe away the dried clumps. When the alcohol fumes gave way again to the thick smell of peppers, the man pried his other eye open.

"I got some nice stew going. I made it strong, so it'll burn. But it's the best medicine for someone in your condition." She moved over to the boiling kettle on the fire. He could see she'd removed the wrapped military jacket. They were in the main room of a small wooden walled cottage. She had pushed a few chairs and a small table against the far wall to make room for his makeshift bed.

"Thank you," he said again. His dry throat caught on the words. It tempted him to cough, but he suppressed it because he lacked the energy.

"So polite," Macey said. "You're welcome." She brought over a cup and held it to his lips. Sweet grape juice cleansed the sting from his tongue as it trickled down to his throat, coating the imagined cracks there with cool salve. The touch of food after so long set his stomach churning with hunger. Macey patiently administered the whole cup of liquid. Then she set it down and picked up a bowl of pinkish stew. She used the black spoon to crush the meat before each scoop.

He tried to concentrate on her soothing words, but starvation would not let him think of anything except the burning pepper broth and goat meat. When she paused and gave him another drought of grape nectar, the soothing of the burn from her spicy stew made the sweet flavor better than anything he had ever tasted. It didn't mean much, since he could only remember three flavors, and both of these were better than coppery blood.

With unending patience, Macey chattered kindly about their modest accommodation, Bowen's goats, and a high yield of grapes this year. Once in a while, she paused to wet a cloth with water and wash a dribble of blood on his forehead. Then she would sting it with alcohol, apologizing constantly as she reminded him of the deadly infections so common on scratches from sea creatures.

In one such pause, he looked at the fire. She had stoked it high on one side of the large fireplace and shifted the metal grill beneath the stew pot to the other side. The grill caught his attention. Jet black from long use, it was twisted, with sharp barbs sticking down. It was strange and familiar at the same time. Suddenly, it dawned on him. The grill was made of weapons, pounded into a new shape with the barbs and points hammered down to make a smooth platform for the cauldron. Like their clothes, they constructed everything out of repurposed military paraphernalia.

The door creaked open and Bowen came in. Macey rushed to close it behind him as he refreshed the woodpile next to the fire with the load he brought in. His deep voice said, "I'm going back down tomorrow to make another run."

Macey shushed him with her fingers, keeping them on his lips as she whispered, "He's awake."

Bowen turned to the man, a look of guilt and worry knitting his thick eyebrows. "Does he remember his name?"

"Hush," Macey said. "He's barely hanging on to life. No need to worry him with such things."

Bowen scratched his beard and then nodded to the man. "If there's any life in you, Macey'll coax it to make you better. She's got a bit of magic, you see. You're lucky she found you."

"Do you have to go back now?" Macey stared deep into his eyes. It didn't take any effort for the stranger to see Bowen was her whole life. He envied their strong connection.

"Now or never. Gonna be snow before long. And we're about out of water, anyway. Might as well make a trip out of it."

"I hate it when you go without me," she said. "I worry the whole time, them crusty devils will take you."

"Not like you could do anything about it anyway," Bowen said. Despite the hard words, his voice was tender. "They'd just take you, too."

"Better together," she said.

"Nothing's going to happen. It's been a couple days now. They will have gone back to the sea, if we drew them out at all. I'll be back by night tomorrow and we can get the barn ready. Goats'll be kidding soon."

"I know," Macey said. "I'll make a roast and some cake for dinner. With the long grape season, the growing heard, and all the…" Her voice trailed off and her eyes flicked quickly to the stranger and back. "Anyway, we have lots to celebrate."

"Just keep a knife handy," Bowen whispered. "We can't trust a stranger." The soldier pretended not to hear, but he knew their caution was wise.

"I know," she whispered back. "Be safe."

He kissed her; a long, hard kiss. Then he ducked back out, and she placed a long metal bar with a row of barbs into a custom wooden brace on the doorframe. Another weapon they'd given practical use.

When she returned, the man pretended to be asleep. He kept his eyes closed as she went off to work on the never-ending household chores.

# Chapter Two

"We need to call you something," Macey said. She sat at the heavy table, scraping hair off a slab of goat meat with a long, thin stiletto knife. The shutters were open, letting a wide ray of morning light fall on the far wall, where a hand-embroidered picture of a rainbow faded under the bleaching beams. The fresh air was cold, so they both had small blankets over their shoulders.

"I still can't remember my name," he said. His body was healing, but his memory still had huge empty patches after a week. No amount of effort could drag the tiniest scrap of information from behind the blank wall. He could not recall his mother's face. He had no memory of the country represented in the blazing sun symbol on his tunic. After endless hours scratching maps in the ground and describing the citadel, Bowen had failed to ignite any memory of the country called Sel, where the amnesiac must have sworn grave vows of fealty. No father's name, no brother's love, no friend's smile could be coaxed from his gray mind. Was he married or betrothed? No ring offered the slightest hint. However, he sometimes reached for his ring finger, as if to play with one.

"I know." Macey paused to look into his eyes. The wound over his right brow had recovered to only a pink line, but the nick in his eyebrow would never fill back in. "Maybe we can come up with something. Just so we have something to say besides, 'hey you,' until you remember."

"What if I never remember?" He wasn't whining, just dealing with reality.

"Then you'll need a new name, sooner or later."

"Where's Bowen today?" the man asked, trying to change the subject.

"Off helping the neighbors." She flashed him a curt smile to show she knew he tried to change the subject.

"He does that often?"

"There's always lots to be done in the fall. He likes to make sure people are prepared."

"I think he's just preparing so they won't be surprised when they meet me."

"These are hard lands. With the fishmen pushing their borders up and cutting off the main road, everybody's worried."

"We need to take back that road." A deep hatred welled up in his heart when heard the Hyzoi mentioned. It wasn't surprising he would harbor ill will. They no doubt killed many men he knew. He really wished he could remember them.

"It's almost winter," Macey said. Red blood covered her hands to the wrist, like fine kidskin gloves. She pushed the wastebasket of scraped off hair aside, and began flaying the meat from the bone. "The road is blocked. It will be snowed in for months. I don't suppose it matters who owns what then."

"It matters." An urge to march up the road and take it back, single-handed, welled up and subsided. There was no honor in suicide. Yet he knew he would willingly die for a country he could not remember. "Can Winigh sustain itself if we're cut off from the outside?"

"Fishmen can't get to us here," she said. "Even with the dam gone and whatever extended their range, they can't reach our town. Fishmen got no need for grapes or goats anyway."

"Not the fish... Hyzoi," he said. He refused to call them by any but their proper, cursed name. "I mean, are there any supplies we can't get here? What came to Winigh from Sel City along that road?"

"Fabric, spices, and news mostly. We used to get metals, but since the war heated up..." Macey stopped mid-sentence and shied back to her work.

"It's okay to talk about it," he said with a smile. It was impossible not to love this rosy-cheeked woman. "I'm not going to turn you in." Even if he knew who to turn them in to, he doubted he could get there now anyway. "You saved my life. I owe you everything."

"I just... It's still shameful. I weren't raised a scavenger."

"The only shame would be in letting all the metal and goods sit out and rust. Worse yet, if the Hyzoi found some way to use them against us. You said yourself the road is taken. Nobody from Sel City is coming."

"You're just saying that to make me feel better."

"I am. But if the king himself came and tried to arrest you, he would have to kill me to do it."

"Don't say such things." Her eyes, glinting in the light, revealed her approval nonetheless. "You can't have any oaths higher than king and country."

"I gave my life for them," he said. "And they left me for dead."

"That's not true," she said. "Everybody died but you. That's not the same."

"Well, I'm here because of you and your good sense. So, I want you to give me a new name."

"Me?" She tried to look surprised, but her smile worked against modesty.

"Yep. Anything you want."

"I wouldn't know any good names." She stood up, dumping the bone into the stew pot. She began dipping the thin slices of meat into a marinade, made from salt and grape sugar. Then she arranged them neatly onto a flat metal tray, hammered from a breastplate.

"You sure I can't help with that?" he said.

"No, no. This is women's work. You just get better. Bowen will have plenty for you to do when the goats are kidding next week."

Now that he was feeling better, sitting still in this cottage made him crazy. They didn't have any books, except a hand written almanac Bowen used to record natural events every year. "I have to do something," he said. "Please, let me help."

"You know how to use a whet stone? Bowen's been complaining no end about how he can't get an edge on that new axe, since the last one broke. You'd think it was something special to hear him go on about it, instead of how he has six new ones. Well, mostly new."

The man tossed the blanket off his shoulders, welcoming the cold air as a token of the first task she had permitted him. The bruises on his hands were still obvious, but he didn't feel much pain anymore. He grabbed the flat stone and leather strap, sitting next to Bowen's chair on the wooden porch, and brought them inside. He pulled the extra chair free of the table, so he wouldn't contaminate the meat she was preserving for the winter with shards, and picked up the hatchet sized throwing axe Bowen had rested near the fireplace.

He dipped his fingers into the clay cup of water Macey had on the table, and began rubbing each precious drop of water into the thirsty rock. With the reservoir gone and the vineyards sucking up every spare drop of rain, there wasn't much more than what man and beast needed for drinking. Macey wouldn't wash her hands until after she used mud to remove the blood and leaves to scrape away the mud.

The piece Bowen had chosen to replace his broken axe was a very good weapon. Balanced just above the leather wrapped handle, it had a semi-circle blade which curled into a barbed point on the top, designed to dig into flesh and offer leverage against the crusty protrusions over most Hyzoi vital organs. All the weapons fashioned in Sel served two purposes: prying and cutting. Despite the visual appeal of the weapon, the man's soldier instincts knew it would be a poor device for splitting wood. If he had access to more weapons, he could probably find something better. However, his place was not to question Bowen's choice. Macey had given him leave only to work with this one.

After turning the axe every way so he could examine the reflection on the fine edge from many sides, the man knew what to do. Bowen had ground a good angle onto the blade for utility work. However, this axe had a convex bevel. Putting a standard angle on the edge of it worked against the original design. This wedge came from a smith with access to a giant flywheel type sharpening stone, which turned fast and ground metal efficiently. Fixing the edge by hand would be a full day's work, at the least. Carefully setting the head against the stone, he began slowly scraping it across the flat rock.

The rhythm of the grinding took over the small cottage. Macey began humming a song to match. Once her tray was set, she carried it out and set it on a stump in full view of the sun. When she came back in, she took two small handfuls of water from the cup to wash the last remnants of mud off her hands. Then she opened a vaporous bottle and rubbed a teaspoon of clear alcohol on her hands.

At sundown, Bowen came home to see the man gently rubbing a few drops of water across the top of the stone with the blade of the axe.

"Looks like you've done that before," Bowen said as he hung his floppy purple hat on a peg near the door.

"So it would seem," the man said. He scraped the edge carefully along the leather strap, eyeballed the curve once more, then offered it with two hands to Bowen.

"Did you stop for water on the way back?" Macey asked.

Bowen nodded. He held the axe blade up and turned it so he could get a close look at the edge. He almost poked his eye before he stopped copying the unfamiliar action, and just ran his thumb along it. A tiny bloom of blood trailed down the side. Trying to suppress his shock he said, "That's really something."

"Why'd you have to cut yourself to test it?" Macey teased. She began ladling stew into three bowls.

"Didn't think that axe could cut anything," Bowen laughed, smearing the blood on his red shirt. "I'm grateful for it."

"It's the least I could do, after all you've done for me. I won't forget the kindness you have shown me here. I only wish I could do something more."

"Well, there's the kidding coming soon," Bowen said with a nod. "And a lot of grapes this year, I'd be happy to have a hand with the work."

"Of course," the man said.

"And you can't leave before winter with no idea where you're going," Macey insisted.

"I can't burden you so long," the man said.

"Nonsense. We had Macey's brother here until he up and married last spring. And he was terrible company, with his sulking all the time."

"Hush," Macey said. "He just needed some time to find the right woman."

"Never thought Ada would be the right woman for anyone," Bowen laughed. "Anyhow, you're welcome to stay as long as you like. I wouldn't turn down some help tying up vine rows in the spring, either."

Macey brought the extra chair in from the porch, and they all sat around the small, round table. She said, "But if you're going to stay on a bit, we are going to need to call you something."

Bowen nodded and scratched his beard.

"I'm leaving it up to Macey," the man said.

"Is that so?" Bowen turned to his wife and furrowed his brow.

"Elwood," she said.

"Macey?" Bowen reached out and put his rough hand gently on her arm. "Are you sure?"

"I've been thinking about it all day," she said.

"But that was…"

"I know. It was the name I had picked out for our son. But we never had a son. And I always liked that name. So if this is my only chance to give it to somebody, I want to. Anyway, it's only until he remembers his own name."

"I would be honored," the man said, looking at their faces. Just past the prime of his life, he was probably about the right age for their son. "Henceforth, I am Elwood of Winigh."

"Until you remember," Bowen repeated.

"Maybe," Elwood said. "Or maybe forever. If my old name was so great, why can't I remember it? This one will probably suit me better anyway."

They both shrugged. Macey wiped a tear from one eye.

"Thank you both," Elwood said. "It is a name better than I deserve."

"Hush," Macey said. "Now eat… Elwood."

# CHAPTER THREE

Elwood of Winigh sliced into the side of a wind-blown berm of snow with a round metal shield. His thick goatskin mittens were sticky, but they kept his hands from freezing to the metal. He lifted a tall mound of icy white drift and carried the heavy load to the chute, which Bowen had fastened years before on the outside of the chimney. The heat from the fire would melt the snow and deliver water through a tube to the cottage. It always amazed Elwood how little water came out of such a huge volume of snow. He'd even checked for leaks a few times.

Next, he mucked out the stable and pulled a bale of grapevine down from the rafters. He removed the old, gnarled branches the goats chewed on but usually left behind, preferring the dried leaves and soft shoots. After the kidding last fall, they'd thinned the heard down to twenty. The shaggy white mountain goats rushed in to start gnawing on the new bale before he could even cut the twine. He laughed as they pushed him aside with their wide, curled horns. They'd eventually gnaw the tie off.

Pulling his soft fur hat down tight over his ears, he left the goats behind and went to the chicken coop. He lifted half a dozen warm eggs out from under the hens, and dropped a handful of dried grape seeds onto the frozen dirt. The birds clucked and raced in to gobble the soft pits.

These simple actions served as meditation. The mechanical work felt good to his muscles. There was a kind of peace in the tools and maintenance of everyday life. Heat, food, and clothing were his entire world, and he wouldn't ask for anything more. In these snowy mountains, Elwood found a piece of heaven. Yet in his soul he felt as if he were lost or hiding. It didn't matter. He couldn't remember those things. He felt satisfied, and for reasons he could not explain, the honest labor felt like a relief from stresses he could not name.

He took the eggs to Macey before they froze in his basket. Then he went to the huge vat where they stored frozen grape juice all winter. When they harvested the ripe purple grapes from the maze of vines, running on wooden fences all up and down the side of the mountain around the cottage, they smashed them into juice in this great wooden press. They collected the seeds for the birds, and baled the vines for the goats. Once the juice froze in the cold winter, they slid it out of the barrels, and stored the ice cylinders in this vat. Elwood hacked one of the cylinders in half with a nearby sword, stained red. Then he tied the cover back over the vat and carried the brick of juice into the cottage.

"Bowen'll be mighty grateful for you taking over his chores," Macey said.

"I just like a chance to get out and move around," Elwood said. He placed the slushy red cylinder into a barrel they kept near the fireplace just for melting grape juice. Then he pulled his mittens off and set them by the fire to dry. The grapes juice made his gloves sticky. They were tinted a reddish purple. It didn't match the red and purple of the salvaged clothes, however. Those were bright colors. The grape stain had a natural brownish hue. Elwood preferred the grape stain. It felt earthy and real, while the brighter colors felt pretentious and fake.

"I worry about him," Macey said. "If I'd have known he was going to be sick so long, I would have planted more peppers. At this rate, I'll be out of them before winter's up. Stew's going to be mighty bland in the spring." She carefully removed the spicy seeds with her cooking stiletto and placed them on a piece of plate mail hammered into a flat tray. When she finished, she set the tray near the fire, but not too close, to dry the seeds.

"He's a tough old badger," Elwood said as he patted her shoulder. "He'll be up when there's anything important to do next spring."

"He'd be up now, if you two hens would stop clucking and let him sleep," Bowen interrupted from the small adjoining bedroom.

"Time for breakfast," Macey said with a smile so bright it almost made up for the sun being behind dark clouds outside.

"No stew," Bowen said with a groan.

"You need it," she insisted.

"Not for breakfast. No more peppers for breakfast."

"I hate to say it," Elwood interjected, "but it's lunch time."

"Can't I have some bread this once?"

She was already cutting a slice of brown bread with raisins, and smearing thick goat butter on the top. "You want jam?"

"Jam with milk, butter with juice." Bowen coughed. Elwood had heard this chant fifty times in as many days. He knew how it would end when Bowen cleared his throat. "God gives goats 'n grapes."

"Juice it is." She already had the tray ready. This was a wooden tray with inlaid stones arranged as flowers beneath a thick lacquer. Elwood had ordered it especially for her from one of the trade wagons. It was her most prized possession. She carried it in and fussed over Bowen the whole time while he ate.

Bowen insisted it was part of her magic. Whenever any neighbors were sick, Macey would show up with her hot pepper stew and minty salve.

Elwood crouched by the fire, warming his hands between removing layers of clothing and untying strips of fabric. Macey quilted heavy coats, of course. But she always insisted on wrapping everybody's arms in strips of purple fabric before they went out in the cold. When he put all his outerwear into the basket of cloaks and similar fabrics, Elwood sat down with his whetstone and began slowly applying drops of water. He was grinding away at a twisted and barbed hunting knife when Macey finally came back in.

"Guess he just woke for food, because he's fast asleep again already."

"It's been two weeks," Elwood said between long slides across the rock.

"I've never seen him so down," Macey whispered. "It worries me."

"Not me." When she looked up in surprise, he winked. "He's got your magic to keep him alive."

"Hush, you. I'm no witch."

"Is exactly what a witch would say."

"I'm so glad you're here," Macey laughed. "I'd be out of my skin with nobody to talk to for so long."

"He'll come around. Two days ago he didn't have the strength to ask for bread."

"That's true. That's a good sign."

"I'm thinking of building another grape press in the summer," Elwood said. He paused to look closely at the edge he was sharpening. He rolled the blade so the firelight would show him the tiny bumps along the curve. Those tiny bumps gave the cutting line a fine serration, which made the knife so much sharper. "Last fall we had too many grapes for just one."

"Wouldn't that be fine, having two. We'll be the envy of all the neighbors."

Elwood laughed.

"I hope you will stay until summer," she said. "You're welcome as long as you like. Heaven knows, Bowen's feeling his age. An extra pair of strong hands is more than he'd ever hoped for."

"I'll stay as long as you let me."

"Can't be keeping you too long." Macey stirred the perpetual stew. "You'll be up and wanting a wife of your own, no doubt."

Elwood rolled his eyes. This conversation had been going on for over a month. "I don't know what I want. Maybe I already have a wife. I can't remember."

"I think you'd remember if you had a wife."

Elwood concentrated on the blade's edge. Like so many times before, he tried to remember something that simply wasn't there. "I don't think I'm going to remember anything. I think that part of my brain was ruined in the battle. As far as I know, I was born the day you pulled me out of the mud."

"Well, then you have to make your mind up about what to do. It's not right, a man living alone into his years."

"I rather think you have already made up your mind about somebody you'd like to see me with." Elwood narrowed his eyes and tipped his head to one side.

Macey turned from her pot and sat down in her chair. It was a rare moment when her hands were not doing something. "I wouldn't presume to say…"

"Out with it, woman," Elwood said, lowering his voice so it sounded exactly like Bowen.

She smiled, but didn't let it break her stride. "Well, there is the winter holiday coming up, and my family's expecting us to visit."

"Macey, you wouldn't happen to have a younger sister you never mentioned before?" He felt a sense of dread gnawing inside him. Why should it bother him? These people had given him his whole life. Why did he cringe inside when she tried to give him even more?

Against their nature, Bowen cooed and whipped two goats into pulling the three of them on a sleigh through the snow. The soft snow had crusted on the top, so the tips of the skis stayed above the crunching plates of ice despite the back of the vehicle dragging below the surface and leaving a churned wake behind them.

Well after noon, the mid-winter clouds kept the day dark and cold. Instinct or forgotten training urged Elwood to keep his mouth closed to preserve heat and water. Nothing prompted Macey to do the same. "It never ceases to amaze me how you keep those beasts running."

"Have to," Bowen said. "If they stop, this whole thing'll sink, and we'll have a terrible time getting it going again."

Elwood continued to scan the trees as he held a basket of cakes Macey baked for the feast. He felt at ease in the mountain forests. He stopped to talk occasionally. Then habit drew him back, and his eyes began darting from space to space between trees and rocks. He scanned the ridgeline above them and the distant valley below.

Having never left the household before in his memory, Elwood felt a surprising amount of apprehension on this trip. He didn't expect trouble. He knew he came from far away, originally. But this felt new and he couldn't relax.

"My parents passed on, of course," Macey said to Elwood, over the top of two chickens she plucked so they would be ready to start cooking the moment the sleigh reached the party. "But my aunt Lanny, who lived with them, is still around. My oldest sister runs the place. She never married, poor thing, but she keeps a few young families around to run the old vineyard. My nephew stayed with us before you came. Now he's married and living back at Aunt Lanny's homestead with the rest of the family."

Elwood had already heard the family roll a dozen times in the last two weeks. He knew where this was headed, and decided to cut it short. "What about your younger sister?"

Macey half blushed and half smiled when he asked. "Jewel's probably your age, best I can tell by looking. She's thinner than me, with lighter hair. Keeps it longer. I was almost married when she was born. My mother died soon after. That's when Aunt Lanny came and raised us. For me, it wasn't long. But Jewel's never known any other. Calls her mother and everything. Of course, I was there for a lot of Jewel's upbringing. She's stayed with us years and years, off and on, in your same bed."

"Is she kind and friendly like you?" Elwood asked. His eyebrows were raised enough to make Macey blush all the way.

"Don't be silly. Sisters are as close as can be."

"Not your older sister," Bowen cut in, between praises and curses for the goats. "She doesn't have the magic."

"Hush," Macey said. "It's true, though, Jewel's more like me."

"She has the magic?" Elwood asked.

"It's nothing so grand," Macey said. "What we do is really just mercy. Our mother had real magic. She could make a fire without flint, and drain the poison out of bad meat. Some say if Aunt Lanny had been there, mother wouldn't have died after Jewel. Aunt Lanny bears it as a terrible burden, but she's often said she loves Jewel as her own and…"

In that instant, Elwood, searching habitually through the woods above the small cliff they sloshed next to, saw the green glint of a mountain lion's eyes.

The story continues in...

# Salvation

By James Wymore

Available Wherever Books are Sold

# Thank You for Reading

© 2014 **James Wymore**
http://jameswymore.wordpress.com

Please visit http://curiosityquills.com/reader-survey to share your reading experience with the author of this book!

**The Actuator: Fractured Earth, by Aiden James & James Wymore**
On a secret military base tucked in a remote desert mountain, a dangerous machine lies hidden from the American public. Known as "The Actuator", this machine is capable of transforming entire communities into alternate realities. Meanwhile, an unknown saboteur dismantles the dampeners. The affect is catastrophic. The entire world is plunged into chaos, and familiar landscapes become a deadly patchwork of genre horrors. It's up to Red McLaren and his band to set things right again. They must survive their journey through the various realms that separate them from the Actuator, where ever-present orcs, aliens, pirates, and vampires seek to destroy them.

**Theocracide, by James Wymore**
At a time when everybody lives isolated lives behind computer glasses showing them whatever they want to see, Jason must abandon his idyllic life. Just as things are coming together with his new girlfriend, his father drags him into a plot to assassinate the Undying Emperor. With aliens invading the world and his sister dying of an incurable flu they brought, he plunges into a dark game of intrigue and conspiracy against the most powerful people in the world. Is there any way to keep the girl he loves after committing *Theocracide?*

**Sweet Dreams are Made of Teeth, by Richard Roberts**

How does a nightmare hunt? He tracks your dreams into the Light, and chases them into the Dark.

How does a nightmare love? With passion and obsession and lust and amazement.

How does a nightmare grow up? With pain and grief and doubt and kindness and learning and dedication and courage.

First Fang hunted, now he loves, and soon he'll have to grow up.

**The Department of Magic, by Rod Kierkegaard, Jr.**

Magic is nothing like it seems in children's books. It's dark and bloody and sexual—and requires its own semi-mythical branch of the US Federal Government to safeguard citizens against ever present supernatural threats.

Join Jasmine Farah and Rocco di Angelo—a pair of wet-behind-the-ears recruits of The Department of Magic—on a nightmare gallop through a world of ghosts, spooks, vampires, and demons, and the minions of South American and Voodoo god shell-bent on destroying all humanity in the year 2012.

### Tattoo Rampage, by "Gusto" Dave Jackson

Evangelina Marquez-James gets her first tattoo, a symbol of courage to carry on after her husband dies in the line of duty as a police officer. The skin art is of an elite yet obscure super heroine created by a forgotten 1940s artist.

A solar disturbance triggers a metamorphosis in her new ink, enabling Evangelina with the ability to transform into the embodiment of the character complete with powers. She sets out to wage war against the types of vermin who murdered her husband.

### Wolf, by Jim Ringel

Johnny Wolfe carries his dog Sindra in a vial that he keeps in his pocket. He carries her out of loyalty. He carries her out of guilt. He carries her because there are no more dogs in this world. He carries her to feel her animal wildness. On his way to work one day he comes across a colleague who is killed by a dog. But with dogs now extinct, how is this possible? Johnny discovers the colleague's rather sizeable sales order. Except he can't figure out what product the colleague is selling. As he gets closer to understanding the product, Johnny starts to realize it has more and more to do with why the dogs might be returning, and why they're so angry.

**Caller 107, by Matthew Cox**

When thirteen-year-old Natalie Rausch said she would die to meet DJ Crazy Todd, she did not mean to be literal.

Whenever WROK 107 ran contests, she would dive for the phone, getting only busy signals. At least, with her best friend, even losing was fun—before her parents ruined that too.

Her last desperate attempt to get their attention goes as wrong as possible. With no one to blame for her mess of a life but herself, karma comes full circle and gives her just a few hours to make up for two years' worth of mistakes—or be forever lost.

**Sin, by Sharron Riddle**

My name is Sin. I killed a man in self-defense when I was sixteen. My dad wanted me committed, but Mom sent me to my druid priestess aunts in St. Charles, IL. I'd barely unpacked before the aunts sent me to find the stolen hellhounds. Without the hounds to herd them to the underworld, the souls of the dead are flocking to the cities. If they're still hanging around after three days, they'll turn into zombies. Van, an annoying Fey Prince, joins the hunt to find the hounds before the zombies overrun St. Charles and turn the cities into cemeteries.

CPSIA information can be obtained
at www.ICGtesting.com
Printed in the USA
FFOW02n0216270814

9 781620 075555